Praise for *Billy Dead*

"A stunningly bold debut." —*The Boston Globe*

"A searing account of a deeply troubled family . . . features an arresting, suspenseful plot . . . [Reardon] is a master of descriptive and psychological detail." —*Atlanta Journal-Constitution*

"Moving, heartbreaking, and always vividly told."
—*The Detroit Free Press*

"Reardon's wild, mesmerizing first novel is not for the faint of heart. . . . *Billy Dead* turns out to be far more about the importance of knowing what—or who—lies at the root of your being."
—*The Cleveland Plain Dealer*

"Reardon's tour of upstate Michigan may not be scenic, but it's not soon forgotten." —*Los Angeles Times*

"Reardon's novel about family abuse pulls no punches. . . . Ray's voice is beautifully raw and honest."
—*Time Out New York*

"A heartwrenching debut . . . the real brilliance in this tale lies in the author's choice of narrator, for it is only Ray's sweet, bruised voice that makes any of it tolerable. . . . This is a compelling work, reminiscent of both Dorothy Allison and Carolyn Chute, that evokes empathy for those who lead bleak, savage lives."
—*Publishers Weekly*

"Vivid and often gripping." —*Kirkus Reviews*

"Startling, alarming, altogether original, and one of the most challenging novels of recent memory . . . Reardon dares to challenge the very nature of sin."—*ALA Booklist*

PENGUIN BOOKS

BILLY DEAD

Lisa Reardon has written half a dozen plays and two novels, *Billy Dead* and *Blameless*, and received her MFA from the Yale School of Drama. She runs a writing group for adolescents at St. Luke's–Roosevelt Hospital. Ms. Reardon lives in New York City with her husband, Mick Weber.

Lisa Reardon

BILLY DEAD

a novel

PENGUIN BOOKS

PENGUIN BOOKS
Published by the Penguin Group
Penguin Putnam Inc., 375 Hudson Street,
New York, New York 10014, U.S.A.
Penguin Books Ltd, 27 Wrights Lane, London W8 5TZ, England
Penguin Books Australia Ltd, Ringwood, Victoria, Australia
Penguin Books Canada Ltd, 10 Alcorn Avenue,
Toronto, Ontario, Canada M4V 3B2
Penguin Books (N.Z.) Ltd, 182–190 Wairau Road,
Auckland 10, New Zealand

Penguin Books Ltd, Registered Offices:
Harmondsworth, Middlesex, England

First published in the United States of America by Viking Penguin,
a member of Penguin Putnam Inc., 1998
Published in Penguin Books 2000

1   3   5   7   9   10   8   6   4   2

PUBLISHER'S NOTE
This is a work of fiction. Names, characters, places, and incidents are
either the product of the author's imagination or are used fictitiously,
and any resemblance to actual persons, living or dead, business
establishments, events, or locales is entirely coincidental.

THE LIBRARY OF CONGRESS HAS CATALOGED
THE HARDCOVER EDITION AS FOLLOWS:
Reardon, Lisa.
Billy dead: a novel/Lisa Reardon.
p.   cm.
ISBN 0-670-88224-0 (hc.)
ISBN 0 14 02.8051 0 (pbk.)
I. Title.
PS3568.E26825B5   1998
813'.54—dc21   98–18721

Printed in the United States of America
Set in Janson
Designed by Kathryn Parise

To Milan Stitt,

who taught me how to write

A C K N O W L E D G M E N T S

Thank you to:

Jennifer Rudolph Walsh for saying yes to the book despite everything.

Courtney Hodell for her intelligent, graceful editing of the manuscript.

Todd Komarnicki and Julia Mueller for acting as miraculous midwives.

Ian Grey for loving the first eight pages.

Simon Fill, Julie Hamberg, Angela Hicks, Shawn Hirabayashi, Stephanie Lehmann, Michael Ornstein, and Liz Ross for their positive response and general support.

Ellen Grasso and the Second Shift at PaineWebber for their patience and humor.

Ivy and the staff at DTUT for two years of coffee, oatmeal cookies and ambiance, which fueled the writing each day.

Pat Walter for sticking with me through the worst.

My love and gratitude to Mick Weber for the ring and all that goes with it.

BILLY DEAD

O N E

People lose people. I don't know why we're all so damned careless. Folks lose their kids, men lose their women, even friends get lost if you don't keep an eye out. I look through the windshield at the houses going by. For every person sitting in them houses, watching TV or eating a ham sandwich, there's someone somewhere wondering where and why they lost them. All those lost people, carrying on their everyday business like the air's not full of the sound of hearts breaking and bleeding.

I'm driving up Barkton Road, Johnny Cash on the AM radio, grumbling "Folsom Prison Blues." Johnny Cash makes me think of my old man, on account of they both did time in prison. Not me, though. I never did time in a cell. But every time I hear Johnny Cash, I think of the old man. I look over at Sally next to me. Her and me just getting back from the Dairy Queen. She's picking the colored sparkles off her vanilla cone, one at a time, popping them in her mouth like she always does. Time she gets to the ice cream, most of it's running down her arm, but she doesn't care.

I ask her, "Why don't you just ask for a handful of sparkles, skip the ice cream?"

She give me one of her looks. We pull into the yard, me steering with the left hand and balancing my root beer float on one knee with the right. Kick the door open on my side because it sticks, and step down into the dirt. No grass ever tried to grow in our front yard. Samson come running out from behind the house, barking and snarling like he don't know it's us. Stops when he sees Sally, and sidewinds up to lick the ice cream off her arm. She lets him, like she always does.

"This dog isn't very smart," she says.

"He knows it's us. Just showing his form."

"Someday, his eyes go bad, he'll rip us up." She's patting his good ear.

"His eyes go bad, he'll run out in the road, get hit by a car, and we won't have to worry about it." I have her there, and she knows it.

I pull the sack of groceries out of the bed of the pickup, toss the last of the root beer float in Samson's direction, and head for the house. Humming "I Walk the Line" between my ears. Sally isn't so keen on my singing, so I try to consider her feelings. But I can hear Samson over my shoulder, humming along with me as he finishes the root beer.

It isn't till I get in the screen door that I hear the crying. Someone crying back in the kitchen. I'm headed that way anyway, so I don't yell, "Who's there?" Figure I'll know soon enough. Not Sally, though. She must've heard it from out on the porch, because her voice comes past me, high and dusty. "Ginny Honey? That you?"

Sniffle, snort, gulp from the kitchen. "Sally?"

I didn't even notice her car outside, parked off to the side of the house. I know right off that I don't want to be in the middle of this, but I got the groceries in my arm and I can feel the hamburger dripping blood through the bag, so I keep walking. Sally catches up with me about the time I see Ginny Honey sitting at the kitchen table with her eyes all black and runny with mascara, wiping her nose across the back of her arm. Time I'm through the kitchen door, Sally's got her arm around Ginny Honey's shoulder.

"Ginny Honey, what's wrong? You okay?"

I don't say anything, just set the bag on the floor and open the fridge. Ginny Honey's been sniffling in somebody's kitchen since the day she married my brother Billy and started popping the kids out. I dig around and check the eggs to see how many of 'em cracked on the ride home. Three.

Ginny Honey doesn't lift her chin this time, doesn't make a show of being brave. I don't see any bruises; can't even smell any liquor on her. But she does not look good, like her skin's gone gray. I pull the hamburger out of the bottom of the bag, which is all soggy by now. Making a mess.

"Billy's dead." No fresh wails out of Ginny Honey, no sound out of Sally, nothing. Silence. I think maybe I didn't hear her right.

"Huh?"

Ginny Honey looks at me and I see her eyes burning red underneath all that smeary black. I guess I did hear her right.

"Someone killed him."

I don't know what to say, so I don't say anything. Sally and Ginny Honey are looking at me like I'm supposed to know the punch line. I feel my gut turn over a few times, think I might throw up, but don't. Sally's voice meets me halfway across the kitchen, higher than ever.

"Put the hamburger down. You're dripping."

I look down and see the watery blood making a little puddle on the floor. *Oh look, Billy's dead.* Like the two go together in my head.

Billy was a son of a bitch. I could picture him doing a lot of things but getting killed. Just about anything but that. Whoever got him must have been even meaner than him. Only one person I know like that. The thought scares me so I light a smoke, toss the match in the sink, and squat down on the floor. Butt on my heels, back against the cupboard door, lying low when the shit flies. Done it ever since I was a kid. Sally and Ginny Honey have stopped looking at me and I'm breathing again, almost normal. Sounds are coming in, people talking, but it's like they're out in the yard, behind the lilac bush.

". . . found him early this morning. Head bashed in. Had his wallet on him still, or they wouldn't have known who it was. How was I supposed to identify that mess? Your ma was there, looking at me like I done it or something. Crazy old bitch. Sorry, Ray. Raises herself a goddamn animal and looks at me like it's my fault his head is pounded into scrambled eggs. Ain't never gonna get that out of my eyes, seeing him like that. Why'd they make me look at it? Why'd I have to go look at it?"

She's crying now, so she can't say anything more. Sally's making clucking sounds in her throat, patting Ginny Honey on the shoulder like I used to do with Ma. I can see it's doing about as much good. I feel the fire of my cigarette burning down between my fingers, but I don't toss it aside. The heat runs up my hand, past my elbow like a lightning shot. Time it hits my shoulder, I feel almost okay again, back here in the kitchen. I smell the skin on my fingers burning and sneak a look at Sally.

She knows that smell. I figure this is not the time to piss her off, so I snuff the cigarette. She'll see the blisters and give me hell for it later on. She puts up with a lot.

"You want something to drink?" It's all I can think of, but I know before it's out of my mouth that it's the wrong thing. Sally looks at me like I'm about to get what Billy got. Ginny Honey doesn't answer. I pour myself a half jelly jar of whiskey and leave the bottle on the table. There if they want it.

"Do they have any idea who did it?" Sally trying to distract Ginny Honey from that picture of scrambled eggs she can't get out of her eyes.

"They got some kind of rock. Say they're sending it into Jackson to get some information off the fingerprints."

"Well, that's good, isn't it? That's something."

"They was talking about skin samples and hair samples and I don't know what they was talking about half the time on account of I'm not even there, like my head's floating around ten feet behind my shoulders the whole time."

Hair and skin samples. Hearing that sort of puts a picture in my head. Dirty rock covered with blood and bits of bone, and Billy's nails with skin or maybe hair in 'em and God knows what else, but I don't want to know so I blink a couple of times, finish off the jelly jar, and light another smoke. Damn.

Sally plows ahead, patient and steady in her teacher's voice.

"You have to figure he died right off," she says. "You have to figure he didn't suffer much."

Ginny Honey opens her mouth to say something. Her cheeks puff in and out a few times and an awful sound comes out of her. Sally pours another shot into my jelly jar and hands it to Ginny Honey, who wraps it in her two hands and huddles over it like a tiny campfire on her lap.

"They said it looked like he crawled clear from the corner of Mc-Gregor up North Lake Road to Dewey's Tavern. Found him in the ditch just short of the parking lot. I guess if he was— I mean, he left a smudge line of blood in the dirt shoulder all that way. I guess he was—" Ginny Honey breaks off and stares at her whiskey, forgetting to drink it.

Well, that didn't work. I look over to Sally to see what she's gonna try next. She leans back in her chair, bringing her bare feet up to rest on the table, balancing on the back two legs of the chair.

"You're gonna go ass over teakettle, leaning back in that chair," I tell her.

"Hasn't happened yet."

"Don't mean it won't."

"Call up Joe Lee and have him bring the kids out," she says.

Oh. That's right. Billy's dead. Seeing her bare feet on the table fooled me to thinking everything was the same as yesterday, or this morning. Or just a half hour ago. I feel bad about forgetting Billy being dead, then I wonder if maybe it isn't shock or something. People do all kinds of shit when they're in shock. I wonder if they ever just forget. I call Joe Lee at the garage and he picks it up on the eighth ring.

"Joe Lee's Sunoco."

"Hey, Joe Lee."

"Hey." I can't hardly hear him on account of an engine fifteen feet away from his end of the line, having its idle adjusted.

"Ginny Honey's out here, gonna stay for a couple of days." I'm trying to bring the volume down, but that engine is revving even higher. "Sally wants you to bring the kids out."

Joe Lee doesn't miss a beat. "They home or next door?" he hollers.

I look over at Ginny Honey. "Home or next door?"

"Home." Ginny Honey doesn't even look up.

I hold the top part of the phone away from my ear, killing the engine sound. "Home," I yell.

"Right. See ya." And he hangs up. Only now do I think to ask him if he's heard about Billy. Joe Lee's picked up Billy's kids and brought 'em out here so often he wouldn't ask what for. Just figure Ginny Honey run out again, talking divorce, restraining orders, hiding out with the kids until she got sort of lonely and Billy come around and talked her into coming back. Ain't none of his business—he's just an old friend doing me and Sally a favor. I feel funny talking to Joe Lee like everything's all right. I want to light another smoke, but even striking a match feels funny and wrong all of a sudden. Like I'm supposed to sit here like a stone until someone tells me it's okay, go on with your day, your brother ain't dead anymore.

I tell Sally that Joe Lee's on his way. Ginny Honey seems to be in a dead zone now, where it's useless to try and tell her anything. Sally rocks easily up off her chair, lifts Ginny Honey like a idiot child, and walks her out of the kitchen. By the time they're up the hall to the bedroom, I finally got my match lit. Salems lay on the counter where I left 'em, but I stand by the phone and don't move. Watching the flame on the match, I count up to twenty-three before the smell coming off my thumb brings me back and I pinch it out.

I'm thinking, Does this mean he's not my brother anymore, now he's dead? Can't say, "He's my brother." Supposed to say, "He was my brother." But if he *was* my brother then, what is he now? Not my brother anymore. My dead brother. "Yeah, you remember Billy, my dead brother." Or is he just nothing? The last idea gives me a stab of comfort that I erase as quick as it comes. Bloody rock. Hair samples. Somebody made Billy into nothing. Somebody took that thing full of mean and made it nothing at all.

"Damn," I say out loud to the warped tile floor. *Who did that? I want to see him. I want to meet him. I want to—*

Sally comes back in the kitchen for the whiskey bottle. Ginny Honey already carried the jelly jar into the bedroom.

"You okay?" She's standing with one hip cocked sideways, like she does when she's had to ask me the same question two or three times. "You want another shot of this?" Nice of her to offer, when she hates me drinking so much. She looks the same as she always does when Ginny Honey shows up. All steady and matter-of-fact: We'll deal with the situation at hand and feel bad about it later. Meaning not now. Meaning not ever. This of course makes me think that it's just another fight, just another case of Ginny Honey getting the hysterics.

"Is Billy dead?" Just checking.

"Looks that way." Sally clucks her tongue once, for emphasis and sympathy. "Sorry, Ray." She looks sorry for me, sorry for Ginny Honey, maybe even sorry for the kids. Sorry for everybody but Billy. Not a reason in the world why she should be sorry for him.

●

The summer I'm ten, I collect beer cans with a buddy of mine, Randy Keilman. This is before recycling and deposits and all that. He picks up any kind of can, but I grab just Budweiser, what my old man drinks. We go out on the back roads on our bikes with empty garbage bags and come home at the end of the day with those bags full. I have my own room, in the basement. The heater and hot-water tank are in the corner, but it's mine and it's private. I take those cans and I stack them up so one entire wall of that room is solid Budweiser beer cans. Billy come in there one day, chasing the cat, who runs into my room whenever it can. For safety, I guess. Same reason I'm in there. Billy come running in, drags the cat out from under the bed by its tail. Cat turns around and smacks Billy's hand with a front paw, laying open the skin all along his thumb. He calls the cat a cocksucker and throws it hard against the wall, the wall of cans. Throws it at an angle so it skids across kind of, and takes out pretty much the whole damn thing. Beer cans are flying and clanging, and the cat's hissing and screaming, and by the time it hits the floor it can't walk on its hind legs, because its back is broke this time. Billy thinks this is about the funniest thing he's seen since Randy Keilman's baby brother took a foul ball right between the eyes and got knocked off the back of the bleachers at our Connie Mack tournament. Three years old, sitting next to his mom, and next thing you know he's out cold, laying on the ground, and his mom's screaming and Billy's busting a gut.

My old man has to kill the cat. It's no good to no one, can't walk. He doesn't take it to the vet or nothing. Just goes out back behind the shed, holds it steady with one boot, and chops its head off with a shovel. Makes a good story. Randy's almost peeing in his pants laughing when I make the sound of that cat flying across the wall. But I throw the beer cans away after a couple of days. Rolling around on the floor all hollow, and some of them have dirty old cigarette butts in them anyway.

•

"Okay?" Sally's looking at me, waiting for an answer. I panic, thinking it's a test I'm gonna flunk.

"Sure. Okay." I keep my hand curled so she won't see the redness on my finger and thumb.

"I'll just get her to sleep, then." Sally finishing up a whole conversation I just missed. Try to breathe normal, breathe through my nose like Randy taught me. She's not trying to trap me. Just ask her. Tell her I didn't hear her. *"Okay" what? What did you say?* Don't panic. Just ask her.

"Sally?"

"Yeah?" She's halfway down the hall and turns, whiskey in one hand and the other on her cocked hip.

"Nothing." Smile to show her I mean it. She smiles back like she does sometimes; like she sees all of me and doesn't mind. Then it's quiet voices in the bedroom, and I put away the rest of the groceries. It's a typical Michigan August, hot and muggy as hell. Food'll go bad whether Billy's dead or not. I work my way past the bologna (put it in the meat drawer, I remember), past the Cheez-Its. Time I hit the canned pears, I wonder again if I can just forget the whole thing. Call Billy up and go out to Dewey's Tavern for a couple of beers. Drive like hell up North Lake Road and laugh at the trail of blood on the dirt shoulder.

"Hell, just forget about it," Billy'd say, and pop open another beer.

I dial his number, figuring I'll give it a try. No one answers, so I hang up and put the canned pears on the top shelf above the sink, in the back. The phone rings and I jump out of the top of my skull thinking it's Billy, but it's not. Joe Lee's hollering into the phone out of habit, even though he's not in the auto shop, he's over to the house.

"Kids ain't here. Neighbor says Jean took 'em."

I close my eyes, lean my forehead against the doorframe. Let out a whoosh like whales do out of those holes in the top of their heads. Jean took 'em. Means she already stopped at Ginny Honey's, saw she wasn't there, and figured the only other place she'd be is my house. Means her truck'll be pulling up into the yard just about now, full of kids and full of Jean. I tell Joe Lee thanks and hang up. Check my watch against the clock above the fridge. 11:36 A.M., and my watch is running three minutes fast. Shit. Sally comes into the kitchen.

"Who was it?"

"Joe Lee. Jean got the kids already."

Sally's mouth and chin flatten out like a frog's, with the lips turned straight down at the sides. Not happy about the news, thinking.

"She's on her way here, then," she says, frowning deeper.

"Sorry," I say, trying to erase the frown. "I didn't call her."

Sally doesn't look at me.

"Let me put something on your finger." She leads me into the bathroom for a B&B. Bacitracin and a Band-Aid. It's a joke I never shared with her yet. Now is not the time.

I look at the top of Sally's head while she patches up the burns. A single gray hair sits grinning up at me. I kiss it, turn to look out the window. Best to see Jean coming from a distance. Breeze from the east smells sweet for half a second, like rain might fall, like it smelled one afternoon years ago when Jean's voice was somewhere above me and little red foxes were running in a pattern across the bedsheets. I glance at Sally's head, afraid she can read my thoughts. There's a rabbit at the far end of the yard, chewing away at one of Sally's tomato plants. I wonder where Samson is. I watch this rabbit chewing like hell, and it takes me a few minutes to realize that he's looking straight at me.

"I never saw Billy. I never knew Billy. Billy never laid a finger on me." The rabbit's talking with his mouth full, so the words are all muffled.

"What'd you say?" I whisper, but the rabbit drops the tomato leaf and makes a dart back out of the yard.

"I didn't say anything." The top of Sally's head is bending sensibly over my burned finger. "Be careful with the matches. All right?" She's not gonna lecture me. She's letting me know it's okay. She stands up and rubs my back absently, looking out the window. I want to stay just like this for the rest of my life. Safe.

"I love you," I tell her. But it's the wrong thing, because her eyes look sad and the frog frown comes back. I look out past the yard to see Jean's truck coming up the road. She's trailing a cloud of exhaust and dust, a space shuttle taking off sideways across the earth, coming straight at me. Like saying the words "I love you" made her pop up like magic. I turn back to the safety of Sally, but she's disappeared.

I come out the front door as the truck stops, dust blossoming, three kids erupting from the truck bed like soup boiling over in a rusted pan.

"Pile everything on the porch. Stay near the house." Jean's herding 'em toward the backyard. Each kid has a pillowcase filled with underwear, pajamas, toothbrush, clothes for two days. They know the drill. Trish, already eleven, keeps hers packed and under the bed. Ready, waiting, hoping. A pile forms on the steps: pillowcases, sweatshirts, lunch bags, even a library book. *From the Mixed-Up Files of Mrs. Basil E. Frankweiler.*

"I read that," I say to the red-haired one, whose name I never remember.

"Did not."

"Did so."

"Did not read it." The red-haired kid is looking at me like I'm something he found under a wet log. His whole hair is wobbling back and forth in defiance.

"Kid runs away with her brother, lives in a museum with some mummies, steals quarters from the fountain to buy food." I let it roll out casually, like I spend every morning of my life discussing books on the front porch with twerps like him.

His nose bunches up in suspicion. "How's it end?"

"Ain't telling." I can't remember, to tell the truth. But I'm right not to give away an ending, and he knows it. He takes off with his sisters without another word. That leaves me on the porch, with Jean standing three feet away from me. She's wearing a blue bandanna rolled up for a headband. The same one she had on yesterday out to Billy's, when we were all out there for the barbecue. Yesterday when Billy was alive. I can smell the sun and dust on her freckles. Sally's inside, where I hear the muffled clink as she puts away the whiskey bottle.

"What are you grinning at?" Jean, pinning me to the doorframe with a direct question.

"Sally putting the whiskey away."

"Where's Ginny Honey?"

"Laying down."

"You seen him?"

"No. She and Ma went."

"Sheriff been here?"

"No."

"Asshole woke me up, banging on the door. 'Sorry to bother you, ma'am.' 'Then don't,' I says. Bang, bang, bang, 'Your brother's dead, lady.' 'Which one?' 'Billy.' 'Kill himself?' I'm hoping. 'No, ma'am. Somebody did it for him, ma'am.' Fucking ma'am this, ma'am that, and I'm in my bathrobe and I'm squinting at him with his hat in his hand. Jesus Christ, he's asking so many questions, you'd think I did it."

"Did you?" Two little words hanging in the dust between us, like they came from far away. She's looking at me like she knows everything I ever thought. This is going on for a long time, and I'm starting to think about hollering for Sally to come out here, just for the hell of it, but now it's Jean's turn to grin.

"No. I didn't kill him."

My heart sinks with relief, collapsing my chest so I suck in a deep breath, just like Randy always told me not to do. I get dizzy and sit down hard on the top step.

"Jesus, Ray. Take it easy." Jean's boots clump past me, the screen door bounces twice against the wood frame, and I hear her voice echoing off the summer walls of the breezeway.

"Hey, Sally. Kids are out back, but I promised 'em lunch when we got . . ." The rest of her voice is swallowed in the shadow of indoors. Now it's just the insect buzz of August sunlight, and kids screaming on the other side of the house, a hundred miles away. She's in the kitchen now, but I can still see the dark outline of her in front of me, close enough to reach out and grab. And the smell of her freckles lodged in the back of my nose. Not a word about sorry or how was I doing. Not even a blink when I asked her if she killed him. The only person in the world who scares me more than my brother Billy is my little sister Jean.

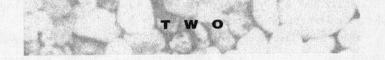

TWO

It's the spring I turn nine when Billy and I take Jean out behind the toolshed and take her shirt off. She's only seven, so it's not like there's anything to see. Billy makes her open her mouth, and he sticks his dick inside it. He's thirteen, so he knows what to do. He holds her head so she can't yell or pull her face away. I can hear her trying to breathe through her runny nose. I'm afraid she'll suffocate or choke to death, and then we'll catch hell. When it's my turn, I do what I saw Billy do. Nothing much happens. I give it six or seven quick jerks and pretend I'm finished. Billy tells Jean that if she tattles to anyone, he'll stick a red-hot poker up her ass. She doesn't cry or nothing. Just sits there buttoning up her torn shirt and wiping the snot and jism off her face. I don't think she knows what a red-hot poker is, but she never tells. At least, we never catch hell for it. I'm surprised, because Jean's a mean little kid in her own right.

●

My arm is warm against the sun-hot metal of my truck door, driving up North Lake Road. On my way to town, to the police station, taking the long way around. I know Billy's at the morgue, but I also know that if I look hard enough, I'll find him in the ditch, head flattened. If I look hard enough, he'll show up. I know that about Billy. I park the truck and walk along the sloping shoulder. The ground is hard, the dirt packed silky firm and soft. There are rocks in the dirt. Some are flat and gray, some are quartz-like and sparkle in the sun. Some are buried in the dirt, so only their iceberg tips show. Those are the kind that break your toe when you absently give 'em a kick in midstride. The kind that make you yell "Goddamn son of a bitch!" and hop on one foot, so the cars going by think you're crazy or something.

I see something in the powdery dirt. A groove, like a wide skid mark or a sled track. I don't see any blood. He had to have been bleeding. I walk right in the track. I know I'm leaving footprints all over. I might even be interfering with police evidence. The whole side of the road from McGregor to Dewey's Tavern, police evidence. You can't bring the side of a road into the courtroom. Pictures. They must have taken pictures. I wonder if they got any pictures of blood. I think about the silver ear clip Billy wore. Looked like a tiny naked woman was climbing up the outside of his ear. I'm trolling for a glint of silver in the dirt, or smears or spots or some sign of my brother. If I can find the blood, I'll find him. Maybe fifteen, maybe twenty feet further up the road, there he'll be, in the ditch. But instead I see flattened bottle caps; the only silver is a bit of gum wrapper. My eye jumps to shards of reddish-brown glass. I know it's just bits of a broken beer bottle, though the color is blood in the sun. A faded Doritos bag, a flat beer can, and a black plastic comb turned gray from repeated rains.

I pick up a piece of the broken glass, finger the edges to see how sharp. *Where are you, Billy? What the hell?* He ain't here. Someone took him off somewhere else, somewhere I can't find. Who? He's my goddamn brother, not theirs. It starts low in my gut and squeezes into my lungs. *So mad. So mad.* Want to find them and kill them. My whole body is turned into one long muscle all tensed up and wanting to kill, like a snake. Gonna find the sons of bitches and take their heads off.

The jagged edge of the glass slides against the skin of my palm. Like butter or cheese, the skin's ready to give up and let it slice through. But I don't let it. I don't do it. I hear tires behind me. Drop the glass, shove my hand in my pocket.

It's a county car, which means the sheriff's office. That's where I was going. I'd gotten into the truck, telling Sally I was heading to the sheriff's office. Needing someone to tell me what the hell was happening. Car door slams.

"Ray Johnson?"

"Yeah." I smile like I'm glad to see him.

"I'm Sheriff McCutcheon. Keith McCutcheon." No deputies. The big man himself. He ain't pulling anything on me, though. Takes his sunglasses off to talk to me, real polite. "Can I ask you a couple of questions, Ray?" Yeah, he's polite, but he ain't calling me Mr. Johnson.

"I was just looking for—" I stop. What was I looking for?

"Looking for something?" he asks.

"I was coming to see you guys." It sounds lame and defensive and guilty as hell, even to me.

"Yeah, that's what your girlfriend said."

"My girlfriend?" I guess he means Sally. I never think of her as my girlfriend. I think of her as my Sally.

"Stopped out to your house," he says. Sounds like he's sorry. What for? I think of the yard with no grass, Ginny Honey's kids screaming out back, Samson with his sidewinding walk. Now the sheriff's looking at me funny. "You been gone a couple of hours," he says. "That your truck a few miles back?" *A few miles?*

"Blue Ford. That's mine."

"You want a lift back to it? Then you can follow me in to the station?" Sheriff bending over backward to respect the next of kin. *A couple of hours?*

"Sure." I follow him to the car. I start to get in the back, but he says I can sit up front. Boy, is he embarrassed. I slide in next to him and concentrate on my breathing. I'm staring at three empty Taco Bell bags on the floor as he pulls a U-turn. That's when I hear a voice clear as water come up out of the ditch.

"Ray, wait." It's Billy's voice all right. But Sheriff McCutcheon's sitting there next to me, so I don't pay it no mind.

●

Take a long pull at the iced tea I got balanced on my knee. Nestea Instant, no lemon, no sugar, four ice cubes. Swallow big and hard, trying to peel away the dry, dusty leaves coating my throat. Feel the familiar dark pounding at the back of my head, drinking too cold too fast. "Ice cream headache," Sally calls it. I set the iced tea down hard on the porch railing, making the ice cubes rattle.

"Ouch," says the cube at the bottom of the glass, nursing a jagged crack up its middle. I turn my eyes away and lean back in the aluminum lawn chair, feet on the railing of the porch. Look out at the stars above the black outline of the substation across the road. Low voices in the kitchen and Ginny Honey hollering at one of the kids to stop goofing around.

"You want me to come in there?" she threatens. Stifled giggles from the living room, Sally telling Ginny Honey to never mind, they'll settle down eventually. I can hear the thin whine of the radio that sits on the sill above the sink.

"Chet from Bakersfield, California, you're on the air. What's on your mind?"

"Hello, Jim. How are you doing?"

I know I ought to turn it off, but I don't want to move.

"I'm doing fine, Chet. How are you?"

"Uh, I'm okay."

"What can I do for you tonight, Chet?"

"Well, you know, I just want to say . . ."

This flattens me out and makes me so tired I can't open my eyes. I try to tune it out, but Chet won't be denied.

"I just want to say, all this baloney about, you know, the satanic cults and little kids—I mean how can you believe that?"

"I don't know, Chet."

"These kids make up these wild stories to keep from getting in trouble—"

"Fuck you, Chet," I mutter softly at the moths fluttering noiselessly against the porch light. Fifteen minutes until I go to work. Graveyard shift at O'Donnell's Metalworks. Footsteps are moving back and forth in the kitchen. Voices low and comforting. Like falling asleep when you were a kid and hearing the grown-ups talking in the next room. A little bit of laughing. No crying, no hollering, no clench in the pit of the stomach. Safe for tonight.

"You can make a kid say anything. These women want to get back at their old man—" Chet, the voice of the people, breaks in and destroys whatever peace the porch has to offer. Squashed, flattened, stopped cold and unable to move. Stopped by Chet. The number of stupid things one Chet can say, and the number of Chets there are in the world, just in this town alone, all the wrongheaded stupid Chets and— I can't get out of this chair. I can't move. I have a quick vision of Billy's skull turned concave, blood fantailed across stones and dirt, and I wish for a second that it was mine. My head split open to let out the pushing, pushing pressure feels like it's gonna blow the top of my head off. The rock coming down again and again— I catch myself. Turn my head and yell in through the screen door.

"Turn the damned radio off, will ya?"

No answer. Jim is agreeing with the caller, adding his own dash of stupidity to the stew. He's cut off in midword with an efficient click. Thank you. Thank you. Over and over, like an automatic prayer inside my head. Thank you for a minute's peace. Thank you for a minute's peace.

Think about the visit to the sheriff's office, Sheriff Keith (not "Sheriff McCutcheon," too scary), the questions he asked. How does a person let himself ask questions like that for a living?

"Where were you last night between ten and eleven?" *Did you kill Billy?*

"At home." *No, I did not kill Billy.*

"Doing what?" *Are you sure you didn't kill him?*

"Changing the oil in the truck." *Absolutely sure.*

"At ten at night?" *Are you lying?*

"Before I went in to work. I work nights." *Not lying.*

"On a Saturday?" *You killed him, didn't you?*

"Overtime shift." *No, I did not.*

They bring me a cup of water when I first get there. Very polite and courteous, but they don't bring refills. I can see the dark sweat stains on Sheriff Keith's uniform when he leans forward to make a note in his notepad. That notepad seems to hold a lot of secrets. Secret things people are telling him about my brother. *You lying? No, sir.*

Then the question I knew was coming. The question that I figure has to account for the bulk of secrets in that notepad.

"Billy have any enemies that you know of?" *Who killed him?*

"Oh well, quicker to give you a list of who *didn't* kill him." The words are out of my mouth and hopping around the table before I can suck them back in. Sheriff Keith watches them somersault over one another for a minute, then brushes them away like bread crumbs.

"Can you be more specific?" He wants names.

"Nobody liked him." A pause. Another pause.

"Tell me about the last time you saw him." Sheriff Keith (the more I call him that in my head, the better I feel about him) smiles and leans back in his chair. All set for more than a three-word answer. He wants to know. So I tell him.

There was this lousy barbecue yesterday. I hate barbecues. The smells get stuck in your throat. There's bugs all over the food. The hot dogs have bits of black char on 'em. The hamburgers taste gritty, like someone dragged 'em in the dirt and brushed 'em off on the seat of their shorts. Me and Sally over to Billy's house, out in the backyard. Jean's there, but I can't figure who invited her. Ginny Honey doesn't hardly speak to her, and Billy ain't one to give out invites.

It's one of them thick, soggy days in August. Hot and gray like breathing oatmeal. Deena and the red-haired kid are out behind the garage, fighting over turns on the dirt bike. But Trish is keeping close to her ma.

Ginny Honey says, "Go on out and ride with the rest of 'em. What's the matter with you?" But Trish doesn't want to ride the dirt bike. She doesn't want to eat a hot dog, or a hamburger, or even a potato chip. The more she sits there moping, always keeping her ma in sight, the more her ma tries to get rid of her. I figure the kid's got a stomachache or something, just leave her alone. But Ginny Honey won't leave her alone. Trish is a tough kid. She's the oldest, so she'll lead the other two into all kinds of trouble. But today she doesn't even mouth off when her ma lights into her. Just mumbles about wanting to stay here on account of she's tired. Which Ginny Honey says what the hell you got to be tired about, it's not like you do anything all day. I can feel Jean getting pissed at the other end of the picnic table, but she ain't saying nothing. Yet.

"Why don't you shut the fuck up?" Billy says to Ginny Honey.

But Ginny Honey ain't about to shut up. She looks over at Billy drinking his beer at the grill and rolling wienies back and forth.

Then she says to Trish. "Just 'cause you're so proud of them ti... you got now don't mean you're grown up. Go on and ǀ kids."

I look down at my hamburger, pretending I didn't hea

embarrassed, though. I look over at Billy, and he's mad. Really mad. But he ain't glaring at Ginny Honey, he's boring a hole into the top of Trish's head. Who has her back hunched and her shoulders slumped over, like she's trying to hide the two sad little nubs that are barely starting to show through her tank top. The crazy growl of the dirt bike is loud in my ears. Sally's asking Ginny Honey about the potato salad, and even I can tell she's just trying to change the subject. I steal a peek at Jean, and she's looking at Trish like all of a sudden she's a bug or a germ under a spyglass, like she never saw her before. Trish has her head bent over her plate, her stringy hair hanging down and hiding her face. But in the half second that I look over there, I see her wipe a hand across her nose like she doesn't want anyone to see her crying. My heart jumps I swear to God to the back of my chest. Like it's backing as far away as it can against the bars of its rib cage. Jean's voice crashes through.

"Trish, come and show me where I can find more napkins."

And in the next minute, Jean and Trish have disappeared and I'm watching Billy rolling the wienies. He catches my eye and looks away, finishing off his beer the way guys do when they know they done something wrong. Sally's still talking to Ginny Honey. Panic is creeping around the outside corners of my brain, nibbling and pecking. I wish I was at work, with the familiar shoulder ache and the greasy sweat on my face. I wish I had my Ginch Littlefield book in my back pocket. I wish it wasn't so goddamn hot and muggy you can't even hardly fucking breathe, for Christ's sake.

"Them dogs ready?" I kind of yell it at Billy, who's twisting open another beer.

"Yeah, 'bout." He stabs one with a fork and shoves it into a bun. "One or two?"

"Give me two."

He does. And while he's doing it, he's muttering to himself, "Stupid bitch."

I don't ask who he means. I hope it's Ginny Honey. Or even Jean. The first bite of the hot dog turns to sand against the roof of my mouth. Me and Sally, having a friendly family cookout with Ginny Honey and Billy. I get up and walk over to the garage to call the kids to come and ·t. While I'm calling to 'em, I'm picturing Ginny Honey's face beaten a bloody stinking mess.

Quick enough, the dirt bike's abandoned behind the garage and the kids are flopping down on the blankets laid out on the brown grass, paper plates sagging full of food. There's a lot of laughing and bickering going on, a lot of kid squeals. Why do they do that? Too much excitement? Too small to hold it all in, so they let out a squeal like letting out steam? In all the noise, I barely make out what Jean says to Billy when she comes out of the house, alone. I wouldn't be listening except she's standing there looking directly at him, and she doesn't usually pay him any mind at all. And the way she's looking at him, it makes the hair on my arms cold.

Finally he can't act like he doesn't see her there, so he grabs a plate and says, "You want another hamburger?" But the way he says it, it's more like "Get the fuck out of my face." That's when the kid squeals start up in earnest, so all I get is Jean's mouth moving and then Billy calling her a crazy bitch.

Jean left not too long after that. And that was that. I didn't tell Sheriff Keith about Trish, though. I didn't tell him none of that. Just a friendly family cookout.

T H R E E

Sally opens the screen door and comes out onto the porch, rests her butt on the arm of the aluminum chair. One arm across the back of my shoulders, one leg over mine.

"Ginny Honey's gone to bed. I got your lunch packed." Her sensible voice is quiet, and I wonder if I would starve if I lived alone. Probably. "You sure you want to go in to work tonight?"

"Yeah." I lean my head back so it's resting on her arm. Turn my face toward her, trying to get the smell of her, but there's only a faint whiff of Prell. Still, this is nice.

"Deena's sleeping on the couch, and Trish is in a sleeping bag by the long coffee table." Her voice is really quiet, like we're already at the funeral. "I got the light off, so don't step on 'em when you go in." I get a mental picture of Billy's kids draped all over my living room like yesterday's work clothes thrown off and forgotten.

"How long they thinking on staying?" Not that I mind 'em staying, however long. She knows that. I'm just wondering if I should get the rollaway bed out of the basement.

"I don't know. Jean offered to take 'em at her house, but you know how well that went over. Trish wanted to, but Ginny Honey wouldn't let her."

As most times happens when Jean's name is mentioned, there's a sad sort of quiet hole that opens up between us for just a few seconds. Not sad because it's something we never talked about or never could, not like that. Sad because there's nothing more to say.

"I guess I'll go, then." But I don't move and neither does she. We got a houseful of company, and here we are out on the porch all by ourselves. I bury my face in her neck, still trying to get the smell of her. She starts a tiny march of kisses from the top of my eye down to my chin. I know I'm gonna be late if I don't leave in the next five minutes. But I don't figure they're gonna holler too loud if I'm late tonight. A just-dead brother ought to count for something. I stand up and take hold of Sally's hand. She smiles at me like she used to on her parents' porch. We slide out behind the garage and I take my shirt off and lay it down as a blanket for us. We start to make love with the moon looking politely away over the lilac bushes. But after a little while she's holding my head on her shoulder, while I cry like I always do when I can't love her like I ought. When I can't keep that other face out of my mind.

"It'll be all right," whisper the lilacs over Sally's head. But I don't believe them.

A little bit later, I step real careful going through the living room on my way to change clothes for work. A fuzzy voice, muffled by a pillow, stops me right next to the TV.

"Uncle Ray?" From the couch. Deena.

"Just me." I don't know what to say to these kids.

"I know who killed Pa." Voice still muffled, like she's afraid to unbury her face from the pillow.

" 'S that so?" I'm standing there and can't think of a graceful way to get moving again. I take a soft step, but Deena feels me moving away from her and stops me again.

"But I ain't telling who."

"Why not?" I'm all of a sudden real worried about how late I'm gonna be at work, and I just want to keep walking.

"I don't want 'em to get caught."

"How you know who did it?"

"I just got a feeling about it."

"Does Trish know too?" I ask her. But she doesn't answer. "Well, all right, then. If you don't want to tell, don't tell." I guess that ought to settle it okay. And Deena must feel the same way, 'cause she lifts up her head, and I can see two little-girl eyes looking at me under bangs that need cutting.

"Really?" She's trusting me.

"You keep it to yourself if you want."

Deena gives me a smile and lays her head back down. I'm three or four feet down the hall toward the bedroom when I hear her voice, muffled again.

"I love you, Uncle Ray."

This time I don't stop walking, don't try to think of an answer. She knows I heard her all right.

●

O'Donnell's Metalworks is on the south end of town, near the mill and the railroad. I been working there since January of 1989, after going away for a couple of years. Came back to town, got a job, and slogged my way through one semester at Jackson Community College. I guess I figured I'd pay my way as I go, semester at a time, taking time off from work or maybe part time one, part time the other. I don't know anymore what the hell I was thinking, exactly. One semester's as far as I got. English and American History.

I'm changing a tub full of metal coils for an empty one, liking the familiar stretchy ache in my shoulders and arms as I pull the three-hundred-pound tub away from the open mouth of the oven. I transferred into heat treat two months ago, when the summer help came on. No one comes out to heat treat, clear at the end of the plant. No summer help anyway. I flap off the greasy work gloves and pull the pen out from back of my left ear. I check my watch against the clock on the wall behind me; two minutes fast. Scribble out the tub number, tub weight, time finished. The metal coils lie in a blue-black heap, shining up at me like some robot's pubic hair. I smile because this is what I think every time I pull out a full tub, five, six times an hour, eight hours a night, six nights a week. I stuff the job ticket in the tub pocket and set the oven to Go for the next batch.

Ten minutes to wait near the mouth of an eight-foot oven in August. I pull my book out of the back pocket of my work pants, open to the turned-down page, and push the safety glasses up further on my nose for the eight thousandth time. The book is part of a series I'm reading. All about a small-time crook named Gregory "Ginch" Littlefield, with a lifelong streak of bad luck. Each book is one more scheme that goes wrong. There's nine in all. Three I haven't read yet, not counting this one. I like to space 'em out. Six months go by, all this shit happens in your life, and you pick up the next book and nothing has changed after all. Tonight, when Ginch cuts his finger on the shower nozzle at his girlfriend's place, like he does every time he has to take a shower at his girlfriend's (her name is Sally, believe it or not), I can pretend everything is the same as it was last night, when he locked himself in the cooler of the meat shop he was robbing. Last night, when Billy was still alive. While I numbered my tubs and pushed the green Go button and red Stop button on the oven's conveyor belt and read about Ginch's hard luck, Billy was alive.

"Hey, Ray." Randy's voice is behind me, shouting through my ear-plugs. He's standing about four feet back. All I got to do is turn around, there he'll be. *Damn.* Randy works at O'Donnell's too, but he and I don't speak anymore, not if we can help it. All through school we were best friends, until one summer (perfect summer, awful summer) when it all exploded, when I tried to kill him with my old red Malibu. That was ten years ago, and still I can't stand it. I pull the foam plug out of my left ear and turn to face him. Randy Keilman, his work gloves tucked under his right armpit and his safety glasses staring back at mine.

"Breathe, man. How many times I got to tell you?" He sounds like he's been saying this every day without interruption forever. I can see us out on his back porch when we were younger, practicing slow, deep breathing through our noses. According to his martial arts comics, a true warrior always breathed through his nose, especially in times of trouble or battle. And we were warriors then.

"What d'you want?" I say.

"I'm sorry about Billy." He wants to say a hell of a lot more than that. And I know what it is he wants to say most.

"Yeah." *Go on, now. Go on back to work and leave me alone.*

"Ray—"

"I got to get this tub out." *Don't fucking say it. Don't fucking say her name.*

I turn away from him, but his voice sidesteps around and corners my left ear, jumping in before I can get the earplug in place.

"It's been ten years, for Christ's sake," he says.

"Forget it, Randy."

"When you gonna forget about that thing with Jean? I told you then I was sorry."

I guess nothing I say is gonna shut him up now he's got started, so I shove him. Twice, hard, both hands like pistons shooting right into his shoulders. Knocking him up and back, on his tiptoes, arms swinging wide for balance. One more shot into the chest to knock the wind out of him, and he shuts up. Picks his work gloves off the floor and limps back to the grinding room, where I can see a couple of the guys turning away like they didn't see the whole thing. Like they don't know the whole damned story. Randy's put on weight. I think I sprained my wrist. I slam the butt of my palm into the side of the oven half a dozen times. I stop when my hand is numb. No one comes back to see what all the noise is. *Jean. Jean. Jean.* Her name coming out of his mouth, it wakes up shit I put to sleep a long time ago. I close my eyes, and the smell of rain soaks through me.

●

Four years went by, and Jean never said a peep about what we did to her out behind the toolshed. Not until I have the chicken pox, in my last year of junior high. I'm sick like death, and I have these sores all over me that itch and drive me crazy. No one else is home. Ma's gone to pick up some kerosene for the floor heater. Dad and Billy are who knows where. Jean comes home from school like any other day, stomps down into my room with a pack of Salems my old man left next to the La-Z-Boy. Lights one like she does it every day of her life.

"Hey, Ray," she says, puffing hard so the red ash glows like a taillight.

"Old man'll kick your ass, he catches you with a cigarette."

"Itches, don't it?" Jean leans close over me to inspect the chicken pox sores on the skin inside my elbow. This is the first time I notice the warm, dusty smell of her freckles. Ain't nothing else in the world smells like that.

"Get lost before I smack you." I'm not feeling good. All weak and watery and hot, and I don't need any company.

"You sorry for making me suck your pecker?" Jean doesn't take her eyes off the skin inside the crook of my elbow. Puff, puff, out of the side of her mouth.

"What you talking about?" I pretended so hard that it never happened, I sort of forgot all about it until now.

"You and Billy. Sucking your peckers behind the toolshed."

"Go fuck yourself." I don't like remembering it, hearing her breathing through the snot in her nose, seeing her face all red.

The cigarette comes down like an arrow, smack on one of the chicken pox sores. My arm shoots through with an electric jolt and I holler, trying to push her away.

"You sorry?" Jean's watching the white burn, the skin jumping in tiny spasms.

"Hey! You crazy?" But I can't move enough to stop her. I'm too sick. I can push her away, but I can't hit her hard enough to scare her away. Each time the cigarette comes down on another sore, she asks me if I'm sorry. I sure as hell am sorry by now, and I tell her so. Figure that'll stop her crazy shit. But she doesn't stop. Keeps right on pressing that cigarette into one sore after another and asking me questions.

"Do you love me?" *Burn.*

"Yes. Shit, yes." I'm playing by any rules she wants; it hurts that bad at first. She starts to give me little kisses on the corner of my mouth.

"Do you love me?"

"Yes." *Burn.*

"Are you sorry?"

"Yes." *Burn.*

"Do you love me?"

And after a while, the press of hot cinders blurs with the press of her lips on my mouth, and I don't say any more and neither does she. The basement window's open just a couple inches, enough to make the green curtains suck in and out with the breeze blowing down across the bed. Jean pulls down the waist of my pajamas and holds my dick in her hand while she keeps kissing me just on the corner of my mouth, never flat out on the lips. It's raining. I can hear a car going by on the wet road outside while her hand jerks up and down. The cigarette burns down to the butt, goes out when she brings it down one last time, and I come in her hand.

"You tell anyone," she whispers, wiping her hand on my pajamas, "I'll stick a red-hot poker up *your* ass." She straightens up and I figure she's leaving, but she stays sitting on the side of my bed. I can hear the sprinkler still spitting in the side yard; no one's shut it off, even though it's raining. Jean's not moving and neither am I, except I shift my hand so it's touching hers and she doesn't look at me but she links two fingers with mine. The cinder-block walls of my basement room swell up into the gray sky, past the rain and the clouds and into the black orbit where there's no one else besides her and me, and there never has been and never will be. The red foxes on my sheets come alive and skitter across my knees, their red fur flying. We stay quiet like that for nearly twenty years, until we hear one particular tire hiss get real loud, and a car door slams back on earth. The walls collapse, the foxes dive back into the pattern of the sheets, and Jean leaves the room with a half smile.

Ma doesn't ask about the burns. Just chicken pox scars all up and down the skin inside my arm, wrist to bicep. They stand out white even now whenever I get a sunburn. I don't know what Jean did to Billy. I never asked. But you can bet it was bad. That's how Jean is.

For lunch break, I go outside the delivery entrance of the metalworks, where the air moves black and hot but there's not a lot of company. There's picnic tables set out on the edge of the parking lot, off the main door, and I can hear the caps twisting off the bottles of beer, the laughter and voices, the occasional crunch of paper unwrapped from a sandwich. I stay put, watching the red dots of their cigarettes jump and weave in the dark. There's no clouds tonight, so the 3:00 A.M. moon is bright enough to cast shadows behind the trash bins. I take a couple bites of the cold meat loaf sandwich Sally made me. Some peace, some quiet. Not a lot, but enough.

I finally see the damn thing after God knows how long it's been sitting there watching me. Biggest raccoon I ever saw, at least in Michigan. Sitting near the fence separating the metalworks from the mill, looking at me. No blinking, no sniffing or switching its whiskers trying to figure out what or who I am. This raccoon knows who I am.

There's something wrong with him, though. One side of his head is flat and caked with blood. He stays half in shadow so I can't see the rest of the damage.

"I saw it," he says. His voice is a horrible wheeze. "Smelled fear, smelled blood. A man screamed in a ditch. A rock came down and down."

From inside the delivery door, I hear footsteps coming up the stairs from the break room in the basement, guys talking. The raccoon sits quiet until they're gone.

"He crawled, choking on blood."

I lean forward. I can hardly understand him. The torture of the raccoon's breathing goes on for a minute.

"Someone followed, held his hand. Waited."

"Who?" I whisper. But already he's turning back toward the shadows.

"Then I licked the blood and hair. Dead." He flattens into the dark, disappears.

I don't feel a chill. I don't feel disoriented or weird. I finish my smoke and go back inside. The lights are morgue white and bore right into my skin until I'm full to bursting with the pressure of the heat, the metal shavings on the floor, the spinning of this machine or that on either side of me and all around. Nothing will stay still. Just machines moving, the electric buzz in the air, the whiteness of the overheads, until I can't hold it in anymore. I watch the ceiling rear up as my knees fold into jackknives and I go down.

I open my eyes and three guys from the coiling department are looking at me, one holding a paper cup with coffee in it.

"He don't need coffee, he needs orange juice or something."

"Where the hell we gonna get orange juice?"

"I got a sister-in-law does this shit all the time. Diabetes."

"He ain't got no diabetes. It's just Ray."

"Get some water."

"Hey, Ray. You okay, man?"

I'm thinking about the Three Stooges, and how I never thought they were funny but Jean and Billy did. Can't act like I didn't just fall down on my face right in front of these guys, so I gut it out.

"I'm okay." All three grin at me like on cue or something, and they all talk at once.

"Too goddamn hot in here."

"Guys dropping like fucking horseflies."

"Got to get more fans."

I head back to my oven, pretend I didn't hear what I heard, walking away from 'em.

"What's his problem?" Summer help walking up to the group. Stupid, stupid summer help. Guy I went to school with shuts him up.

"Ain't nothing wrong with Ray. That was his brother got killed last night."

Another voice adds, "Someone should'a got that sister too, while they were at it."

Embarrassed quiet, since I ain't all that far out of earshot yet. Then Randy's voice.

"Hell, it ain't her fault. Ain't no one's fault."

Sally's frog mouth and sad silence at the mention of Jean's name. Ginny Honey screaming earlier this afternoon. "Get that cunt out of this house. Get her away from my kids!" Jean smoking a Marlboro out on the porch, hearing every word, picking a stray bit of tobacco off the tip of her tongue and grinning at me through the hysterics coming from the bedroom. I wanted to stay on the porch with her, where I belong, but I got a home life to preserve, so I went in to help Sally. For the millionth time, I wonder what Jean's doing right now. It's 3:25 A.M. Is she up? Is she looking out the screened window at the black sky and thinking how easy it is to move through empty space?

I'm thinking I should've listened to Sally and stayed home tonight. Five more minutes left of lunch. I pull the book out of my back pocket, open it up, and jump headfirst blind into it as hard as I can.

When the shift is over, I pull out of the metalworks into a world full of cool morning. I got the window down, no radio on. I'm thinking about Billy and about Sheriff Keith. About Sally and Jean and Trish. About the raccoon. I turn just before the bridge and head through town instead of home. I'll just stop in, see if they nailed anyone yet, got any ideas, got any clues.

Sheriff Keith isn't in yet, but he's due in three minutes, and I can sit over there if I'd like to. What the hell, I drove out of my way, so I sit. Check my watch against the clock above the door. I'm a full five minutes behind.

"Is that clock right?" The girl behind the desk looks surprised, like it never occurred to her whether it was right or wrong.

"I don't know. I guess so." She smiles to take the too-early-in-the-morning edge off her voice. But it's not a smile inviting further discussion. She's young, skinny, with one of those clips in her ponytail like Sally wears sometimes. I can't tell if she's a receptionist, county clerk, or deputy sheriff. She's got nice shoulders for being skinny. She glances up and I look away, not wanting her to think I'm looking her over even though I was. I take my baseball hat off and set it on my lap, like it's a layer of protection I'm putting between her and me. I think about Jean's laughter when she said how I'd let Sally castrate me. I jerk the hat back onto my head and pull the bill down over my eyes so she can't tell where I'm looking. All the same, I keep my eyes on the clock.

Seven minutes go by. I'm trying to read my book. Ginch Littlefield is changing a flat tire on the Ohio Turnpike, with a vanful of live stolen minks screaming in their cages. Three patrol cars pass by, not one of them stops to offer help. Ginch is glad they pass by. But on the other hand, what the hell is he paying his taxes for? The girl behind the desk is on the phone. I can't tell if she's taking information on a missing person report or talking to a girlfriend about a date gone bad.

"When's the last time you saw him? Did he say anything? You think he was seeing someone else?"

I think about Sally at home, probably wondering where I am. Just getting up and pushing the button on the Mr. Coffee. Every night she fills it with water and gets it all ready so she doesn't have to think about it in the morning. I'm feeling in my pocket for a quarter, thinking I'll call and let her know I ain't lost, just visiting Sheriff Keith, when I see him walking by the window, and then he's in the door and talking to Sue. (That's what he calls her: "Morning, Sue.")

Sheriff Keith doesn't look surprised to see me. We go into his office this time, not the room we were in yesterday, since this is just a friendly visit. He's carrying a Taco Bell bag, which I know by the smell is a bean burrito, maybe two. I tell him to go ahead and eat, don't mind me, hell, that's his breakfast and sorry to interrupt it. Sue brings two cups of coffee without being asked and offers me sugar.

"No, thanks." My voice is anxious and overly friendly, so I decide to shut up for the count of twenty while Sue closes the door on her way out. (Really great shoulders. Broad and straight like those swimmers at the Olympics.) Sheriff Keith looks like he appreciates the quiet, so I stay shut up until he's done. One bean burrito, one plain tostada.

"You're wondering what we have so far."

I nod, feeling like the fake that I am. Concerned next of kin, demanding action.

"Time of death turns out to be three-thirty A.M., although the initial assault could've taken place one to three hours prior, judging by the distance covered by the deceased." Apologetic look. "We got verification you were at work from eleven P.M. to seven A.M., which means you are no longer a suspect, if that's what you're wondering."

"I could've done it before I went to work." Arguing my own guilt like a dumb ass. I can tell he's thinking the same thing.

"We have a witness saw him alive at midnight. And whoever did it stuck around for the whole show."

That's it. That's it right there. "The whole show?" Casual interest. *Gee, Sheriff Keith. What do you mean?* I take a sip of coffee and burn the hell out of my tongue. I press my lips tight to keep from hollering, but tears are boiling up.

He's crushing the Taco Bell bag and taking aim at the trash can by the door, but stops himself when he sees my face. "You sure you want to hear this?"

"Sure."

"The son of a bitch followed him all the way up North Lake Road." At first I'm confused, because I think "son of a bitch" refers to Billy. Sheriff Keith sees the blank look. "Must have been afraid your brother would actually make it to Dewey's Tavern, and finished him off just before he hit the parking lot." Close enough to the version I heard last night.

"That's some kind of son of a bitch," Sheriff Keith goes on. "To watch a thing like that. To let the poor bastard drag himself—" He interrupts himself by swinging the paper cup to his mouth and taking three pissed-off gulps. I wince, waiting for the explosion of scalding coffee, but he wipes his mouth on his cuff and grins through the tiny bits of lettuce in his teeth. "Sorry."

I sort of smile back and shift my eyes to the wall behind him, where there's an old movie poster of *The Magnificent Seven*. It hangs between an Allstate Insurance calendar and a black-and-white photo of a kid standing by a monster steer and holding a blue ribbon near as big as the animal.

"Grand Champion?" I ask.

Sheriff Keith grins wider and looks over his shoulder. "Two years ago. Took the county and went on to place at state. Fourteen years old."

"That's great." What else can I say?

"They're all great. He's got two little sisters."

"Yeah?"

"They look like their mom, thank you Christ. How many you got?"

I see Billy's kid, the red-haired one with the book, with a yellowing bruise above one ear, disappearing into his hair. "Walked into the car door," he says. Deena with red welts on the back of her legs just beneath where her shorts leave off. Saw me looking and didn't say nothing at all, didn't try to cover up, either. I remember one of them as a baby, skin blistered and scabbing because Billy set it out in the yard on account of its crying. Sat there and burned like bacon till Ginny Honey come home and found it two hours later.

I look at the black-and-white photo on the wall. Think about my old man. A small laugh sneaks out of the corner of my mouth. Halfway between a snicker and a sneer, it isn't a nice sound, and right away I feel sorry. Sheriff Keith's eyebrows come down a quarter inch. I cover by saying the obvious.

"Don't have any kids."

"I saw a mess of 'em when I was out there yesterday. Figured 'em to be yours."

"Billy's."

"Yeah. Anyway."

There doesn't seem any point in hanging around anymore, but I do.

"So no ideas, huh?"

"Nothing I can say officially, you know."

"No, I suppose not." Pause. He's figuring I got something to say and need to work up to it, so he waits. Takes his shot at the trash can and banks the Taco Bell bag off the wall and in. Then he pulls a toothpick out of his drawer and sets to work quietly on his teeth, which I'm glad to see.

"Any fingerprints off that rock yet?"

"Some."

"Yeah? Whose?"

"Can't say."

"How come you think the guy was still hanging around at the end?"

"Someone was there either at or after the time of death. Someone playing games. Can't imagine it being anyone else but the one attacked him in the first place."

"What do you mean, 'playing games'?"

"Can't really discuss it at this time."

"Yeah, I guess not." I get up to leave.

"Hey, you got a smoke? I'm trying to quit, but you know how it is."

I pull out my Salems and hold one out to him. I see his eyes go to the pack. To his credit, he actually inhales once it's lit. I light my own and think for a minute.

"What brand you looking for?"

Sheriff Keith grins again and looks me in the eye. "Four fresh Marlboro butts right next to the victim's head. Someone waited a long time for your brother to die."

I call Sally from the pay phone outside the sheriff's office and tell her I'm talking to Sheriff Keith and so I won't be home before she leaves for work and I love her and yeah, everything's okay. Tell her to go on to work, it's all right. I know she'll go. The thing about Sally, she believes what I tell her.

My truck's parked right smack in front of the sheriff's. I start her up and ease out onto Main Street. I take it slow through town and don't let myself think about anything but making sure I use my turn signal, keeping under the speed limit, hands on the wheel in the ten o'clock–two o'clock position. Turn right at Carter's Diner and follow Sullivan Street clear out of town, where it becomes Sullivan Road. I've gone down this road a couple of thousand times, never stopping, always driving right on by.

Jean's yard is as green as mine is brown. Sally pulls teeth to get a few vegetables or geraniums to show themselves around our place. But Jean's house is all tropical with its greeny colors and purple smells. She's got flowers hanging, creeping, spreading, climbing, spilling up over the porch and down the long driveway clear to the road. Her truck is next to the back door. I stop halfway up the dirt driveway and sit still. I can see Jean working in the backyard. Breathe. Breathe. I ain't supposed to be here. I know that. But something's starting to squeeze in on me, and I need to talk to her. I don't want to get out of the truck until I'm feeling steadier. But Billy's face keeps pushing through my closed eyelids. Shit that I haven't thought of in years.

FIVE

Ten years old and my old man takes me, Billy, and Jean to the carnival they have set up down at the 4-H fairgrounds. Not the kind of county fair where Sheriff Keith's kid took the Grand Champion. No livestock here, no tents with vegetables, canning jars full of fruit, needlework, and homemade cakes or pies. The carnival is all lit up with harsh reds and yellows. The carnival has live music coming from the grandstand, and concession booths selling nachos and beer. The carnival has rides that look dangerous and too fast, and I can't wait to get on 'em.

Me and Jean are inside out and beside ourselves, happy to be going anywhere with our old man. Billy's quiet, but he comes along just the same. The old man hands us each five dollars and takes off walking. Not sure what he wants, we follow him along the midway, stopping whenever he stops, staring at the rangy men with tattoos and cigarettes who holler for us to come on and take three shots for a quarter. "Can we, Dad? Can we?"

But he walks on. I keep looking over my shoulder at the out-of-control lights on the Tilt-A-Whirl, the Scrambler, the Helicopters. But we stick close to the old man. Except Billy, who disappears before we hit the cigarette game, where the old man stops and lifts Jean up onto the counter so she can see. He flips her a quarter, tells her to pick a color from all the different-colored squares on the counter. Jean puts the quarter down on pink, which makes me duck my head and cringe. *Pink? Jean?* The booth is crowded with men and women, all slapping quarters down on colored squares. The rangy guy at this booth has two tattoos:

a pirate ship on his left arm, and a cross on his right hand holding the microphone.

"Throw the ball, throw the ball, where will it land? Pick your color and throw the ball. Only a quarter, pick your color." Everyone has a quarter down, and the rangy guy makes eye contact with the old man, who nods. The guy tosses the ball in our direction, singsonging into the mike, "Here we go, here we go, what's it gonna be?" The old man catches the ball with one hand. I never saw him do that before. He hands it to me and tells me to toss it into the center of the booth. There are little crisscrossings of squares, all different colors. I can barely reach over the counter, but I throw it as hard as I can toward the squares. It bounces around from aqua to tan and rolls over black, right smack into the pink square.

"The lady wins," the rangy guy sings. "The pink lady takes it all." Jean looks quick at our old man out of the corner of her eye, to make sure it's okay to be the pink lady who won. He's grinning, so she claps her hands and laughs. The rangy guy's scooping up the quarters from all the colors and dumping 'em in a pouched apron around his waist.

"Salem, Camel, or Marlboro?" he asks.

"Salem," says the old man, and a carton of cigarettes appears on the counter in front of Jean.

"Good job, boy." That's my old man, and he's talking to me.

He lets us stay at the cigarette game for about twenty minutes, long enough for him to have three cartons of Salems in front of him. Jean keeps picking the colors, and on the fourth win, the rangy guy (pirate ship and cross tattoos) tells my old man he can trade in the cigarettes for another prize.

"Four cartons gets you one of the big dogs up front," he says. "Pick one for your girlfriend there," he says. Jean's looking down at the scab on her knee, her hands lying flat under her legs.

"We got Saint Bernards, poodles, collies. All different colors. Take your pick." The rangy guy is singsonging again, attracting new players. Now, this is when cigarettes are only thirty-five cents a pack, but four cartons is a pretty good stash for the old man. So I figure the guy's wasting his time talking about stuffed animals, and I'm waiting to get on with the game so I can throw the ball again. I see Jean still looking at her scab, not up at the old man and especially not at the dogs. The old man shoots the rangy guy a dirty look, but he doesn't say anything for what feels like a month or two.

"Go on, pick the one you want," he finally says. Jean lights up like a Fourth of July twizzler and a freckled, sunburned arm flashes out straight at the poodle, finger pointing like the tip-up bobber we use for ice fishing. Third from the left, a giant pink poodle with green jeweled eyes. Of course she's had her eye on it all along. The rangy guy pulls it down and hands it to the old man, who hands over the four cartons of Salems. He lifts Jean off the counter and hands the poodle to her. She's glowing full beam now and trying not to hop up and down like she does when she has to go to the bathroom. The old man tells us to go on now, ride some rides. He hands me another couple of dollars. Either he forgot about the fives earlier or he's afraid I'm gonna start wanting a dog of my own.

Jean says something and he leans down to hear her under the music and the screaming and the bells going off on all sides. When he's in reach, Jean grabs his shirt, kisses him on his bony cheekbone, and quick lets go and backs up two steps toward me. The old man laughs and turns around to the game, while Jean and I hurry to a quiet spot behind one of the ticket booths to inspect the dog. We check the fur under his belly. White. So are the paws. Plastic toenails. Black plastic nose and white fur again inside the ears.

"Those are emeralds," says Jean, poking the eyes with cracked, dirty fingernails.

"Yeah?" I don't ask what emeralds are.

"His name's Bojo," she adds. Bojo's as good a name as any, so I don't dispute it.

"Let's go," I say. And the three of us head out into the glare of the carnival lights.

Later, we are locked into our car on the Tilt-A-Whirl, Jean and I sitting stiff-backed against the metal dome enclosing us. We have Bojo wedged between us. Jean's legs stick straight out from the seat edge. We have tried the Bullet, buzzing like a big gray hornet; the Helicopters, which actually went out over the surface of the river on their upward swing; and the Avalanche, with its too-loud rock music, five years out of date.

Now we are on our familiar old Tilt-A-Whirl. Our car is a giant clam holding two live pearls and a stuffed one, swinging on its circular hinge. Jean juts out her elbow between us, using it as an added safety bar for the poodle. His green plastic eyes are glittering like a crazy fly's. They do not blink as we start to move.

"Scared, Bojo?" I ask him.

"No," he answers, staring straight forward.

Jean grins, first at the stuffed dog and then at me. She leans into the turn as our car lifts up and over its first curved incline. I lean with her, and the force of our shifting weight whips the car around so my head knocks against the rusty wall behind me. I'm smiling, jutting my elbow so it crisscrosses over Jean's, keeping the dog more firmly in place. Then we are leaning the opposite way, bringing the car almost to a standstill on its hinge as we crest the second hump. This'll give us the best momentum for the third hump. It's during these few seconds of holding still that I see Billy.

I'm surprised to recognize him in that crowd of people waiting along the makeshift metal fence with the mothers, and the little brothers and sisters too young to ride, and the people holding tickets, waiting for this ride to be over and the next to begin. So surprised to recognize him that I stay suspended in the air as the car lowers on its track, and the top of my thighs bang hard against the safety bar across my lap. He's got his favorite shirt untucked from his jeans, the plaid cotton as thin as a spiderweb, unbuttoned all the way in the heat of summer and carnival sweat. Cigarette in his mouth, which I know the old man would belt him for, so I figure he must be well out of sight, probably still at the game where we left him. But the thing that makes my body hang suspended in the air is the surprise of realizing that he's looking at us. Watching me and Jean on the Tilt-A-Whirl. He ain't talking to some girl standing next to him, he ain't even talking to the rangy guy running the machine (this one has eight tattoos, one on the back of each knuckle, R-O-C-K and R-O-L-L).

Billy ain't doing nothing but smoking his cigarette and watching us. Jean sees him a second after I do, because her thighs bang even harder than mine on the safety bar. But the thing about Jean is, she waves. Just waves because she's glad to see him standing there. And the most unbelievable thing of all is, Billy waves back. Not just a quick nod of his head, not just a lift of one shoulder, but a full wave like he doesn't care who sees it. And he's smiling. I look close to see if he's drunk. At four-teen, he can't hold any liquor at all. But he's sober. And he's waving, looking at me. I'm waving back and I'm smiling back, and the domed clam suddenly sinks from underneath me and Billy is whisked to the side and out of sight as the world becomes a blur of horizontal lines spinning green gold blue white redorangeyellowblackgreengoldblue until I close my eyes against them.

We hit the crest of the third hump and catch it perfect, like riding a wave. Jean and I lean and sway, throwing our shoulders first to the left, now the right, now bracing against the back as the spin takes over. Bojo navigates between us, already losing bits of pink fuzz-fur in the hot whooshing air.

Jean and I go faster than any car has spun all night. And between the blurred racing stripes of color I can see Billy watching us, looking for the first time I can ever remember like he's glad that we belong to him.

When we come to a complete stop and the rangy R-O-C-K and R-O-L-L guy comes around to take the pin from the safety lock, we wobble out of our seat and land like water on the grass. We ripple over to Billy, who's still standing by the metal fence. Jean swings Bojo by one ear as if, in surviving the Tilt-A-Whirl, he's ready to handle any rough treatment she can dish out.

"Ready?" Billy says when we come to a full stop in front of him, our knees still vibrating. By "ready," he means "time to go." We nod. No topping the Tilt-A-Whirl, no sense trying. He's walking out toward Pe-terson Road, where Woodley's cornfield stretches back for two miles before it butts up against Cutler Road. Our road. Our house.

"Where we going?" Jean asks, now bouncing Bojo against her hip.

"Home," says Billy.

We haven't seen the old man in over an hour. I don't have to look over at the parking lot to know the gold Pontiac's not there. This isn't the first time we been left. So we follow him across Peterson Road with no more questions. We stand on the shoulder for a few minutes, Billy looking up and down the road, trying to figure something out.

"You got to figure we're right opposite the cornfield, huh?" He's dis-tracted, but the question is definitely directed at me. And not like I'm a kid, either.

"Our house?"

"Yeah."

"I guess so. Close enough."

So off we march—Billy, then Jean with Bojo, and finally me—straight into the corn. Just five feet in, and the corn muffles the music and the screaming and the bells ringing. Ten feet in, and the lights of the carnival go out like a giant battery's been switched off. Fifty feet in, and all I can see is the back of Jean's head and Bojo's green eyes glittering at me over her shoulder. Looking up, I can see stars peering in at me, twinkling and squinting in an effort to make out that movement down there. What are those children doing in a cornfield in the middle of the night? Shouldn't they be in bed? Where's their father?

We take turns telling ghost stories to keep ourselves from getting tired. I'm not gonna be scared, for Jean's sake, so I pound my teeth hard together and tell the most bloody, gruesome stories I can think of. Billy's are worse. Jean tops us both, setting her stories in a cornfield. Of course we get lost and come out a mile or so from the house, and we make it home after nearly two hours. Ma asks where the old man is. Billy won't answer until Jean and I leave the room, then their voices are too low to make out. But it don't matter, Jean says. It's still the best night we ever had. All the pent-up willies from the walk in the corn finally take over once I'm safe in bed, and it takes forever to fall asleep. Two weeks after that, the old man's arrested for beating some guy near to death in a bar.

"Broke his neck bone. I heard it go *c-r-rack!*" Jean tells me. She was with the old man when it happened. Got to ride in a cop car and run wild all over the sheriff's station until they tracked down Ma to come get her. The old man stayed in jail for two years that time.

S I X

I hear the crunchy gravel sound of tires pulling into Jean's driveway behind me and lift my eyes to the rearview. A dark-blue Buick stops a few yards back. Now I'm trapped. Now I can't get out of the driveway unless I drive over Jean's front yard, over the damned flowers. Ma and Ed sit in the Buick. Why don't they get out? Then I see Ma's mouth moving. I look away from the rearview and see Jean, still out behind the house. Either she hasn't heard the parade of cars in her driveway or she doesn't care. I want to stay in my truck until the Buick goes away, but here we are, and there's no way out of this.

I think of Sally at home, getting dressed for school, me lying on the bed, fighting back sleep for the sake of seeing her cross the bedroom to the closet, to the bathroom, in from the kitchen, back to the bathroom again. Same thing, Monday Tuesday Wednesday Thursday Friday. Teaching summer school. Poor hot kids in a room, everyone else out swimming and riding their bikes or doing who knows what down by the mill. It's got to be just god-awful, even with Sally there.

Behind me, the passenger door opens, then the driver door. Heads, then shoulders, looming outward and upward like giant ears sprouting from either side of the Buick. I kick the door and jump out of the cab of the truck. Feet land hard on the ground and I slam the truck door. It's probably stuck shut forever now. Sally'll say, "Why'd you slam it?" And I won't have an answer that makes sense.

I stand with my feet wide for balance, dug in and spread. Ma's in front, Ed hanging back a little, letting her have the lead like he always does when any of us kids are around. I wait to see what she'll do. Burst into little-girl tears and slump her shoulders in a miserable hump, demanding comfort. Reach her arms up and pull me down by the back of the neck, giving awkward love whether I want it or not. Pout, hanging on Ed's arm for reinforcement, because I ain't phoned since I heard the news. Or ask what the hell I'm doing there: the most natural impulse, given everything she knows or refuses to know. She walks to me without a word, holds my hand, and kisses me on the cheek.

"You okay?" It's a real question. And she's waiting for an answer, looking me right in the eye. Hers are brown with gold flecks.

"Yeah, I'm okay." Out come the words in formation, like the trombone section of a marching band. Ye-ah-I'm-o-kay-hup! But my face feels funny and my nose is full of the after-school smell of her chocolate no-bake cookies. So I'm the one in the miserable shoulder slump and she's got two arms around me, not saying nothing. It's what I need. Goddamn Ma, you never knew what you were gonna get with her. After a minute, Ed comes up and offers a hard, reddened hand.

"I'm real sorry."

"Thanks, Ed."

They walk up the drive and I fall in behind. Jean looks up from a wheelbarrow full of flagstones she's bringing from the barn. She lives on an old farm. Not much left except the original stone house and a half barn, also made of stone. She's rigged it up as a sort of greenhouse, storage shed, furniture repair shop. She looks up from the wheelbarrow, and I'm too far away to see, but I know her face registers nothing. We could be strangers come to ask directions, for all she shows. I think about my own face and what's written all over it. For a second I feel sick, because I'm afraid she's gonna think I came with Ma. Like it's some sort of prearranged visit. But Jean knows better than that. I'm in for a long wait, though, if I want to talk to her private. Ma'll try to out wait me, like she always does. She doesn't want to leave us alone together. Locking the barn door after the horses are out and long gone.

"Jeannie! Oh, Jeannie, baby!" There it is. The little-girl wail out of a forty-nine-year-old woman. The brown with gold flecks are just flat glass now, swimming in easy tears. On and off like a light switch.

Jean's standing under Ma's hug about the same as she was standing over the wheelbarrow. Ed waits, of course. I'm looking out to the stone shed, thinking how cool and quiet it must be inside there. Old stones. I listen, but they don't say a word, just breathe real quiet. I can't turn my eyes back to the people behind me. I remind myself it's just my sister and force myself to look at her. It's like a punch in the ribs, because she's looking at me over Ma's bent head. A look that doesn't say anything, but it goes on for three seconds longer than it should. Then she's walking Ma into the house, thanking Ed for his clumsy "Real sorry." I always used to try to get her to play poker, but she said poker was for assholes.

I keep hanging back, the last one to go in the house. Tagging along on someone else's business. What was I gonna say to her anyway? *Were you with Billy? What's going on? What did that look mean just now?* Someone puts a glass of lemonade in my hand. The glass is white with red chickens on it. Two red chickens facing each other. I look inside. Four ice cubes, the way I like it. I look up at Jean, but she's got her back to me, closing the refrigerator door. Mom and Ed are sitting at the kitchen table. Like kids waiting for their report cards. I stay where I am, in the doorway.

". . . all set for Wednesday at one o'clock. Up to Snell's." There are two funeral homes in town. St. Joseph's for the Catholics, Snell's for everyone else. When I was eleven and my grandpa died, I fell in love with Snell's. The look of it hasn't changed in the seventeen years since. The thick cream carpet soaking up all the echoes in the room, the sheer curtains hanging in a perfect line a quarter inch above the floor. Even the heat ducts, covered with little plastic hoods. Never disturbed, no matter how many dead people are wheeled in and out. I go to pay my respects to every non-Catholic in town. A work buddy's ma, an old teacher, the guy behind the bakery counter up to Grant's supermarket.

". . . want you both there at seven sharp. Are you listening?" Ma's looking at me, all out of patience.

"Sorry."

"You think I'm made of money?" She's pinched her mouth tight tight tight, in her talking-about-money voice. Ed's looking at the chickens on his glass. It's a matched set, except Jean has roosters.

"No insurance, no savings." Pinched so hard, her teeth almost squeak. "You kids think you can just go off living however you want, but someone's got to pay sooner or later, and always it's me. I don't see your father coughing up anything to help out." Her mouth screws all the way shut at the mention of the old man, so the words are squealing out like tiny mice. Ed is riveted by those chickens.

Jean raises innocent eyebrows. "Anyone told him yet?"

"The sheriff, from what I understand. He won't even show up sober, let alone help pay for it."

Jean gives a small sigh, thinking. She flicks a half look at me. She knows Sally and I ain't got a pot to piss in.

"I got a couple, three thousand," she says. "If that'll shut you up."

In midsip, I snort lemonade up my nose and reach quick for a paper towel. No one pays any attention. Jean and Ma are looking at each other, and Ed's practically counting chicken feathers by now. Ma tries to look like she might say no to the money, but she can't pull it off and quits trying.

"That'll be a help, yes. Thank you, Jeannie."

The mood gets light all of a sudden, despite Jean's tone, now that the real purpose of the visit is over. I'm adding up the Buick and the house out on the west end of town and the new patio furniture Ma bought earlier in the summer and the vacation cabin they keep up north. And the motor home.

"That's all Ed's money. You know I don't have money of my own." She's said this as long as I can remember. They've been married nine years now, but it's still Ed's money. All of a sudden I'm tired. For some reason, I think of old Chet in Bakersfield.

"The obituary'll run tomorrow in the Jackson paper, but it's too late for this week's *Chronicle*. I got a list of people that have to be called. Ray?"

"Yeah?"

"You think you and Sally can make some of these calls?"

I nod. Ma tears off part of the list, copies down the visiting times, hands it to me.

"Wednesday at one. That's day after tomorrow." She's all brisk and orderly now. Like a five-year-old playing mother with her dolls. Bossy, bossy. Jean stares out the window at the wheelbarrow full of flagstones. I wonder if she's wishing me gone as well as the others. No one's asked me what I want here. I look at the list in my hand. The old man's name,

third from the top, his telephone number next to it. Just below Joe Lee
Phillips and above old Mrs. Barnes, who used to baby-sit us. I thought
she died a long time ago.

I look up and see Ma watching me. She's itching to go, but there I
am still and she doesn't know what to do.

"How's Sally?" Her voice is still in a pinch. Holdover from talking-
about-money or a start of why-don't-you-marry? "I don't see why you
two don't get married." Oh.

"No need to." I raise the glass to my mouth to ward her off.

"I see a need to. I see a definite need to." She has those awful lines
around her mouth from smoking too long. Make her look like that fe-
male gorilla from *Planet of the Apes*. Zira? Zora? I told Jean this once,
thinking it would make her laugh, and it did. Ma's looking at me now
like she can't forgive me for not turning out better. Like why can't I pretend I was raised by Ed, with the Buick and the patio and weekends at
the cabin? For Ma, the past dead-ends nine years ago. The thing about
being rescued is pretty soon you're an awful hard judge of the ones you
left in the shit to fend for themselves. I think she honestly can't understand why all three of us didn't end up doctors.

"Not everyone can get married, Ma." I say it gentle enough, but I
see it land anyway.

"If you let Sally get away, you're a fool." She's talking blind now,
mouth forming words but eyes locked on the screen door. I know what
her brain is flashing in ten-inch neon: Escape. *You rotten coward, you rotten coward.* But I don't know who I mean, Ma or me. They are getting
up to leave, declining Jean's bloodless invitation to hang around for a
while, maybe lunch later.

"You don't forget to make those calls, okay?" She's digging around
for the car keys before she remembers that Ed drove. "And don't leave
it for Sally to do all of 'em." She's kissing me on the cheek, eyes still on
the screen door. Ed's giving a sort of shamefaced nod by way of good-
bye. Like we don't know he bullies the life out of Ma when we're not
around. She'd wither and die if he didn't.

Jean walks with them out to the car. Stands absently nodding while
Ma continues to talk at her from inside the car, waves too lightly in response to the parting toot of the horn, and they are gone. I stay in the
kitchen, watching out the screen door. Jean turns toward the house,

walking up the driveway past my pickup. *Now we are alone, now we are alone.* The lemonade bites at my stomach.

"C'mon," she says as she passes the door, not looking at me. "You can help with the stones."

I dump the rest of the lemonade, rinse out the glass, and set it in the sink. I feel a little panic at leaving the red chickens. Magic chickens. Charm chickens. Protection against disaster.

The day has heated up by the time I've emptied the third load of flagstones. Jean doesn't mind the heat, kneeling and digging out earth, testing the lay of the stones, leveling the ground some more with a yellow-handled trowel. She's biting down on the Marlboro sticking out of the corner of her mouth, like she always does. We're building a flagstone path from the back porch out to the shed. We've finished about ten feet and haven't said more than a dozen words. "Here?" "Yeah." "Smaller?" "No." There is quiet between the two of us, quiet that would make Ma sick with panic if she heard it. The question buzz that hummed so loud earlier is gone. Right now, with my shirt off and the sweat standing out on the back of my neck, with Jean's hands broad and square as they place the stones, with her worthless gold tiger cat stretched out on its back on the grass and watching me upside down, the questions are gone. The sky is wide and flat, and I don't care if she killed him. A ladybug lands on the outside of my thumb, and if she held his hand while he died, at least she's quiet with me now.

I got a ridiculous wide-open space in my chest, full of hot sunshine and white daisies and robins singing and all that sort of shit.

I go to move the wheelbarrow, but when I hit a bump in the grass, a big flagstone balanced on top tips back toward me. I lift the handles to adjust the pile, but the stone keeps coming. It slides down and I hop back, but I know before it lands I'm screwed. I'm thinking, It's got to weigh forty pounds easy, and then it lands. On its jagged side. Just where the toes meet the rest of the foot. Just where all the balancing and walking stuff happens. Crack. Five toes. Five simultaneous cracks.

"Fu-u-u-uck!" I go straight down. The worthless cat doesn't twitch an ear. Just cocks his head back a bit further, the better to see my upside-down thrashing.

"Fuck you, cat," I think.

"Fuck you too, Ray," it says.

"Oh shit, you okay?" I hear Jean drop the trowel. "Let me see." I don't answer. I'm trying to breathe through my nose, but my ears are pounding so hard my nose is blocked with noise.

"Fu-u-u-uck!" comes from somewhere again.

"For Christ's sake, Ray. Take your boot off so I can see."

"Nonononononono! Shit!" The cloud of red that bloomed in front of my eyes is starting to clear. I see Jean sitting back on her heels, wiping the dirt off her hands onto her shorts. I'm rocking back and forth now, a sick sweat making my forehead all of a sudden cold. The sunny day in my chest is gone. Jean tugs on the laces of my Red Wings. I'm sitting up, leaning back on my hands, fingers digging in and clutching clumps of grass.

"It's broke," I say.

"What is?"

"All of it. The whole foot."

"These are steel-toed boots," she says. "Probably just bruised." Okay, maybe. But when she slides the boot off, I throw myself back hard on the grass. My head lands on something soft and warm. It is a fur-covered stomach. In the next half second, I feel something sharp lay open my left eyelid. Then both of us, the cat and me, are screeching and clawing in unison. From about six miles away, I can hear Jean's laughing interrupted—

"Ha ha humpht—"

—as my leg jerks up in the struggle and my poor broken foot makes contact with something solid, which turns out to be her face. A fresh bloom of red erupts inside my eyeballs. Ouch plays leapfrog up my leg. The old brain is scurrying in little circles like a panicked rat, hollering, "Crippled and blind, crippled and blind!" I'm not breathing. Jean's laughing again. When I open my eyes, I see she's got one hand over her mouth and there's blood on her fingers. I can't tell if it's hers, mine, or the cat's. She's laughing so hard, tears are starting up.

I say, "He took my eye out." Ha ha ha.

"Naw, it's just your eyelid hanging down." Ho ho ho. We go on like that for I don't know how long, flopping around on the grass, howling and crying.

"You knocked my tooth out." Hee hee hee.

"Naw, just a split lip." Ohmygod, haw haw haw. Ohmygod, ohmygod, and we've rolled into each other. There we are, lying right next to each other, with her warm, bare arm next to mine. The sun is high and bright behind a torn red eyelid. I don't move, afraid she'll disappear. *The grass is green, the sky is blue* . . . I'm grabbing at facts. Holding myself down with 'em so I don't fly off to heaven. *The grass is green, the sky is blue, buttercups are yellow* . . . Where is that from? Jean has picked a long blade of grass and she's trying to stick it up my nose. I swat her hand away, but she keeps doing it.

"The grass is green," she starts.

"The sky is blue," I follow.

"Buttercups are yellow."

"And I love you," I finish.

The blade of grass at my nose disappears and Jean sits up.

"That ain't how it goes." Her voice is flat and hard like a dull penny, the back of her head staring me down. I don't answer. This is closer than I've been in ten years, and my heart is lodged somewhere up under my jaw. She picks a dandelion and twirls it against her cheek like we did when we were kids. If it leaves a stain of yellow, that means you'll marry your true love.

After a couple minutes, I reach over and put a finger real light on her elbow. She doesn't pull away, but she says, "You gotta go home now."

I sit up, not too close to her. But I don't leave. She's still giving me nothing but the back of her head. Concentrate on the burning of the torn skin over my left eye, like the pain is gonna give me some kind of magic word to say to her. The tiger cat sits licking his wrinkled fur at the edge of the yard, one killer eye on me.

"What do you want, Ray?" The sound of my name off her tongue hits me hard. *What do I want?* I take the coward's way out and misunderstand the question.

"Wanted to see if you were okay," I tell her. This is met with a snort, and she throws the dandelion hard toward the work shed, making the cat jump in midlick.

"I'm fine," she says. "You go now."

But I can't go now, I can't. And I hate her for pushing me away like this.

"Don't you even care that he's dead?" I want it to come out hard like a bullet. It doesn't, but it has the effect I wanted.

"Go fuck yourself," she says. And then she's heading for the house. I'm up and limping after her, grabbing an arm to make her stop. But she's stronger than me and not only yanks her arm away but gives me a shove backward while she's at it.

"You gotta be the stupidest person on earth, you know that?" She's walking away from me again, yelling over her shoulder. "I don't know why I ever bothered with you."

"Why did you?" I yell back. We neither of us move now, 'cause this is the closest we come to talking about it, ever. My head's filling up with static and bubbles, static and bubbles, until I take a big breath.

"Because I thought you was something you ain't," she says. The screen door screeches and she's gone.

Well, there it is. There's my answer. Now I don't have to wonder about it anymore, wonder what's on her mind. I get in the truck, gun the engine, and drive away from her.

SEVEN

Got home from Jean's around 2:00 P.M., grateful that Sally was still at school. Laid down, had to get up and be at the funeral home by seven for two hours of torture. Even in my favorite place in town, two hours of torture. Ma's self-righteous sniffling, all the folks reaching for something nice to say about Billy, most of 'em coming up with some of the lamest-assed crap I ever heard.

"He's with Jesus now." *Jesus?*

"At least it wasn't a long-drawn-out illness." I think I'd have a tough time choosing a head bashed in with a rock over cancer, but there you go.

"You're looking well, Sherry." Sherry's my ma. And she looks like hell.

It's sort of fun for a little while, watching everyone make small talk and act like there isn't a dead man in the room. Coffin closed, but a dead Billy in there, no doubt about it. And four feet away from him, Ed's listening to Mrs. Norris (the organist for the Methodists) tell the plot of a TV movie she saw last night. About some people with thirty-six foster kids.

"And these kids were every color you can think of. Some of 'em were just as cute as any kid you'd see anywhere."

After about a half hour of this crap, I tell Sally I'm gonna head down to the smoking lounge. Partly I'm gonna die if I don't have a smoke. Partly I'm wondering if Jean's here yet, and I'm thinking I might nose around a little.

The smoking lounge is a room downstairs where the bathrooms are, and the little kitchenette area for coffee, and the general offices and God knows what else. There's dark paneling on the walls, a clock that looks like a captain's wheel, and green ashtrays made of dark, heavy glass. I'm wolfing down a cigarette on the corner couch, holding one of the ashtrays on my lap. Two women come in, pour themselves coffee, talk real quiet in a far corner. Trying to walk that line between respecting someone's privacy and ignoring 'em completely. So I wander upstairs, even though I don't want to go back into that room where Billy is. Not just yet. I ain't seen Jean since we got here, and I'm wondering if maybe she's wandering around, not wanting to be near Billy's coffin either. And that's what I'm doing, avoiding Billy's room and keeping an eye out for Jean, when I run into Elizabeth Rollins. She's laid out in the small chapel, which is all pink and kind of hokey. Actually, I was afraid it was for kids only. So I'm glad to see old Elizabeth laid out here.

She's got to be at least ninety years old. She looks like a nice person. Tiny. I can actually see where they've sewn her lips closed, see the stitches. Must be because she's so old and her skin isn't so good anymore. The chapel's tiny. I feel like I walked into a dollhouse. She's all alone in here, which makes me feel awful. Where's her family? Doesn't anyone care that she's in here, dead, alone? I look at the guest book. She died the same day Billy did. I sneak another look at her in the coffin, checking in spite of myself to see if she took a rock to the head too. No signs of violence. She's got a rosary in her hands. There's a thing to kneel on in front of the coffin, like they have in Catholic churches. I went to the Catholic church in town a couple of times when I was a kid, with Randy and his ma, so I know what it looks like. I'm surprised, though. Because I never saw a Catholic laid out at Snell's before. I wonder why she ain't over to St. Joseph's. It occurs to me that maybe she was excommunicated, tossed out of the church. Randy told me that's when you do something so bad even the Pope can't stand it. I sign the guest book, paying my respects. Say good-bye to Elizabeth Rollins and take another swing past the smoking lounge. No Jean. I'm thinking I might apologize for this morning, for whatever I did to make her so mad. But she ain't here.

When I finally get back to Billy's room, some guy's standing next to Ma, talking to her. Acting awfully friendly, considering her kid's laying there dead, fifteen feet away. I'm practically on top of them, and this asshole puts his arm around Ma's shoulder and says something in her ear. She ducks her head and puts her hand up to her mouth, looking all of a sudden like she's the Queen of England trying to hide a smile. Who is this asshole? Ed's on the other side of Ma, talking to someone I don't know. He's paying no attention to this. Ma's giggling like a virgin now, leaning her head toward this guy. I half-step my way a little closer to her, trying to hear what this dickhead is saying.

". . . and she had ugly toes," he says to her.

"Oh stop it."

"She did. Long skinny old toes like a monkey, I swear to Jesus."

Ma's shaking her head, but her eyes are all sparkly like they used to be when the old man was in a good mood and started in with her.

"Now I remember someone else," says this piece of shit. "Someone else had the sweetest little toes in the world."

"How would you know?" Ma's voice sounds about fifteen years younger. The Zira lines around her mouth are gone.

"You used to wear white sandals with—"

"Oh Lord, those white sandals!"

". . . and paint your toenails pink."

That's about all I'm gonna stand here and listen to. I move in on the two of 'em, sucking in air and holding it to make me a little taller.

"Hey, Ma," I say, not bothering to look at this jerk.

"Oh, honey," she says all innocent. "Here's someone you ought to meet."

"Yeah?" I flick him a look like he's something you pull out of the bathtub drain when it backs up. He grins back at me.

Ma's voice cuts in. "This is Shiner LaVonn."

"Shiner LaVonn?" I say, louder than I mean to. "Jesus Christ," I practically yell. "Shiner LaVonn!"

He looks at Ma like to say, *What the hell you been telling this guy?* Sticks out his hand and I grab it and shake it a little harder than I would with just anyone. This is Shiner LaVonn, for Christ's sake.

"You look just like your old man," he tells me. "No doubt about that."

"Damn," I say. "I heard a lot of stories about you."

He grins wider and the arm goes around Ma's shoulder again. "They was all lies, all lies," he says. "That was your old man did all that shit, going home to your ma, laying all the blame on me."

Ma laughs at this one, losing another five years off her face. The smell of stale cigarette smoke is coming off his clothes, a little bit of liquor when he talks. Shiner LaVonn's a real living legend, and I can't take my eyes off him.

He's swearing up and down to Ma how it was my old man, not him, who stood up on the table and proposed to Joy, the bartender at the Watering Hole, when they was up north deer hunting. But it was Shiner who tipped over the snowmobile when they was ice fishing over to Clark Lake. Took a snowmobile with a sled hooked to the back and run it up a snowbank off the side of the lake and tipped the whole thing over. The two of 'em went rolling back down onto the ice, covered with minnows from the bait bucket, cans of Budweiser, tip-up bobbins, and fishhooks. Drunker than hell and laughing their asses off. It was Shiner stuck a lit firecracker back in the burn barrel up to the hunting cabin so it went off when Abel Williams took the deer guts out back to dump. Abel thought he was having a heart attack, but it was just a firecracker and a little sunstroke. Shiner jumped up on the Watering Hole float during the Fourth of July parade and danced with the go-go girls in just his Bermuda shorts, rubber flip-flops, and a purple felt hippie hat.

The old man told Ma once that Shiner had over fifty women in six months.

"I swear to Jesus, Sherry," he's saying now. "That was Bill." He means the old man.

Ma says, "Believe me, Bill didn't have it in him." Shiner throws his head back and barks up to the ceiling. It's loud enough so I jump a little.

"Ar! Ar! Ar!" he laughs. "Ar! Ar!"

I heard the old man imitate this laugh so many times it's like I'm having an old familiar dream. I got no idea what they're talking about, but I laugh too. Just looking at Shiner LaVonn, I got to laugh. A couple people look in our direction, wondering who'd be gross enough to laugh that loud in a funeral home, relax when they see Ma.

Shiner was the old man's best friend in high school. They played football together and won the district championship their junior year.

The old man was quarterback on account of being so skinny. Shiner was known for getting his fist through the space above the face mask and popping the defensive linemen right in the eye. No ref ever caught him, but there'd be at least three black eyes by the end of each game. That's how he got the name Shiner. His real name was Bernard.

Started out Ma was dating Shiner, and the old man stole her away. So the two guys kicked the holy hell out of each other one afternoon behind the bleachers and got back to being best friends. But Shiner carried a little torch for Ma all the time after that. Every time the old man came home from a three-day drunk, after fucking everything in sight, he'd accuse Ma of cheating on him. Say how she was giving it to the gas meter guy, Dr. Summer next door, just about everyone, except he never said a peep about her and Shiner, no matter how drunk he was. He didn't want to give her any ideas. Shiner got married and moved to Florida when I was too young to remember him.

And now here's the guy in front of me, barking at the ceiling and flirting Ma's head off. She's looking almost pretty, she really is. This guy could've been my dad instead of the old man. Ed finally decides to join Ma and see what the hell she's been up to right under his nose.

"Still after my wife, you old son of a bitch?" But he's smiling.

"I'll get her sooner or later," Shiner says, patting Ma right square on her ass. "We're just waiting for our moment, aren't we, Sherry?"

Ma gives Shiner a slow smile, and I can believe the old man stole her away in high school. It's dawning on me that Ma was a real pistol.

I go to find Sally so she can meet Shiner LaVonn, and that's when I hear Randy's voice behind me, talking low to someone.

"Billy was a son of a bitch, but he didn't deserve this."

Then her voice her voice her voice, sounding strange because it's coming from that same direction in the room; not whispering in my ear like it ought to be. And her laugh. She *would* laugh right then. She *would* laugh about it. I don't even catch what she says. Sally's next to me now, and I can feel that she's heard it too. I look at her, but she smiles at me like it's okay.

Now that Jean's here (I was afraid she would-wouldn't, would-wouldn't come), I feel like I'm standing around naked. All of a sudden, everybody's looking at me. Not staring, just little looks. Like being attacked by gnats. Tiny looks taking tiny bites out of me. They're looking at both of us, me and Jean. Like they're waiting for me to tear my hair out of my head in big handfuls and jump around howling like a baboon. Which is what I want to do.

I breathe through my nose and duck my head slightly, scratching at the cut over my eye to cover my quick look back. Sure enough, Randy's standing fucking *right next to her*. He's got some dishwater blonde glued to his hip. I'd heard he was living with someone. She looks all right. But blonde or no blonde, he's still standing fucking *right next to her!* I forget about the apology I was gonna make earlier.

Sally takes my hand in hers and starts us away from their side of the room. She's spotted a couple of empty chairs by the corner and I can feel her brain figuring the safest route. But Ma pops up on our right, and even though she's been talking to Sally on and off since we got there, she sort of swoops at her and gives her a hug and a kiss. I position myself behind Sally, out of reach, and wait for what I know is coming. What I knew was coming the minute I saw the dark-blue Buick behind me in Jean's driveway. I look around, but Ed and Shiner LaVonn are talking on the other side of the room. No help there.

Ma isn't letting go of Sally, holding her by the neck with a circling arm. It's uncomfortable because it keeps you off balance. A real Ma specialty.

"Jean promised me she'd be here right at seven o'clock, and look what time it is." Ma's little-girl-hurt voice. Clinging to Sally but pulling back her head to include me. "You heard her, Ray. You heard her."

"Yeah, Ma." I try to stop her, agree with her, shut her up.

"Over to her house this morning, standing right there in her kitchen, you heard me tell both of you that you had to be here at seven sharp."

"Don't worry about it, okay?" I try not to sound pissed, but I am.

"And she said she'd be here. She said she would. And waltzes in here an hour late without saying a word to me. She does it on purpose."

"No, she probably just got running late and—"

"She does everything she can to hurt me."

I know that if I don't look Sally in the eye right this second, then I am a bastard and a prick and a coward and a son of a bitch. Because I didn't tell her I'd been to Jean's house. I lied and told her I cut my eye on the cupboard door. I look up, and Sally's right there. I don't look away. I don't let my eyes slide off across the room like the old man would. I look her in the eye even though I don't think I can stand it another minute as Ma finally lets go of her, mission accomplished.

●

I think about shivering with my head under the covers as a kid. Snow beating on the windows. The sound of Ma crying in the kitchen downstairs, the old man hollering. For a skinny guy, he had the voice of a cannon shot. I hear the sick thud and crash of dishes or chairs hitting the wall. The cold knot in the stomach, like a giant nail right through my gut, pinning me to the bed. Don't move. Don't breathe. Don't move. Her voice high and thin and pleading with him to stop please stop please stop. Until the next thud is different. Heavier, and I know it's her hitting the wall. The covers fly off and Billy's voice hisses in the frozen dark, "Don't go down there."

But I'm on the stairs. The bare wood floor is like ice picks on the bottom of my feet. I'm still holding my breath, but my feet are landing flat, hitting each stair hard, loud enough for him to hear, loud enough to give him time to let go of her. I'm in the kitchen door and no, he hasn't let go of her. Has her by the hair. She sees me and covers her face with her hands like she's the one caught doing something wrong.

"Leave her alone! Leave her alone!" My voice sounds tiny and scared and I hate myself for it.

"Get your ass upstairs." He takes a half step, like he's coming after me. I don't fall for it, though. I take two full steps forward, right up against the kitchen table, and I take a deep, deep breath. Enough breath to yell it out as loud as I can.

"I hate you. We all hate you. We wish you were dead."

It really surprises him, drunk as he is. He drops his hold on Ma's hair and looks at me, and now I am scared. Now I am plenty scared. The window above the sink is a black hole full of cold cold cold. Tiny bits of snow and ice throw themselves against the glass: "Let us in! Let us in!" But inside, where it's light, we're frozen too. I hear Ma tell me to "Get upstairs. Ain't none of your business." I look at her, still keeping him in the corner of my eye, and she's scowling at me.

"Git!" She says it like she hates me. "Go on!" She's not saying it for my own good. Not saying it to protect me.

So there we are. Two people and a kid in the kitchen. And the kid finally gets it. Figures it out. This ain't got nothing to do with him. It's like he doesn't exist. I go back upstairs without another word and lay there in bed, thinking about the snowflakes outside. Don't never try to rescue Ma again.

E I G H T

There's a hand on my arm, and when I look down I see it's Sally's hand with the square nails all short and sensible. It's pulling me over to those two chairs that are still empty in the corner, and I follow and I sit and I feel her sit next to me and there we sit together. I think about how the old man felt, throwing Ma across the kitchen. I think of the weight of her in my hands, slamming her head against the counter, how that might have felt. I suck my cheeks in hard and bite down. Harder.

"I'm sorry," I finally say, tasting blood.

Sally doesn't answer, but her fingers squeeze my arm. My eyes are on the soft, deep carpet. I want to kick off my shoes and smash my toes into the soft fur of it. No way I'm gonna have a single word with Jean. Not now.

Two boots appear in the little circle of my sight. Two black boots plowing through the tall grass of beige and stopping right in front of me. Clean blue jeans, and what looks like a two-mile stretch of Harley-Davidson T-shirt. Arms like mountain logs and hairy hands with most of the oil and grease scrubbed off but not all of it, never really all of it. Bushy red beard and mustache, and somewhere behind all that explosion of hair, two little blue eyes looking at me. Little blue eyes hiding under more bushy red hair, eyebrows sprouting and springing.

"Hey, Joe Lee," I say. He's so big he blocks out the whole room. Joe Lee's been waiting for a chance to kick my ass since the day Sally first said she'd go have a beer with me. They grew up two doors away from

each other, down at the end of Redfield Road, where the new tree nurs-
ery was built a few years back.

They were best friends all through elementary school, even when it
wasn't cool for boys to talk to girls. They climbed the water tower together, ran away (twice) together. Sally told Joe Lee about the birds and
bees. Joe Lee taught Sally how to hang by her knees under the Stritch
Road bridge when the train went over it. Something Jean tried to get
me to do, but I was chicken. One time Jean hung there by just one knee,
even though I hollered and hollered for her to climb down, even when
the train went over and drowned me out. I was so mad I kicked her ass
on the way home.

So Joe Lee and Sally stayed best friends, and I guess this made prob-
lems with her keeping boyfriends in high school, on account of sooner
or later they all got jealous of Joe Lee. So they ended up going to the
senior prom together, because ain't neither of 'em got a date. I seen a
picture of her at the prom in a strapless dress with flowers in her hair.
Real pretty. And Joe Lee in a green tux, all red-haired and red-faced,
like a sweaty tomato. But they're having a good time. You can see just
looking at the picture what a good time they're having. That was two
years before my senior year, before that summer. Sally was going to
Adrian Teachers College by then.

The reason I think Joe Lee's just waiting to kick my ass is, he was
working up to Jack's Sunoco station that summer. Got questioned by
the cops the night I tried to kill Randy. Had I come in for gas? *Yes, sir.*
Had I seemed drunk? *Yes, sir.* What time was that? *About ten P.M., sir.* Joe
Lee knows all about me. Ain't a soul in town don't know some version
of what went on that summer, most of it all twisted around and wrong.
But I was used to that, people getting it wrong.

Only time Joe Lee ever said anything to me directly was just after
Sally moved in. I take my truck into his shop with the radiator leaking a
gallon of antifreeze a week. It's Joe Lee's Sunoco by now, because Jack
retired six months before. I don't see Joe Lee's LeMans in its usual
place, so I figure it's safe to bring her in. But I'm stepping out of the
truck and he comes out from behind a tan station wagon, big greasy
wrench in his hand like a club. I try to play it off real cool, telling
him the problem with the radiator. He's not saying nothing, but that's

Joe Lee. Sometimes he talks your head off, sometimes he don't say a word.

Then he says, "Won't get started on it for another couple of hours. You gonna wait?"

"No, I'll leave it," I say. Then I got to go and say something else. Can't just let it be. "Sally's gonna pick me up in a half hour over to Carter's."

Carter's Diner, three blocks west on Main Street. French fries thick as your thumb and black cherry ginger ale to wash them down.

But we aren't thinking about Carter's right then. Joe Lee puts the wrench on a workbench behind him and wipes his hands with an oily rag hanging out of his back pocket. I think he's getting himself cleaned up so as to land a neater punch on the left side of my whole head. But he stuffs the oily rag back in his pocket, pushing the waist of his work pants so low I don't know what's keeping them up besides the will of God.

He's looking a hole through me with his tiny blue eyes. That's a habit he's got, staring straight at people, right dead in the eye. Makes the hair on my arms stand on end.

"She know about your sister?"

This ain't the time to get on my high horse about anything, so I just say yeah, she knows about it.

"I don't know what happened to you. I don't care," he says.

"Thanks." Stupid, but how do you answer that? He stops for a second, decides I ain't being a smart ass, and goes on.

"You okay now?"

"Yeah, I'm okay."

"You ain't gonna go berserk again?"

Oh. He thinks I'm a nutcase.

"No." I say it real steady, but what I want to do is pound his fat face into the side of that tan station wagon. I don't do it, but my chest is ballooning with that old black air and I'm glad for the pole I'm leaning back on.

"Okay," he says. He still hasn't blinked.

"Okay," I answer.

"Tomorrow morning all right?"

"Yeah. I'll give you a call."

"All right." And he turns back to his work. And I beat it over to Carter's. And that's that. I say I ain't gonna go berserk again, and he believes me. And he's nothing but friendly ever since. Still, you can't tell me he ain't just waiting for a reason to kick my ass.

Now I'm looking up at him from my seat in the corner of Snell's and he just looks like he goes on forever. So I stand.

"Hey," he says. "Go on and sit down." He pulls a folding chair over from the other side of the window and sits on it. I wait for the crash, but the chair takes the weight. He's next to me now, on my left, with Sally on my right.

"I'm real sorry about it," he says.

"Thanks," I manage.

Sally's talking to him now. The two of 'em back and forth over top of me, around behind me, right through me. Making a kind of sticky web out of words, wrapping me up like a fly. I want to buzz and beat against the web, but I know at the same time that it's for my own good.

"I'm thinking of bringing in another kid after school," says Joe Lee.

"You that busy?" asks Sally.

My eyes flick up off the carpet for a second. Jean's hand pushing a piece of hair behind her right ear. I feel Joe Lee's weight just a foot from me and flick back down to the carpet.

"Tomason kid didn't work out so good, and I need someone gives a shit about cars." Joe Lee acting like the rest. Like Billy ain't across the room. I look up to see Jean turn away from whoever she's talking to. Who is she talking to? The dishwater blonde? Where's Randy?

"I got a kid, he's young, in my Family Living class. He's young, though." Sally talking.

Billy's just over there. I wonder how long before he starts rotting. I know they pumped him full of that shit that keeps 'em fresh for a while, but when does that start to wear off? Is he already starting to go soft inside?

Joe Lee says, "Don't care if he's young. Just a couple hours a day, after school."

Sally throwing the sticky lines of the web back to him. "Only fourteen, but all he cares about is cars. Can't get him to pay attention . . ."

Jean's out of my view. Where'd she go? There's Ma. There's the carpet. God bless this carpet.

". . . nothing but cars. Give him something to do, keep him out of trouble." Sally loves her kids.

I wonder if I poke my finger into Billy's shoulder would the skin bounce back, or would it stay indented, sort of bruised and pushed in, like a peach that's gone half bad? I think about rotting. On and on it goes like that, and it don't stop until nine o'clock, when we all leave. Everyone in a clump, like we're stuck together in a huddle until we're safe out of there. I'm hoping to maybe hang around, just for a minute, sort of by myself. I tell them I have to go to the bathroom, excuse myself, saying, "I'll meet up with you all out front." But much as I take my time in the bathroom, no one budges until I get back. Soon as I reappear, the clump of people surrounds me and we move out the door.

I was thinking maybe I might have a talk with Billy, with no one around. Just to ask him a couple of questions. Coffin lid's closed, but still he'd be able to hear me. But it ain't gonna happen, not tonight. And Jean left a half hour ago. Alone. Surrounded by no one. Free to walk in and out of there whenever she felt like it, no matter what Ma or anyone else wanted or thought or said about it. She'd made a point of keeping a clean distance from me all night. Not so's anyone else'd notice, but steering clear just the same. *I thought you was something you ain't.*

Me and Sally don't say much on the ride home. We both climb in the passenger side of the truck, me sliding across the seat to the steering wheel.

"Door stuck again?" she says.

"Yeah."

"Did you slam it?" she says.

"Yeah. I'll take it in to Joe Lee tomorrow."

She doesn't say anything after that, except when I ask if she's hungry, want to stop at the Burger King drive-through? No. So we drive home with just the glow from the dashboard lights, and the crickets loud like thunder once we're out of town. But the quiet inside the truck is louder than all the crickets on earth. And it's not like she's mad. Sally's no brooder. If she's mad, she yells. Quiet just means she's thinking. But what she's thinking about, that's what's making the quiet so loud.

It's not until we're almost home when she says, "Where'd you go today?"

"To Jean's." I'm surprised how blank my voice sounds when I say the name. Sally doesn't say anything. I keep driving.

"Was it some sort of family meeting? Did your ma ask you to be over there?" She's giving me the way out right there. She's handing me the lie that'll get me out of this. And I'm ready to jump on it, tell her how I didn't want to go over there but Ma insisted. We had to make decisions about the funeral. We had family stuff to talk about. I'm all set to jump on it, but I don't want to lie to her. I'm screwed up in a hundred different ways, but I do not lie to Sally.

"No," I answer.

"Did Jean ask you over there?" she says, keeping her voice level.

"No." Jean would eat glass before she'd ask me for shit.

"Why were you there?" Sally asks. I can feel her tensing up on the other side of the truck.

Why was I there? What made me take Sullivan Street out of town when I left the sheriff's office?

"I was scared," I say.

Anyone else would've said, "Scared of what?" right off the bat. But Sally just looks at me as we pull into the driveway, trying to answer it for herself. I don't know if she's been doing any guessing on her own about who killed Billy. I don't know if she has any theories that she's keeping to herself. But she doesn't ask me what I'm scared of. I pull around back, kill the motor, but I can't open my door so I just sit there. So does she. Finally I'm feeling so bad I say, "I'm sorry."

"Don't say that." She doesn't sound mad. But she sure sounds like she doesn't want to hear me say I'm sorry. So I keep my mouth shut, feeling like I'm on the edge of a slippery cliff. One more wrong word out of me and the cliff crumbles and I go down, down, down. I don't move at all, don't even breathe, thinking maybe that'll stop time, stop everything, so disaster won't strike. I count as far as fourteen before she says, "I don't want to talk about this tonight."

"Okay."

"I want to talk about this tomorrow."

"Okay."

"We've got to talk about this tomorrow, after I think about it."

"I love you." Jesus, I just can't shut up.

"I know that," she says. And she gets out of the truck, leaving her side open for me. See, that's Sally. She didn't slam that truck door, even though I know she wanted to. Slam it so I'd have to open it to get out. It's a little thing, but still it would've been shitty. And she didn't do it. That's Sally.

I don't wait too long before I follow her into the house. Into the house where Ginny Honey and the kids are watching TV. Ginny Honey wasn't feeling up to going to Snell's.

So we all sit together and watch TV. Ginny Honey pops some popcorn for us. Sally is on one end of the couch, I'm on the other. She ain't necessarily looking at me, but she ain't necessarily not looking at me, either. The red-haired kid is falling asleep between us, with his head on my knee. The two girls are sprawled out on the rug, faces about an inch from the TV screen.

Couple of minutes into one of them real-life search and rescue programs, Sally's taking the orange and brown granny-square afghan off the back of the couch and putting it over the boy, when Ginny Honey says, "Did you hear that?"

"What?" says Sally.

"I heard a car door," says Ginny Honey. I get up to look outside. The kid grumbles in his sleep, his head falling onto the couch cushion. Ain't nothing out there.

"Ain't nothing out there," I say, turning back to the living room. And there's Ginny Honey sitting just like she was a second ago, but her face is all wet. And it's eerie because she ain't making a sound. Just tears falling all over her face while she's looking at the TV.

"Yeah, I guess not," she says. "But I thought . . . you know, I thought I heard him."

Sally looks at me, and we neither of us know what to say about that. All the nights that we'd be sitting here eating popcorn and watching TV, then a car door slams and Ginny Honey goes outside to talk to him. Until she comes back into the living room and says to the kids, "C'mon. We're going home."

Billy would carry whoever was asleep, carry 'em out to the car. And Ginny Honey'd make sure all the pillowcases were loaded up. And she'd thank us every time like it was the last time. But tonight there ain't nothing out there. I'm watching Ginny Honey cry. I'd been sort of waiting for him too.

"I think me and the kids'll go home tomorrow," she says.

"You sure?" asks Sally, frog-mouthed, not thinking it's a good idea.

"Yeah. We ought to be home."

"All right, then," says Sally.

None of the kids say a word. It's real quiet, except for the rest of the search and rescue program. I been keeping one eye on Trish. She's quiet. Younger two been crying on and off all day, but not her. Maybe it hasn't sunk in yet. Maybe she just takes after her old man and doesn't cry no matter what. At eleven, I leave for work with the lunch Sally packed for me, just like usual. Just like nothing's wrong.

NINE

Work is quiet, seeming normal. I get one chapter of Ginch Littlefield read on my breaks. He drops his wallet in a jewelry store he's robbing. Has to go back and try to break in a second time to find it. But by now the store's due to open in fifteen minutes. So what he does instead is, he acts like he's a customer and waits for the manager to show up. Once the store is opened, he's in there like a shot and sees his wallet on the floor behind one of the cases, but he can't get to it because the manager's standing almost on top of it, screaming and hollering on account of being robbed. And a bag full of stolen rocks is in the trunk of Ginch's car, two blocks away.

After about six heart attacks and seven or eight prayers to God about never breaking the law again, never never never, Ginch gets his hands on the wallet. The cops arrive and now he's a witness, sort of, and they're taking his statement. *How long were you out front waiting for the store to open? Did you see anyone in the area? Hear anything? No? Thanks for your help, sir.* And Ginch is getting a kick out of this, having a ball, until he looks up at the camera mounted in the corner. The security camera. Of course he taped over the lens before he started. He isn't a rookie. But it's cheap masking tape, because Sally (!) used up the duct tape for caulking the tub. It's such cheap masking tape that it came unstuck, and it's dangling there in the breeze of the ceiling fan. And there's the naked lens, recording Ginch's face as he stares back at it. When did it come unstuck? When? He beats it out of there and doesn't even stop for breakfast but goes to unload the rocks with Sergeant (his fence) as fast as he can. That's Ginch Littlefield. That's just one chapter.

I come straight home from work this morning, you can bet on that. No stopping to pass the time with Sheriff Keith, no stopping nowhere for nothing. Sally still doesn't want to talk. I don't lay in bed, half on my way to sleep, watching her get ready for school like I usually do. I'm all wired and wide awake. So I start in on the phone calls, the list Ma gave me. Getting a sort of mean kick out of the fact that people are having a heart attack, hearing the phone ring at eight in the morning. A phone ringing at that hour only means someone's dead or in the hospital. Oh yeah—someone is dead. Billy.

I try dialing the old man's number, but I get a message it's out of order. "No further information available about—" I move on to the next name. Sally leaves. Kissing me good-bye like always, saying, "I want to talk this afternoon." Not like a threat, just a friendly date sort of. I'm still all wired and wide awake, so that's when I decide to go out and see the old man. I gotta tell him when the funeral is, and I want to get it over with.

The old man lives out on Old Route 29 past the Bowl 'n' Bar, in a white cinder-block house with light-purple shutters and front door to match. I don't go out there much if I can help it. But now I'm driving down Old Route 29 and Samson's butt is in the passenger seat with the whole front half of his body out the window, paws scraping the paint off the outside of the door, mouth grinning wide, tongue flapping.

"You look like Goofy when you do that," I tell him. He does look a little like Goofy, and he hates it when I tell him that. He flicks me a quick look out of the corner of his eye.

"Try it," he says.

"Try what?"

"Head out the window."

I shift my weight to the left and keep my right hand on the top of the steering wheel. It's just Old Route 29, so there's no traffic front or back. I stretch my neck and stick my head out the window as far as it'll go. The wind hits me hard and sucks the breath out of me. The hot air rushes into my eyeballs, so I scrunch 'em down to slits. The left one, the one the cat tore, stings a little. My ears are roaring so hard I want to yell. I open my mouth wide and I'm hollering loud as I can, but the wind carries it away behind me like a trail of sound bubbles following the truck.

Old Samson and me, and no one around for miles. Samson and me and the wind whipping our yells out into who knows what the hell. I wonder if I yell loud enough, who will hear me.

"Billy!" I'm laughing and yelling, "Fuck you, Billy! Fuck you!" which takes the last of my breath out of me. The hot wind bites at my slitted eyes, pulling tears back across my face to somewhere above my ears.

"Owowowowowowow-haw!"

I don't know how the truck is staying on the road. Samson starts howling too. I can feel his tail thumping hard on the seat between us. I holler again, feel my face turn red with the strain.

"Yaaaahhhh!" I'm yelling.

"Yooooooow!" Samson answers.

A bug flies into my mouth. Flies in so hard and so fast it hits the back of my throat, and I half swallow it before I know it's in there. I kick at the brakes and Samson scrambles for footing as he falls under the dashboard. I land the truck on the shoulder and kill the engine. I'm coughing and gagging, but the bug doesn't move. He's wedged in tight and he's not coming back up. So I work up some spit and swallow hard a few times. No good. I swear to God I can feel the bastard moving around right behind my Adam's apple. He ain't dead.

I can hear him in there: "What the hell?"

I think for a second of him just flying along, wind in his face, yelling a little bug yell for the hell of it, and wham! Makes me feel like everything's just useless. Just absolutely goddamn useless. The old gag reflex is taking stabs at me. I'm leaning out of my window, hot metal from the side of the truck sending flashes of scorch marks onto my arm, spitting and phlacking onto the gravel below, when a spot of blue and white comes into my vision from up the road. A patrol car. Coming up Old Route 29. I know right away who it is, and I know where he's coming back from. I think of me with my head out the window screaming down the road a few seconds ago, eyes closed, mouth open wide, driving smack into that patrol car. How it would seem, head-on collision, murder investigation going on. Sheriff Keith's boy, the one with the blue-ribbon steer: "Naw, my dad's dead. Some guy did a kamikaze in his Ford pickup."

I rest my forehead on my arm. "Thank you, thank you, thank you."

Sheriff Keith pulls over onto the opposite shoulder. Takes his sunglasses off even though now he has to shield his eyes with his hand to cut the glare. A naturally polite person.

"Hey, Ray."

"Hey, Sheriff."

"Everything all right?" *What the hell are you doing?*

"Yeah. Just swallowed a bug."

"How's that?"

"Swallowed a bug."

"Must've been one hell of a bug." He's looking at the pavement behind my truck. Dark slashes of skid marks going back about fifty feet. *Jesus Christ.* How fast was I going? I picture that head-on collision again.

"It was. Still stuck in there."

"You want some Coke? Flush him down?" He's reaching for a Taco Bell cup wedged between the dashboard and the windshield.

"No, thanks. I'm just going up the road here a bit."

Sheriff Keith nods. "You headed over to your dad's?"

"Yeah." Samson scuttles over half onto my lap, eyeing the patrol car.

"Just came from there."

"I figured. He under arrest?"

Sheriff Keith laughs on cue. "No. Just some questions for him, you know."

"Yeah."

"What's his name?"

"Bill Johnson."

"No, I mean the dog."

"Oh. Samson."

"Good-looking dog."

I turn to look at Samson on the seat beside me. He's looking from me to the patrol car and back at me again, just his eyes moving, cocking first the left eyebrow, then the right, then the left again, the way dogs do. I look at the mud-colored bristles that pass for hair, the bent tail (wind blew a door shut on it), his good ear standing straight up like a satellite dish. This ain't a good-looking dog.

"Yeah," I agree. "He's all right."

"Well, I better get back, then." He hunches a shoulder forward, moving for the ignition.

"Any new leads?"

"Well . . ."

"Can't really talk about it?" Me backpedaling fast as I can. *Don't tell me. Tell me. Don't tell me.* There's a span of quiet that sprouts up and grows like the weeds on the stretch of pavement between us. I start to think maybe he didn't hear me.

"It's a terrible thing that happened." He's not looking at me. He's looking up the road at a car coming, dark plume of dust wagging behind it like the tail of a tornado.

"Yeah."

It's a lame answer, and even I can hear the lack of feeling in it. But Sheriff Keith doesn't seem bothered by it. We neither of us say anything for another stretch. The car comes closer, slowing down a bit but not too much. Three girls, high school. Three carefully blank faces driving past the sheriff, who of course knows them, knows their parents, knows they're driving around sneaking cigarettes. Once they're past, the one in the back seat can't help herself and steals a quick, guilty peek back at us. Sheriff Keith grins and shakes his head a little. He isn't gonna bother them.

"The thing about investigating a murder is, you get to know your victim awful darned well," he says. "Pretty soon you're talking to him, asking him questions, like he's sitting right next to you, sort of pointing the way." He's playing with his side mirror, moving it up and down, making the reflection of the sun slide up and down his arm. "I've worked on two murders before this one. That's what it felt like."

"Yeah?" I'm getting a little hypnotized by that reflection bouncing around on his arm, but I'm listening.

"Yeah. Kind of nice. I get to thinking of these dead folks as friends, almost."

I'm having a hard time picturing Billy and Sheriff Keith being anything but two faces staring hard at each other from opposite sides of a set of bars. It's like he's reading my mind, because the next thing he says is:

"But not with your brother. The more I learn about him, the more I get nothing. Like there's no one there."

I have to laugh at this. I really have to laugh at this. He waits until I'm finished before he hits me with it.

"You seen your sister recently?" He's still playing with the mirror but stops now and looks straight at me.

"Saw her yesterday."

"How's she taking it? Pretty hard, huh?"

"We all are." I'm looking at the spot on his arm where the sun's reflection has stopped. I think how if he doesn't move soon, it's gonna start to burn. Smoke rising up like a magnifying glass held over a dry leaf. Poof, fire.

"Well, you know I'm real sorry about it."

"Yeah. Thanks."

"I'll see you around, Ray."

"See ya, Sheriff."

He pulls out slow and easy. I imagine him driving away, sipping on his Coke, wondering if I'm hiding something or if I'm really just stupid.

"What's his name?"

"Bill Johnson."

"No, I mean the dog."

Jesus Christ.

I watch the patrol car get smaller, head resting on my arm. When the last tiny speck of him is gone, I start up the Ford. Samson is looking out his window like he never saw such an interesting field of soybeans in his whole dog life. By the way his shoulders are set, it looks like he's waiting for me to hit him. Even though I ain't laid a hand on him since he was a puppy. Not since the time he turned around and took a bite out of my thumb.

"It's okay, boy." But he still won't look at me. He's laughing. I swing back out onto Old Route 29. Both of us are pretty quiet until we pull up to the old man's house. He's still driving the same gold Pontiac. It's parked in back, floating and rippling in the furnace blast of noon. My ears are pounding. It's too bright. I look up at the sky, but I don't see the sun now. There's nothing but a white overcast haze. No breeze. Misery.

Samson falls over into a small patch of grass next to the cement porch. I grab the hose lying in the dirt and give him a soaking. Take a long drink, which finally sends my friend all the way down my throat. Knock quick two times and open the screen door in the back. No answer. I hear the TV in the next room talking too loud. Bells are clanging and buzzers jumping, the audience laughing. Some guy in a suit and pretty hair and heavy jaws is talking to three contestants. Two flower-print dresses and a short-sleeved striped shirt. All with eager Play-Doh faces. One of the flower prints is answering a question.

"Well, Ned, I'm a systems analyst from Sacramento."

What's a systems analyst? What does that mean? And why did she call him Ned? Why do people overuse names until you can't stand to hear 'em anymore? I think about my own name. Ray Johnson. Ray Johnson. Ray Johnson. Ray Johnson. See how you get sick of the sound of it? I flick the TV off. The old man's voice comes down the hall.

"Who's that?"

"Ray Johnson," I yell back. It just comes out that way, I don't know why.

"I'll be out in a second."

I figure from the tone of his voice that he's in the bathroom. Hell. I walked in on the man taking a shit in the peace of his own home. Probably waited and waited for Sheriff Keith to leave, and now he's in there finally, and here I come. I figure I'll just tell him what I got to tell him and make like I'm on my way somewhere, running late, and get the hell out. He comes into the living room, wiping his hands on his plaid shorts. Black socks with brown shoes, no shirt. I think it's the same plaid shorts he's had since I was about seven. He's still skinny, but he's got a gut now.

"You want a beer?" He's already at the fridge, pulling out two. There's an empty couple of cans next to the La-Z-Boy. Could be from last night, but I doubt it. It's just about noon. I think what that beer's gonna do to me in this heat, but I take it when he hands it to me. I bring the can to my mouth and feel the beer land on a stomach empty but for a bug.

The old man throws himself backward into the La-Z-Boy and kicks the footrest up in the same motion. He looks in a better mood than I expected. He looks like he can look sometimes, like an overgrown leprechaun, those Lucky Charm guys, the little Irishmen. I read once that leprechauns aren't necessarily nice, and that's when I thought of the old man with that look on his face. Smile wide in a flat line, and the eyebrows up high and innocent. The old man can get going sometimes. Once in a while I'll say something just on purpose to make Sally laugh and sure enough she laughs and looks at me and there are my eyebrows all high and innocent and it makes her laugh even more and I know I'm just like him just like him just like him and I wonder if he got as much of a kick out of it, making us laugh.

On Sunday mornings, hung over and lurching through the house in boxers and black socks, hair straight up in the air and one eye closed against the hard hard daylight, he'd be singing under his breath, just loud enough for us kids to hear but not Ma in the other room (she was always in the other room on hangover Sundays), singing softly Ma's favorite hymn:

"Oh, what a friend we have in Jesus."

Then the eyebrows go all high and innocent and the mouth flattens out at the corners.

"Jesus Christ, he is our pal.
He will lend us his last penny,
And bail us out when we're in jail."

His head is stuck in the fridge, looking for pop or juice to cut the fuzzy paste that's grown up overnight all over his tongue. He's ignoring us, but we know the singing is for our benefit. Jean and I giggle at the breakfast table. Billy looks away, not wanting to admit it's funny, even though he knows it is. There are five or six verses the old man made up. I never heard him sing it except on hangover Sundays.

TEN

One time my cousin Harold stayed a week with us. It's right after my eighth birthday, and I just got a new transistor radio, which we spend most of that week listening to while we try to build a fort.

For the fort, we start off with the doghouse, which is under the box elder tree behind the garage. It's Shadow's house, but he died about a month before and the old man hasn't gotten another dog yet because he says he don't have time right now to train a new pup. We had Shadow since the year I was born. Same month, even. So when he dies of heatstroke a few weeks before I turn eight, I wonder if maybe I'll die too pretty soon. So for the rest of that summer, I spend a lot of time in the shade, trying not to get heatstruck. And since the dog's house is in the shade of the box elder tree, I figure this is a great place to build a fort.

Me and Harold get a crowbar out of the garage and pry half the back wall planks off Shadow's house. We're gonna use the flap of the doghouse as the front door, so only kids our size can fit into the fort. The next morning, we steal a bunch of scrap sheet metal from the old storage sheds over by the mill. We have to carry it home on our bikes, which is not easy. Harold's using Billy's bike, and he's afraid of scratching the paint with the metal and getting killed, so we have to keep stopping so he can shift his grip. We got about half a dozen balls of twine that Randy brought from one of his dad's barns. Harold didn't want to let Randy in on building the fort at first, but we needed the twine.

So we get hammers and nails and a rusty old saw that hangs on a nail in the garage, and we snag a tire that's leaning against the back garage wall. We get Billy to take it off the rim by daring him that he can't do it. Even then he won't give us the tire until we give him three dollars and the use of the transistor for the rest of the day.

We got a piece of sheet metal braced against the box elder tree, and we're tying it in place with twine when the old man says, "What the hell are you doing?"

We didn't even hear him drive in. Randy says he has to go home, but the old man tells him to stay where he is.

"I asked what're you doing?" he says.

"Making a fort," I say kind of low.

"What you doing with my tools?"

"We only took the old ones," I answer. He looks down at the hammer at my feet. "We didn't take any of the Craftsman."

The Sears Craftsman are the old man's good tools and they stay in a huge red metal box that says CRAFTSMAN on it. I'd chew my fingers off before I'd touch that toolbox. The old man looks at the tire, which we've already sawed in half with the rusty handsaw. Harold's watching me and Randy to see how much trouble we're in: if it's really bad or just a little. It's really bad.

"Where's the rim?" the old man asks, kicking the pieces of rubber just a little.

"In the garage."

"You do that yourself?"

"Billy got it off for us."

The old man turns toward the house and yells Billy's name like he's really gonna get it.

"I asked him to," I say, trying to lighten the ass kicking I'm gonna get later from Billy. The old man doesn't answer, probably doesn't even hear me. He yells for Billy again and then inspects our work so far. We can't get a nail through the sheet metal, so mostly it's all tied in place. The sun's shining hard and slanting against the back of the house, which looks real far away right now. The old man doesn't say a word until Billy comes out on the back steps with my transistor in his hand. He doesn't even bother to turn it down, even though he knows it's gonna get the old man's goat. He stands there with the sun popping off the metal of the radio and says to the old man, "What."

I look at the ground. It's one of those "what"s that make people say,

"It ain't what you said, it's how you said it," just before they smack you across your mouth. I sneak a look at Harold, who's probably wishing real hard for the green hills of Tennessee right now.

Then the old man says to Billy, "Go get my toolbox."

Billy keeps his trap shut, does what the old man says. Honest to God, my first thought is that the old man's gonna bust my ass with one of them big wrenches he's got. But he doesn't.

An hour later, we got the whole thing held together with C-clamps and shit, and the old man's letting me and Harold and Randy take turns using the electric drill to make holes for the metal bolts. The transistor's propped up on a tree branch, playing tinny Motown music. Billy's mostly just standing around watching, but he'll hold stuff steady for us and sort of help in a half-assed way so no one can accuse him of really helping us build a fort.

The old man's telling jokes that all start with, "This guy walks into a bar . . ." Harold's looking at me like I got the coolest old man in the world. And I'm thinking maybe it's gonna be like this from now on. Maybe whatever was bugging the old man and making him so mad all the time, maybe that's gone. By the time Ma calls us for supper, it's pretty much done. Big enough for me and Harold and Randy all three to stand up once we're inside, once we crawl through the dog flap.

Randy calls his ma to see if he can spend the night, and later Ma makes root beer floats for everyone after the old man says it's okay. We all watch *Chitty Chitty Bang Bang* on *The Wonderful World of Disney*. Dick Van Dyke's pretty cool with that flying car, but I can't see him telling jokes about a guy in a bar. Harold and me and Randy stay up playing Chinese checkers half the night, and I can hear the old man's muffled voice and Ma laughing in their bedroom. I wonder if maybe Harold can come live with us for good.

Looking at the old man now in his La-Z-Boy, I think maybe this visit won't be so bad. Maybe it'll be okay.

"Funeral's tomorrow," I say. "One o'clock." He nods like I'm telling him the Pistons made the playoffs. "Phone's out, you know that?"

"I got this corn on my toe," he says. "Can you believe that? Outside of the little toe. I go up there to Benson's to get something to put on it, and I don't see the Dr. Scholl's display anywhere, so I'm standing there with my thumb up my ass, staring at the deodorant, and this girl comes up and wants to know if she can help me."

There's a layer of dust on the table next to me. I make ring designs in it with my beer can while he talks.

"And I mean, she's got a pair of tits that make me want to cry. Not real big huge, just nice. Beautiful tits on this girl, and I'm trying to look at the deodorant so as not to stare at those tits and get tossed out of Benson's on my ear, and I can't think what I came in there for."

"Yeah?" I nurse the beer, staring at the dust rings, letting him go. Can't resist clearing my throat a few times, even though I know there's nothing in there no more.

"And she's waiting, all polite. And I say, 'No, thanks, I got it,' and I grab some deodorant off the shelf and go up to the counter and she's right there, boy. Right behind me. She rings me up and asks if I want anything else and this corn is screaming, I mean screaming, on my damned toe, but I can't say it. I just can't say it to this girl who's maybe sixteen, I don't know. But she probably don't know what a corn on your toe even is. Her feet are perfect, right? Perfect sixteen-year-old feet. And just thinking about it, I get a hard-on."

I slide the beer can back and forth lightly, erasing the ring patterns on the table.

"So I pay for the deodorant and I leave and I still don't have nothing to put on the damned corn. But you know what I got in the medicine cabinet? Secret. I fucking bought Secret. I swear to God. That's what a pair of tits'll do to a man. You think maybe Sally could use it?"

"What?"

"The Secret. I ain't gonna use it."

"No, that's all right."

"You can help yourself. It's in the medicine cabinet."

I get up for an ashtray. He's got one on the floor next to the La-Z-Boy, spilling over with butts and cellophane from old packs. I look in the kitchen and there's an old metal ashtray on the counter. Coated black with ten-year-old ash, but butt-free. I stop when I see the open pack of Marlboros. Right there on the counter. I don't touch 'em. Just look closer. A little crumpled, less than half left. My veins are cold all of a sudden. Tingly. I look in the trash at the end of the counter. See a

couple of Marlboro butts. Look closer. No lipstick smears. Pinched at
the end like they been bitten down on. I count four of 'em and reach in
to push aside a paper towel full of coffee grounds for a better look.

"Where'd you go?"

I don't jump at the sound of his voice. It's far away, not like the next
room. My veins are cold cold cold now. Like old lead pipes left out in
the snow. I think about lead pipes. Cold and solid and a good grip. A
lead pipe in my hand swinging like a baseball bat perfect swing right up
the middle caving in the old man's face with one blow. I picture it con-
necting with his gut, folding him in half, but it's no good. It's got to
be the face, the crunch of cheekbones, the nose an explosion of blood.
Eyes wild and glazed, not getting it. "Why?" the eyes ask the ceiling.
You know why.

"Ray, bring in another couple, will ya?"

I open the fridge. A box of Velveeta, an old jar of horseradish crusted
shut, and two cases of beer. I grab two cans in one hand and the ashtray
in the other. Pause at the La-Z-Boy long enough for him to take his
beer before I ease back into the far end of the couch. The cushion sinks
so low my knees are about chest level. He's talking about some waitress
up to the Bowl 'n' Bar got a wet spot for him.

". . . young too. She got a kid in school but she can't be more'n
twenty-three, twenty-four. She's always telling me to go put something
on that jukebox for her. 'Bill,' she says, 'you know what I like.' You bet
your ass I know what she likes."

"When was she here?" I ask like it's a casual thing.

"She ain't never been here. She got a kid in school and—"

"I don't mean her. You know who I mean." Breathing through my
nose.

"No, I don't know who you mean." But his eyes are sliding off away
from me because he damn well does know.

"Whose Marlboros on the counter out there?"

"Them are Marge's."

"Who's Marge?"

"Gal used to work over to Adrian, the hi-lo driver, Marge. Crazy
Marge. You remember her?"

"Yeah, Marge." I do remember her.

"Well, she come over to watch the Tigers Saturday. You can have 'em, I can't stand the goddamn things. Taste like smoking dirt. You want 'em, help yourself."

I remember Marge. Hair the color of Fritos and frosted orange lipstick. Tons of lipstick that'd smear all over a cigarette butt like two coats of wet paint. He's lying to me. Smooth as always, lying and warming up to the lie and then enjoying it, believing it, telling it like he can see the whole thing in his head, so that when you tell him he's lying he's already convinced himself it's the truth.

"Who won?" I'm talking through the aluminum can at my mouth, my voice tinny and hollow.

"Goddamned Tigers lost it. Can't even say the Royals won it; it was the goddamned Tigers lost it. In the last inning, three runs up and they pissed it away. Six batters and one long steady stream of pissing it away. Marge is crowing on account of she's a Missouri girl. That's how come she's over to my house. Being a Royals fan, no one else'd watch it with her. Old Marge is all right, though. She's a good girl."

Which means he's fucked her. Anytime the old man says someone's a good girl, he's fucked her.

"Sheriff was here just now," I say like he don't know.

"Nice guy," says the old man.

"He come in the back way or the front?"

"What?"

"He come in the back door?" Breathe, breathe, breathe.

"Yeah. Why?" Shit shit shit.

"I got to go."

"What's your rush?" He's putting out his Salem in the ashtray, knocking old butts onto the floor.

"I just stopped to let you know about the funeral. Tomorrow, one o'clock, at Snell's."

"Yeah," he says. "Shiner told me."

"You coming up there tonight?"

"What for?" He's looking at the TV now.

"Visiting. You know."

"Who the hell I wanna visit with up there? Your mother? All her people?"

"I got to go." I'm up off the couch and moving across the room.

"How's that Sally?" He stays in the La-Z-Boy.

"She's all right." I'm heading to the back door.

"She's a great little gal. You tell her I said hello." I'm relieved he didn't say that she was a good girl. He's still not moving.

"I will. I'll see ya later." I'm at the screen door. His voice follows me out into the shimmer of heat.

"Better watch out I don't steal that girl away from you."

Down one cement step, down two.

"And don't think I couldn't do it. There's a gal up to the Bowl 'n' Bar—"

I don't hear anymore. I get in the passenger side of the pickup, scootch across the hot vinyl seat, and fire her up. Samson jumps in the back. I drive slow and careful along Old Route 29 back toward town. My stomach is growling. Thoughts like bats flapping in circles inside my skull.

Jean hates the old man. She ain't seen him or talked to him in years. Now all of a sudden she's over to his house. The old man knows it, I know it, and Sheriff Keith can guess it if he came in through the kitchen. No way he missed seeing those butts. That's what he's trained to do. Paid to do. See shit like that. I picture the cigarettes all around the pulp that was Billy's head. I see them bitten flat at the end. Jean never wore lipstick in her life. Billy told her she ought to once, but she told him to go fuck himself.

The cab of the truck is closing in on me. Why'd the old man lie about her being there? And did he lie to Sheriff Keith too? I want to stick my head out the window, get some air, but I don't. You can't send a person to the chair for biting the ends of her Marlboro butts and visiting her own father. Sheriff Keith didn't have any real evidence. Jean wouldn't leave a fingerprint. She's too smart to get caught doing something if she don't want to get caught. If she don't want to get caught.

I hear Sheriff Keith. "It's a terrible thing that happened."

A cold weight settles low in my belly. I don't know yet what any of this is adding up to. I don't know why it scares me so much that she was out there. But my knees feel like two bowls full of guppies. She's always been around. Whether she was near me or not, talking to me or not, she was always around. I think of the world without Jean in it, and my mind slams shut. As if the *really* terrible thing hasn't happened yet but it's closing in fast.

The two beers kick in, and I'm so tired I want to pull the truck over and go to sleep right there in the ditch with the chicory weeds and the Queen Anne's lace. I'm tired, I'm starving, I'm lost. Like all my strings have been cut and I'm just floating loose in the middle of the week. That's the worst thing about working a graveyard shift. You never know what damned day it is. I'm swaying and swinging somewhere between Monday and Thursday. But I know it ain't Wednesday, because that's the day of the funeral. I can see Ma's face if I don't show. "Sorry, got my days mixed up." I have to laugh.

I park the truck in the shade two doors down from Carter's Diner. I need to get some food in me. Samson lays down in the bed of the truck, stretching out as if there was a breeze. A little bell jingles over my head when I open the door to the diner. Feels like a meat locker in here.

When Lynette sees me, she pulls the pen out from behind her ear and bounces it up and down against her index finger. "Hey, Ray."

"Hey, Lynette." I lean on the counter. "Can I get a pie pan with a little water?"

"Sure." She pulls out a pan, fills it up, sets it on the counter, all in silence.

"Thanks." I'm turning back to the door when she works up the nerve.

"Sorry about Billy," she says, pen bouncing off her finger like crazy.

"Yeah, thanks." I don't know what to say after that, standing with a pan of water in one hand, the other hand on the door. I got stuff I got to ask her, but I can't let on that I know Billy was fucking her. Her and just about every other woman for five miles around.

"You want the usual?" she asks.

"Yeah." I love that about her. She says stuff like "You want the usual?" She's smiling at me, really nice. I can feel my face burning hot and red, so I duck out the door. A couple weeks ago, Billy said how old Lynette would be fucking me if she could, but she couldn't so she was settling for him. I never thought about her that way. I don't cheat on

Sally. Lynette's got a great ass, though. You got to give her that much. Lousy taste and a great ass.

I take the pie pan out to the truck, setting it down careful in the back so I don't spill any. Samson waggles me a lazy thank-you with one eyebrow. I dip my fingers in the water and flick 'em at his face. He grins and stretches one leg in the air. Damn stupid dog loves getting water flicked in his face. I give him a few more shots, not ready to go back inside yet. Billy named Samson. Billy gave him to me, tell the truth. He had a litter he wanted to get rid of. I took Samson, Billy killed the rest.

I got back inside. Carter's is air-conditioned so hard, Lynette's got her sweater on. I sit up at the counter so she don't have to walk out to one of the booths. Sip my black cherry ginger ale and wait for my fries. The thing is, I get gravy on the fries. That's what makes it a full meal.

"How's Ginny Honey taking it?" she asks, bouncing the pen half a dozen times, then tucking it neatly behind her ear.

"Oh, 'bout like you'd expect, I guess," I say. I don't know how Ginny Honey is taking it. I want to say, "Straight up, with olives," but I shut up for once in my life.

"I'll check those fries," she says. And she's gone like smoke. I guess she used up all her nerve just saying Ginny Honey's name. They were friends from back in high school, Billy told me.

I don't know why I had to come in here when the lunch hour's just starting up. There's three—no, four booths full. That's considered a rush for Carter's. Out of the four booths that have people in 'em, I know the folks in three of them. Don and Carol Wainer back against the far wall. They fight like no two people you ever saw. Everyone says it's a public scandal the way they fight. Always have. They live out on Three Mile Road, where the mud holes get real bad after a hard rain. One night, after a big old fight, Carol Wainer jumps in their car and come tearing down Three Mile Road about seventy miles an hour and hits those mud holes and damn near gets herself killed. Worst accident ever, and everyone said so who saw it. But she lived. And they're still married. And they still fight like that.

Up closer to the counter, in one of the smaller booths, there's Mrs. Thompson, my old eighth grade history teacher. She used to play cribbage with us kids on Wednesdays, in the cafeteria. Wednesday was her day to be cafeteria monitor. But she got bored I guess, standing around. I don't even remember now how it started, except that for that whole year there was about a dozen of us kids in and out of that cribbage game every Wednesday. Mostly us boys, but there were two girls too. Jane Ellwey and Susie Thacker. Jane got killed in a car crash after the homecoming game my junior year; her boyfriend was driving drunk. Lots of people died in cars out on those back roads over the years. I generally try to be real careful, especially at night.

Mrs. Thompson, sitting in a booth across from Ella Platt. Ella Platt writes the "Tell It to Ella" column in the *Chronicle*. It's really just a gossip column, but she thinks of herself as a real journalist or something. She's a huge pain in the ass. She writes stuff like So-and-so's daughter finished basic training, stationed in Buttfuck, Virginia. Or So-and-so's getting married again and honeymooning in Aruba. Or Billy Johnson got murdered the other night.

I'm looking over at the two of 'em—well, really I'm looking at Jill Thompson (that's Mrs. Thompson's name, Jill) and thinking how she seems pretty young for being my eighth grade history teacher. She looks over and gives me a smile. Jill Thompson looks straight at me and smiles. Like she remembers who I am. And it ain't a showy smile, and it ain't a polite smile, or even a casual friendly smile. It's more a smile like we never stopped that cribbage game. It's an "I'll see you Wednesday" smile. I sort of nod and duck my head into a gulp of black cherry ginger ale, like the charming asshole that I am. She's pretty. I never thought so then, even though some of the guys at that lunch table thought so, and I know for a fact that Susie Thacker damn near went out of her mind, she was so in love with her.

Lynette comes by with my silverware and napkin, and that's when I ask her, "You seen Jean around?" She's about to haul ass back to the kitchen but stops.

"Jean?" she says back at me.

"Yeah." I wait.

"No, I ain't seen her in a while," Lynette says. "She come in a few weeks ago with a bunch of 'em from the lumberyard." She takes another couple of steps and looks back at me. "She all right?" Lynette really is a nice person. She's looking me in the eye and everything.

"Yeah, she's all right," I tell her. Then the pen starts bouncing again and she's gone back to the kitchen. Lynette knows all about what happened with me and Jean, just like every other person in this lousy town.

I hear Ella Platt talking to Jill Thompson real quiet, trying to emphasize something she's saying without saying it too loud. The only thing I hear exactly is ". . . the whole Johnson family . . . ," and the rest of it's garbled. Sounds like ". . . if you ask me."

I'm just waiting for my fries. Waiting for my fries. Trying not to feel Ella Platt's eyes boring into the back of my head like two milky-blue maggots. "Tell It to Ella." I'd like to tell you something, Ella. I'll tell you to fuck yourself.

Up to Snell's, people could be so nice. People could really give a shit about the fact that you felt terrible. People *decided* to be nice to you, to give a little damned human kindness. So why did people like Ella Platt decide to be such miserable shits? Why be shits? Why? Billy could be terrific too. Billy could say things like "I knew you'd be the only one who'd appreciate that joke, Ray." And you'd believe you really were the only one in the world smart enough or funny enough for Billy. But most of the time, he was giving Ginny Honey a smack, or yanking one of the kids around. Just being a miserable shit. Why? And why was I a miserable shit too sometimes?

I get up and grab a paper off the end of the counter and go back to my stool. The daily paper out of Jackson. I'm starting the crossword puzzle, wondering what the hell happened to my fries, when a plate full of heaven slides under my nose at the same time the bell tinkles over the front door.

"Thanks," I say. But Lynette don't even break stride. She's on her way out to one of the booths by the front window, where Whaley just sat down. He's at least a hundred years old. Still drives. Lives alone. Don't know if Whaley's his first name or his last. Don't know if he even knows anymore. I hear him order boiled chicken, and Lynette shoots off to the kitchen. I tuck the paper under my arm, pick up my fries and soda and carry 'em to the front booth, slide in over the hot vinyl. It's air-conditioned, but the sun's been beating in on that booth all morning, like through a magnifying glass. I'm surprised my butt ain't smoldering.

"Hey, Whaley," I say.

He looks at me over his sagging eyelids. I swear to God, his lower eyelids hang halfway down his cheeks. It could really make you sick if you weren't used to it.

"Hey, Ray," he sort of whispers. His voice is high and wobbly, but his brain is all there. "What ya doing?"

"I was just wondering why I'm such a miserable shit sometimes."

Whaley listens to this like he'd listen to me talk about the weather.

"I don't know," he says after a while.

"Yeah," I answer. I'm so happy to be sitting there with Whaley I want to yell or sing something. I want to sing a couple of lines from "Got the World on a String," but I don't. Instead I spear a french fry, thick as my thumb like always, and whirl it around in the gravy a few times, pop the whole thing in my mouth.

"Heard about your brother," says Whaley. Lynette comes back with his coffee. He's trying to tear the ends off four packets of sugar all at the same time. I chew, watching, not offering to help. I wouldn't do that to Whaley.

I swallow finally and say, "Yeah."

"Funeral tomorrow?"

"Yeah. One o'clock."

"Shot a woodchuck this morning," says Whaley, stirring his coffee.

"Yeah?"

"Got him with my shotgun."

"Anything left of him?"

Whaley shakes his head like he's disgusted. "Hit him from four or five feet. Nothing left but the tail."

Four or five feet. How the hell did old Whaley get that close to a woodchuck?

"Where'd you get him?" I ask.

"Behind the TV."

At first I think he said, "Behind the tepee," which would make about as much sense.

"In the house?" I'm talking with a mouthful of fries and gravy, but he understands me okay.

"Bastard come right in the damn window, the one with the woodpile just outside it, right? He's walking through the goddamn living room. Grabbed the nearest thing I had and shot."

"No shit." I don't know what else to say.

"Missed him the first time." He pauses but then goes on. "Under the couch. Missed. Then I got him wedged, right? Behind the TV by the end table there. That's when I hit him."

I think about what a shotgun shell would do inside a house. Tear a pretty good hole in the floor, spatter a woodchuck halfway up the wall. I look at Whaley to see if he's pulling my leg, but he's sipping his coffee (loud) and looking out the window like he can still see it all in front of him.

I say, "Bet it took a while to clean all that up."

"Yeah. And now I got to get a new TV too," he says. And he starts to chuckling. And I start to chuckling too, thinking of Whaley in his overalls that he only washes once a month maybe, on his knees with a shotgun under the couch, missing the damn thing.

Whaley's saggy eyelids are shaking back and forth. "I *told* him to git the hell out," he says. And this is really funny. I don't know why it is, but this is about the funniest thing either of us ever heard. Whaley's so old he doesn't make any sound when he laughs. Just a silent wide grin, and shoulders hunching, and crinkled droopy eyelids that start to water. And he's pounding his fist on the table. Not too loud, but that's what he's doing, laughing his ass off. So am I.

A hand touches down real soft on my shoulder. It's Mrs. Thompson. Jill Thompson. I look up with my own eyes watering because I'm about to choke on a fry.

"I'm sorry to hear about your brother," she's saying. I cough a couple times, hoping nothing comes up onto my lap.

"Thanks," I say. Whaley's got his hand over his eyes, but I can feel the table shaking a little still. I try to look at Jill Thompson, but I can't. I can't look at her. I look over her shoulder a little to the left, where Ella Platt is looking grim and not at all surprised. *The whole Johnson family . . .* I'm trying to look all torn up about my brother, because Jill Thompson is really trying to offer some kind of sympathy. She's being a decent person. I try to stand up, because I know it's rude to sit when I talk to a woman, but she's in my way and I'm trapped in this booth and I can't think of anything to say and the whole thing is so stupid all of a sudden I don't even care. I don't care if I'm saying everything wrong or even if Ella prints the whole damned thing in her stupid paper.

"That's nice of you," I say, looking Jill Thompson right in the eye.

She smiles and says, "Well, I'll see you tomorrow."

And I think she means the cribbage game, I swear to God, so I say, "Yeah, see you then," like it's no big deal. And I realize two seconds later, as they're walking out, that she meant tomorrow at the funeral. Whaley's cradling his head. He's shaking hard, but still no sound. I think about what it's like to be a hundred years old.

By the time Lynette brings over Whaley's boiled chicken, he's calmed down a bit and I'm pretty well into the crossword, my fries all gone and the gravy turning hard on my plate. I know Billy's obituary is somewhere in the folds of the paper under the crossword, but I ain't in any hurry to see it.

"Give me a four-letter word for a seabird," I say.

"Cardinal."

"Not a *c* bird—a seabird like the ocean."

"Pelican."

"Got to have four letters."

"Duck."

I know ducks hang around lakes, so I try it.

"Don't fit," I say.

Whaley looks surprised. Chews his chicken and thinks for a while. The door chime tinkles and a blast of oven heat hits my back. It's Phil with the mail, which means it's about 1:00 P.M. I check my watch, which says 1:00 on the button. He drops the mail at the far end of the counter, then goes around behind and helps himself to a cup of coffee (Lynette's in the kitchen) and brings it up to the front.

"How you be doing, gentlemen?" he says.

I'm in the middle of my last sip of black cherry ginger ale (third glass), so I don't answer.

"Gull," says Whaley, bringing his palm down flat on the table so the silverware jumps. I try it.

"Don't fit," I tell him. Whaley looks at me like I'm lying.

"What don't fit?" Phil wants to know. He's keeping an eye on Lynette's ass as she walks past the table.

"Four-letter word for a seabird," I say.

"Tern," says Lynette over her shoulder.

Phil looks back at me and says, "Jesus Christ, that's tough about your brother." I start to slide over for him to sit, but he shakes his head.

"Nah. Got to be going. But let me tell you something about Billy. He was one of the funniest men I ever knew."

"Yeah, he could be pretty funny," I say. Having Phil talk about Billy in the past tense is making me want to smash his teeth in.

"And he was a damned good friend too. You know that, don't ya?"

"So I hear." I smile all nice and pleasant.

"I'll tell you who killed him, too. It was that bunch of Satanists over to Clark Lake."

"Oh, I don't know, Phil."

"They probably sacrificed him at one of their meetings, is what they probably did."

The Satanists are really just some commune, I guess you'd call it, of nature-lover vegetarian types that have a big old house out on Clark Lake. I think they worship Mother Nature as being God's wife or something along those lines. I only met one of them in the five years they been out there. Seemed like a nice guy. But Phil's never warmed up to them.

"You tell McCutcheon to go check on 'em?" he asked. " 'Cause I told him yesterday, and I don't think he's done jack shit about it. Maybe you tell him, it'll light a fire under his ass maybe, see? Don't you think?"

"I don't think it was them people," I say, still all nice and pleasant.

"Well, who the hell else would do something like that? Cut a man's head off and—"

"No one cut his head off," I say.

Phil looks offended by that. Personally offended. He says, "Well, that's what I heard."

"You heard wrong. Nobody cut his head off."

"That don't necessarily mean it weren't them," he says, hating to give up his theory.

"Well, thanks anyway," I say. I don't know why I'm thanking him.

"Right. I mean, it's a damn shame. I got to go." He slugs back the last bit of coffee as he's walking over behind the counter, drops the cup in the bus tray with a loud clink. "Thanks, Lynette!" he calls, laying a dollar on the counter. He gives me a wave on his way out the door. "Say hi to Sally for me." And he leaves.

Thinking of Sally, I look over at the clock. I'm feeling a little sleepy now, after the fries and gravy. I figure maybe I ought to head back, try to get a nap in before she comes home.

When I stand up to go, Whaley says so long. I leave the crossword for him, and money for Lynette. I want to yell thanks to her back in the kitchen, but I don't want to sound like Phil. I step out into a wall of soupy heat. Samson's lunging to his feet at the sight of me. Whaley nods through the window. I give him a sort of half wave as I start up the truck.

That's when I remember the goddamn pan of water in the back. I shut her off, climb out the passenger side, dump the water in the street, and take it back into the restaurant, setting it on the counter. Whaley, one hundred years of patience, nods again.

TWELVE

Once I'm on the road, all alone except for Samson, I think about what Phil said. About them folks up to Clark Lake killing Billy. But I know better than that. Where was Billy's truck on Saturday night? How'd he wind up on the corner of North Lake and McGregor anyway? Who's the last one to see him?

So Lynette ain't seen Jean in a couple of weeks, which means Jean wasn't anywhere near Dewey's Tavern the other night. Lynette's been up there pretty near every night, drinking with Billy. But were they there Saturday? Maybe Jean was at Dewey's, knocking back a few while old Lynette was out somewhere caving in Billy's head. I laugh out loud. Lynette beating his head in with her bouncing pen.

Maybe the old man did it. Jean drives out there, they get in a fight, the old man goes berserk, hunts down Billy and kills him. But that doesn't make any sense. And if he was gonna kill any of us, he would've done it a long time ago.

Ginny Honey? She doesn't have the nerve to kill a cat. Truth is, there's no end of folks Billy knew that wouldn't be sorry to see him go. But there's only one person I can see lifting that rock and bringing it down over and over again. I swallow a big wad of air and my head swells up like a balloon. I switch on the radio. Switch it back off again. I dread the memory that's knocking on my skull, that one summer knocking and knocking, knowing I got to let it in sooner or later.

The summer me and Randy graduated high school, there was no humidity, no rain, nothing but blue sky and sunny for three months nonstop and endless. I got a job up at a truck stop outside of Houghton Lake. Good enough pay for the summer, and I could live up at the hunting cabin.

Jean's sixteen, got her own driver's license, decides she's gonna move up there too, just for the summer. Says she's gonna get herself a job at one of them farmers markets, picking strawberries. Me and Randy had it figured that he'd come up every weekend (he was working on his dad's farm during the week) and we'd be drunk for two days straight, bringing girls back to the cabin, doing whatever we felt like. So I throw a big stink about Jean coming up there too. But she's goddamn determined to get away from Ma and the old man, and all my threatening to break her neck don't make a dent. So Ma decides we'll be able to keep an eye on each other, and that's that. I got Jean living up there with me all summer, screwing up all me and Randy's plans.

It don't take more'n a couple weeks to settle into some kind of routine. I'm at the truck stop by seven every morning. Smell of gasoline. All the years after and for the rest of my life, the smell of gasoline makes my heart beat its fist and holler for her. I'd be back at the hunting cabin by three-thirty, take a bath, and generally lay down for an hour or two before Jean come home from picking strawberries or washing cucumbers or whatever the hell they had her doing up to the farmers market. Sometimes she'd pick up something for us at the Little Skipper: chili dogs, onion rings, and a couple of jumbo-size root beers. Some nights we'd drive into town for pizza or maybe up to the Watering Hole for burgers. Later, we'd hang out down at the park by the beach with some of the guys from the truck stop and their girlfriends. Maybe hit a movie all the way over to Cadillac if it's something we really want to see, or stay home and watch *Wheel of Fortune*, which I kick her ass every time.

But on Fridays I stop and pick up some meat—hamburger usually or a cut-up chicken. Steak a couple of times, but that's a lot of money. We get the charcoal going out on the back porch and Randy rolls in around eight or eight-thirty. We eat barbecue and drink a couple beers before hitting the bars, all three of us. Jean may be sixteen, but she's got big bones and no one's checking ID. Having a sister tagging along must make us look like we're decent guys, because the girls are all over us. So for a while anyway it's shaping up just like we figured, me and Randy bringing girls back to the hunting cabin every weekend and Jean sleeping on the back porch or a few times stretched out in the back seat of my Malibu when it's raining. She doesn't complain because hell, we're getting her into the bars and buying rounds all night. And I don't give her shit on the nights she doesn't come home at all.

A lot of times on Saturday afternoons us three go down to the ball diamonds and watch the fast-pitch softball leagues, since I work with some of the guys playing. Or we go to the beach and swim or screw around looking for snail shells and quarters in the sand. We all three cram into Randy's yellow convertible MG that he bought with money he earned selling a couple of steer. We buzz all over that town, and it's okay having Jean around. The three of us, we have a good time.

It's the Friday before the Fourth of July and Jean just finished a bath and she's got her head under the faucet in the kitchen sink, washing her hair. I'm looking in the cupboard for paper plates, slamming around the kitchen because I was supposed to get more paper plates and I forgot and now I'm gonna get stuck washing the real plates we got to use instead.

"Fuck me," I say under my breath, stepping around Jean to the other side of the sink. "Fuck me, fuck me, fuck me."

"No, thanks," she says under the running water.

"Why didn't you remind me to get paper plates?" I ask her.

" 'Cause I ain't Ma. Give me a break." She turns the water off, wrings out her hair with one hand, and reaches for the towel with the other. I grab the towel and toss it on her head, sort of rubbing it back and forth a little, drying her hair.

"We got any potato chips?" I ask.

"There's a half a bag next to the TV," she says, taking hold of the towel and rubbing hard, head down. I'm standing behind her, and that's when I drop a kiss on her neck before heading over to get the chips. I don't think about it, I just do it.

"You left the bag wide open," I tell her.

"Sorry."

"They're gonna be all stale and gummy."

"So get off my ass," she says, friendly like, heading into the bathroom for a comb. On the way past me, she stops for a millionth of a second and plants the littlest kiss in the world right on my mouth. Then the room's empty and I'm holding the potato chips and that's all it was, really. The whole thing takes less than thirty seconds and it's no big momentous thing but that's when I first know in my brain that I love her like that. Got no idea how long I knew in my heart. But it's like looking through the glasses they use in seventh grade to test if you're colorblind. You see a page full of dots and then you put on those colored glasses and there's a picture all of a sudden. It was there all along; you just didn't see it. That's how it is with me and Jean. And I guess we both know, from that minute on, where we're headed. We don't give it too much thought, because what's there to think about? You can give a person a hundred damned good reasons not to love someone, but when it's too late, it's too late.

So Randy rolls in at the usual time, and tonight it's hamburgers and gummy potato chips, but I never tasted anything so good. It's all taking turns in my mouth. The ketchup, the mustard, the tomatoes Jean brought home from the farmers market. The beer's going down cold and smooth, and even the air tastes good. Jean's wearing a pair of old cut-offs and a Detroit Lions T-shirt, and she's so beautiful I can't look anywhere else. She's barefoot like she always is, only slipping on her sandals when we leave for town. We always take two cars in, so if any one of us wants to go our own way later, there's no wondering how to get home. Me and Jean pile into my Malibu and Randy follows in his little yellow MG.

Everything's working overtime tonight, my eyes, my ears, my skin. It's after 9:00 P.M., but it ain't dark out yet. Spot six deer on the way into town, Jean sees another two. I can hear the crickets starting up already at the far edges of the fields where the woods rear up. The wind's ruffling the hair on my arms. Jean's just two feet away on the seat beside me, sandals kicked off and bare feet up on the dash. She's got my hand in hers.

The town's packed full of weekenders on account of the Fourth of July. The Watering Hole is swelling with sunburns, rubber flip-flops, and shorts tugged on over bathing suits. Everywhere there's a ponytail flying against my face, a cold and wet beer bottle pressed against my arm, the smell of coconut tanning lotion mixed with sweat, heavy and sweet and stale. We get our Miller drafts and Jean threads her way through to the back, me right behind her. It's quieter in the back, locals and "summers," which is what they call me and Jean. People living up here full time from June till September.

Hours go by, no different from all the other Friday nights. There's a girl, Diane, I took home with me a couple times, and she's sitting at the table with us. She's talking to Randy about some shit I don't hear half of. Jean's leaning back in her chair, got her leg propped up on mine under the table. We ain't neither of us saying much, just grinning a lot. Diane puts an arm around me, like she owns me or something just because I fucked her. Jean gives her a big friendly smile. Real big and warm and chummy, and I see trouble coming. So I stand up to get the arm off me, and ask Jean if she wants another beer.

"Dance with me," she says.

"No," I tell her.

"Asshole," she says.

"I'll dance with you, Ray." Diane, like a kid playing in a snake nest, not seeing what's coming. I sidestep that one by pretending I don't hear.

"You want another beer or not?" I ask Jean.

"We'll bring back a round," says dumb old Diane, standing up with me.

I figure I done about all I can to head this off, so I stop trying. Jean doesn't get up. She doesn't turn around in her chair.

"Hey, Didi," she says.

"Diane."

"Don't matter what your goddamn name is."

"What?" Diane's still friendly, not sure she heard right.

"Ray says you grunt like a pig when you're getting fucked," Jean says. "That true?"

Randy's been missing most of the action at the table, but he hears this clear enough. He coughs and dribbles a little beer down his chin. Diane opens and closes her mouth a couple of times like a trout on the beach. I just stand there, which is what I do best. Just stand there and let shit happen. Finally Diane pulls herself together.

"What a bitch," she says to no one, and no one answers. Then she looks at me like it's my turn. I do an eyebrow shrug and turn my head to the TV above the bar, where the Tigers are playing the Orioles. A few more seconds go by while we're all waiting to see what someone else is gonna do. All except Jean, who looks like she's said all she had to say.

Randy's voice breaks the weirdness. "You want to dance?" he says to Diane. She nods. So they head off to the dance floor, and I go get a couple more beers. Back at the table, I sit down next to Jean and think. The message is clear. If we're gonna do this, there ain't gonna be any games. No screwing around with anyone else, no jealousy, no bullshit. No Dianes, no Tammies or Debbies, no Ricks or Jims or Zeds. (Honest to God, she told me later she'd fucked a guy named Zed. "Had a dick looked like a cactus, too.") No one but Ray and Jean, dealing straight with each other like we always did. None of that was gonna change.

It's near on three in the morning. Me and Jean are lying on our backs under a black bowl of night. The stars are bright, looking like someone took a lit cigarette to the lining of the sky and poked tiny holes for the light of heaven to shine through. We see two shooting stars. I let Jean have the first, but on the second one I wish that I'll have her with me until I die. We spent the last hour and a half making love. It felt like me sinking into myself, like having a layer of skin put back on after it'd been torn off.

Randy took off from the Watering Hole with Diane around one o'clock. Said he'd see us tomorrow. So we beat it home fast as we could. Dragged a blanket out to the backyard by the dock. Now I can hear water flapping slow and sleepy against the half-rotten wood, and Jean's fingers are brushing real light up and down the inside of my arm, up and down over all the scars, some old, some new.

"It'd make you puke if you saw it," she's telling me. "Big old hunk of broccoli I got to hold down in this salt water."

"Salt kills slugs," I offer.

"They wasn't no slugs, they was worms," she says.

"Does it kill 'em?" I ask.

"I don't know. I think so. They let go of the broccoli and then they float up to the top."

"How many?"

"Dozens of 'em," she tells me. "The whole top of the water's squirming with these floaty worms and I got to skim 'em off and shake out the broccoli and then they go ahead and sell the shit."

"Don't bring home no broccoli."

"So what do you think that garbage can looks like after about four hours of slopping these little green fucks in there?" Her fingers stop on my arm, waiting for an answer. I tell her it must look pretty gross, and the fingers start moving again.

"I had about a hundred great ideas what to do with that garbage can, too. But hell, it's too late to get hired on anywhere else. So I bagged 'em up and left 'em out back." She reaches up over her head for her Marlboros at the edge of the blanket. Lights one with her purple Bic, hands it to me, lights one for herself.

"So what happened?" I want this story to go on for weeks and weeks.

"So it's one of them clear plastic garbage bags, okay? And I leave it sit out back where we dump all the garbage. And the sun's beating down all afternoon and pretty much baking 'em. And after a while, they're popping like popcorn."

I roll over and kiss her. It's the feeling you have when you're finally dropping off to sleep. Familiar. *At last, at last.* I roll back again.

She's left off with my arm, and now her fingers are running currents through my hair, running down past my shoulders. We're quiet for a while.

"Jean?"

"Yeah?"

"Let's sleep out here," I say. "All night."

And so we did. After that it's hard to remember what it was like when I didn't have her there. Like trying to remember what it was like before you were born. Blank.

July into August, days filled up with pumping gasoline, shooting the shit with the truckers or the other guys working the pumps, thinking about Jean and wondering what's she doing right now, what's she thinking about? Then home and our usual routine at night, except we stay home more than we did before. There's a couple of days when we both call in sick because we can't leave each other. Can't do it. Go swimming off the dock out back, spend the rest of the afternoon stretched out on my bed.

We have nothing to hide from each other and nothing to hide from anyone else. Jean'll kiss me right smack in the middle of Wagner's Grocery and not think anything of it. Every weekend, when Randy comes up, we keep our distance and act like nothing's different. Jean doesn't want to, but I make her. I don't know why I thought we could fool him. Maybe because I always been keeping secrets from Randy when it come to my family. I always been able to fool him, is what I thought.

On the weekends, the three of us still go to the softball games, eat snow cones and elephant ears on the beach. On the weekends, it's the three of us just like usual.

There were an awful lot of minutes wasted during those months, time spent at work or sleeping or running some stupid errand without her. Like we thought we had all the time in the world. So we pissed away a little bit every day. I don't think about that summer if I can help it. The two months between the Fourth of July and Labor Day, they're like a butterfly under glass. Frozen perfect and sitting on a shelf somewhere in my mind where no one can get at it or mess it up. Me and Jean and perfect.

But what came after, it still comes after. Can't think about the time at the hunting cabin without remembering what went down back home after. I know no one ever loved me like she did that summer. For ten years since, I been pretending I ain't been ripped in half. Like my leg got torn off and I'm hopping around, acting like my leg's still here instead of across town living alone with a lousy tiger cat.

I don't know if she loves me anymore, or if she hates me, or if she just don't care one way or the other. She ain't shown a thing to me since. Smooth, friendly, nothing. It's all I deserve after what I did to her.

THIRTEEN

Coming home from Carter's, I pull into the driveway and Samson jumps out the side window, heads for the back. It's no later than two o'clock, and Sally isn't supposed to be home for another hour at least. I head in, hoping I'll sleep a little, knowing I won't. When I walk in the bedroom, I see the bed's not made. It looks terrible, with the covers all tangled and twisted like a pile of fat snakes. Looks like a bed where someone didn't sleep too good. She was running late this morning, on account of Ginny Honey and the kids. I think about Sally walking in and seeing that bed. I think about it making her feel as bad as it's making me feel.

I pull everything off and dump it on the floor. I tuck the sheet back in at the bottom and try to pull it straight. I have to retuck a few times until I get it right. Then the other sheet. One at a time, I know that much. She's gonna be surprised. Maybe it'll put her in a better mood for when we have our talk. Maybe it'll keep Jean's bare feet from trampling on my nerves for an hour. I toss the pillows around a few times to make them look fat, then lay them at the head of the bed, side by side and real close together, like Sally and me. I pick up some socks and underwear off the floor and carry 'em into the bathroom, where she keeps a clothes hamper. That's when I see all the hairs in the sink where I shaved last night before going up to Snell's. I dump the clothes and rinse the sink, pushing the little hairs down toward the drain with my fingers. Jesus. One little thing leads to another little thing and it's goddamn hopeless hopeless hopeless, there's so much needs doing.

I walk back into the bedroom, pretending I'm Sally coming home from teaching. I see a bed all made and a clean floor, and it makes me happy. I move on into the rest of the house, still looking through Sally's eyes. The living room has blankets and pillows stacked on one end of the couch (I remember Deena folding blankets this morning). There's bowls with a few popcorn kernels left in them, newspapers piled on the floor in one corner.

The kitchen's where I have to sit down, I feel so sick in my heart. There's breakfast dishes all over the counter, all over the table. Cereal boxes left out, and an empty milk carton with its sour-smelling mouth open wide and screaming. Toast crumbs and sticky gobs of jelly.

I start by taking the papers out back and tying them up. A headline flops over on its stomach as I'm knotting the twine:

Area Man Killed on North Lake Road
Police Question Family in Brutal Slaying

How many times have I read headlines like that and come to my own conclusions, without knowing a damn thing about it. Now, being inside one of them headlines, I'll never believe anything in the paper again. Now that I'm the family being questioned by police in the brutal slaying, I see the lie behind every headline, every word ever printed about anything. You can't know from reading about it. They tell you stuff, like then you'll know about it. But you can't know. You can't know anything until it happens to you.

I stack the bundles of papers out by the back porch, return to the kitchen, get sick at heart again looking at it. Living room first. Blankets already folded; just stick them in the hall closet, top shelf, where I pulled them down that first night. Three popcorn bowls, paper towels soaked with salt and butter. I empty the ashtrays into the bowls and right away wish I hadn't, on account of the smell. Take them into the kitchen (that kitchen! that kitchen!) and toss them onto the counter by the sink.

Now I don't know where to start. Can't wash the dishes because they need to be stacked up. Try clearing the table and get the crap off it first. But can't throw away the empty milk carton because the trash basket's overflowing. So I got to empty the trash, but there's shit all over the bottom of the trash bag when I pull it out from under the sink, like something leaked, and now there's wet, sludgy stuff that I can feel on the bottom of my feet. It's like a circle that you can't ever find the start to.

So what I do is, I breathe slow through my nose, and I count to ten. I glance up at the wall to check the time, and that's when I figure out how I'm gonna do it. I'll act like the kitchen is a clock. I'll start at 12:00 and go clockwise around the room until I'm back at 12:00 again. Just make a big circle. The sink is 12:00. Just wash what's in the sink right this second, and to hell with the rest of it. Then move just one foot to the right and wash that. By the time I hit the 9:00 position, things are sparkling. I click on the radio, and this is what's playing, I swear to God: "I Got the World on a String." And it's Frank Sinatra singing it, too. See, that's the kind of stuff that happens, and I think that's all that matters really in the world. You got a song in your head, and then you hear it on the radio. Times like that, jobs don't matter and fights don't matter and even mad Sallys don't matter. So I'm sweeping the kitchen floor with the straw broom, got all the chairs pulled out from the table, and I'm singing out loud, just like I wanted to do in the diner with Whaley. Ain't no one around to tell me what a crappy voice I got. I think how if I was Ginch Littlefield, this is exactly when his Sally would walk in on him. But my Sally doesn't walk in yet. She must be running a little late. I didn't think there'd be any way I'd get it all done. But it's done, and the dish towel is hanging all straight and perfect on the handle of the oven, and there's nothing left to do, and she ain't home yet. So I go sit out on the back porch and light a cigarette.

This is what I see while I smoke a cigarette and wait for Sally to come home: The beans are growing thin and stringy in the garden. Tomatoes are doing okay, if you aren't particular about the size. I walk across the yard (crunch, crunch on the dead grass) and squat on my haunches, taking a better look. Two tomatoes come right off in my hand. There's another, a little bigger, but it's still a kind of orangey red. Another couple days for that one. And it's got a worm hole on the back side, under the leaf. That's okay, though. I'll just cut it out, make sure I get all the gross part out, and the rest of it's good.

I take the two tomatoes into the kitchen, put one in the wire basket over the counter. I rinse the other one under the faucet, careful not to splatter water on the counter. Trying to keep everything perfect until Sally comes home. I dry it off on the front of my shirt, take another look for worm holes, and go back out to the porch. No matter how careful you are, the first bite always sends tomato juice all over your face.

I wipe my chin with the back of my hand. Thinking how Sally's gonna be so surprised. She's gonna know I'm sorry for yesterday, and I won't even have to say it, probably. And it'll be okay. Damn, this is a good tomato. Something flashes brown out at the edge of the soybean field. Probably a fox or a coyote. You wouldn't think we had coyotes in Michigan, but we do. Big ones, too. Farmers get permits to shoot them because they eat the lambs and the ducks and even a calf once. They come right up into the fields, next to the subdivision developments, and the town people go all ape shit when they look out their kitchen window and see a big old coyote skulking along the fence to their backyard. They almost always think it's a wolf and call the police and don't let their kids play outside for week or so. Randy told me about it. How his dad shot a dozen one summer, had 'em stuffed (full body), and sold 'em to local bars. Said he made more money on coyotes that year than he did on his wheat. There's one up to Dewey's Tavern still.

Sally pulls into the driveway. I never even heard her coming up the road, but there she is, closing the car door and walking toward me. She looks tired.

"What you doing up?" she asks, sitting down next to me on the porch, tossing her purse behind her against the screen door.

"Waiting for you." I offer the last bite of tomato, which she takes.

"You slept at all?" she asks.

"Not yet." That's what I said. But what I meant was, *Not until after our talk*. And that's what's echoing loud now over the backyard and into the field beyond. She's looking out there, like she can see each word rolling and bouncing along the rows of soybeans.

"I was up most of last night, thinking," she says.

"Yeah?" I ask. There's a little pause, so I say, "I almost called on my lunch break." Which was true. I almost called her, but I didn't want to wake her up at 3:00 A.M.

"I was awake," she says. We're quiet for a minute. "Why were you gonna call me?"

I don't answer at first, because the real answer is something I don't want to say. It's something I'm afraid to say. But I don't want to lie to her. I hate lying to her. So I don't answer at first. But finally I say, "I don't know."

Which probably drives her crazy. But at least it don't lead us in the direction we'd be heading if I said the real reason I wanted to call.

"Just to say hi?" she says. There's a little bit of meanness in her voice, but only just a little bit. Sally's not a mean person unless her feelings are hurt pretty damn bad. Which is how I know for sure that our talk is gonna be a real bad one. Which is what I was afraid of. Which is why I wanted to call her last night, to ask her to please promise me she isn't walking out on me. Please put my mind at rest and tell me she's not leaving.

"I got a surprise for you in the house," I say instead. It'll be okay once she lays eyeballs on that kitchen. By the time she sees the whole house, the bed all made and everything, she'll forget all about what kept her up thinking last night.

"I want to stay out here," she answers. I look over at the tomato plants, where I was kneeling just a little while ago. I wonder if there's indents in the dirt where my knees were. I wish I was back over there now, inspecting the tomatoes, picking out the ripe ones.

"Look, you already know what I'm gonna say," she starts. *No, I don't. I don't know what you're gonna say.* But she goes on, not hearing me thinking beside her. "And it's not like I'm even mad anymore. But I'm going."

One leaf on the tomato dips just a tiny bit, and I look real close and see a grasshopper's landed on it. He holds steady and doesn't move until the leaf stops dipping. Sally's next to me, her steady voice pouring itself into my ear.

"I'll stay with Barb until I get something of my own." Barbara's her sister. Lives just this side of Adrian.

"That's a forty-five-minute drive to school," I say, like that's reason to stay.

"Just till I get something of my own." We're quiet for another minute. I want to say something to make her stay. This is my cue for it, this quiet minute. But every time I think of something, I can already hear her answer. And it's an answer I can't argue with.

"Can't we talk about it first?" I ask.

"We are talking about it," she answers. And I can't argue with that. See? We are talking about it. What I really mean is, *Can't I talk you out of it?*

"Can't I talk you out of it?"

She looks surprised. Thinks for a second, really thinks. God, that's one reason I love her. Because she'll think before answering a question like that.

"No," she finally says.

Well, then. That means I got nothing to lose. So I say, "I didn't fuck her."

The frog mouth comes, quick as lightning. I feel her turn her head and look straight at me. But I'm keeping an eye on that grasshopper over on the tomato plant. So I can't look at her just now.

"It doesn't matter, Ray. It doesn't matter if you did or not."

I think it matters. I've spent the last ten years not fucking her, and it matters a whole hell of a lot to me.

Sally goes on. "We had a deal. You knew the deal, and you knew what would happen if you broke it."

See, we *did* have a deal. The deal was, I don't go near Jean. That was the deal. That was it.

"I know," I answer. I sound like a kid. Like a rotten kid getting punished for something he knows damn well was wrong, but he doesn't like being punished anyway.

"It feels like you're using me as a rest stop, like you're killing time," she says. "I want someone who loves me like I'm the end of the road."

The grasshopper's eating a corner off that leaf. He'll probably keep eating until the whole damn leaf is gone. I ought to go over there and brush him off. Scoop him up and toss him out into the grass. Sally keeps talking.

"Ray, you're with me 'cause you're afraid to be somewhere else. I'm thirty years old now. I don't want to waste any more time on someone who isn't planning on staying to the end."

"I'm not the one who ain't planning on staying," I whisper. I don't mean to whisper, but that's how it comes out.

"If you were gonna die tomorrow, who would you want to die with? Me or Jean?"

Hearing that name come out of her mouth right now makes me feel sick, like someone punched me. It's all I can do to sit tight and not run across the yard to knock that goddamn grasshopper clear into the next county.

She takes a deep breath and gets to the point. "I'm not making any judgments about you and her. But I'm not your first choice, Ray. And I don't want to be the one you just settled for."

She sounds so tired. Not urgent, like she's trying to convince me. Tired, like she knows damn well that I know she's right.

"You ain't happy here?" I ask, sidestepping the whole point.

"It's a fake kind of happy," she answers. "I want the real thing."

"I want you to stay." I blurt it out like a sheep or a goat.

"I deserve better." She isn't crying. I wish she would. I try to think of something to say that'd make her cry. But there's nothing that's gonna get a rise out of her. I can tell that by the tired voice. She's already gone. So I keep my mouth shut.

"I'm sorry for you, Ray," she says. "Sorry for both of you." And it isn't snotty. She really is sorry. I pick up a little stone off the porch step and throw it hard at the tomato plant. Miss.

"I'll stay till after the funeral. I'm not gonna run out on you," she says.

"Right," I answer, sounding like a prick.

"We're better friends than for me to run out on you," she says. "That doesn't change."

I know. My friend's leaving. My friend's leaving!

"You ain't got to stay," I say.

"Think about it," she says.

"I'll be all right."

"We'll see." She gets up and goes in the house, grabbing her purse on the way. I stay out on the porch. I picture her walking from the kitchen to the living room, down the hall to the bedroom. Same as I pictured it the last couple hours.

I walk over to the garden, crunch crunch crunch some more. I bend down and look; the grasshopper's gone. Get a deep grip on the stem down near the base and a good stance with feet squared and knees bent. Then I pull. It ain't easy. I pull with my legs and shoulders, keeping my back straight. I feel a few roots give way, like a tooth letting go of a jaw. Finally the whole thing comes up in my hand. I throw it hard as I can toward the soybean field in back. I reach for the next one. Rip it out by the roots. I make my way down the row, pulling until they're all gone. Then I reach for whatever's next. String beans. They come up a lot easier. So much easier that I damn near go over backward into the dirt. So I rip 'em out one-handed, moving at double speed down the rows. Pulling until I get 'em free, standing up straight and throwing 'em out toward the back. String beans, squash, zucchini, cucumbers no bigger than my hand it's such a lousy garden. Everything is flying out of the earth. Flying rootless and cut off. After the tomato plants, there's nothing that holds on very tight. They all let go at the first sign of trouble, and up they come.

It doesn't take long until I'm done. By now I got a buzz roaring in my head, and every part of me is coiled up and hissing. *So mad. So mad.* Want to go in there and kick the living shit out of her. Can't hardly hold my eyeballs still enough to see straight. I go in the garage and there's a rusty X-Acto blade on the wooden shelf by an old snowmobile battery.

Want to kill Sally for leaving. Want to kill Billy for leaving too, but I can't. Ain't a fucking thing I can do about any of it. I pull the blade across my upper arm three times hard and quick. Right away there's the burn and tingle of blood, and I'm breathing easier. They aren't deep, just hurt like a son of a bitch. *Thank you thank you thank you* for some hurt I can hold on to.

I'm thinking maybe I'm not so strong after all, staying away from her for ten years. Maybe it was a hell of a lot easier to stay away than to go near her. And maybe I'm a coward. Maybe that's what I've been doing all this time, being a coward, hiding behind Sally.

After a bit I'm back to myself, and the blood on my arm is the last thing I want Sally seeing right now. There's an old greasy sweatshirt on the other side of the battery. I throw it on for cover. Go get in the truck and start her up. Samson's trying to jump in, but I tell him no. Sally comes out on the back porch as I'm putting her in gear.

"Where're you going?" she says.

"I don't know," I answer, trying to sound normal.

"The place looks great," she says with a smile. "Thanks."

"You ain't got to stay for the funeral," I tell her. "You can take off whenever you want."

"You shouldn't be alone—"

"I think you ought to just go." I give her a little smile so she knows I ain't saying it to be mean.

"I'm just taking a couple things, then. Just for a few days." She looks less tired already. "We'll worry about the rest after." After what? The funeral, I guess.

"Sure. Yeah. That's fine."

"You got the number. Up on the wall." For Barbara, her sister. We got a phone number list on the wall next to the phone.

"Yeah," I say.

"All right, then." She waits for a second, then she says, "I'll be gone when you get back, Ray." And it's not a threat. And it's not revenge. She's just being clear so I won't be surprised.

"Okay, then," I say. And she turns and walks in the house, and I pull out of the driveway. And that's it. That's all. Six years of living together, and treating each other pretty decent, and it's over.

I'll be gone when you get back.

Okay, then.

And that's it.

Sally pretty much says what she means. If there was something else to say, she'd have said it. Besides, I know she's right. I ain't giving her the kind of love she was talking about. Any argument out of me would've been a lie.

So now I'm driving down the road and I feel like someone unscrewed my head and put it somewhere, like the back bumper or under the hood. I remember Ginny Honey said something like that the other morning. Going to identify Billy, and seeing Ma there, and feeling like her head's floating a couple of feet above the rest of her. Maybe that's just how you feel when someone leaves you. Maybe that's what people are talking about when they say, "So-and-so lost his head" or "Now don't go losing your head over it."

I yank the sweatshirt off. First one sleeve, then the other, one hand on the wheel, and up over my head. I'm tired now. I want to lay down and sleep, but I can't go back to the house. I could pull over somewhere and sleep in the truck, but I don't want Sheriff Keith stumbling on me again. I do a mental rundown. Ma? I ain't comfortable over there to Ed's house. The old man? No. He and Shiner are probably somewhere half stewed by now. I don't want to go back to Carter's. And Joe Lee is not gonna be glad to see me when I tell him why I'm not home. In fact, I'll be surprised if I don't have my ass kicked by the end of next week. I'm figuring he'll give me a week's break out of respect for a death in the family. I light a cigarette and let it fill me up with smoke.

"Where the hell are you, Billy?" That's what I say out loud in the truck. Because that's exactly where I'd be headed if this was a normal time. If anything was normal anymore. If the whole damned world hadn't gone into the toilet in just a couple of days. Me and Billy, we could grab some beers and go squirrel hunting. Or I'll hang around the garage while he adjusts the timing on his old Harley. Shooting the shit until he gets too drunk, accuses me of fucking Ginny Honey (!), and lets me have it with a socket wrench. Still, there's times when it's worth a black eye so as not to be alone.

F O U R T E E N

That deal I broke, it was the one condition of Sally and me living together. We'd only been dating a few weeks. I was up to the Bowl 'n' Bar, out by where the old man lives. I'm there with a couple of guys from work, getting drunk before our shift starts. I never make it in to work, though. And Jean's up there too, because it's Thursday night and she bowls in a league on Thursday nights. And her and about half a dozen people on her league, they wind up in the bar after they're done. And we're all shooting pool and getting drunk. John and Mike Tiller—they're cousins—and me, blowing off work for the night. And it's a mixed league, so it's something like two or three couples and Jean and her friend Pebbles and some other people I don't remember.

Jean and me are playing partners in pool. She's a little better pool player than me, but only a very little better. Mostly because she doesn't usually get as drunk as I do. And we've been running the table for a couple of hours now, and John Tiller and some guy I never seen before or since were putting up a pretty good fight. But this guy, he's all over Jean, and she don't seem to mind it too much. I keep waiting for her to tell him to fuck off, but she doesn't. So I screw up a shot, a pretty simple bank shot around behind the eight ball, but I screw it up like I'm shooting with a hockey stick or something. And Jean sort of gives a snort and says, "You're drunk," and laughs.

And for a second it feels like she's laughing at me. I mean in a real nasty, ugly way. So I tell her to shut the hell up, and I give her a shove up against the jukebox, which makes the music jump all to hell. (It's

Willie Nelson, "Poncho and Lefty.") And she hauls off and cranks me upside the head with her bottle of Stroh's. Not like she gets a grip on the neck of the bottle and swings. She just busts me up against the ear with her left hand, and she's got a beer bottle in that hand, is all.

Tells me, "Don't fucking tell me to shut up." And I say something about whipping her ass for her, and she says, "Come on and try it, Ray," and throws her pool cue on the table—screwing up the game—and walks back to where the rear exit is, past the pay phones and bathrooms, leading out to the parking lot, which is separate from the rest of the bowling alley. Everyone sees this, of course. And I'm standing there drunk, and my ear's ringing where she cuffed me, and everyone's looking at me like I'm a jerk.

So far this is no different from one hundred and eighty-seven other fights we've had. And what I ought to do here is let it go. She'll stay out in the parking lot until she's cooled off, and come back in, and we forget about it. But I can't let it go tonight. It's not so much that I've been drinking more than usual, but I switched over to Jim Beam a few hours ago, and that's a different kind of drunk than a beer drunk. It's the kind of drunk that makes you follow someone out to the parking lot instead of letting it go.

So I go after her, out the back door to the parking lot. I'm still carrying my pool cue, which I'm thinking I might use to knock the shit out of her if I have to, if she won't settle down. I'm half expecting her to land a punch right in my nose the second I'm out the door, but that ain't what happens. She's walking across the parking lot, heading for her car. I yell her name and she stops, hops up on the hood of Mike Tiller's Grand Am, and rests her feet on the bumper. Waiting for me, but not saying nothing at first. Not until I'm a few feet away.

"You gonna whip my ass with that pool cue?" she says, scooching over on the hood so I can hop up next to her, which is what I do.

"No," I say. The metal is cold against my ass. It's early November and the nights are pretty damned cold. I'm wishing I'd grabbed my coat on the way out. She's looking up at the sky, clear and black. The moon looks like a frozen dime up there. It's never looked so far away and small.

"You're still a goddamn coward, Ray," she says. But she says it sort of sweet like. Even leans against my shoulder.

"I know," I say.

We're both thinking about it, about that summer, but neither one of us is gonna say a word more. It's cold, as if the rest of the world and everyone in it got frozen solid except us. After a while, she says, "I heard you got a girlfriend now." I can't pick up anything from her voice. No feeling.

"Yeah," I say.

"What's her name?"

"Sally Brosnik."

"I saw you guys up to Bell's the other night." Bell's is a restaurant outside of town where Sally's other sister, Berry, works a couple nights a week. We went up there so Sally could drop off some baking pans she'd borrowed, and also so Berry could meet me. I was nervous as shit, which makes me act like a jerk. I never saw Jean that night, had no idea she was around. Which is a good thing, because it would've made me a hell of a lot more nervous and more of a jerk.

I'm thinking how Sally seems far away and frozen with the rest of the world right now. With Jean against my shoulder, all of the things that were right and familiar about Sally now seem as foreign and strange as a Russian sled dog.

That's when I hear this sound next to me. It's not a gulp, and it's not a snort, and it's definitely not a sniffle. But it's a sound a person makes who's not gonna cry, no matter what. It's a sound that stops the whole frozen world. My arm goes around her and I've got my face buried in her hair. It smells the same as her freckles smell, even now. I'm saying her name over and over. And it's like no time has gone by at all. It's still that summer, and we don't know yet how bad it's gonna get. Like nothing's ever been interrupted between us.

She's not saying anything, just holding on to me tight. It's not cold anymore. And then I'm kissing her. And the world is the place it should be for a little while, just a minute or two, until the sound of a door slamming open freezes everything again. It's the guy who was playing partners with John Tiller. I never did find out his name. And he stands there about thirty feet away, looking at us, and finally turns and goes back inside. Maybe he came out to piss. Who knows. Jean jumps off the hood of the car and walks toward the bar. I holler for her to stop, but she won't.

"God damn it, Jean. Wait a minute." I'm off the car and following her, though I don't know how the hell I'm gonna walk back in that door.

"No," she yells, still walking. "I ain't waiting. I ain't doing this, Ray. I ain't doing this with you." She's almost to the door.

"What do you want?" She's pissing me off, I can tell you. "What the hell do you expect?"

But she's gone inside. I stand out in the parking lot, freezing my ass off and wondering what she's doing in there. She can walk back in there alone and face everyone down. She'd walk back in there and let people say whatever the hell they want, rather than be out here with me one more second. I stand in the parking lot and I remember the pool cue leaning against Mike Tiller's car. I grab it and snap it in two across my knee. It's cold and it snaps easy, leaving jagged points where the break is. The reason Jean's so mad is this: When we heard that door slam, I pushed her away. Hard.

I grab the jagged end of the pool cue and scrape it hard up and down the inside of my arm. Digging a trench of cuts until the whole arm is burning and I am calm and calm and calm and calm again. I find my truck, dig in my pocket for the keys, and drive to Sally's house. I leave my jacket in the bar. Fuck it. (I never do see it again.) My arm's smeared pretty good with blood, and it's comforting in a way I can't ever explain. But mostly I don't give a shit, I'm so disgusted with myself.

What makes me think it's a good idea to go visit Sally right this moment, I have no idea. It's got to be close to 3:30 A.M., because they announced last call just before I screwed up that last shot. Sally's living at the time with her ma and her dad, before he shot his brains all over the wall of their bedroom. Sally's ma finally sold the house. She kept feeling bits of his teeth in the bedroom carpet.

I pull the truck into their driveway and feel around in the cab for an old windbreaker that I know damn well is in there somewhere. I finally find it under the passenger seat, and I'm slipping it on because for one thing I'm freezing, and for another thing I don't want Sally to see my arm. It's still burning like hell all the way from my wrist to my bicep, all along the inside skin, but mostly the blood is dried. And that's a funny sensation when the cold air hits it, I tell you. Overall, though, it's doing the trick.

So I'm just getting this windbreaker on when Sally's ma comes to the front door and looks out, sees it's me, and goes back inside. Pretty soon Sally comes out on the porch, with a big furry bathrobe over some sweatpants. I get out of the truck, shivering like a hairless cat, and I come up on the porch and lean on the railing.

"Hi ya, Sal," I think I say. Sally remembers this conversation better than I do.

She just looks at me sort of skeptical. I guess she figures there's no point trying to have any kind of conversation that makes sense, judging from the whiskey smell. So she's looking at me, not very friendly, and I get a little defensive and I say, "What?"

She says, "What're you doing?"

I say, "Coming to visit."

She don't answer.

So I say, "That okay with you?" There's something not very nice in the tone of my voice. Even I can hear it.

So she says, "No, not if you're gonna be an asshole."

And I say, "Yeah, that's me. I'm an asshole. I'm an asshole." And that's not enough, either. I got to start hollering as loud as I can about what an asshole I am. Loud. And I guess I'm waving my arms around, because she grabs me to stop me from flapping around like some asshole chicken with its asshole head cut off. But it's the hurt arm she grabs, and I nearly fall down because it sends a shot of fire through me. And then there's blood soaking through the windbreaker where her hand squeezed it.

Sally sees this and says, "Jesus, Ray!" And she's about to call for her ma, who's an RN, but I shush her real quick. Because it's one thing if you've been in a fight or you've been shot, but if it's something you did to yourself on purpose, you don't tell people that. And my brain is too soaked to try poking around for a passable lie.

"It's okay," I whisper. "Shut up a second."

"What happened?" she wants to know.

"I'll tell you. I'll tell you all about it. Just quiet down, will you?"

So she drags me in the kitchen and sticks my arm under the faucet, which burns in a very *not* comforting way. Once she's got the blood all washed off, she sees that it ain't all that deep after all, just ugly and raw. So she goes to get some gauze, and this is the first time she cleans up a mess I made all over myself. She wraps up the whole arm like I'm the

Mummy, which is kind of comical, because her ma's the nurse, not her. Once I'm all set, she gets me a winter jacket from the basement.

"Let me see it," she says. I hold out the mummy arm for inspection. "If it starts to bleed again, you're gonna have to get stitches."

"Okay," I say, reaching for the coat.

"Promise?"

So I promise, and she helps me get the coat on. Then we sit at the kitchen table with just the light above the stove, and we smoke cigarettes, and I tell her all about it. By this time I'm not drunk anymore. I got sober the minute that warm water hit my arm and scalded me from the inside out. But it's the kind of sober that comes on the other side of being drunk. The kind of sober that sets you outside of the day-to-day and makes you quiet like tomorrow's never coming so nothing counts. That's why I'm able to tell her. Because I'm that kind of sober and it's 4:00 A.M. and there's just us and the little light above the stove.

I tell her about that summer after high school, about me and Jean, about Randy and how it all blew up, how I went away for a couple of years, and how I came back and it's been four years now and it sure ought to be out of my system by now, but then something like tonight happens and I don't know what I hate myself for more, the giving in or the resisting. And Sally just listens. She doesn't interrupt. She doesn't give her opinion. And she sure as hell doesn't give me advice or try to make me feel better.

And by the time I say everything I have to say, the little light above the stove feels dimmer, because the patch of black outside the kitchen window is turning purple, then pink. It's warm and quiet and still in that kitchen, and a few birds are singing at the top of their lungs outside, even in November. And Sally's still sitting next to me at the table. She hasn't jumped up and run screaming from the room. She hasn't thrown me out for being a disgusting creep. All she did was get up once to grab some wheat crackers, which we ate until they were gone. And it's a relief to have said all that shit out loud. All of that unsayable shit. I want me and Sally to run away together now and get married. That's how relieved I am.

So I say, "Hey, why don't you move in with me?"

I guess I expect her to be a little surprised, since we ain't been seeing each other very long. But she doesn't look surprised at all. She's quiet for a minute and then she says, "Let me think about it." That's something I already learned about Sally: She never speaks without thinking, something I do all the time. But when she does say something, you know she means it. And you know there's not much use in arguing at that point.

So the next day I remember everything that went on the night before and I have no idea if Sally's gonna live with me or tell me she doesn't want to see a crazy pervert like me anymore. At the time, I'm living in the apartment above Phil's Barbershop. (Phil Senior owns the barbershop; Phil Junior's the mailman.) Sally comes over there in the afternoon and wants to know how my arm is doing. Brings me some more gauze so I can keep it covered and it'll heal better. I feel funny with her, like all the words that came out of my mouth last night are still buzzing like mosquitoes around our heads. I can hardly look at her.

Then she says, "You still want me to move in with you?"

I say that yeah, I do.

She says, "I want an agreement first." *That's it. It's over. She's gonna tell me no more drinking.* But it ain't that. "As long as you and me are together, it's just you and me. I don't want to be wondering about anyone else."

We both knew who she's talking about, but it's still a jolt when she says the name out loud.

"You have to promise me you won't hang around with Jean anymore." I don't say anything. "I don't mean family stuff. She's your sister and you live in the same town and you can't pretend she doesn't exist. I know that."

Pretend she doesn't exist? That makes me smile.

Sally goes on. "But no getting drunk together, no visiting out to her house, no being alone with her." I guess she realizes how hard she sounds, because she reaches over and touches my hand like it's a two-week-old kitten. "Look at what it does to you."

She means my arm all torn up. I say, "I know."

"I'm not a jealous or suspicious person," she says. "And I don't want to turn into one. So we have to keep this just you and me."

And I know she's right. I know that. And I feel safe with Sally. So we find the place out on Barkton Road because the apartment over Phil's is too small, and Samson comes to live with us a few months later. Billy told me that when Jean heard I was shacking up with Sally, she laughed.

So that was our deal. That's the deal I broke. That's why Sally's leaving now. And that's why I can't argue with anything she said back there on the porch, because she's right.

I'm on Junction 10 now, coming up on Billy's house. I pull into the yard and there's their car, but no sign of Billy's truck. It must be impounded as evidence. I figure how Ginch Littlefield would be proud of that little bit of detectiving. I hear music loud in the house. I get out of the truck and I hear a voice say, "Uncle Ray? Uncle Ray?"

I look around and don't see anyone, and that same voice says, "Up here."

I look up into the red maple by the west side of the house, and there's the red-haired kid up in the tree, legs dangling over each side of a wide branch, back leaning against the trunk, book in his hand.

"They're at the museum, where the mummies are," he says.

"Yeah?"

"Yeah." He looks pretty excited about it, swinging his legs back and forth. "Do they crawl inside with one of the mummies? Do they get inside one?"

"I ain't telling," I say. But I know. They don't crawl inside with one of the mummies. They hide their violin cases in one, but they don't get inside themselves. I was disappointed about that when I read it, so I don't tell him what I know.

The loud music is coming up from the basement, where Trish's bedroom is. I holler into the house from the front porch, but no one answers. I come down the steps of the porch and walk around back. Along the fence me and Billy put up a couple summers ago. We poured the cement ourselves for the post holes. Bought the chain link from Kelsey's Lumber and Lawn Supply, where Jean got us a discount. Took us three weekends to finish it, and about six cases of beer. But it's still looking good, straight and even.

I come around the corner of the house and see Ginny Honey out back, hanging clothes on the line. She's got a plastic laundry basket at her feet. There's lots of rips in it, from when the kids were smaller and played mousetrap with it, just like me and Jean and Billy used to do. Tore Ma's laundry basket all to hell. Ginny Honey's hanging shirts on the line. Billy's work shirts. There's six of 'em up already, hanging by their tails, arms dangling straight down in the no-breeze. They look useless, hanging like that. They are useless, I guess. She's got single socks hanging willy-nilly between the underwear, the dish towels. Ma always hung the socks in pairs, hung all the underwear together, towels, etc. Common sense will tell you that makes it easier to get it all folded and sorted and put away. Seeing all those clothes mixed up like that, I ain't surprised. That's Ginny Honey all over.

I don't want to scare her. The music from the basement's not so loud on this side of the house, so I give a little holler. "Anyone here? Ginny Honey?"

She turns her head toward me.

"Hey, Ray," she says, reaching for a wet apron and another clothespin.

"You all right? You need anything?" I don't feel easy and comfortable with her, like I do when Billy's around.

"I'm all right," she says. "You look like shit. Ain't you been to bed?" She knows I work nights.

"Naw." I don't know what to say after that. She's got the apron pinned up, so I reach into the basket, pull out a towel, shake it out and hand it to her. She's got the clothespins in an old plastic milk carton with the top cut open, its handle hanging on the line. It's all streaked and gritty from old rains.

"I know I'm supposed to be up there," she says. She means the funeral home. There was a lot of talk about the fact that her and the kids didn't show up.

"Ma's there," I said.

"Yeah." It comes out of her mouth like she's spitting poison.

"I mean she can take care of everything. You ain't got to worry about it." I can see that this line of talk ain't helping, so I move on to something else.

"What you gonna do with all this?" I give one of the shirtsleeves a flip.

"You can take it if you want," she says. I shake out a pair of blue jeans and hand 'em to her.

"I don't want it." That sounds too harsh. "You know."

"Yeah." She stops and gives a big old Ginny Honey sigh. A real long hard one. "You think anyone'll want it?"

"I don't know." Another line of talk that ain't doing the trick. No subject's safe now.

"If you want, I can take the kids up there. Or Sally can take 'em." But this is the worst yet. Ginny Honey throws the blue jeans back into the basket and puts her hands on her hips the way Ma and Sally and Jean and every other woman in the world does.

"Ain't no one taking my kids anywhere. You understand that?" she hollers. "Just keep the hell away from my kids." Then she's standing there like she's waiting for an answer. What am I supposed to say to that?

"Okay."

"And tell that to your whore sister too."

"Okay." The reason I'm just laying down and taking this is because I learned what to do with people who are in this state of mind. I learned it when Sally's dad blew his brains all over the bedroom. She was all crazy and not making any sense, and the best thing to do was just agree to everything. She called me from the police station, told me to come pick her up. I get there, and she's gone. She's over to Joe Lee's. She tells me that's where she *said* she'd be and I was a stupid bastard and on and on. And if I tried to make sense out of it, she got more hysterical. So the rule is, you don't say nothing but okay when they start going off their head like that. And if Ginny Honey wants to call Jean a whore, I just say okay.

"I know what she says about my kids. But she ain't getting 'em away from me. I'm their mother."

"Okay."

"And I don't give a goddamn whether Billy's dead or not. Just keep away from us."

"Okay." I can see she's running out of mad already, on account of how I ain't offering any fight.

"What'd you do to your arm?" she says.

"I cut it on something out in the garage," I tell her. She picks up the blue jeans and reaches for a clothespin. I don't know what makes me say the next thing out of my mouth. "You want to go for a beer?"

"What?"

"Want to go get a couple of beers?"

She's quiet for a minute. Hangs another sock (single) and then she says, "No, thanks." But she's not pissed that I asked her. She sounds tired, like Sally sounded earlier. A few more minutes go by. I can't think of anything more to say. One thing I know is, this is getting me nowhere.

"You tell me if there's anything needs doing around here," I say.

"We're all right," she answers. I can't figure the tone of her voice now.

"I mean it," I go on, trying to get a little control over the situation, "Mowing the lawn or stuff."

"Deena mows the lawn. That's her chore."

"Oh." I feel dumb and uncomfortable as hell, standing there as useless as Billy's shirts. So I walk around. I make two rounds of the backyard, past the barbecue grill and the red picnic table. I finally stop at the willow tree, where a tire swing hangs unmoving. Me and Billy hung that tire when they first moved into the house. Trish was big enough to hang on by herself. But Ginny Honey'd climb in and hold Deena on her lap. Billy would twist that rope tight and let go. They'd spin so fast it was a blur of arms, legs, and hair flying. Time it stopped, Ginny Honey was green and Deena was screaming, "Do again! Do again!"

I spin the tire a couple of times. Then I decide for no good reason whatsoever that I want to swing. Ginny Honey's paying no attention to me. So I get both legs through the tire and push off with my feet. That's when I remember that you got to check inside the tire for water. Because it's always there, from the last rain. I soak the seat of my work pants. I know it'll dry quick enough, but it takes the fun out of swinging anyway.

Ginny Honey's walking toward the house, the empty clothes basket under her arm. I climb out of the swing. Getting out of it is harder than getting into it. I follow Ginny Honey through the back door of the house. The kitchen looks like ours did before I cleaned it. Dirty dishes and half-empty cereal boxes, toast crumbs and gobs of jelly, mail and newspapers all over the counter. Bottle caps and matchbooks are scattered at one end. That's Billy. That's evidence Billy's here. Probably right in the next room. I can't stop myself from doing this, looking for him. Ginny Honey feels it too, because she says, "He's a pig."

And she sweeps up the bottle caps with her arm, dumps them in the trash, and drops all the matchbooks into a drawer next to the spare batteries, twist ties, road maps, scissors, masking tape, and a couple of unopened Cracker Jack prizes. I clump across the kitchen in my work boots. The music from downstairs stops. The quiet after the noise is strange, something to be afraid of. Ginny Honey's nowhere to be seen all of a sudden. I run some water and splash it on my arm. Dry it off with a dish towel. It's giving off a familiar ache, keeping me quiet.

There's a bunch of coats hanging on the wall near the basement stairs. Billy's hunting jacket. Brown Carhartt with the orange vest draped over the shoulder. Billy hunted whatever was in season. Duck, pheasant, deer, didn't matter. Early most mornings and again at dusk, he'd be out somewhere in the woods with his gun, waiting. Said he liked the aloneness of it, out there by himself. Between that and the nights up at Dewey's and all the women on the side, it's a wonder he was around enough to give Ginny Honey three kids.

I open the fridge. A twelve-pack of Stroh's is on the bottom shelf. More Billy evidence. A jar of pickled tomatoes sits inside the fridge door. Something Billy picked up from the old man. I can't stand the taste of that shit. And it used to make the old man fart something awful. It got so bad some nights that Ma told him to stand on the back porch until it was all worked out of his system. I don't think I ever smelled anything that bad since.

"What do you want?"

I turn around toward the hall, and it's Trish. She's staring hard at me like she's looking at a ghost.

"Hey," I say. "I was kind of looking for you."

"I thought you were my dad for a minute."

I close the fridge. "Nope. Just me." It comes out too cheerful, like I'm some kind of goddamn cartoon animal or something. Trish don't react much one way or the other, just keeps studying my face. This is the first time I notice that she's a good-looking kid. She takes after Billy in that. He was a very good-looking guy, which is why he could get away with fucking every woman in three counties. And it's not like Ginny Honey didn't know about it. One time when he hadn't been home in about a week because she kicked him out, I was drinking with him up to Dewey's. And I asked him why he couldn't keep his dick in his pants, and he said why should he? And it wasn't like he was being a smart ass. It was like a real question. Why should he?

This is what's running through my mind when I realize that Trish is still staring at me, like she's looking for something, looking for Billy just like I am, except she's looking for Billy in my face. And in one split second, when my eyes meet hers, I know something. It must show on my face that I know, because I can see Trish harden just like she's some kind of quick-dry cement. Hardens and gives me a smirk that's a lot older than eleven-year-old Trish. She thinks she knows what Uncle Ray is gonna think of her now. Because he's looking at her the way her dad used to look at her. And eventually he'll get her all alone. And it'll be just what she deserves. This is what's all over her sharp little face, and neither of us has said a word. I feel my stomach heaving up like that old Tilt-A-Whirl, and I keep a hold on the handle of the fridge. Because now that I know for sure, I realize I've known for at least half a year. Like having a rumor confirmed that you barely remember hearing. *Billy's been fucking this kid? Yeah, I knew about that.*

"I'm sorry," I say, still looking at Trish. But she's too far inside that dry-cement face, and I don't know if she hears what I'm saying or not.

"You ain't got to be sorry," she says. "I done it."

"Done what?" I ask her. But Ginny Honey comes back into the kitchen, sees us watching each other, and tells Trish to get back downstairs. Trish makes for the basement door, and Ginny Honey puts out an arm to stop her. Takes Trish's chin in her hand so the kid's forced to look her ma in the eye.

"He say anything to you?" Trish mumbles no, but Ginny Honey ain't done. "You don't gotta put up with no one saying nothing to you." Trish doesn't answer, just keeps her eyes on the floor. Ginny Honey brushes the hair off the kid's face, which is about all the touching Trish is gonna stand for, because she disappears down the stairs. Ginny Honey watches her go and then she says something without turning her head, so it takes a second to figure out she's talking to me.

"Sorry I went off on you out there."

"That's okay."

"It ain't okay, really," she says. Shoots a look in my direction before she starts brushing crumbs off the table. I can tell by the hunch of her shoulders that she's crying.

"I love them kids. I can't be letting no one take 'em away from me now." She's brushing and brushing, even though the table's clean now. "I'll be a lot better mama to 'em now that son of a bitch is gone." And here she goes, really crying hard now. "I don't mean that. I don't mean it."

I wait for her to get a grip on herself. It takes a while.

"Trish don't talk to me no more, and Deena's breaking windows faster than I can get new ones put in," she says from behind the back of her hand, which she's using to wipe her nose. "And I don't even see Kyle half the time no more. I got no idea where the hell he gets off to." Kyle, that's the kid's name. What the hell kind of name is Kyle?

"He's up in the maple, side of the house," I tell her. "Reading a book."

This doesn't make her feel any better, though. She drops down into one of the kitchen chairs and sobs all over again. I bite my lip. Partly to shut up, and partly because biting down hard gives me something else to think about while I watch her cry. Finally she gets it back down to a sniffle and says for me to go on, let her finish up with the washing. No, there ain't nothing they need. No, but thanks for looking in on 'em.

I walk outside, hop in the truck, and pull out of Billy's yard. Head west toward town. Wish I'd brought Samson with me, because I don't like being alone right now. There's a dark spot coming up on the left shoulder of the road. Almost looks like someone hit a dog, it's so big. I slow down a bit when I get up close to it. Raccoon. It's been lying there a day or two at least, in this heat. All bloated and blown up like those giant balloons in the Macy's Thanksgiving Day Parade. But it's the size of him that sets me shivering. He's about eighteen inches wide at his middle and over two feet long, stretched out. Even without the bloating, this is a huge raccoon. About the size of the one come to see me out behind the plant the other night. Got to be the same one. Even if he had to cover six miles to get from there to here. As I slow down and pass, I can see his face covered with flies and blood. I step on the gas, hurrying to the Little Creek Party Store as quick as I can.

Hope Gary Keilman's working. (Randy's brother, the one got knocked off the bleachers.) I wouldn't mind shooting the shit with someone right now. But he isn't around, so I buy a six-pack of Bud and a fifth of Jim Beam and stow the fifth under the driver's seat. I'm on the road again, an open Bud balanced on my knee. Can't go home; Sally might still be there. Sally. *My friend's leaving!* The old black balloon fills up in my chest.

I drive down to the park with the six-pack, leave the truck, and find a picnic table out of sight of the road, down near the river. There's a group of ducks poking around, quacking no particular welcome. They watch me out of the corner of their hard pebble eyes as I climb on top of the picnic table, kick off my boots, and pull the T-shirt over my head. The cuts on my arm are standing out all red and swollen. Still a little burn to 'em. I snap open another beer and start pulling my thoughts together. Sally pops up, but I set her aside for now. That's for later. I got to pull my thoughts together about Billy, about Jean, about Sheriff Keith.

What do I know?

I know Jean was out to the old man's place sometime in the last few days. Could have been before or after Billy got killed. Was it Saturday night? Or maybe she just drove out there Sunday to tell him Billy was dead. But she hates the old man's guts, so she wouldn't bother about telling him anything.

I know Billy was pissed as hell at Jean the last time I saw him. I also know that Jean was pissed as hell at Billy the last time I saw her.

I know now the reason she was pissed was on account of Trish. On account of what Billy was doing to Trish.

I have to repeat that one a couple of times in my head, to nail it down. There's some thoughts that are always trying to fly off out of your head, like your head can't hold 'em, so you nail 'em down hard. Billy was fucking Trish. His eleven-year-old kid.

So Jean goes out to the old man's house on Saturday, asks him to kill Billy for her, and he says "Okeydokey." No.

That leaves Jean. What'd she say to Billy at that barbecue? It seemed like a threat, that look on her face. But she told me flat out she didn't do it. And she has never lied to me.

How much of all that does Sheriff Keith know?

He knows that the last time I saw Billy, Jean was there.

He knows that Jean was out to the old man's house.

Other than that, I'm not sure. You got to figure folks have been lining up to tell him not just all the dirt about Billy but all about Jean. All about what a slut and a whore she is. But you never hear about the beatings the old man gave her after I left home. Wasn't until she had a busted nose, couple of broken ribs, and a bruised kidney that she finally left to live with her girlfriend Pebbles. Stayed there through half of her junior year, until he got sent back to prison for hurting a couple people while he was driving drunk and Ma finally divorced him.

Jean told me later she took the beatings because it was okay with her so long as he didn't stick his dick in her no more. But she said the real torture didn't come until that last year of high school, at home with Ma after the divorce. She said she'd rather have the old man fucking her every way sideways than listen to Ma call her a slut day in and day out.

The sun's finally about to slip down below the willows where the river turns. Did I leave my damn watch on the kitchen counter when I was doing the dishes? How long have I been sitting here? Long enough for the ducks to make their peace with me. Most of 'em have their heads tucked up over one shoulder or under a wing. There are still a few awake, bobbing like decoys, watching the trees and me and each other. I gotta get up to Snell's sometime tonight, but I got no idea what time it is.

Sally comes to mind, and I wonder if she's over to Barb's yet. I let myself wonder that for about four seconds, then I open my last Bud and think about something else.

I got to come up with some kind of plan. Which is something I am no good at. I can't just sit here staring at the headlights while the train runs smack the hell over me. I got to do something about things. I try to think, but I get hit with a wall of tired. I want to lay down right here and sleep for three days, but I got to be up to Snell's in a little while, or Ma'll have my ass. I reach in my back pocket and pull out Ginch Little-field, hoping that'll keep me awake.

Someone starts humming. I shove Ginch back into my pocket, quick slip the beer into the paper bag with the empties, and look around. Don't see anyone. There's a few last shots of sunlight playing over the ducks, and I realize they're all awake now. And they're humming. Ducks don't sing, so it's just a steady murmur that goes up and down. But it's a song. And it's a sad song, no mistaking that.

The sun sinks behind the willows. Ducks bob out into the middle of the water and start to move as a group, downstream. The music they're making floats above 'em, and then I recognize the song. It's "In the Gloaming," I swear to God. A breeze has started, which is sweeping the willows and carrying the music back to me, even when the ducks are far away. There's no other sound in the park. Ma used to sing that when she was putting the wash through the hand wringer before hanging it out on the line. Made me sad even when I was a kid. I watch until they're out of sight in the gray flatness that means dusk. After that, there doesn't seem to be much point sitting here any longer. I pull my boots on, finish the last beer, grab my shirt, and head back to the truck.

I pull out of the park and head into town. Drive past the Dairy Queen, where the high school kids hang out in the parking lot, sitting on the hoods of cars, on the crumbling picnic tables. They got their radios going loud, filling up the summer dusk with a drumbeat. Randy and me used to sit in that same parking lot, watching the girls, flirting sometimes, just hanging out, being kids in summer.

When we were fifteen, me and Randy took the old pickup his dad kept for hauling calves, and we went for a drive. Didn't know where we were going, just driving. Ended up on I-94, headed west. Randy had never been out of Michigan, unless you count the Upper Peninsula when we went with his family up to Mackinac Island for two days. We got one of those two-people bikes and rode our asses all over that island. No cars allowed. Spent the rest of the time dodging his brother Gary, who was a real pain in the ass, wanting to follow us everywhere. Gary ended up getting sick on account of eating all the fudge his ma bought to take back to the folks at the church.

Other than that, though, we never really been anywhere to speak of. So we're heading west on I-94, me and Randy, and we pass a sign that says:

KALAMAZOO   90
CHICAGO   238

And I say, "Let's go," and Randy give me a look like to say, *What the hell you want to go to Kalamazoo for?* And I'm grinning and then he gets it. I know what he's thinking, though. Neither of us got our driver's license. And this truck's been nowhere but the livestock auction and back in about ten years. Randy doesn't even know what model year it is. I got about nine dollars in my pocket, and I know he ain't got much more. And we'll be crossing over state lines. We're figuring up how many laws we're breaking and how much of an ass whipping we'll get if we're caught. And we're setting that against the glory of doing it. Really just driving all the hell the way to Chicago with no maps, no clue except to follow the highway signs.

Randy knows a hog farm west of Jackson where we can siphon gas out of a tank they have back of the storage barn. We look all over for a gas can, but all we find is a dirty old pail and a tin funnel. Randy's doing the siphoning. I won't do it no more after getting a mouthful of gasoline the first time I tried it. Randy calls me a pussy, and I still won't put my mouth on that hose. I'm looking around, waiting for someone to spot us, trying not to gag on the smell of pig shit in the April air. I see something laying on the ground about twenty feet from us, by the other corner of the barn. The second I see it, even before I figure out what it is, I feel my skin prickle. Like when you just know something's not good, and you don't even know what it is yet. I walk up closer and look, not wanting to look but not having a choice. It's a piglet. I don't know what got ahold of it. Looks like it might've been a fox killed it. It's real small, no older than a couple of weeks. It's all chewed up around the stomach and the hind legs. And half of its face is pushed into the ground where it's starting to thaw out from the winter. The other half is smiling. One of those really cute piglet smiles, except it's been there awhile, thawing and rotting, the face sinking in on itself. It's really gruesome as hell.

I walk around it two or three times, inspecting it end to end. Then I grab a heavy stick and poke at the ground until I pry it loose. I flip it over, and the underside is covered with movement; grubs and maggots and roly-polies. I start to scrape 'em off, but then I jam the stick into the chewed-up end and lift the whole thing, bugs and all, into the air. It's even more gruesome waving around like that. Randy's bent over a pail full of gasoline, getting a good grip. I carry the dead piglet over to him, hold it about six inches from his head, and yell, "Randy!"

Lucky for him, he drops the pail straight down before he even sees the piglet, on account of I startled him. So only a little bit of gasoline sloshes over the sides. He turns his head and sees this thing in his face, and he falls back right on his ass and yells, "Jesus!"

I wave it at him a few times and say, "This is my friend Moe. Say hello, Moe."

"Hello, hello." That's me in a fake dead-piglet voice.

"What the fuck is that?" asks Randy when he picks himself up off the ground.

"Knock-knock," says Moe.

"Who's there?" Randy's picking up the pail of gas, heading for the truck.

"Dead pig on a stick. That's me!" Moe twirls around.

"That ain't even funny," says Randy, handing me the tin funnel. "Hold this, will ya?"

I set Moe down in the bed of the truck, and I hold the funnel while he pours the gasoline into the truck's gas tank. He does a pretty good job, but we still get some spilled on our jeans and on our hands before we're done.

"Damn, I wish we'd found a gas can," he says. "This ain't gonna get us there and back. And we can't carry an open pail of gas back there." Randy's a worrier, like me. That's why this trip is so glorious.

"Yeah," I say.

"Fuck it. Let's go." He hops up into the cab while I toss the empty pail and the funnel into the back of the truck with Moe. I got to backtrack a little to find the rubber hose. I'm climbing into the truck, and Randy says, "Get the damn pig out of there."

"No way, man," I say. "Can't ditch Moe."

"Come on," he says. "It's covered with maggots."

"Look at that face," I say, turning to look back at the piglet. Randy looks back. Moe's lying at an angle because the stick's propped against the side of the truck bed. One forehoof is outstretched into the air so it looks like he's waving at us or, worse yet, reaching for us.

"You're a sick fuck," says Randy. "What are you gonna do with it?"

"Team mascot."

So we're back out on I-94 without getting caught, Moe riding shotgun in the back. I light a cigarette, being real careful with the match on account of the spilled gasoline. It's a blue-sky day, with the sun beating down hard and clear on everything in sight. It's cold but not freezing. A perfect day for hawks to hunt, perched on the telephone poles and the tops of dead trees. We spot eighteen; that's what kind of a blue-sky day it is. A perfect day to be flying free down the highway.

Randy clicks on the radio. We're still within range of the Detroit stations, so he spins the dial to WRIF, and the DJ says, "We got the Tigers playing their season opener today, so this one's for the boys." And then the song comes on, and it's Thin Lizzy singing "The Boys Are Back in Town." Randy grins real wide and cranks it up loud as it'll go. I roll my window halfway down to let out the cigarette smoke. The wild spring wind stirs us up even more. I look over at Randy, and he's still grinning. So am I. Me and Randy are singing along: "Won't be long till summer comes, now that the boys are here again." There ain't no two better friends in the whole damn world than me and Randy, and we're going to Chicago.

Thinking about Randy like that makes me feel like shit. Going back through town from the park, I pull up to the light on Main Street and see Ella Platt through the window of the *Chronicle*. Rotten bitch. I'm heading toward Randy's street, just to see if he's home before I head to Snell's. See if his car's in the driveway. Still three blocks to go; time to turn off somewhere else. But damn, I could certainly shoot the shit with someone right now. I really could. And it wouldn't have to be any big deal. I think the Tigers are on tonight; we could have a few beers and watch the game and not have to talk about anything. I think about the old man at home alone, watching. Or maybe with Shiner. The two of them knocking back beers and having a ball. I probably could go out there. But I don't want to be around the old bastard tonight.

I pull onto Randy's street and there's a patrol car in front of his house. My first instinct is to floor it and get the hell out of there. But I got to be sure. So I drive by nice and slow like a hundred other trucks have driven by, and there's a Taco Bell cup wedged on the dashboard. Sheriff Keith. He's a nice guy, all right, but he's a slob. I keep the speed down low until I turn the corner back toward Main Street. So Randy's out of the question. Doesn't matter. I've done all right without him long enough. Think about checking on Jean. Wipe the thought out of my head, if I know what's good for me.

I head over to Snell's. Realize I'm still wearing the same thing I wore to work last night. Work boots. My T-shirt all greasy, plus the tomato stains on the front where that first bite squirted, blood on the sleeve. I figure I can at least get a clean shirt, so I stop over to Lon's, which is sort of a dime store, except now they sell more candles and knickknacks. But the lower level, in the basement, that's where you can get stuff like underwear and T-shirts and batteries and sunglasses and useful shit like that.

Lon's is air-conditioned to death. I buy three white cotton T's (long-sleeved) for fifteen dollars. I tell Shawnlea that I'll just change right there in the dressing room, if she doesn't mind. "Shawnlea" is what it says on her name tag. She can't be more than fifteen years old. Any girl under eighteen has a name like Shawnlea these days. I like a name like Sally. You really can't go wrong with it. Shawnlea says she doesn't mind me changing, so I put on the clean shirt, stuff the dirty one in the shopping bag, comb my hair while I'm at it, and pick right up where I left off on my way over to the funeral home. All I want to do is get inside there, where all the sound is muffled and no one ever runs, for any reason whatsoever. Where nothing bad ever happens, because the people are already dead.

I pull into the parking lot and see Ed's car; he and Ma are here. I don't see Sally's Skylark, which I didn't really expect to; I was only just a little curious. I know she'll be here tomorrow for the funeral. I don't see Jean's truck. I slide out of the passenger door and walk up the sidewalk. The breeze is really picking up, which keeps the mosquitoes from hovering. It smells like raspberries for some reason.

I go down the hallway, past the big Bible opened to John 14:18—"I will not leave you comfortless." *Right.* Past the coat closet, with boxes of tissues stacked on the high shelf. I walk slow, letting the calm seep into my skin and my veins. But the second I walk into Billy's room, I know it was a mistake to come here tonight. I don't know why, even. It's just a mistake.

The place is full of relatives. Everywhere I look, I see someone who looks like me. All Ma's brothers have come up from Tennessee with their families and their families' families. Cousins and second cousins I ain't seen in twelve years, and kids I ain't ever seen except for school photos stuck in a Christmas card. I have no idea who belongs to who. I'm not even sure I got the right names for the people I do recognize.

Those six beers I killed in the park come to mind, and I start a slow slide backward, out toward the hall. That's when I bump smack into

Mrs. Dollar. (I swear to God, that's her name. It's pronounced "Doe-lar.") She's being real sweet to me, saying how sorry she is, but I can see she's got one eye sweeping the room, looking for Ma.

"Ma's here somewhere," I say.

"That's all right," she says. "I know she's got people to talk to." One eye's still sweeping.

"She'll want to know you're here," I tell her. "I'll see if I can't find her downstairs." And I duck out and head down there. I figure I'll hide in the smoking lounge, suck on some of them peppermint candies to kill the beer breath. When I walk in, I think at first there's no one there. It's all still and dead quiet. This is a good time for a smoke, to take advantage of the peace. So I'm lighting up, and that's when I see Ma. She's in front of the mirror hanging on the far wall. It's in a round wood frame that looks like a captain's wheel, just like the clock. She's standing there, but she's not looking at herself. Not checking her lipstick (which is faded) or her hair (which is okay). She's just standing in front of it, facing off to the side, looking at nothing as far as I can tell.

"Ma?" No answer. I walk over to her, talking as I go because I don't want to sneak up on her and startle her. She really, really hates that. All three of us used to get the shit kicked out of us for doing that to her when we were little.

"Ma? Mrs. Dollar's here. Upstairs." Still she ain't moving. I don't think she's hearing me, so I stop a ways from her.

"Ma?" There's another stretch of quiet. Ma don't usually act like this. It's the old man that never answers you. Especially if the TV's on.

"Hey, Dad?"

"Hey, Dad?"

"Hey, Dad?"

"Hey, Dad?" Like he's stone deaf. Then twenty minutes later, he'll say, "What?" So I'm starting to feel real weird, when Ma finally notices me.

"I don't know what to do," she says.

"Huh?"

And she turns, but only for a second does she look right at me, and her eyes are *not* flat colored glass. Then she looks at my feet and says it again.

"I don't know what to do."

"About what?" I say.

"About Billy."

How do you answer that? You can't answer that. Try it sometime. You can't.

And she looks like she lost her glasses or her keys and she can't think what the hell she did with them. Or someone just clocked her a good one with a two-by-four, and she's got that really surprised, confused look you get right before you go flat on the floor. She looks like all of that at once.

She puts out her hand; she's lost her balance a little. I take it and hold it, but I don't know what to do about Billy either. I'm still trying to think of some way to answer her, but like I said, you can't.

So she says to me, "Ray," like she's stating a fact. Like she's laying a finger on the couch and saying "couch." I think of Helen Keller, that girl who was blind and deaf and dumb. I think this must be how weird it was for her family, except Helen Keller couldn't even say "couch." This is the kind of stuff that's running around inside my skull while Ma's turning into some kind of freak show right in front of me. And it feels like twenty hours since I came downstairs. I figure people got to be wondering where she is.

"Where's Ed?" I ask. Probably this whole thing feels so weird because it's the first time I've seen her without Ed standing next to her in nine years.

"I don't know," she says. Then she turns liquid for half a second, but it's long enough for her knees to give out, and down she goes except I get ahold of her in time and she straightens up a little.

"Let's sit down," I say.

"I don't know," she says, which seems to make sense. I get her over to one of the couches, and we sit next to each other. She takes hold of my hand again. Hard. Footsteps are coming down the stairs. Some old guy, I don't who he is, pokes his head in the door, sees the two of us, and says, "Oh, Sherry. I'm just gonna use the bathroom." And he disappears quick as he came. Ma gives a little laugh. I think she's laughing at the old guy, but she's not. She's still kind of looking at nothing. She's looking a little happier, though.

"You kids," she said. "Sometimes you really made me laugh."

"We made you laugh?" I ask, keeping up the conversation.

"Oh, you were so funny." Then she really does laugh. And she says, "Lots of times you just . . . I don't know. You just made my day."

All of this is news to me. I'm about as surprised as I can be that we ever made her day—even once. Mostly all I remember is how much better her whole life would've been "if it weren't for you goddamn kids!" I'm thinking about this, saying nothing. I figure about now is when she starts crying. But she doesn't.

"You know, Billy used to brush my hair when he was little," she says.

"Yeah?"

"Real little, two or three. He'd just brush and brush for hours." We're quiet then. I'm trying to imagine what Billy was like before I came on the scene. I seen pictures of him little, but they don't seem real like the pictures of me do.

After a while, she says, "You okay now?"

"Yeah," I tell her. I think I'm okay. Hell, I don't know. I have no idea what just went on.

"I'm gonna head back upstairs." She's smiling at me. I'm smiling back at her.

"I'll come up with you," I say.

"That's all right," she says. "Finish your cigarette."

"You sure?" But she looks all right again.

"I love you, Ray." And she stands up and walks out of the room. But the last thing she does is, she sort of ruffles the top of my head. Just half a ruffle, really. But it's something she hasn't done since I was a kid. So I sit there for a little while.

When I get back upstairs, there's a cluster of aunts hovering like a bouquet of flowers a few feet from Billy's coffin. How do I even know Billy's in there? How do I know they didn't just throw him in a garbage bin at the morgue? A shiny dark-gray metal coffin like the barrel of a Winchester, which he would've liked. But empty. How do I even know they have the pretty pillow and the pleated satin lining and all that shit inside? Maybe they charged Ma full price but gave her a half-ass coffin. Just empty air, gun-barrel gray. How do I know he's really dead?

Ma's back to her usual self, smiling all brave through her tears and bossing everyone around. She spots me in the doorway and drags me over to the flower cluster of aunts. The first one to go for me is Aunt Lois, married to Ma's oldest brother, Bub. No shit, we call him Uncle

Bub. She give me a big hug and kiss, and the smell of her perfume makes my stomach heave, just like it did when I was a kid. White Shoulders. I know because I'd spend a week down in Tennessee with them every summer when I was a kid. Me and my cousin Harold got into Aunt Lois and Uncle Bub's room, looking for the *Penthouse* he kept under his socks in the top drawer. There was a bottle of White Shoulders on top of the dresser. So we grabbed that along with the *Penthouse* and we buried the perfume out in the backyard with a trowel we found in the toolshed. He hated the smell of it even more than I did. Harold and me did a lot of raising hell when I went down there.

"Oh, honey baby, I'm so awful sorry," Aunt Lois says.

"Glad you're here, Aunt Lois," I say, putting my arms around her as lightly as I can get away with. I don't want that smell clinging to me. When Aunt Lois is done mauling me, she passes me off to Aunt Weazy. Her real name's Louise, but she's been Aunt Weazy since I can remember. Anyway, she claps her hands twice on my shoulders (hard enough for me to make a face and hope she didn't see it) then sucks me into a billowy hug, squeezes for a count of five, and lets go. I have to make an effort not to bounce back off her like a rubber ball. She's a pretty hefty gal, around two hundred eighty pounds, and stands five feet eleven inches in her socks.

"Look at this good-looking man," she's saying. "This good-looking man can't be little Ray." We all laugh a little, uncomfortable. Her voice is booming all over Snell's, echoing down the quiet hallways and plowing through the fields of plush carpet. Aunt Weazy's all right from across the room, but up close she's hazardous. She's married to Ma's second-oldest brother, Hal (namesake of my cousin Harold). Uncle Hal's damn near as big as his wife. They only had but one kid, and he died when he was four. I never did know what he died from. I was seven when it happened. I remember I saw him just a couple times, at family reunions. He was puny. I always had it in my mind that Aunt Weazy and Uncle Hal overfed him, like a hamster, until he burst. I took care to keep that theory to myself.

"Look at him, Evelyn," she says. "Look at our little skinny Ray. He's damn near as tall as I am." Ho ho ho. I'm only five feet nine inches, as if that matters. The aunts are irritating the shit out of me. This is exactly how they've always treated me, and Billy too. The aunts would say shit to him made my hair stand on end waiting for him to land a punch square on one of their noses. He could've raped and robbed all three of them and they'd laugh and tell him to quit showing off. Maybe that's just the way women are in Tennessee.

They're all older than Ma, who's the baby. Three boys and then her. Aunt Evelyn is standing quiet next to Ma, smiling at me but making no lunges for a hug.

"Hey, Aunt Evelyn," I say. "How you doing?"

She smiles even sweeter and ducks her head for a second.

"I'm doing pretty well." She talks kind of quiet, so I have to lean my head down a little. "I'm sorry for Billy," she says, like she really means it. I want to swoop her up in a big hug and tell her I love her. And I damn near do it too. Except I remember those beers, and I don't want her smelling that on me. So instead I just look at her with a big stupid grin, nodding my head. She was married to Uncle Jerry, who died about twelve years ago. I think that was the last time I saw these people. They had six thousand kids, it seemed like. She finished raising them by herself, with Aunt Lois and Aunt Weazy helping.

The thing about Aunt Evelyn, she's real quiet and religious, but not in just the going-to-church way. Even so, she used to teach me songs like "Riley Is Dead" and "Do Your Ears Hang Low?" which she said were old sailors' drinking songs.

"I been trying to track you down all day," says Ma. "Where you been?"

"Just doing stuff. You know." Typical Ma. Like what just happened downstairs didn't happen at all.

"You're gonna have Aunt Lois and Uncle Bub stay in the spare room," she says. Bossy, bossy, bossy again. "I got nowhere to put everyone. Harold says he don't mind sleeping on your couch."

"Harold's here?'

"Yeah, he was just over there," says Aunt Weazy.

I look, but I don't see him. Ma goes on. "Ginny Honey don't have any room over to their place." So Ma's doing it too, forgetting Billy's dead. *Their place.*

Aunt Lois breaks in. "She doesn't need any strange people in her house now anyway."

"You're not strangers, you're family," Ma flips back. Then she turns to me again. "I got Pastor and Mary Hodges to take Hal and Weazy. Evelyn and her kids are staying at the house with me and Ed."

All this information is making the room feel hot and stuffy. Real hot and stuffy.

"Where's Sally?" asks Ma.

"She ain't here."

"Well, call and tell her to make up the bed and set out some sheets for Harold."

"She ain't there."

Ma stops, waiting for me to come up with some more information. I can't think of anything to say, so I say, "She's at Barbara's."

"It don't matter. I gave Lois my key to your house, so they can just come and go as they need."

Lois must feel something coming off me that's not perfect joy. She says, "We don't need any looking after, honey. You won't even know we're there."

"That's okay. Glad to have you." I can smell that White Shoulders all over my house. It's gonna be harder to get rid of than termites.

"We've all heard very nice things about Sally," says Aunt Evelyn.

"She'll be here tomorrow," I say. Jesus, the room is hot. I'm thinking how I'm probably gonna drop dead right in the middle of the aunts because I can't think of any way to get out of here.

Uncle Bub comes up behind Ma and says, "Lois, you got the car keys?" She opens her purse and roots around for 'em. "I need my pipe." He sees me and says, "Hey, Ray, good to see you."

"Hey, Uncle Bub." *Pipe?*

"This is the bad times, huh?"

"Yeah. How long you guys in town for?"

Lois finds the keys and says, "Bub has to be back to work on Saturday."

Tonight's only Tuesday. Between the pipe and the perfume, I'll have to burn down the house when they leave.

"Harold's downstairs," says Uncle Bub, taking the keys. Then he's gone.

"Maybe I'll go say hi," I tell Ma.

She pats my arm. "You go on. You boys always had such a good time together."

I give a smile and a nod that includes all three of the aunts, though I look at Aunt Evelyn when I say good-bye. On my way out of the room, I don't see Jean anywhere. Once I'm out in the hallway, the front door opens and someone walks in, someone I don't know. But in those few seconds, I feel the breeze blow in from outside. Relief trickles down from my forehead and I can breathe a little easier. I pull out my cigarettes, go downstairs to find Harold.

Harold's real tall and real blond. And he has this small head. Small and triangle-shaped, like the head of a praying mantis. I saw one up close once. It swiveled its head at different angles and looked at me and I thought, Jesus, that looks like Harold. The other thing about Harold, he smiles out of only one side of his mouth, the right side. It makes him look like a bit of a smart ass, even when he's not being a smart ass at all.

I'm remembering Harold and that week when he came to stay with us, how I wished he could come and live with us for good. Think about the old man and what happened the next night, the night after we watched *Chitty Chitty Bang Bang* and me and Randy and Harold stayed up playing Chinese checkers while Ma and the old man were laughing on the other side of the wall. Because the next night the old man don't come home for supper, and he don't come home when we watch TV, and he don't come home when Mom says me and Harold can spend the night in the fort. She even says Harold can use Billy's sleeping bag, which means we don't have to bribe Billy.

So we grab all the stuff we think we're gonna need, like two flashlights and the Chinese checkers and a bunch of graham crackers that Ma puts in a lunch bag. Jean starts in, rolling up the blanket off her bed and saying how she's gonna sleep in the fort too. Me and Harold tell her no way. We get two cans of Vernors ginger ale, two pillows, and half a dozen comic books. Jean starts screaming and slamming the screen door over and over again, but we tell her no girls allowed and Ma sides with us. So we load up a brown grocery bag with all our stuff, plus the transistor radio. Harold's got a sleeping bag and the grocery bag in his hands. I got my sleeping bag and both our pillows. We're heading out the back door and Ma's in the living room. Jean's not giving up, though.

"I'm sleeping in the fort," she says, standing in front of the door with her blanket and blocking our way.

"No you ain't," I tell her.

"Why not?" she wants to know.

" 'Cause you're just a stupid girl," says Harold. I'm not sure I like hearing anyone else talk like that to Jean except me. But Harold's my best friend this week. Better even than Randy, better even than Jean. So when she looks at me to see if I agree that she's just a stupid girl, I say, "Go on now, we're sick of you."

And she bites me. She flies straight at me and bites me hard on my shoulder. I holler and drop the sleeping bag and both pillows. She starts to run past me, but I grab hold of her blanket and yank it hard. She swings back toward me and I shove her as hard as I can across the kitchen. She's all tangled in the blanket and crashes into the kitchen table, landing under it and sliding into the chair legs. She's only six, and she looks pretty small under the table all of a sudden. Ma hollers at us from the living room, so me and Harold quick take off out the door before she gets in the kitchen and sees Jean, who's not exactly crying, but sputtering and saying how she hates my guts and she's gonna get me good.

No one comes out to the fort to bother us, so I figure I'm not gonna get in trouble, at least not tonight. I feel a little knot in my stomach because I wouldn't have really cared if Jean slept in the fort or not, but I didn't want Harold to think I was a pussy. I also got a little knot because she said she was gonna get me good. And when she said that to Billy a couple weeks before, she took the old man's lighter to his hair while he was sleeping. Only reason she didn't burn him bald is because I was awake when she come into the room and I just pretended to be asleep to catch her at whatever she was up to. Saw her flicking that silver lighter, and once it caught fire, she held it right to the ends of his hair. I didn't move at first because I was curious to see what would happen. But it really caught fire. Fast. I jumped up and hollered and pushed my pillow hard over Billy's head and held it there.

Billy wanted to beat the living shit out of her, but the old man did it for him. Used the belt on her bare ass, but she didn't cry. Then he laid her arm across the kitchen table with the big turkey knife in his hand and told her he'd cut her fingers off if she ever touched his lighter again. Still she didn't cry. She thought she was in the right, no matter what the old man said or did. So I'm afraid of what she's gonna do to me, because I know I acted like a jerky asshole, which is taking some of the fun out of sleeping in the fort.

That night I wake up fully alert and on guard all at once. A feeling of *oh, no* is already creeping up my legs, through my gut, and closing over my chest, even before I hear the hollering. The old man's home. He's drunk. I turn my head and look to see if Harold's awake. He's laying on his back, eyes open and staring straight up, holding one of the flashlights across his chest. I don't say anything to him, just listen to the sounds coming from the house. I don't know what time it is, or how long it's been going on. Maybe he just got home, maybe they been fighting for an hour. They're both yelling, him looping up and down, her thin and whiny. But she ain't crying yet, so maybe he'll just fall asleep. I lay still, pinned in place by the same old nail through my gut.

It gets quiet for a few minutes. Then glass is breaking and I can tell it's his dinner flying across the room. I can see the fork flying off the plate in midair, the corn exploding against the cupboard door and landing like yellow raindrops on the counter and the floor. Hamburger gravy trailing across the Formica tabletop, across the chair where Ma was sitting a second ago. She's shaking the glass out of her hair, crying now. I can see the whole thing behind my closed eyes. I hear another crash, and it's his chair shooting backward when he jumps up after her.

"Bill, no! Please!" It's coming out full scream now. But he ain't gonna stop and just go to sleep. Not now.

"I don't need to come home to this shit from you," he's hollering. More dishes are flying around the room like they're in a panic and trying to get away. "I don't need to come home at all." His voice is loud, going in and out of the other sounds. The scraping across the linoleum when she lands against the table just like Jean did a few hours before, the muffled noise that skin makes when it hits other skin.

"Stupid cunt, can't even comb your fucking hair."

His voice is like a thick black ribbon wrapping up the whole house, tied up in a hard bow along with Ma's ribbon, red and silky, twining to get out of his way. I'm picturing this giant Christmas present, our house, wrapped up in red and black. I hear the pounding of his feet. He's heading up the stairs. I look at Harold again out of the corner of my eye. He ain't moved. I watch him for a long time, but he doesn't even blink. I can hardly see his chest move at all. I want to reach over, take that flashlight out of his hands, and beat his face in. I hate him for not letting Jean sleep in the fort with us. I hate him so much right now I don't know how I'm gonna live until he goes home. No way in hell I'm talking to him. He can damn well sleep with Billy until Saturday, because I hate the little cocksucker.

A door bangs open in the house. Like a gunshot. Ma's voice has followed his footsteps up the stairs. She's quieter now, trying to get him back downstairs or get him into their bedroom, into their bed. But it's not gonna work tonight. The noises just keep on. And there's some sounds that you don't know what they are, no matter how many times he comes home like this, because you can't imagine. You just can't imagine. So you listen and you try to figure it out, try to picture what the hell's going on. But your brain's gone blank. So you count to ten and then see if those sounds have stopped. Six, seven, eight. Each number punched through with Jean's squealing little-kid scream. "Daddy! No, Daddy!"

And Ma crying again and singing the same old song. "Bill, she's so little. Stop it!"

So much noise. Most of it old and familiar, like an old teddy bear. But still, there's some things you're hearing that don't make sense. It won't stop. So you count some more. Twenty-three, twenty-four.

"Leave her alone." Billy's voice, shaky but loud.

"Gonna get it worse . . . stupid little shit . . . get your ass over here . . . my goddamn house . . . all of you someday . . ." The old man's black ribbon is garbled and only coming through in bits. Footsteps running light down the stairs. Whose? What's happening now? Yelling gets all of a sudden too loud. It's just too loud now. One house can't hold all that sound, all those ribbons screaming at the top of their lungs, pulling tighter and tighter. But it only lasts a second or two, because then there's a whole row of thumps, one after another, clumsy noise. Someone falling down the stairs. Then nothing but Ma saying, "Oh my God, oh my God," about a hundred times, very soft. Like she doesn't understand what's happening, like she doesn't believe it.

I don't hear Billy or Jean, so I figure one of 'em got killed this time. Maybe both of 'em. Nothing's happening now except voices talking low. Can't make it out. Ma's still crying, but she's making an effort to calm down. Which means it must be something really bad. I get out of my sleeping bag.

"Stay here," I say to Harold without looking at him. I crawl to the flap of the doghouse and peek out across the yard. Every light in the house is on. Like a lighthouse warning the whole county where the danger is. Like ambulance flashers screaming, *Look out! Look out!*

I hear Billy's voice, but I don't hear Jean. That's when I know that she's dead. Dead of a broken neck from falling down the stairs. I don't want the old man looking at her laying there dead with her neck broke. I got to get her out of the house. Me and Randy can bury her tomorrow. We'll put her out by Ma's honeysuckle bush, next to the fence. In the meantime, she can stay in the fort, where the old man can't get at her. I'm not about to ask Harold to help me carry her. I'll just drag her out here myself. I crawl out of the flap and start across the yard. That's when a voice hisses out of the dark. "Ray."

I turn around and it's Jean. She ain't dead. She's up in the box elder tree.

"Where you going?" she whispers.

"To get you."

"Hang on." She climbs down. All she's wearing is her pajama top, and she's got the matching bottoms all balled up in her hand. Ma just got those pajamas for her last week. We were up to Lon's, and Jean took about nine hours picking them out. Short sleeves, with little ladybugs all over 'em, and buttons to match the ladybugs. They're all torn. I figure she tore 'em climbing up the tree.

I say, "Ma's gonna kill you when she sees them pajamas."

Jean looks down at her pajamas and her mouth screws up like she might cry, but she doesn't. That's how I know she didn't rip them in the tree.

"C'mon," I tell her. She pulls on her pajama bottoms and follows me into the fort. Neither one of us says anything to Harold, who still ain't moved. We climb into my sleeping bag. Not much room, so we're both on our sides. She scootches until her back's against my stomach. I wrap my arms around her tight as I can and smell the back of her head. We lay like that for about ten minutes, all three of us wide awake, trying to read the voices in the house. The back door bangs open and the old man calls out into the yard. "Jean!" Nobody moves in the fort. Like we turned into three cocoons that won't open till next spring. He calls again a couple times, then Ma's voice comes through the door.

"You go to bed. I'll find her."

I don't hear what he answers, but the door bounces on its frame and it's quiet again. The whole house holds its breath for a few minutes and then it sags in a loud sigh. The old man's gone to bed. The three cocoons in the fort stay just as they are. No sounds at all from the house. Jean's hair is tickling my nose, so I pull my head back a little. She nuzzles her cheek deeper against my shoulder, which hurts a little because it's right where she bit me earlier. The door creaks and Ma comes across the yard. She's outside the fort.

"Ray?" God, she sounds tired.

"Yeah, Ma."

"Jean in there with you?"

"Yeah."

"She okay?"

"Yeah, Ma," I say. "Billy okay?"

"He's all right. You kids go to sleep." Quiet.

"G'night, Ma," I say.

"G'night, Ray." Pause. "G'night, Harold." Quiet.

Finally Harold answers. "G'night, Aunt Sherry."

Ma goes back across the yard. The door squeaks again, and she's gone without ever saying a word to Jean. I rub her head a little and scratch the back of her neck because I know she likes it.

Finally I say, "I could hear everything." She doesn't answer, but she knows what I mean. I mean the Petersons two doors down, and Dr. Summer, who lives on the other side of the big fence, they could hear it too. I always thought the house kept it all inside, but I was wrong. We're never gonna be able to play over to the Petersons' again. We're never gonna be able to leave the yard or look any of them people in the eye. We were kidding ourselves that we could act all normal and no one would know.

"I'm sorry I pushed you into the table," I whisper.

Quiet for a while, then she says, " 'S okay." She sounds small, though. I turn my head into the pillow so Harold won't hear me blubbering.

"What's the matter?" She turns and whispers in my ear.

"I thought you was dead."

"Oh," she says. I stay awake a long time after I'm done crying, listening to a couple of dogs barking across the yards to each other. I can tell by her breathing that she's awake too.

The next morning, Harold's up before any of us, like usual. Early enough to make a phone call that no one hears. Ma drives the old man to work so she can have the car to take Billy to the doctor. He's got a broken arm from falling down the stairs. Me and Harold have to baby-sit Jean till they get home, around noon. I ain't talking much to Harold, and he ain't talking much to anyone. Late in the afternoon, a strange car pulls into the driveway. Harold's out the front door and sitting in the passenger seat before we even know who it is.

Uncle Bub comes in the house and talks to Ma for a long time. Me and Jean stay in the backyard, Billy's upstairs sleeping. Jean goes to peek around the house every five minutes to see what's happening, then reports back to me.

"What's going on?"

"Same thing," she says. "Harold's sitting in the car with his stupid triangle head and Uncle Bub's still in the house." About the hundredth peek around the corner, she waves me over. Uncle Bub's coming down the driveway carrying Harold's duffel bag (army regulation, from Uncle Bub being in Korea). He gets in the car, they pull out and drive away. Me and Jean don't wave good-bye and Harold doesn't look back once. After that, we still went down to Tennessee to visit, but he never came to stay with us again.

SEVENTEEN

At first I don't see Harold down in the smoking room. He's talking to Uncle Hal in the corner, but I don't know that's him until Uncle Hal says, "Well, goddamn, is that Ray?"

"Hey, Uncle Hal." I walk toward the two of 'em, and that's when the other guy smiles crooked and I realize it's Harold.

"Hey, Harold, how ya been?" I guess everyone can hear in my voice how glad I am to see him.

"Doing okay," he says. "Sorry about Billy." The smile turns up even further at one end.

"Yeah," I say. The name sort of hangs there in the air like a cloud of poison gas. What the hell do I say to this guy? I ain't seen him in twelve years.

"So how you doing?" This is Harold, asking me how I'm doing. Hell, I don't know how I'm doing.

"Hell, I don't know." This gets a big laugh out of both of 'em.

"Yeah," says Harold. "This is weird, isn't it?"

Uncle Hal asks Harold if any of the other kids are coming. He means Harold's three brothers. It's hard to remember they're my cousins. They were always older, never around.

"Getting in later tonight," says Harold. "Where's Jean? I don't see her here."

"I don't know," I say, looking away. Looking around the room. Looking for Jean. I don't know where she is.

Uncle Hal sees someone else related to us and stumps off to talk to him. Uncle Hal always walks like he's wearing big old work boots. Stump, stump, stump. So does Aunt Weazy.

Jesus, I'm tired. The six-pack is hitting me like a twenty-foot wave, crashing and lulling, crashing and lulling. I honestly can't think when was the last time I slept. Harold looks a little blurry. Partly because I'm tired, partly because he's gained some weight around his middle, around his chin. His head's still small and triangle, but he doesn't look like a praying mantis anymore.

"You're looking good," I say to cover the fact that I been staring at him.

"Fat," he says, half his face smiling big. "You look like shit, you know."

"Got a new shirt," I reply, following a logic all my own.

"Shirt looks great," he agrees. "You sick or something?"

"Tired."

"Yeah."

"I work nights."

"Hmm."

We sit down, neither of us talking, smoking in peace and quiet. I want to kick my feet up on one of them couches and die. A redhead walks into the smoking lounge. She's real pretty. Real pretty. Uncle Hal gives her a big hug.

"Who's that?" I ask Harold.

"That's Nan."

"They're here?"

"Yeah, Marty and her." He blows out a long, loud sigh of smoke. "I haven't seen Carol yet, though." Carol, Nan, and Marty are more cousins of ours, Aunt Evelyn's girls.

"The guys here?" I ask.

"Somewhere." He waits a second or two and says, "They haven't changed much."

I think of 'em all down there in Tennessee, growing up together, living close by. Having Thanksgiving together, Christmas. Going to the same schools. Ma and Ed go down there every year at Easter. She was always pestering me to go down there with 'em. I never saw any reason to go. I didn't know how much I missed Harold.

Carol, Nan, and Marty were all three pretty, even when we were kids. We hit thirteen or fourteen years old and they got to be knockouts, while Harold and I got uglier by the day. Still, Nan let me feel her up one time when we were all five of us camping out in their basement. We had our sleeping bags laid out on a piece of green carpeting under the pool table. After that I spent six months in love with Nan. I even wrote her a couple of letters.

That was the summer Jean come down for a week too. I stay with Harold, and Jean stays with Aunt Evelyn and all her kids. Nan and Marty give her a beauty parlor treatment one afternoon. Curl her hair and put makeup on her and nail polish, even. Spend all afternoon tarting her up. Me and Harold come over there to ask 'em to play neighborhood war with us, and there's Jean looking like a goddamn clown. They lead her out to show me and Harold, and we bust out laughing. I laugh because she doesn't look like Jean at all. I laugh because I hate how she looks. She's only twelve, and I hate it.

She doesn't like us laughing any more than I like that shit on her face, I guess. Because she walks upstairs to the girls' bedroom and doesn't come down all night. Nan won't talk to me and keeps shooting me dirty looks all through two games of Trivial Pursuit, which we have to play instead because Aunt Evelyn says the folks down the block are getting pretty fed up with neighborhood war and we'd better stay inside tonight. The dirty looks are driving me crazy and make me want to break Jean's neck. I go upstairs and knock on the door to apologize, but she won't answer, so I go in. She's laying there on the bed. She took a shower, because her hair's still a little damp and the makeup is gone. Nail polish is gone too. I tell her I'm sorry for laughing at her and she tells me to go fuck myself. I tell her to quit pouting and come downstairs and play Trivial Pursuit with the rest of us. She tells me to go fuck myself again. I tell her she can be on my team, and she doesn't even bother to answer. I can't blame her. She stays upstairs all night. But Nan softens up after that and lets me keep my hand on her leg under the table.

The next day, Nan finds her Barbie on the floor out in the hallway with no hands, no feet, and all the hair cut off. She's fourteen already and hardly plays with it anymore. But she's pissed off anyway. She says Marty did it, Marty says Carol did it, Carol accuses Marty, and no one confesses all through two hours of Nan crying and throwing a fit. Jean watches me, daring me to say something. I know damn well she did it. Hell, she did the same to her own dolls. But I don't say anything.

A few months later, she locks herself in the bathroom and I can hear her in there, humming to herself. I know that sound. It's the humming she does to keep herself calmed down, so she won't cry.

"Jean?" I say to the bathroom door.

"Go away."

"What's the matter?"

No answer. Quiet.

"Jean?" I try again. "What you doing in there?"

"Leave me alone." So I start to go, but then I hear, "Ray?"

"Yeah."

"I'm bleeding." I can tell by now that she hasn't cut her finger or anything like that. "It's bleeding."

"Hang on a minute," I tell her. I go down the hall and reach up to the very top shelf of the hall closet. The reason I know they're there is because Billy showed me once, both of us giggling, afraid to get caught. I take her the pad and tell her to put it in her underwear.

"Don't come in," she says, unlocking the door.

I hand it to her through the door. After a minute she says, "I need a safety pin." So I get one off Ma's dresser, in her music box. Hand that through the door, too.

"Wait for me," she says.

When she's done, we go sit outside on the back porch. It's October, and the leaves are just starting to go.

"Didn't Ma tell you what to do?"

She shakes her head. Said her friend Pebbles told her this would happen, but she didn't believe it.

"Am I gonna have to wear these things every day till I die?" she says.

"I think just till you have kids."

Her face is white and she looks small, tired.

"Does it hurt?" I ask her.

"Yeah." We sit for a long time, not saying anything. She kicks a couple of stones off the lowest step. "I guess I'm really fucked now," she says.

I can't argue with her. She's a girl. Boys'll be coming around pretty soon. I try to picture Jean with a boyfriend. I close my eyes at the thought of it, try to shut it out. She puts her head down on my knee, and I twist a finger through one of her brown curls. Neither of us say much after that.

●

So there's Nan, standing on the other side of the room, pretty in a woman way now instead of a girl way.

"Come on and say hi," says Harold. We're sitting on one of the red plaid couches. He's making a move to get up. I can't get up. I can't think what to say to her or to Marty or to Carol.

"Naw, I'll wait," I say.

"Wait for what?"

"She's talking to Uncle Hal."

"Okay." Harold's perfectly happy to sit there or talk to Nan or go upstairs where the aunts are clustering. Doesn't make much difference to him. Ain't his brother lying dead up there.

"I'm gonna go outside for a minute." Harold looks at me, so I add, "You want to come?"

He nods his weird triangle head and stubs out his cigarette in the glass ashtray.

"You still smoke?" he asks softly.

"Yeah," I answer. "Once in a while."

"I got some out in the car," he says.

"Okay," I say, moving across the room. I know it's not possible to get out of there without speaking to Nan. I know it's not humanly possible to get away. But I'm taking one step after another with my eyes on the door, picturing myself already out in the parking lot where maybe the breeze ain't died down yet, smoking a joint with Harold and wiping the beads of nervous off my forehead.

"Ray?" Well, there you go.

"Hey, Nan."

"You gonna walk right by without saying hello?"

So we stand around and chitchat, me and Harold and Nan and Uncle Hal. I need to get outside pretty soon. Nan's wearing a pin on the lapel of her black blouse. It's a little gold bunch of lilies of the valley, and the flowers are made of little pearls.

"When's Carol getting in?" says Uncle Hal.

I seen that pin before, because I remember thinking how pretty it was.

". . . so nice to see all the . . ."

It was Grandma Loreen's pin. She wore it all the time.

". . . and she says, 'Who the hell are you?' " Everyone laughs, so I laugh too. Lilies of the valley meant the whole family around and the old man on his best behavior and Ma smiling.

". . . probably leave Thursday morning."

I'm getting so I can't breathe, looking at that damn pin.

"I got to go," I say real quick, and I'm on the stairs, and I'm at the door, and I'm outside finally. Outside where the breeze has turned into one of those winds that only come on August nights. Winds that are restless and wild, not ready to let go of summer yet, not ready for the death that autumn brings. I'm outside in that August wind and I'm standing in the middle of the damned parking lot with my head hanging back and my arms dangling like dead things at my side. I'm looking straight up in the air and the stars are wheeling around the sky, blowing around in that wind. I know I got to get in that pickup and drive like hell. Just drive like hell.

I hold my arms out straight to the sides like a human cross while I walk slow and steady across the pavement to my truck. Maybe I'll get picked up and carried off into the wild night. Land someplace where nobody knows my name. Live the rest of my life a polite guy no one really knows. *A nice guy, but keeps to himself.* I'm ten feet from my truck when Harold hollers at me from the steps of the funeral home.

"Hang on. I gotta get something."

So I lean against the truck and look back up at the stars again. The sky is one big black coffin lid closing down on me. I know I ought to be doing something, but I can't think what it is. Something about Jean, who's nowhere around tonight. But I can't do anything more now, except get the weight of all this shit off me for a while. I'm at the end of something, but I don't know what.

We never make it back to the funeral home. After Harold rummages around in the back of his minivan, he hops in the truck with a shaving kit in his hand. I ain't even out of the parking lot and he's pulling out a couple of joints, a little tray, and some coke.

"Where we going?" he asks.

"This bar I know."

We hit the Bowl 'n' Bar first. See some guys I know from work. We shoot pool until I get in a fight. I don't remember the guy's name, but Billy used to know him when he hung out with the Night Angels, a bunch of half-assed biker pricks with a clubhouse out on Redfield Road, past where Sally grew up. Anyway, this guy starts running his mouth on Harold, so I take him out back and kick the shit out of him. Two other bikers are there with him, but they don't stand up. From the look of it, I was doing them a favor because this prick was chasing away every bitch in the place.

Harold decides we oughta take off, so he's heading for the truck and I rifle through the guy's wallet, take the cash, and put the wallet back in the prick's pocket. I drive us to the Lakefront Bar and Harold counts over two hundred dollars this stupid son of a bitch was carrying. We switch from beer to whiskey at the Lakefront and I think for a second how I ought to lay off the whiskey because Sally doesn't like it. Then I remember what the bitch pulled earlier today and fuck her. But the bartender cuts us off after three, so we leave the Lakefront and head up North Lake Road toward Dewey's.

Harold's driving on account of he's the one found the truck keys when I dropped 'em in a big ditch full of ragweed out front of the Lakefront. North Lake Road's been patched and mended with new tar on just about every other square inch of it, so it feels like you're riding along some old-time road made of logs or bricks. The rumble of the tires on the pavement makes the seat of the truck vibrate, so my legs are tingling. The windows are down and I got my right arm out the window, cutting the air at all sorts of angles, feeling how it blows my arm hairs. That's about all I'm made of right this second, tingling legs and arm hairs blowing first this way, then that way. All my thinking's gone, all my worrying, all my figuring anything out, all gone. Just tingling and blowing from here on out. I look up and the moon jumps into the sky, lands somewhere high over my right shoulder, and hangs there like a round glow-in-the-dark kite we're towing behind the truck.

"Hey, moon," I say over the rumble of the tires.

"What?" says Harold.

"Just stay on this another few miles."

"Ought to get yourself a new truck, Ray."

I look at the busted heat vents where I put my fist when the radiator froze up a couple years ago. On the floor under the dashboard there's some sort of green shoots, look like pea pods, growing out of the dirt on the floorboard. The rear window's cracked and won't slide shut anymore, so I got to cover the open window with a plastic tarp in the winter. There's rips in the vinyl seat from Samson's toenails.

"Yeah," I say finally.

"This thing handles like a forty-year-old whore," Harold tells me.

"Broken in," I tell him.

"Broken down," he says. I don't say anything, digging into one of the vinyl rips with my forefinger. "The point is to trade 'em in before you run 'em into the ground, for Christ's sake." He's fighting the wheel, which pulls pretty hard to the left if you let it. "I mean, this is a piece of shit you're driving."

"You're driving," I correct him.

"It's a piece of shit."

"It's my goddamn truck," I mutter, and turn back to the window to shut him up. We're on North Lake, just passing the corner of McGregor Road. I see someone kneeling in the ditch, swinging both arms high

in the air. What the hell? I turn with my head out the window. The
arms are coming down hard, like driving a railroad spike. My face turns
clammy cold because there's another person there, lying in the ditch,
his head—

"No!" I fumble with the door handle. "No! No!" Is it too late to stop
it? Maybe I can get there in time and Billy won't die. Me and Harold
got drunk and so now it might be too late. Now someone's killing him
and I can't stop it. It's all my fault because I got drunk, and now Billy's
being killed and I can't get to him.

I open the door and Harold's slamming on the brakes, trying to hold
the steering wheel to the right so we don't plow into the Winnebago
coming the other way. I'm leaning out, looking back at Billy, and
Harold hollers for me but I jump out and oh shit we ain't stopped yet. I
roll for about eight hundred miles and come up running back toward
the corner.

"No! Stop! Billy!" I'm running hard as I can, seeing in my mind that
rock coming down again and again. "No!"

Behind me the truck's whining in reverse, trying to keep up.

"Ray? Ray, what the hell?" Harold's hollering out the back window
of the truck. I run down into the ditch, hoping to tackle the bastard
with the rock, screaming, "Fuck you! No!" But I can't see anyone. I stop
short to look around and fall over backward and knock most of the wind
out of myself. I try to get up but roll over on my face instead and then I
can't move.

"Stupid son of a bitch. Dumb motherfucker. Ray?" Harold's pretty
much keeping up a steady river of calling me every type of asshole. He's
got the truck in park and he's running up and down the shoulder, looking for me. I stay where I am, facedown in the weeds. There's nobody
out here. No one but me and Harold. I'm too late. Somebody already
killed Billy. This all happened already, and I wasn't here to stop it.
We're still a ways from Dewey's. I try to imagine crawling all that way
along the ditch. Even without my brains bashed in, it'd take forever. *Oh
Jesus, Billy.*

Someone's watching me. Someone's in the woods and they're watching me. I turn my head and look through the weeds at the dark spaces
between the tree trunks. He's sitting behind a half-rotted log, blinking
yellow eyes at me. One paw's sticking straight up in front of his face,

like I interrupted him in midbite. The same raccoon I saw out back of the metalworks. But he was dead and bloated and swarming in flies this afternoon, wasn't he? How many forty-pound raccoons are there in Monroe County? The yellow eyes are looking at me.

"Too late," he says.

I'm all set to ask him what the fuck's going on when I hear "What happened?"

I look up and Harold's sitting next to me, surrounded by Queen Anne's lace. He looks like some sort of spaceman, with wild, weedy starbursts growing out in all directions from his little triangle head. I look back toward the woods, but the raccoon's gone.

"I thought I saw something."

"What?" He doesn't sound mad anymore, but still I don't answer. Then he says, "This is where he was, ain't it?"

"Yeah," I tell him.

Quiet, then he says, "Fuck."

I sit up straight, moving each bone just a little to make sure nothing's broke. Everything works okay, but I took all the skin off my right shoulder. My T-shirt's torn clean through, and I try to brush the tar and gravel off the torn skin. Harold's quiet now. We get back in the truck. I open up the bottle of Jim Beam that rolled out from under the seat when Harold hit the brakes. Look out the window for a pair of yellow eyes in the trees, but there's nothing there. Harold throws the truck in gear and we take off for Dewey's.

First thing we do when we walk in is buy the bar a round with the money from the prick I took out earlier. This was mostly Billy's bar, and there's a shitload of guys in here tonight who turn around and buy me and Harold drinks and talk our ear off about Billy. I'm feeling like I'm on strange turf, even though I been up to Dewey's plenty of times. They keep the stuffed coyote on a wooden platform just above the jukebox. He's posed laying down, head up and looking sideways. So when you go to pick out a couple of tunes, the damn thing's grinning right smack into your face, with all them sharp teeth showing. Like he thinks it's funny that he's lounging there on top of the jukebox.

Billy'd bring Trish and Deena here from time to time, even though it wasn't any place for kids. Started out because Ginny Honey'd send the girls up there on their bikes to tell Billy to get home. So he'd show 'em off, teach 'em darts, treat 'em like they were his girlfriends. He was hardly ever home, so they took what attention they could get. He never brought the boy. For one thing, he said Kyle was a faggot name. And for another thing, the kid always had his nose in a goddamn book. No way was he taking that faggot bookworm anywhere. Claimed it wasn't even his kid, with all that red hair.

The bar itself is long and curved at one end. There's pool tables in the back, and darts, and tables to sit at. But mostly you go to the Bowl 'n' Bar if you want to shoot pool, you go to the Lakefront if you want to dance with some girls, and you go to Dewey's if you want to get good and drunk. Which is just as well, because me and Harold are in no shape for anything but drinking by the time we get there.

Harold's next to me, talking to Rick behind the bar about Brittany spaniels. I gotta piss on account of drinking so many toasts to Billy. I push off the bar and head for the back, and that's when Alan Halsey puts his hand out to stop me.

"Hang on, Ray." Al is or was or is or was Billy's best buddy.

"Hey, Al."

"Rick, get him a JB, will ya?"

Rick nods and pours the whiskey, setting it down near me without breaking off his conversation with Harold. You start a man talking about Brittany spaniels and it takes a fire breaking out to shut him up.

I look at Al. The jukebox is playing "These Boots Were Made for Walking" for the third time in a row. Jean used to sing that song and do a go-go dance with it when she was only five or six. Used to crack us up. Even the old man laughed. Al picks up his drink and holds it in the air.

"To Billy," he says.

"To Billy," says me and everyone in earshot. This is about the five hundredth toast I drunk since I walked into Dewey's.

"Where is he?"

Al laughs a little and ducks his head closer to me, saying, "What'd you say?"

So I shout it in his ear. "Where's Billy?" Al doesn't answer, just looks at me, so I tell him, "I ain't seen him tonight."

I still ain't getting an answer out of him, so I go on. "I stopped over to the house, but he ain't there."

Al's not the only one hearing this. A couple of guys laugh a little, thinking I don't know what. I'm looking at Al, waiting to see what he's gonna say.

"Ray, fuck." That's all he can think to say. I guess Harold and Rick can feel the change in the air over at this end of the bar, because they stop talking. Rick doesn't move, but he's watching me. I know I ought to leave. But I don't.

"You seen him?" I'm asking a simple damned question, and no one's giving me an answer. It's quiet now. Nancy Sinatra's done singing. It's so quiet in that goddamn bar I can hear the buzz of the neon Miller Lite sign in the front window.

"Knock it off, Ray," says some asshole.

"Supposed to be funny?" says Al.

It can go either one of two ways now. Everyone's looking at me and Al, waiting to see what I'm gonna say now. Lots of guys smiling, like they can still pass it off as screwing around or something. I'm looking at Al, who's looking around the room all of a sudden. Then he turns to Rick behind the bar and shrugs.

I hate Al Halsey. He and Billy were a couple of lousy shits and no way I'm gonna stand here and have a goddamn JB with either one of 'em. Al used to punch me in the arm when I was a kid. "Hey, punk," he'd say, and punch me in the arm hard as he could. Ha ha ha.

Billy and Al are in high school, almost sixteen years old. I'm eleven years old, which makes Jean eight or nine. I remember because that's the year Billy gets this rat that he keeps as a pet. Gets it when his sophomore biology teacher has to get rid of the rats he's had in the classroom for about a hundred years. There was half a dozen of 'em given out six months ago, but Billy's is the only one still alive. He names it Old Yeller, on account of it's really yellow. This thing is so tame it sits on Billy's shoulder while he's walking around, eats off his fingers, the whole works. Billy loves this lousy rat.

"Old Yeller!" he calls, and that thing come following him right down the stairs. Ma's given up trying to get rid of it. Jean feeds it M&M's on the sly and tries to get it to sleep in her room, but it's pretty loyal to Billy.

It's a white-glare summer day. I'm looking for my Wiffle ball and yellow plastic bat. There's a storage area at the back of the garage. I walk into the garage and I hear voices. My stomach turns because I can tell the voices aren't good. Even before I recognize who's talking, I know they're doing something bad. I start to turn around and go back outside, tell Randy the ball and bat are in the basement and let's go look for them there. But I don't. I walk slow across the garage. There's cat litter scattered along the cement floor, soaking up patches of motor oil. My gym shoe scrapes on the cat litter and I stop, freeze, listen to the sounds coming from the back of the garage. There's a plywood door to the storage area and it's open just a little bit. I hear scuffling and Billy whispering to hold her still. My stomach goes to stone and I take another step. It's Billy and his best friend, Al, and they got someone in there with them. Randy's out in the yard, waiting for me. I got to turn around and get out of there, but I don't. I take two more steps and I'm right next to the door. Just got to lean in a little and look, see what they're doing. Because I think I know what they're doing, and I want to be wrong, and I can't walk away until I find out. It's dark in the garage because all the doors are shut. There's a daddy longlegs walking along the handle of a rake leaning against the wall. He stops when I look at him, like he's listening too.

"Don't look in there," he whispers, then runs up the rake and onto the wall, getting far away as he can.

I hear muffled whining, and Billy laughs under his breath. The laugh is scared but excited. I move my head a couple of inches and look through the door. I let out a little breath of relief because all I see is Billy and Al and the Doberman that's been hanging around the house bothering our bitch, Lula, who's in heat. The Doberman's crouched over, humping, and they're watching. Getting off on watching two dogs going at it. I start to take a step back when I see her hand. I stop, can't move, can't make myself look away. It's clenched in a little fist and the knuckles are bone white. Then Al shifts his weight from one knee to the other, and it's not Lula there, it's Jean. She's trying to wiggle away, but they're holding her down on her back under the Doberman. Billy's holding her face so the dog's penis, all bright red and wet, is at her mouth. I only see a second of it, but it burns right into my brain like a picture on a calendar.

"Lick it," Billy snarls at her, giving her head a jerk.

"No." It's muffled because she says it with her mouth clenched tight. I step back and turn around, pick my way back through the cat litter. Randy's standing at the garage door, looking at me to say what's going on? I give him a look to stay quiet until we're both outside. Then I slam the door hard enough to shake the whole garage. After that I take off running. I run out of the backyard and down Cutler Road. Past the doctor's house, past the Petersons' house, across to Woodley's cornfield. I can hear Randy's footsteps falling fast behind me. I keep running, even when my chest is burning and my skin turns cold like it does when you have diarrhea. I cut through the corner of the field, letting the cornstalks cut my cheeks and hands as I whip past them. I keep running until I come out at the alfalfa field and step into a woodchuck hole. My whole body slams down facefirst in the dirt.

I don't move. Everything hurts. I concentrate on one pain at a time, letting each one take all my attention in turn. My lungs are burning dark purple. I let the purple fill up my brain until I'm nothing but a lung on fire. When that eases a little, I feel the cramp in my side from running too hard. It's blue. Sharp and clear blue, stabbing into my gut. Blue, blue, blue, and no room for anything else. Ankle swelling up a little from the woodchuck hole, a dull dirty yellow ache. I go deep into my ankle and throb yellow hurt.

It's a relief to hide inside the pain. Pain you can point to, say "Here! It hurts here! I made it hurt!" Pain that erases everything else even for just a minute or two. Erases the picture in my mind of Jean's face. Her looking straight at me before I step back from the door. A little-girl face with eyes already hopeless. A face that knows no one's gonna come help her. Even when she saw me standing there, she knew no help was coming, ever.

One time when she was younger, I heard Jean say to Ma, "Daddy peed white stuff on me." Ma hauled off and smacked her hard enough to knock her onto the floor.

"Don't you ever let me hear you talk nasty like that again!" So Jean never told Ma anything after that. Neither did I.

Randy catches up, sees the woodchuck hole, looks at my foot.

"You break it?"

"Don't know. Don't give a fuck."

He doesn't ask me what I saw in the storage room. He never mentions it. I tell myself he's got no idea what all goes on in our house. That it's a secret no one knows but me and Jean. That he thinks I'm just like him, with a family just like his. Long as I can tell myself that, he'll still be my best friend.

The next morning, I'm out behind the garage digging up night crawlers and I hear this squealing sound. I come around the side of the garage. Jean's got Old Yeller tied around the legs and hanging from the box elder tree. She's swinging at it with Billy's Louisville Slugger like it was a tetherball. It ain't dead yet either, all bloody and squealing so I hear it when I'm trying to go to sleep for a couple weeks after. Jean doesn't even stop when she sees me. Just beats on that thing until finally it slips out of the string and lands on the ground, dead. She picks it up by the tail and tells me to keep a watch for Billy or Ma. We run upstairs with it and Jean puts it on Billy's pillow and pulls the covers up over it.

Billy come about as close to crying as I ever seen when he finds Old Yeller. He wants to know what happened and she flat out tells him she done it. He kicks her ass up one end of the house and down the other, but she ain't sorry. Neither am I.

⬤

I haven't thought about that in about a hundred years. Fucking Al Halsey, reminding me of that shit. He's got his back to me now, leaning against the bar. I'm all coiled up, tense and tight. *So mad. So mad.*

"You're a fucking prick. You know that, Al?"

He turns around. He don't even know what to say to that, so he says the first dumb-ass thing that comes into his head.

"Your brother's dead, asshole."

"Lay off him, Al," says Joe Lee. I didn't know Joe Lee was there. "He's drunk."

"Fuck it. Forget it," Al says.

Me and Al are looking at each other. I haul back and send my fist square into Al's fucking prick face. I can feel his nose give way against my knuckles. Tension drains out of me when I feel his face cave in, and I'm so happy at the feel of it I could cry. Blood flies in two different directions at once, far enough to land a spray of drops on the mirror and bottles behind the bar.

Everyone's moving at once. Half the bodies pulling me away from Al, the other half pulling Al away from me. Someone steps on my foot, the one I dropped the flagstone on. I let out a holler, but they don't let go.

"I know he's dead, you dumb fuck." That's all I say, but I figure it's enough. I guess the old death-in-the-family code of conduct kicks in, because Al's the one they hustle out of the bar, not me. Hands let go of me, eyes slide away from my face. I tell Rick to get me another JB, but he says that was last call for me. Dumb son of a bitch cuts me off. I look around for Harold, and he's right next to me, leaning against the bar.

"The guy's a pussy," I tell him.

"Yeah," says Harold in no tone of voice.

I guess it was an asshole thing to do, picking a fight with Al Halsey. But that cocksucker thinks he can drink a toast to Billy with me, like now we got something in common. But I got nothing in common with that stupid son of a bitch Al Halsey. Not one goddamn thing.

"Let me finish this and we'll get out of here," says Harold, picking up his glass.

"Ain't no one going nowhere," I growl back.

My hand keeps reaching for the drink that ain't there. So I shoot a look over to Rick to let him know what I think of his pussy bartending. Light a smoke. Suck in as much as I can hold and leave it in there, holding my breath till my ears start to buzz and pop. Finally blow it out and turn to Harold.

"Give me a joint," I say.

"Not in here."

"Give me a goddamn joint."

"When we leave."

I think about giving Harold a little bit of what old Al just got. But I don't remember if he's got the shit on him or if it's in that shaving kit in the truck. So I stare hard at him for a minute, but he ain't paying me any attention. He's asking Rick what we owe him.

"We don't owe him shit," I say real loud. "Cocksucker cuts me off like a pussy. Fuck him."

Rick and Harold both ignore me. But not Joe Lee. He lays a hand on my shoulder feels like someone dropped a whole side of beef on the side of my neck.

"Hey, Ray," he says. "What's up?" Like all of a sudden this son of a bitch is my best friend in the whole goddamn world. Like all of a sudden he thinks he's Randy standing there.

"Hey, Joe Lee," I say back at him. "Why don't you suck my dick?"

When I wake up, I'm looking straight up at the stars. The wind is blowing over me so hard I think for a second I'm flying. Or dead. Then I feel the metal bottom of the truck bed under my shoulder blades and I realize I'm in the back of someone's truck and that I'm going down the road. I can't hear much of anything because the wind is whistling hard in my ears. But there's no mistaking the steady beat of crickets on either side of me. That means we're on a road out in the country. And it ain't the highway, because I can hear the spit and hiss of gravel flying off the tires. I'm so hot I'm soaked in sweat. The front of my shirt's wet. Jesus, that air feels good. I try to turn my head to look at the truck bed I'm laying in, but I can't move much because it makes my face hurt. My whole face.

We start to slow down, and then we come to a stop. I hear music then, but it's not coming from near me. Then I hear tires on gravel again, but we haven't moved yet. That's when I figure out there's a car ahead of us. With the radio on. Playing an old Led Zeppelin song. We go forward, turning a corner and picking up speed. The turning motion makes my stomach lurch as the stars rearrange themselves.

It ain't just my face that hurts. My right shoulder's bellyaching where I tore all the skin off flying out onto the side of the road earlier. But on the whole, I have to say I'm pretty happy here in the back of someone's truck. I try to think for a second who might be driving, but I don't even know where we're coming from, let alone where we're going to. And that's okay. Got no idea how long I been out. No idea what the hell happened. But someone's driving the truck, and someone knows what happened, and someone knows where we're going. I don't have to know shit. Just lay back here and watch the sky and feel the cool August night brushing over me from my hair down to my boots.

My shirt is really soaked. I run my hand across it. Lift up my fingers in front of my eyes, but it's so dark I can hardly see. It tastes rusty and tangy, which means it's blood. I let my hand drop back down beside me and shut my eyes. Sally's gonna kill me when she sees this. I wonder what my chances are of ditching the shirt and sneaking into the bathroom for a quick scrub without waking her up. It takes a second, but then I remember she ain't there. I open my eyes and the stars are gone. The sky's turned into a black ocean, wavy and watery, and it's leaking down onto my face. Tears run into my hair, hide there. *My friend's leaving! My friend's gone!*

We slow down again not long after that. Pull into a driveway and stop. A car door slams, then the passenger door of the truck, my truck.

"He still out?" Joe Lee.

"Yeah." Harold.

"Someone had to shut him up." Joe Lee.

"Yeah." Harold.

"Dewey's ain't the place to look for trouble. He generally knows that." Joe Lee.

"Just leave him where he is, you think?" Harold.

"Yeah." Joe Lee. "You need a lift somewhere?"

"No, I'm staying here." Harold. "Didn't catch your name."

"Joe Lee."

"Harold Patterson. Ray's cousin."

"I'll be seeing you tomorrow, then." Joe Lee.

"Thanks for getting him home." Harold.

Joe Lee doesn't answer, but he laughs a little. "G'night, Ray."

Then the car door slams and the tires and the music (now it's the Doors) all drive away. *G'night, Joe Lee.* The back door squeaks open and closed real soft. Harold trying not to wake anyone up. And then nothing but the beat of the crickets all around me and that wild August wind that's died down to something tame. I kept my eyes closed all through their conversation, in case they decided to check and make sure I was all right. Now I open them and the stars are back, chirping down on me louder even than the crickets. The smell of raspberries comes back for a second, then it's gone. The pines are rustling secret things back and forth along their top branches.

Where's the moon? I look around the sky as best I can without moving my head. Finally catch her just about to glide behind the poles near the substation across the road. She stops when she feels me looking, and waits.

"Where is he?" I ask.

"Where's who?" says the moon.

"You know." No answer. "Where's Billy?"

She gives a deep sigh and turns the blue of hospital sheets.

"You don't know, do you?" I ask.

"It's hard to hold everyone's sorrow," she answers, dodging the question.

"Don't go."

"You are beautiful, Ray, lying there in my light." Then the moon turns violet and disappears. And I'm left alone.

For some reason, I'm thinking about Billy's Harley-Davidson hat. It was his pride and joy in sixth grade, that Harley hat. It was an old fishing hat that he found. Brought it home from the dump, which made Ma scream and holler for a week. So he washes it in a bucket of bleach and ammonia, which makes her scream and holler even more. Then he starts putting stickers on it. All along the brim, the crown, covering everything. He has one of those "Keep on Truckin' " stickers, and Pink Floyd with the triangle and rainbow colors. A "Have a Nice Day" smiley sticker that he draws fangs and horns on. The Sinclair dinosaur, the Purple Martin, the Texaco star, and a parking sticker for the Monroe County Metroparks. My favorite is the big red Rolling Stones tongue that he has on the back of the hat before it gets covered over by a five-fingered marijuana leaf. But the biggest one, the Harley-Davidson sticker, is always front and center, never covered over.

The Harley hat never leaves his head except when he puts on a new sticker. When he goes to bed, he shoves it under his pillow so Ma can't get her hands on it to throw it out, or me get my hands on it to try it on just once. The night Billy lets me wear the Harley hat, I had taken his bike to go up to the mill. The mill is strictly off limits, but Randy and I go up there with our lunch money and buy the candy they have at the front counter.

We step outside after buying thirty-five cents' worth of Mary Janes, and Billy's bike is nowhere in sight. Randy walks me home, wheeling his bike next to him. We're both quiet, thinking how there's no way out of this. Not only was I up to the mill, where I wasn't supposed to be, but I took Billy's bike without asking. I'm dead.

Randy says good-bye in front of our house. He pedals off and now I'm alone. I decide the only thing to do is find Billy and confess straight out. I'm halfway up the driveway when I see the old man and Billy standing next to the garage. The first thing the old man does is ask what I did with Billy's bike.

"I didn't take it." It's out of my mouth before I can think. And what's worse, it comes out snotty. The old man's arm comes up and a wall slams into the side of my head. My brain jumps and sputters for a few seconds until it stops knocking against the inside of my skull.

"What'd you lie for, boy?" he says. The arm shoots out again, and this time I try to jerk my head away so it doesn't catch me square on the ear. But I'm not quick enough, and the butt of his palm lands on my cheekbone, which makes my eyeball retreat back up behind my nose. He's hitting me with his left hand, on account of his right hand's all bandaged from an accident at work, so I'm taking hits on the side of my face that ain't used to it. And the thing about pain in your face, it's so close to your brain that it scrambles everything. All the brain waves get mixed up and you can't think, you can't talk, can't hardly see.

Billy's keeping his eyes glued to the neighbor's house. He's picturing in his mind how he lives there and the doctor and the doctor's wife are his parents and he has his own room and no one gets drunk and no one gets hit and you can stay up late and watch Johnny Carson on Friday nights and the doctor's wife comes to your parent-teacher conferences and maybe she's even a chaperone on the school field trips to Greenfield Village or the Henry Ford Museum. He's thinking how he doesn't even know the old man and he doesn't know me and it wasn't his bike that got stolen and he doesn't have anything to do with what's gonna happen and he's safe inside the neighbor's house right now having grilled peanut butter and jelly sandwiches.

The old man tells me to go upstairs and wait for him. I go up to the bedroom I share with Billy. This is before I make my own bedroom in the corner of the basement. I can hear Ma still running water in the kitchen. She could see the whole thing out the window over the sink, but she doesn't say anything as I go up the stairs. I make sure the door's closed tight, slip my jeans off onto the floor, and start pulling on underwear, one after another. I got the sixth pair on, bent over with one foot in the air, when the door opens. My heart shoots to the roof of my mouth and then falls out onto the floor, bloody and useless. But it's just Billy. He doesn't waste time looking at me, just yanks open another dresser drawer and dumps half a dozen pairs of his own Fruit of the Loom on the bed next to mine.

"He's still out in the garage," he says.

"Thanks." My teeth are banging together so it comes out like "Tinksh."

Billy still won't look at me, though. "Dumb-ass thing to do. You got it coming to you."

"Yeah," I say. He's right. I do.

Then he hands me two pairs of long insulated underwear that he got last Christmas because the old man was taking him down to Ohio dove hunting for the first time and you freeze your ass off. "Try these too," he says.

"Okay," I say, piling layer on layer as fast as I can.

"And don't cry," Billy tells me. "If you cry, you know what you'll get." He peeks out the window. I know what I'll get. Billy'll kick my ass even worse.

"He's coming across the yard," says Billy, and then he's out the door. Gone. But I know he ain't gone far. Maybe the bathroom or Jean's room, where he can hear me if I cry.

I finish off with the two layers of long underwear, then my jeans. I stand and wait for the old man to show up, trying not to think about what's coming. I'm just standing there waiting, trying to picture the old man coming in the house, through the living room, past the kitchen, up the stairs, and through the bedroom door. I count how many steps it takes to cross the porch, go down the hall. But he doesn't come. I count all the steps three times and still he doesn't come. I start to think maybe he sent me up here just to make me sit in my room for the rest of the day, sort of grounding me and torturing me all at the same time. That's happened a couple of times. After a few hours, you're practically begging him to come up and hit you. I walk-shuffle across the room and try to peek out of the space where the curtain meets the edge of the window. I see a strip of yard, but I don't see him. I nudge the curtain just a little, keeping myself close against the wall where I won't be seen. I can see the top of Billy's head. He's sitting on the back steps right underneath me, where he can hear everything through the window. I want to call out to him, just to have him look up or something. Then I hear the door open and it's the old man. So here he is here it is here we go.

"Down across the bed," he says to me. I walk as naturally as I can over to my bed and sort of flop across it facedown.

"Pants down," he tells me. This is new. This is not expected.

"C'mon, Dad. I won't do it again—"

"Shut up and do what I said."

I know I'm just making him madder, but I can't help it. I'm a coward and a pussy and I know it, but I can't stop.

"I'm sorry for lying. I didn't—"

"Now!" His voice is a wrecking ball crashing through the walls of the room. And in the echo after it, I hear the dry *whish* of the belt whipping through his belt loops.

"Dad please I'm sorry I'll be good I'll be good I'll be good."

He holds the tip of the belt next to the buckle in one hand and snaps the two straps together so they clap like thunder. Not rumbling across the clouds from five miles away, either. This is the kind that cracks your head open as the sky goes white with lightning.

"The more you talk back, the worse it's gonna be." He's got that look on his face and it's like I'm talking to someone from outer space for all the good it'll do me. I get my jeans off with my back to him so he won't see the fourteen pairs of underwear. I push down all the layers together and have a hell of a time getting my feet out. I'm taking too long. He lets me have it while I'm bent over the bed, and the leather lands smack on the knobby part of my backbone. One foot's still stuck in the pile of clothes, but I forget about it and fall forward on the bed. I try to suck in air but I can't. I can't get any air to holler or cry.

"—gonna teach you some goddamn respect—"

Just the start of the thunderstorm coming down. Words and belts raining down. I got my face pushed into the blanket and I reach behind me with one hand to cover my butt, ward off the belt, protect myself. But the buckle comes down this time and it lands on my knuckles. You'd never believe how thin that piece of skin is over your knucklebone. An electric shock runs up my hand, my arm, my shoulder, up the neck to my scalp, where my hair prickles. I jerk my hand away fast and grab hold of the blanket to keep myself from reaching back there again.

"—see if you lie to me ever—"

Now he's speeding up, because he's getting used to the feel of it in his left hand. But his aim ain't so hot and he's getting me everywhere from the back of the knees almost to my rib cage. The air's coming back into my lungs and it makes a sound come out of my mouth. Sounds like I'm crying but I ain't crying, I ain't crying. I bring my other arm up and bend it under my face. Open my mouth and bite down hard until my mouth is full of the skin on my forearm. I remember Billy telling me how a pit bull can clamp his jaws on a tree branch and not let go even if you kill him. I clamp down hard and don't let go.

I can't tell where the belt's hitting me because it hurts everywhere. Just a jolt on the bed each time the buckle comes down, like my body's trying to get away from the belt all on its own with no help from me. My skin is on fire. Like I'm bleeding everywhere and all the blood is boiling hot. But pretty soon the pain in my arm is so bad I don't feel much of anything else. I don't hear the leather whistling like an old train riding through the air. I don't even hear the old man yelling no more. Just the pain in my arm and the growling in my throat like a real pit bull, holding on even if he kills me.

After I don't know how long, the bed stops jolting and the belt slithers back around the old man's waist. He's saying something, but I don't know what. I don't hear him leave the room, but I know he's gone. I unclamp my jaws and there's blood on my face where my teeth broke through the skin of my arm. The breeze coming in the window is ice cold on my burning back. It feels good. It's such a relief, there's no room for thinking. The curtains are waving and whispering, "Oh, Ray, it's all right, it's okay now," over and over again. "Go to sleep," they tell me. "It's all right." Everything aches really hot, but the air blowing across me is so cool I could die happy right then. I close my eyes, give up, and fall asleep.

I doze and half wake up and doze some more. One time I wake up and someone's put a blanket over me and closed the window. The burning of my skin has turned into a warm underwater feeling, and I don't ever want to come all the way awake. It's not until after dark that I wake up hungry.

I got no idea what time it is. Maybe it's midnight and everyone else is asleep. I look over to Billy's bed, but the covers are flat. Everyone's probably downstairs watching *The Love Boat*. No one even notices I'm not there, and I'm sitting here achy and fevery and swollen up like a dead hound. No one's missing me and I'm starving and my bones ache. My throat closes up. I grab my pajamas and hobble down the hall to the bathroom. My skin's still really hot, and I feel like one of those ninety-year-old men you see walking all sideways and bent over at the Memorial Day Parade.

I turn the bathwater on and stand on the toilet to get a look at myself in the mirror. I turn around and crane my neck and try to see everything from my back all the way down my legs. I look like Frankenstein. I got stripes that are red and stripes that are blue and even a couple that are black and purple. I got cuts mixed in there too, from the buckle. And there's dried blood, all dark and smeary in patches. But the worst and scariest part is that it just goes on forever. I don't hardly see a patch of clear skin bigger than an inch. I look like some kid that got radiation contamination like the Incredible Hulk. I climb down off the toilet, slow and careful. I kneel on the tile floor, rest my arm against the edge of the bathtub, and see where my teeth cut deep through the skin. I push my hot face against the tub's edge, first my cheek, my eyes, then my forehead. It's cold like the breeze earlier. It feels the same kind of comforting, all clean and cold on my skin. I cry plenty now, with the bathwater running hard to drown me out.

That's how Ma finds me when she comes up to check on me a little later. She helps me into the tub and I kneel on my hands and knees because it hurts too much to sit on the hard porcelain. Ma doesn't say much, but she's gentle with a soap and sponge. I can tell by her face that she thinks I look like Frankenstein too. But all she says is for me to dry myself off and come downstairs; she'll make us some Tin Roofs.

The bath has cooled off my burning skin. I slip on my oldest cotton pj's because they're the softest. Ma's got a couple of pillows on the couch for me, white and crispy cool. I do a quick scan of the living room for the old man, but he ain't there. Jean and Billy are on the floor in front of the TV, watching *Dukes of Hazzard*, and Ma's out in the kitchen. They don't look at me and I don't say anything, just climb up on the couch and lay my head back on one of the crispy cools. I'm really tired. The old man always says, "I'm so tired, I feel like I been beat with a fucking stick." That's how I feel right now. Jean's looking at me out of the corner of her eye. I can tell she wants to say something, but she ain't sure if it's okay to talk to me or not. Ma brings in a Tin Roof and hands it to me. A Tin Roof is vanilla ice cream, Hershey's chocolate syrup, and Spanish peanuts with the red skins on 'em, all in a cereal bowl. Ma says, "How you feeling?"

"Like I been beat with a fucking stick."

Ma stares at me. I can feel Jean and Billy freeze, and their ears go back like dogs hearing a whistle. Dead couple of seconds before Jean lets out a snort, trying not to laugh, which sets Billy to laughing. Ma shakes her head, trying not to smile.

"He ain't here anyway," says Jean. "He ain't here, he went out."

Ma says, "Ray, what am I gonna do with you?" She smiles then, and ruffles her hand through my hair.

Then Billy and Jean go into the kitchen to get their Tin Roofs. On the way back into the living room, when he walks by the couch, Billy takes the Harley hat off his head and tosses it over my ears. It's too big and I'm blind for a minute, but I nudge it back off my forehead and it stays up okay. Ma and Jean don't say anything, but they sure notice. All night long, Billy or Jean'll say, "How you feeling, Ray?"

"Like I been beat with a fucking stick." And us kids'll laugh all over again. Ma doesn't even tell us to knock it off. She tenses up when tires go by outside, looks toward the window to see if his headlights are turning into the driveway. But mostly she's laughing with us. And Billy doesn't take the Harley hat back until the next morning.

I open my eyes and they're gone. Ma, Jean, Billy. There's just me, laying in the back of the truck, and now I really am alone. Dead drunk, laying
in the back of my pickup where Joe Lee threw me, bloodied up, and at
least one black eye if not a busted nose. Brother's dead, woman's gone,
sister's probably going to prison, and a houseful of relatives. I close my
eyes and laugh.

Something nudges my leg, like a kick. I open my eyes, and there's
Billy sitting on one of the tire wells. He's looking down at me with that
same old look on his face, the look that wonders how he got such a
lightweight for a brother.

"Where you been?" I ask.

"Forget it," he says. "You got anything to drink?"

"Jim Beam under the seat." Me and Harold killed half of it driving
over to Dewey's. Billy stands, jumps out of the truck, opens the driver
door (how'd he unstick the door?), and rummages under the seat. After
a few minutes of quiet, when I start to think I imagined the whole thing,
I feel the truck bed sink under his weight. He's climbing in over the tail-
gate, sitting right back down on the tire well where he was before, taking a long hit of the whiskey. I ain't moved since he showed up. But I'm
following him with my eyes, no doubt about that.

He wipes his chin with the back of his arm and hands the bottle to
me. I stand it up on my stomach, not taking a drink. He rolls his eyes
and grins, looks out at the field behind the house. I don't know what the
hell's got his attention, but he looks at it for a long time. I try lifting my

head. No pains shooting crisscrosses on my face, so I sit up halfway and scooch back, leaning against the cab of the truck. I take a drink. Face and head still doing okay, so I take another and hand the bottle back to him. From this angle I can get a better look at him, even in the dark. He doesn't look any different. Light-brown hair pulled straight back off his forehead and held in a ponytail down his back. Cheekbones standing out in a lean, long face. A handful of freckles across the bridge of his nose. Eyes snowy green. People say Billy, me, and Jean all got the same color eyes. "Them Johnson eyes," Randy's mom said once. Billy's got a wide grin that shows teeth just a little crooked but not too crooked. Makes him look a little like that coyote out to Dewey's. The thing about Billy, when he looks at you, he looks so hard it's like there's no one else on earth but you. Which is a feeling you don't get from a lot of people, which is a feeling you'd like to get more of. But if he was pissed, that same look would come back, like you were the only person on earth and he's gonna wipe you off the face of it. Like you might as well lay down and die right there, because he's gonna hurt you that bad. Women just fell all over him.

Now those eyes are directed straight at me. He looks at me awhile, then he says, "You look like shit."

"Are you dead?"

"Yeah," he says. To hear it like this, all matter-of-fact, it sets me to shivering. "What's the matter with you?" he says.

"I'm sorry."

"What for?"

"Sorry you're dead."

"Are you?" And he grins real wide, showing his teeth.

"Mostly." I figure what the hell, he's dead. Might as well tell him the truth. "I miss having you around."

"Looks like you could've used me tonight." He's talking about my busted-up face. "Who did it?"

"Joe Lee."

"Fat fuck."

"He just wanted to get me home."

"Still a fat fuck."

I think about this for a minute, decide not to argue the point. "I punched Al's face in."

"No shit?" He's got a laugh makes you feel like king of the world if you're the one said something funny. That's how he's laughing now. We each take another hit of the whiskey.

"Funeral's tomorrow," I tell him.

"She better not take the kids over there."

There's only one "she" on my mind right now, so at first I think he means Jean. "Who?"

"That fat cow I married."

I think about that fat cow saying how she's gonna be a better mama to them kids now Billy's gone. I say, "I reckon she's better off now."

I don't know what made that come out of my mouth, but there it is. Billy looks at me like I lost my mind. "What the hell you talking about?"

"You know." I look somewhere over his head so I don't have to meet his eyes.

"Little bitch," he says.

"Who?" I ask him. Ginny Honey? Trish? Jean? Every one of 'em was a little bitch, far as Billy thought.

"You got to do something for me," he says.

"What." It's not what I say, it's how I say it. He takes another pull of the whiskey, and I can tell he's pissed. That's how fast he can turn on you. My stomach clenches in a thick knot. I'm about ready to tell him I'm sorry, sure, whatever he wants, I'll be glad to do it. But I take another look at him and that's just what he's expecting me to do. Just what I always did. Probably just like Trish did.

"I don't know, Ray," he says. "I thought you'd be glad to see me."

This really pisses me off. So I say, "Yeah, well, to hell with you, Billy."

He disappears, bottle and all. He's just gone; empty air, nothing. My last words echo like a scream over my head. *To hell with you, Billy.* My gut turns to ice and I think I wet myself. I can't tell for sure because I'm cold and clammy all over. *Oh Jesus, I didn't mean it.* I look out the side of the truck, in case he fell over backward. Nothing there. *Oh Jesus, Billy, come back.* I stand up in the truck bed and look around, turning in a circle about half a dozen times like Laurel and Hardy. He's nowhere. He was here talking to me, and now he's nowhere.

"Billy?" I say it quiet. I don't want anyone in the house to hear me and think I've gone off my nut. *Billy, Christ! Don't go away.* No answer. No sound. Even the crickets are quiet. The breeze is gone. Everything is still, not moving, black. It's so black I can't even see my hands waving in front of my face. It's a deep black like what it might look like two miles deep in the ocean. And it's pressing down on me from all sides at once, just like the ocean. *Billy, what are you doing? What's going on?*

I open my mouth, but I can't suck in any breath to yell. I swear to God, there's heavy cold black moving into my chest, filling up my stomach. This is about a million times worse than that familiar black balloon in my gut. My legs are dissolving. *Oh fuck, oh fuck, oh fuck!*

Then I hear Billy's voice whispering right inside my left ear, like he's sitting smack on my eardrum.

"How's it feel, Ray?"

"Billy?" I can't tell if my voice is coming out loud or not. "Billy!"

"How do you like it?" And the bastard's laughing. Everything's dissolving in the black. Even my mouth is breaking up and drifting out into that ocean. I'm moving my mouth, but I know my tongue's already gone. I reach up to cover my face and there's nothing there. My hand goes right through empty air. Billy's voice comes back.

"This is what she did to me," he says.

"Nonono-o-o," echoes somewhere in the shifting black. It's me trying to answer.

"You gonna let her get away with it?" His voice isn't even a whisper now, just a feeling. I concentrate on every particle of me that's still me, and I try to yell from there. Sound comes out. A light switches on in the house. The black ocean pulls away and I take shape again, falling down heavy in the truck bed, banging my head and making my whole face hurt again.

The back door opens and Harold comes out on the porch to look around.

"Ray?"

I lay still and keep my eyes closed. I hear him coming down the porch steps. I lay just like he left me, breathing heavy so he knows I'm alive. *Alive. Jesus Christ!* I can feel him looking down into the truck bed. I'm more scared than I ever was in my life, but I lay there and don't twitch. Still, I can't help but think what old Harold would do if I jumped at him and yelled "Yah!" all of a sudden. Finally I feel him move away. The back door opens and closes and he's gone. But I don't move. I'm tired, for one thing. I'm afraid to open my eyes, for another. The last thing in the world I want to see when I open them is Billy. So I stay like I am, wondering what the hell just happened. And the number-one question: Who done it? I didn't ask him. Why didn't I ask him?

A dog's whining somewhere out in the darkness. I listen. There. Again. I climb out of the truck and rummage through the cab, digging everything from the glove box, out from under the seats, until I find a flashlight. Slide Ginch Littlefield from my back pocket, toss him on the dashboard, and climb out of the truck. The noise is coming every few minutes. I come up about fifteen feet from the vegetable garden, and that's definitely where the dog is. It doesn't sound like Samson. I figure if he ain't in the house, he's hiding in the garage until Billy's good and gone. I take another step toward it, but a deep, quiet growl comes out of the dark. It makes the hair on my arms go stiff and prickly. I flick the flashlight. Nothing. Smack it against the palm of my hand a couple times, and light bounces across the brown stubbly grass. I swing my arm slow in the direction of the growl, which gets deeper and more like he means it. I'm wishing like hell I had the .22 I keep under the bed, but then I see him. It's Samson. He's half whining, half growling now, looking into the light with eyes that glow red.

"Samson," I whisper. "Samson, boy."

He's laying next to a pile of the beans I pulled up earlier this afternoon. He's all curled up with his tail tucked under him, his head held low to the ground. I reach out my hand slow and he pulls his head away from me like I'm gonna hit him. I keep saying his name so he doesn't forget it's me. Every part of him is shaking. I run the flashlight all over him, feeling to see if there's something broke or bleeding somewhere. But nothing's wrong with him.

I turn the flashlight off and lead Samson over to the garden, which is just a patch of loose dirt now. I sit down in the middle of it, cross-legged. Old Samson doesn't hold back even for a second. He climbs right onto my lap, as much of him as will fit. I toss the flashlight in the dirt and wrap my arms around him, trying to warm him up or calm him down or do whatever will stop the shaking. Hold him like he's a little kid.

"You think I'll ever have kids?" I ask him.

"Not at the rate you're going," he says.

"What scared you tonight?"

But he doesn't answer. So I just hold on to him, and that's when Jean comes busting into my head. I wonder what she's doing right now in the middle of the godforsaken night. I picture her standing at her back door, looking out at the same moon as it disappears. And it all comes crashing down on me, the end of that summer and how everything fell to pieces. It's been a few years since it's hit me this bad, but I know there's nothing to do but let it play itself out. I close my eyes and let it come.

TWENTY-ONE

It was a week before Labor Day, that summer up at the hunting cabin. Me and Jean been loving each other for about seven weeks. Saturday morning, and she's working a couple hours because she needs the overtime. Me and Randy are out in the boat with a bucketful of bait and a couple of cane poles. It's early morning, so the sun's sparkling hard on the water. I'm facing east so I don't go blind staring at the bobber, which is sitting still because there's hardly any breeze brushing over the top of the water. Just enough for the red and white plastic ball to wave from side to side like an old grinning drunk. We only got one six-pack with us, because I heard enough stories about Shiner LaVonn and the old man drunk as skunks on the boat. The old man swung back to cast with a fresh night crawler on the hook and caught Shiner square on the upper lip. Yanked forward on the cast and that hook sank all the way through. Shiner's yelling and swearing with a hook in his mouth and the live worm still on it. Makes a funny story, but the old man says Shiner still has the scar where they ripped the hook out. Poured whiskey on it to clean the worm guts out of the cut and left it at that. Randy doesn't even hold his beer as well as I do, so we don't drink much on the boat.

We got three bluegills in the basket hanging off the edge of the tail end, and there's something playing with my hook, because the bobber's taking sharp dips into the water but never going all the way under. Probably a twenty-inch pike nibbling the minnow to death.

"Do you think Jean'd go out with me if I asked her?" says Randy.

"No," I answer.

He doesn't ask why not, doesn't get pissed off. I don't even get jealous. We just keep on fishing. The twenty-inch pike finally gets his fill and the bobber floats steady. I reel in to check the bait and there it is. Just a little hunk of dead gunk left on the hook. Bastard.

"Fish me out a minnow, will ya?" I ask him. He reaches into the bucket at his feet.

"Ma sent up a bag of sweet corn for us," he says. "I left it out on the back porch last night and forgot about it."

And the conversation drifts from sweet corn on the grill tonight, to Randy's dog getting hit by a car two days ago, to where he can get a new radiator hose around here for the MG. But all the time I'm thinking back over the summer and how I should've seen it coming. I know how Randy is when he's getting it bad for someone, and he's been showing all the signs. Laughing at her jokes when they ain't funny, bringing her ice cream, offering a back rub. But still I'm not jealous. Hell, I can't blame him.

So I don't give it any more thought until a week later, when it rains all day on Friday. It's Jean's last day at the farmers market, so she knocks off early and she's there when I get home at three-thirty. Randy's not due till eight or eight-thirty, so we lay down and fall asleep for an hour or so. Wake up around five o'clock and make love to the sound of rain still coming down steady outside. We're slow and tender, taking our time because this is the last chance we get for a week. Randy'll be here all weekend and Jean has to move back home in a couple days, start school on Tuesday. We lay there afterward, curled up close, talking. She'll drive up next weekend. I'll think of some reason for Randy to stay down home this time. We don't talk about anything further away than the next time we'll see each other. I don't know how I'm gonna live through a week up here without her. My brain can't hardly take that in, let alone all the months to come and how are we gonna manage?

This is it. This is the last time we got it this easy together. I guess if I'd known it right then, I'd have thrown myself into the lake, in the rain, and settled at the bottom like an old rotten log. But I didn't have any idea what was coming, or how soon it was gonna hit.

Jean's laying sideways across the bed, with her head on my chest. She's giving me shit, saying how I can take a week off from the truck stop, come home with her for a week.

"We can sleep in your old room in the basement," she says to me. "Just like old times." She's talking about the nights she'd sneak down and sleep with me, all turned around the wrong way. Her head at the end of the bed next to my feet, blankets untucked so she wouldn't suffocate.

"I ain't going back there," I tell her.

"You gonna hide here the rest of your life?" she says. I'm on my back, with one arm up under my head. She's tugging a little on the hair under my arms.

"Gonna stay here," I tell her. "Gonna lay just like this and mope until you get back." I smooth out a short curl at the top of her head. It's golden from being out in the sun all summer. I still got that little curl around my finger when the back door slams, and in two seconds Randy's voice barges into the room. "Hey, Ray, you sleeping?" And there he is, standing in the bedroom door. He's never showed up earlier than eight o'clock, but today it's been raining down home too, and it wouldn't take a genius to figure there wasn't much to do around the farm. And we didn't hear the MG pull up on account of the rain coming down on the roof.

No one moves for about a hundred slow, molasses years. Then Jean reaches over my shoulder for my denim shirt. Randy's not looking at her, he's looking at me, and none too friendly. I do my usual: nothing. Except I tug a sheet up over my waist, because even though Randy's seen me naked five dozen times, all of a sudden I can't stand the thought. Jean's slipping that denim shirt on and working on the buttons. Slow and thoughtful, not hurrying or embarrassed. Once she's done she looks Randy smack in the eye and says, "We should've told you."

Randy lets out a big breath through his nose like a moose snorting, like he can't believe what he just heard, like it's either snort or punch Jean's face in. Then he's gone. The back screen door slams once and I'm pulling on my jeans, not all that fast because what am I gonna say when I catch up to him? I can see him through the kitchen window backing out of the driveway at about a million miles per hour, hitting the brakes so hard he damn near slides backward into the ditch across the road. Then he turns the car around and there's just the rain over the sound of his motor going further and further away. Jean's next to me at the window, her arm warm against mine. We neither one of us move for a while, just watch the rain running off the tar-paper roof of the well pit. The little maple tree at the edge of the property line is shuddering under fat raindrops like it's taking a beating.

After a while, Jean goes and flops down on the end of the couch. She's got her baggy gray sweatpants on and she tucks her legs up underneath her like she's cold. I stay at the window a long time, looking out. Whole goddamn world looks like it's hanging its head in the rain. *For shame, for shame.* I don't even know where to start feeling ashamed of myself. Everything in my whole damned life went from being right to wrong in two seconds. I done so much wrong, all of it jumbling over itself and leapfrogging blame across my forehead.

I'm seeing the last couple months through someone else's eyes, anyone else's. I let Randy down by lying and sneaking around behind his back. But I kind of knew that all along. What's hitting me for the first time is what I did to Jean. I'm two years older than her. Ugly words spurt into my head like bloodstains: words like rape and incest. Things that didn't ever occur to me until now. The more I'm seeing this through someone else's eyes, the dirtier it seems. I think how it's gonna sound when everyone's talking about us. "Those Johnsons always been trash." For all I know, they're already saying it up here. Half the people around here know the old man, and some of 'em still remember Grandpa Eddie when he built the hunting cabin. People around here, they know damn well who we are. And maybe we ain't been so secret as I thought. Jean never tried to hide anything except from Randy, and only then because I made her.

We been living in some kind of bubble all summer, and now it's popped. And I know when it gets real dirty and smutty and nasty, it's gonna be worse on Jean than on me. Hell, I ain't stupid, I know that. I think what people are gonna say about her behind her back, and what they'll say right to her face. I got my fingers in the silverware drawer, pushing it closed with my right hip as hard as I can. The wood's cutting into my knuckles, but it ain't hurting bad enough.

"He asked me out," Jean says from the couch.

"Did he?" Fucker. After I told him not to.

"Yeah."

"What'd you tell him?"

"I didn't wanna lie," she says. "I told him I was already kind of seeing someone, and besides, you probably wouldn't like it."

"That was the truth," I tell her.

"But not really it wasn't." She sounds like she's feeling about the same as me. "Not really."

"Where do you think he went?" I ask after another piece of guilty quiet.

"I don't know."

So we finally decide to head out and look around for him. We climb in my Malibu and drive into town. Stop at every bar and hangout spot from the pontoon marina to Judy's Juke Joint, where all the potato pickers up from Ypsilanti get drunk and fight each other until sunup, when it's time to go to work again. But no one's seen Randy.

"Hey, where's your buddy tonight?"

"Where's that good-looking friend of yours?"

"Where's your sidekick?"

About the eighth time I hear this sort of shit, I'm ready to kick someone's teeth out the back of their head. We drive from one place to the next and I'm looking. Behind the billboard for McCarthy's Boatland, under the tent awning set up in the parking lot of the First Presbyterian Church, in the back of a minivan overflowing with half a dozen kids and two dogs pulling into the Dairy Dip. Randy ain't around.

"You know, I been biting my tongue," Jean says. We're climbing out of the Malibu at the end of our rounds. Making a second stop at the Watering Hole just in case he's shown up, and because I got to have a beer. "I kept my mouth shut so far."

"But . . ."

"But I goddamn told you so," she finally blurts.

"Feel better?" I stop short next to the car and look at her like she's a bag of boiled shit.

"We should've just told him, and then if he was gonna get pissed off or weird about it, it wouldn't be our fault."

"Like it is now, you mean?" I ask her. "Our fault?"

"Yeah." She looks half pissed and half miserable. Jean ain't used to seeing herself in the wrong. I did that to her too, along with everything else.

"C'mon," I tell her. "I want a beer."

We never find Randy that night. We figure he drove straight back home to the farm. So me and Jean, we get drunk. Drunker and louder than usual. Around midnight we're at one end of the bar and this kid is sitting at the other end. His old man's playing pool in the back and George behind the bar's keeping the kid stocked in pretzels and Diet Coke. He's one of them skinny, scraggly thirteen-year-olds, not even close to growing into his bones yet. Teeth too big for his skinny face. This kid, he's a character, though. He's telling George jokes down there at the end of the bar. So of course it doesn't take more'n a minute before Jean hears this going on. She slides off her barstool and sits down next to the kid.

"Speak up, twerp," she tells him. So he does. And she matches him joke for joke. This goes on for about half a dozen jokes, minor-league stuff, and folks are starting to listen. Some muscle guy and his muscle girlfriend leave their table by the front and carry their beers up to the bar. Couple of older guys that are always in there from noon onward, drinking Schlitz and watching ESPN, they turn away from the TV and listen. The kid's old man even shows up from the back, just when Jean's finishing one about three guys with one wish each. No strong stuff yet, a couple of barely dirty ones from Jean and one about a Jew and a Polack from the kid. But once his old man shows up, the kid turns it up a little, with the German shepherd on the golf course, and Jean comes right back at him with the priest and the rabbi and the two little boys. The muscle girlfriend tries to break in with a knock-knock, but all she gets is a few dirty looks and her boyfriend telling her, "Shut up, will ya, Josie?"

You can tell this ain't the kid's first time doing this. He's playing it cool, laughing at Jean's jokes before coming back to top them. They fall into a streak of jokes all starting with "This guy walks into a bar . . ." The people crowded around us are having so much fun they don't hear half the punch lines, but it doesn't matter. The kid's sweating by the sixteenth (about a ten-inch pianist), and there's a big gap of quiet while Jean tries to think of another. The kid's watching her close. I think he's run out. Jean's shaking her head a little, frowning down at her beer. I can feel her leg against mine, swinging loose back and forth at the knee. I want to kiss her on the ear but I don't want to distract her thinking, and I can't in front of all these people anyway. But in my mind, I do. In my mind, I brush the curls back and kiss her on the top of her ear.

Finally she says, without looking up, "This guy walks into a bar," and everyone's cheering and laughing so hard it takes forever for her to finish the joke. It's the old chestnut about the crying elephant out back, but no one cares. She topped the kid. But now he's got his second wind, and out comes some ugly, raunchy shit. Couple of women get huffy at the butter brickle ice cream. A black guy from Ypsilanti leaves after the one about the two guys hunting woodcock in Georgia. Other than that, no one's got a problem laughing at blacks, homosexuals, Japs, Scots, Indians, Irish, women, Jews, cripples, kids, and dogs. A real low-class crowd, but Jesus, we're having a good time.

I had enough of beer and switched over to whiskey about an hour ago. I'm not thinking about Randy, not thinking about Jean heading down home soon. Not thinking about anything but watching her next to me, laughing with the kid, who's been growing up in pretty much the same bars we have. Maybe on the other side of the state, but pretty much the same damn bars.

Neither of them feel the need to be polite anymore. Jean tells the hardest thing about eating a hairless pussy. My stomach lurches a little, because I'd sure as hell never tell that joke in front of strangers. That's when the kid comes back with the ringer.

"How do you know when your sister's having her period?" he asks.

"I don't know," says Jean.

"You can taste it on your father's cock."

Maybe it's in my head, but I swear there's a couple seconds of total quiet and everyone in the room's looking at Jean and they know all about her. The whole bar knows every dirty secret me and Jean have had since we were four years old. There's a second where I'm looking at her and she's looking at me and we're both stripped naked of every lie we ever told to cover up our family. And her face is blank and surprised, like someone shot her in the stomach. But it must be in my head, because now she's throwing her head back and laughing up to the ceiling. Laughing so loud it's filling the bar and then haw haw haw everyone else is laughing with her with her with her and so am I haw haw haw. When she settles down enough, Jean takes the kid by the wrist and lifts it in the air like he's a champion.

"That's it," she says loud enough for everyone to hear her. "I'm cleaned out." And she's being good-natured about it, giving the kid his due, making him feel like a million bucks with his old man watching. "That kid's something, ain't he?" she's saying to George. And God, he's grinning, that kid. Grinning and talking to folks and hell he's only thirteen but I want to smash his fucking skinny toothy face in. I take a last gulp of my JB and get up off my stool to head over to him. Jean's arm comes up like an old rusty gate in front of me.

"Where you going?" she says.

"Nowhere," I grunt.

"Let's go home."

"Got to smash his fucking face in first," I say.

"Naw, he's a kid, he's all right." She's throwing money down on the counter. "I just wanna get out of here." And she's pushing her way through people toward the door. I follow the back of her head until we're out in the dark. It makes me stop short, all the dark outside. It always catches me like that, going into a place when it's light and coming out in the dark. Jean's yanking open the driver's side of the Malibu, so I slump in on the other side.

The dark gets thicker and cooler as we head away from the lights of town. A misty fog hangs across the road, turning the windshield furry. Jean turns on the wipers once every minute or so. The air smells good. Like dead fish without the stink. I take in three or four snortfuls and the air rushes up into my head, clearing the whiskey sludge out of my brain.

Jean's handling the Malibu okay for the liquor she's had. We're quiet, listening to "Layla" playing low on the radio, fading in and out. I'm hanging limp somewhere real nice, halfway between awake and passed out. The red dot of Jean's cigarette sits above the steering wheel. I watch it swoop through the dark toward her mouth. It flares for a second, then swoops back again. That's when the deer pops up from the pavement smack in front of the car. A doe, red eyes staring straight at me, froze solid.

"Oh," says the doe in a brown velvet voice. "Oh, no." Like her heart's broke at the thought of dying already. Her disappointment is soft, giving up, resigned to the death about to hit her. My foot slams into the floorboard, kicking for the brake.

"Oh God," says someone. Jean swerves over to the left and the deer shoots straight up into the air. Outside my open window, the white fur of her belly floats like a slow-motion spaceship. There's a slash of black hoof, a white tail racing away. Now nothing but dark. Jean gets the car over to our lane and halfway onto the shoulder, where we stop. She must have laid a hell of a skid to stop so quick. I look behind, but everything's black.

"We hit it?" Her voice is dull and flat.

"No." My foot's still planted in the floorboard, hard enough to lift my ass right off the seat. I unclench everything while Jean puts the car in park. We climb out and look for dents or blood on the hood. Nothing. The dark swells up around us. Soaks into my clothes, my hair. The car is still humming "Layla" to the fog.

The doe's somewhere in the brush now, about a half mile away. She's wondering if maybe she's dead and doesn't feel it. If she's really laying on the road with all her legs broken. Hobbling an inch at a time on broken stumps, lurching and falling until I find a tire jack in the trunk and use it to bash her head in, put her out of pain. Drag her over to the ditch, where she rolls once and stops still. Neck twisted around so she's staring up at us.

But no, she's alive. There's no tire jack, no need for it. Me and Jean get back in the car, sober as hell. I'm looking out into the woods in the direction of the doe. She's in the brush, her heart still galloping full tilt even though she's stopped running. I try breathing slow and steady through my nose for her. Heart's slowing to a trot, still a long way from calm. So it takes a couple minutes for me to figure out that we ain't moved yet. Jean's killed the engine. I turn my head to see what's the holdup, and she's looking straight out the drizzly windshield. Her hands are in her lap, like she's in church listening to a sermon. A really good sermon. She ain't making a sound. There's her face, her profile with the short, freckled nose and her strong jaw, disappearing in the shadows. But enough of her is visible so I see the tears. One's about parallel with her mouth, right where it starts to tickle. Sure enough, her hand erases it, but another one takes its place. I ain't seen her cry since she was three or four. It's like the end of the world.

"Jean?" I reach across the front seat for her. When she hears my voice, that's when everything breaks loose and she's bawling out loud.

Holding on to me hard and burying her face in my shoulder. Pretty soon my shirt's covered with tears and snot. I got both arms around her. I don't say anything but her name, over and over. I whisper it to her hair, to the rearview, to the drizzle fog outside.

"Jean. I love you, Jean."

She's crying so hard I don't know if she can even hear me. But I keep saying it as long as it takes her to quiet down, which doesn't happen for a long time. Finally she says, "I don't care what happens. We ain't letting go of each other."

I get a chill running tiptoe up my arm. Like already I know what's gonna happen to us. "What do we do if people find out?" I ask her.

"What are they gonna do?" she says. "Put us in jail?" She's still crying, but her voice is clear. "I mean, what can they do to us, besides talk?"

"Forget it," I tell her. "Randy ain't gonna tell no one."

She looks hard at me, not bothering to wipe off the tears now, not trying to hide her face.

"Ray. Don't screw up on me."

"What's that mean?" I laugh. But she's serious.

"You're it for me," she says. "Ain't gonna be with no one else. Don't run out on me."

"Well, you're it for me." I want to say more, but she cuts me off.

"I know that. If I didn't know that, I wouldn't be telling you not to cut out."

"Where am I gonna go? Huh?" Pissed now, because she ain't trusting me all the way. Pissed because I'm scared. I'm yelling now. "Where the hell am I gonna go?"

But she doesn't holler back like usual. She lays her head on my shoulder and cries again. This is Jean, my little sister, my love. So I hold on to her. Tell her how we'll figure something, we'll maybe go away and live somewhere else. But I ain't going anywhere without her. After a while we're both quiet, sitting in the Malibu watching the rain mist over us and trickle its way down the windshield. I don't know how much time goes by before she reaches for the ignition and shifts the car into gear. *No. No. No. Stay!* We drive back to the hunting cabin. Go to bed and she falls asleep right away. I lay there, eyes wide for a long time, looking at the shadows crawling in and out of the corners as the cars drive by outside. Jean's got her face half buried under my shoulder. Dug in like a mole. She always did that, even when we were kids. Burrowing under the blankets, the pillows, my arm or my neck. Trying to get somewhere safe.

TWENTY-TWO

The next day, we decide to drive down home, and I'll go out to the farm and talk to Randy. Jean packs up all her shit, we load her big Plymouth, and I follow her home in the Malibu. It's late afternoon when we pull up to the house. I don't bother getting out of the car.

"I'm gonna head on out there," I tell Jean when she steps up to the window.

"All right," she says. She's back to herself, not showing any sign of all her crying last night. She looks me in the eye, clear and smiling. "Take it easy."

I watch her walk into the house before I pull out. Time I get to the farm, my stomach feels like I swallowed a bottle of wood glue. My knees are full of air and I'm breathing through my nose like a son of a bitch. I check the hay barn, the toolshed, out by the silos. Don't see him out on the tractor nowhere. So I knock on the back door and ask his ma if he's around. I'm waiting for her to point a finger at me and scream something nasty and true. But all she says is, "No, he isn't. What're you doing home, Ray?"

"Moving Jean's stuff down," I tell her. "He come home last night?" And right away I know I'm an asshole, because if he didn't come home she's gonna worry.

"Yeah, hon. Awful late, I heard him come in." She's a nice lady, Randy's ma. Don't know why she likes me so much, but she does.

"Know where he is?" I ask her.

"Got up, did the chores, said he'd be back later." She smiles. "You want me to have him give you a call?"

"Yeah. Will ya tell him I was here looking for him?"

"Sure will. You come over for a visit before you head back up north."

I tell her I will, and get back in the car. Shit. I drive over to the Dairy Queen, to the mill. Feels like my whole life has turned into driving around looking for Randy. He's not at the old track field, he's not at the park, he's not anywhere.

It's getting on to dusk now, got to be near eight-thirty. The crickets are starting up a steady beat as I drive around the outside edges of town. Bruce Springsteen comes on the radio, "Thunder Road." Listening to the song, my brain's flooded with Jean. I turn the car toward home, missing her. Randy can wait until tomorrow.

I hear hollering when I pull into the driveway behind her Plymouth. Jean and the old man, going at it. The front door's open, so the sound is pouring out the screen door. I'm running up onto the porch when I see Jean go by like a blur on the other side of the screen door. She disappears up the stairs and Ma's face, scared and white, is at the screen. She looks at me coming toward her for a second before she says to me, "Oh no, Ray."

She tries to shut the heavy wood door on me. I bust past her and see the old man's legs going up the stairs, hard and heavy on the bare steps. I look at Ma, but she turns away like she can't stand the sight of me and goes into the kitchen. A chair scrapes across the linoleum and then she's crying. I take one step toward the kitchen, but there's a big bang like a gunshot upstairs. Heard it a thousand times, the explosion of a bedroom or bathroom door hitting the wall after the old man's kicked it in. Right away the stairway's full of screams and hollers sliding tumbling swooping down the banister and all over me. I start to run upstairs, but I got to sidestep around Ma's white pine rocker that Jean upended behind her, trying to block the old man's way. There's a TV tray with a glass of milk and something looks like a liverwurst sandwich knocked over by the couch.

Time I get up the stairs, he's got her across the bed. The old man ain't that big. Medium tall, skinny as hell. And Jean's big-boned. But he's been drinking all afternoon, from the smell coming off him sharp and sour. So he's mean and wiry, and she's only sixteen. Her T-shirt's tore along the front and she's got blood on her face. I can't tell where it's from. But she's screaming loud as she can. She's got the old man's voice. So it's filling up the room, the house, the whole county. No one's gonna call the cops, though. The neighbors gave that up a long time ago. The old man's got a bony knee pinned into her chest and he's yanking back his belt, flipping open his pants.

"Little goddamn whore, don't care who fucks ya?"

She's calling him a cocksucking motherfucking bastard son of a cunt, every word I ever heard all mixed in new ways. Scratching and swinging with her fists. Bucking her hips hard, trying to send him flying headfirst into the wall. I come up behind and get an elbow lock, lifting him so his knee ain't stabbing into her chest. I pull him up and back, and his trousers dangle halfway down to his knees. I'm fixing to throw him back into the corner of the dresser, when Jean lunges off the bed and buries her face right in his crotch. The weight of her knocks me to my knees, and I let go of the old man. He gives out with a holler makes me want to crawl under the bed and wait the whole thing out. Because at first I think Jean bit his dick clean off. That's exactly what it looks like. There's blood on her face and he's grabbing his crotch, feeling around for his belt. He grabs hold of it and swings hard so the buckle catches her right across the cheekbone. Blood spurts like it's some kind of slasher movie. She's scrambling out of reach, jumping off the foot of the bed and running out of the room. I stop him from following by sitting on his legs. Don't know what else to do. Feet thump like tree stumps down the stairs and the squeak crash bang of someone flying full speed out the screen door. Then no sound, no car door or engine turning over. Wherever she's headed, she's running there on foot. The old man ain't moving under me. He says, "Go git your mother 'fore I bleed to death."

And it looks like he might. His dick is still there, but she bit a chunk out of his leg right up high where the big veins are. And it's bleeding like a bastard. Ma comes up the stairs when I call her. She's still crying, but it's like a nervous tic or something by now, like she doesn't even know she's doing it. She won't look at me, just bends down and takes a look at the old man.

"Run git me a towel and some hydrogen peroxide," she says to his leg. I go into the bathroom and grab an old towel with purple roses that

Ma got out of a box of Tide. Grab the peroxide and some rubbing alcohol while I'm at it. I hand her all of it and stand back. She douses it good with the whole bottle of peroxide, and I watch it bubble white like his leg's got rabies, foaming at the mouth. Then she wraps the towel hard around his leg.

"Gonna need stitches," she says.

"Damned if I do." This is the first thing the old man's said since Ma came in the room.

"Look at it, Bill." She's crying again. "Bleeding right through the towel."

So she helps him to his feet and I grab a stack of towels on the way out and we load him into the back seat of my Malibu, Ma next to him. Got to drive him to the emergency clinic over in Adrian because the old man says he ain't going to no real hospital and we can just kiss his ass. Ma hasn't asked what happened or who bit him. It's pretty goddamn clear. I'm driving slower than I need to, out of spite. Wondering what the old man's gonna say when the doctor asks how'd it happen? The old man breaks through my wondering by saying, "It ain't your fault, Ray."

Ma tells him to shush. "Ain't no need to talk about it," she says. But she still ain't looked at me since I showed up at the house.

"You're a man," he says to the back of my head.

"For God's sake," Ma whines, and she's off again with the tears.

"But that girl's a whore," he's explaining, like to convince himself. "Whole town probably knows by now what she been doing up there."

"Bill, please." Ma's voice stepping up up up higher higher higher, hysterical.

"How's your ma gonna go to church with people talking about what you kids done? You think of that?"

I got my hands in the ten o'clock–two o'clock position on the wheel. Driving slow. Eyes on the road.

"Who told you about it?" I ask him.

"Billy goddamn well told me," he explodes. The back seat bounces, he's yelling so hard. Voice going bang bang bang around the inside of the car before it cuts out the window, with Ma's sniffles trailing behind it.

"Billy run into your buddy last night, got a earful of it. So did everybody else at Dewey's."

Dewey's. Randy's never stepped a toe in Dewey's in his life. I know that for a fact. "What buddy of mine?" I ask, keeping my eyes off the rearview so I don't see his face. So I don't drive us all into the twisted, bent oak tree coming up on the right.

"Randy," he barks at the ceiling of the car. "Who the hell do you think? Who else walked in on the two of you fucking like a couple of cats?"

"Oh God, Ray. It ain't true," Ma says out the window. "You didn't do that." The old man snarls at her like a cornered wolverine. He brings his fist down on the vinyl armrest.

"Bitch admitted it! Weren't sorry, neither." His face is all red and Ma's wrapping a fourth towel around his leg. *Go ahead, bastard. Holler all the blood right out of you.* "I'll teach that whore. I'll teach her."

I pick up the speed a little because I got to get this bastard out of my car before I kill him. Cut a wide path around two kids on their bikes. They're going like hell down the shoulder of the road. Clouds of dirt drift up behind 'em and hang there over the road. They're both hollering loud, mouths wide open, laughing. Making noise for the hell of it, just like me and Randy used to do. Pedaling fast as they can. Once we're past 'em, I drift back over into our lane.

"You ain't gonna do shit," I tell him.

"Ray, honey, I don't—" Ma gets halfway through a wheedle when the old man cuts her off.

"What'd you say, boy?" Him.

"You ain't laying a finger on her no more." Me.

"You're asking for a stomping." Him.

"You ain't hitting her. You ain't pushing her, whipping her, smacking her, or sticking your dick in her—"

"Raymond Edward!" Ma pretending to be shocked, like she don't know what he been doing to her own daughter all this time. But she's not putting on the show for anyone but herself, so we ignore it.

"That whore's living in my house," he says. "I'm gonna teach her how to act."

"Only thing you ever taught her is how to suck dick." That's me talking so big. But I'm thinking about that time me and Billy got Jean out behind the toolshed. What we did. I'm hating the old man plenty right now, but the feeling isn't stopping there. Ma's screaming "Stop it!" in the back seat, full-blown hysterical now. She's swirling like a brunette blizzard back there next to the old man. Ma can put up with just about anything but saying the truth out loud.

"Pull over," the old man's yelling. "Pull this goddamn car over now!" Loud voice. Big voice. Sledgehammer voice beating me into the seat. I slam the accelerator down and three heads jerk back hard. We zoom like a crazy rocket into Adrian.

"Touch her again and I kill you," says someone in the car. "Call her a whore again and I kill you. Look at her funny and I kill you." Whoever's doing the talking, he doesn't care if he sounds like a bad Dirty Harry movie. Truth is, he sounds pretty good. Sounds like a guy I'd be scared of.

"I might kill you anyway," this guy says as I'm watching the speedo move up to 105. Ma and the old man are pressed against the back seat like someone stuck 'em there before the clay was dry. And they stay like that until we come screaming into the emergency entrance of the clinic. I don't turn the car off, I don't get out of the car. Ma helps the old man out the back seat and I peel out before they get halfway to the sliding door. They can take a taxi home, or they can sit there all night. They can go to hell.

I never acted like such a prick in my life. Sure I've been a prick, but mostly by what I ain't done. The quiet, chicken-shit sort of prick. I never been so on top of being a prick before. I've grown nine feet longer. I'm a python snake curled up in the driver's seat of that car. Fifteen feet of coiled-up hate muscles flexing for the first time. I see now how Billy picks bar fights, beats up on Ginny Honey even though they're married and she's all pregnant. So much mean and hate, where else is it gonna go? I head back toward home. I'm thinking how the hell am I gonna find Jean? But underneath that, I'm thinking what I'm gonna do to Randy when I find him. It's not a long ride back from Adrian, but it's long enough for me to wish I'd pulled over and stomped the old man near to death while I had the chance. I don't think I could do it in a fair fight, but he'd been bleeding pretty bad for a while. I had my chance and I kept driving like a pussy. All that hate and nowhere for it to go. Pulling my veins tight like guitar strings, making my ears buzz. I'm coming back into town now, thinking how I got to put my fist through the windshield or else the top of my head's gonna blow off.

Maybe the veins in my arm'll split open and firecrackers come out snapping and sparkling.

That's the state I'm in when I pull into the Little Creek Party Store. Buy a fifth of Jim Beam and drink a third of it before I get out of the parking lot. It takes the snap crackle out of my blood. I pull out smooth and start looking for Jean. Already the world's going wide and easy, the booze starting to soak in. I'm a twenty-foot python by now, getting bigger the more I soak it up. The world outside my windshield gets shorter, stretched out, easier to manage. I'm on top of it. I'm on top of all of it.

I stop at the Sunoco station and have Joe Lee fill it up. Feels like he's looking at me funny. I wonder if he hangs out at Dewey's. Feels like he's looking at me like he knows shit about it. I don't say anything until he comes to my window and I hand him a fistful of singles.

"Why you such a fat fuck, Joe Lee?" I ask him, looking at him all snake-eyed. He tells me to get out of the car so he can kick my drunk ass. But the door's locked and I'm rolling up the window and pulling away. I'm looking for someone to hurt, not for someone to kill me. So I take it at a pretty good clip coming onto Main Street.

It's dark out now, and the Malibu's running smooth under me. Stars are popping already. What clouds there are, they're stretched too thin, like cotton batting coming apart. I drive and think. She ain't at her girlfriend Pebbles' house. First stop once I get back into town is over there. But Pebbles ain't home and her ma ain't seen her since dinner. No, ain't seen Jean all summer.

"Everything okay?" she wants to know.

"Yeah, just . . . Ma was looking for her," I say quiet enough so she probably can't hear me. I come down off the front porch and wave real nice. Like I been taught. Pebbles is all right. No sense getting her ma all worked up.

Looking for Jean. Looking for Jean. I come up on the traffic light next to the Dog 'n' Suds right at the town limits. Red and yellow island of neon in the dark, cars parked with the little trays perched off the windows. Cheese dogs, french fries, root beer. I roll my window back down, waiting for the light to change. Warm greasy smell hanging like a haze in the neon. People's faces smeary and pale, chewing. I take a quick pull from the JB.

"Hey, Ray!" comes a voice from the neon. I turn my head, hand up over my eyes to cut the yellow-red glare. "Ray Johnson!"

Three cars parked back a ways from the building out by the picnic tables, where dark starts taking over. Half a dozen guys; some I know, some I don't. One takes a few steps away from the others. Music that was blaring from one of the cars is cut off. He looks behind him for a second and back at me. "Saw your girlfriend tonight."

Little mean laughs coming up out of the pack of guys. The traffic light's still red. I want to ask where he saw her, but I keep my mouth shut and try counting to ten. Breathe. Get as far as four and holler back, "Where?"

This makes the laughing swell up like a swarm of gnats. The guy hollers back something about two-timing me with my best friend and I can't hear what else. I can't hear him because they're laughing and now the green light's screaming "Go! Go!" and there's a car behind me honking to get through the intersection and I want to ask him, "What? Where is she?" Because I feel like I'm driving around with my arms cut off without her. My foot pushes down and the Dog 'n' Suds fades behind me. I'm so goddamn homesick for her, I just head straight back to the house. I'm sick of driving. Sick of looking and not finding shit. I drive out Cutler Road, finishing off the liquor I been cradling in my lap like it's a baby. To hell with it, she's got to come home sometime. I'm about twenty yards from the house when I see Randy's MG parked in the driveway.

Two-timing me with my best friend.

That guy's voice and the laughing behind him, all dancing in a witches' circle in my head. Is that why Randy was so pissed? Was she seeing him on the sly? She told me he asked her out and she said no. Jean wouldn't lie to me. But it was her said we had to come down home today and find him, talk to him. What the hell's he doing at my house? Is she with him? I pull up front but I don't want to walk in there. No power on earth is gonna make me walk in on them and stand there sucking air like Randy did yesterday. I hit the horn. One long scream of get your ass out here, bastard.

I'm in my car, empty whiskey bottle next to me. My left arm's cocked on the door and my right hand's resting on the top of the steering wheel. Crickets. This is what I see: Jean's face behind the screen door. It opens and she comes out on the porch. Randy comes out after her. He's walking down the front steps toward me, but Jean stays where she is on the porch. She's got a white bandage on the left side of her face. Who put it there?

So because this is what I see, because they come out the door together, I decide that's it, that's proof. Everything I know about Jean goes pop and it's gone. Everything she been to me all summer swallows up on itself and disappears into a whiskey-sogged sinkhole of shit. All that's left in my brain is two things that I know now. First I'm killing him. Then I'm killing her.

Randy's in the middle of the yard now, shouting something at me. Eyebrows pulled down in the middle from trying to be heard. But I'm still laying on that horn. The sound of it tears up the quiet like machine gun fire, like people screaming. It's ripping a hole in people's heads while they're watching TV or sitting out in the backyard with a beer. Pissing them off, getting them all in a knot. I take my hand off the horn, count to five, then lay on it again. Just so people have a few seconds to be relieved at the quiet before the screaming starts up again. Now it's twice as hard to take. It's the last straw after a bad day for someone out there. They're slamming a stack of plates down on the counter, or kicking their dog out of the way, or yanking their two-year-old by the arm so he goes flying across the room.

This is what I hear during the five seconds of quiet: Randy hollering, ". . . it off, man. You want someone calling the cops?" Then when I don't answer, he says, "You getting out—" And then he's cut off by the horn starting up again. So he comes the rest of the way across the yard and tries to yank open the door of the Malibu. But it's still locked from when I was fending off Joe Lee. He grabs my left arm through the open window like he's gonna pull me out that way. My right hand lets go of the horn and lands on the neck of the empty bottle. I swing it around, but he sees it coming. Ducks his head to the side and I catch him on the shoulder. Useless goddamn bottle bouncing off of him and onto the grass. *So mad. So mad.*

So I unlock the door, lean back, and kick the damned door open hard enough to knock him on his ass. The python muscle uncoils and I'm out of the car, roaring up twenty feet tall. Look down at Randy picking himself up off of the ground. Think about him fucking Jean. Think about what I wish I'd done to the old man when I had the chance. I land a kick into his rib cage that damn near lifts him off his knees before he goes over on his side. He might be trying to say something, I don't know. I pull back for another kick, this time into his back.

"Shit, Ray. That's enough," says Jean from the porch. "He said he was sorry."

I land the kick anyway. Randy rolls a good ten feet away from me and gets himself upright.

"Sorry for what?" I holler. My voice is deep and loud like a black river, not really my voice at all. "What's he sorry for?"

"Sorry for telling anyone," Randy says. He's backing up, but I know him. I know he ain't gonna take an ass whipping without fighting back sooner or later.

"Yeah well, fuck you Randy," I yell in my new voice, the old man's voice. "Fuck you all to hell."

"C'mon, Ray," says Jean, stepping off the porch. "He's sorry."

"Shut up, bitch."

She stops at the bottom of the porch stairs. "Don't talk to me like that," she says.

Randy decides this is a good time to send a punch into the side of my head. Stars twinkle and I'm about fifty feet above the yard, floating. Voices below are yelling at me. I open my eyes and they're both in my face. Jean and Randy both, trying to kill me. I punch and kick at everything in sight. Words fly in and out between fists and elbows and chins. *Get off of him . . . Jesus, Ray . . . what's the matter with . . . goddamn it . . . kill you both.* This goes on until someone hits Jean hard enough so she goes straight down and stays down. I drop to my knees and Randy takes a break, hands on his stomach, breathing hard through his nose like the asshole he is.

"Jean?" I say to the back of the hand covering her face.

"What the hell, Ray?" she says through her fingers. "What's going on?"

"You been fucking him?"

"What?" The hand comes away, and she's a mess. The bandage is torn off and now she's looking like hell, with fresh cuts over the bruises and blood all over. "Fucking who?" she asks.

"Him." I jerk my head at Randy, who's muttering something about what a dick I am.

"For Christ's sake," she says. "When would I have time to fuck him too?"

I think about this. But the sight of them coming out onto the porch together, it's eating poison into my gut. And the guys at the Dog 'n' Suds laughing.

"Don't you goddamn lie to me." I jerk her shoulder hard.

"Hey!" Her eyes are on me, clear and open like they were all summer. "It's me. Jean. I don't lie to you."

Randy's muttering to himself some more, keeping a distance. I'm looking at her face, all banged up but still her face. I want to be like we were yesterday. I want my Jean back. The real one; the one I trust. But this one in front of me, I can't tell for sure who it is. I want to believe her. I'm picking my way through the liquor fog, trying to find my way back to her.

Then she says, "Where you been, Ray? We was all over, looking for you."

And when that word comes out of her mouth, that "we," I push her back down on the grass and stand up. "We" is her and Randy. "We" is them without me. The sound of it sets my stomach heaving, and I'm gonna be sick be sick be sick.

"Goddamn miserable bitch," I tell her.

And I'm in the car. Randy's waving his arms and hollering at me to "Hold on, will ya?" Jean's sitting in the grass watching me like she can't believe any of it. Like I'm some kind of nightmare coming true. My right foot lays the gas pedal flat. Tires trying to grab hold of the pavement, engine revving faster than she ought to, guitar on the radio turned up full blast. Then I'm moving and the car's moving with me. Randy gets smaller and smaller as I get closer and closer, pinned there in the headlights. He looks fed up, like "What's this asshole doing now?"

Time he figures it out, I already hit him dead on. But he doesn't go under like I expect. He flips straight up in the air and lands rolling across the roof. Sounds a little like I'm going through the automatic car wash. Brushes pounding on all sides like a hurricane coming from every direction at once. Then two hard bangs as he goes off the back end of the car.

I keep the pedal flat on the floor. Look in the rearview and there's a body in the road, not moving. Jean sits in the grass watching my tail-lights disappear. There's another Ray inside me, banging on the back windshield, crying and begging me to stop turn around go back and get her. But I don't go back. I don't slow down. I keep my foot flat on the floor until I cross the state line into Ohio.

I stayed away for two years. Got a job in Gary, Indiana, laying low. Wrote to Harold a couple of times, but he never told no one that he knew where I was. Harold's the one told me Randy wasn't dead, that he was in the hospital for two weeks and he got a pin in his hip and a limp. Harold's the one told me Randy never pressed charges. I was free to go home whenever I wanted. Harold's the one told me about the old man going back to prison and Ma divorcing him.

I stay away, though. I stay away until Jean graduates high school. By then it's too late. She's moved out of Ma's house and got herself a job up to Kelsey's Lumber. She's hard now, like she never was before. Just as mean, but now there's something around her no one's gonna get through. And she sure doesn't want to have anything to do with me. At first I'm half waiting for Jean to get some kind of revenge on me for running out on her, since she never forgives a thing. But no. Billy gets me a job up to O'Donnell's and I get used to living alongside Jean in the same town, half alive. A couple years go by like that until I meet Sally, and that's that. End of story. And not a word out of Jean. Not a word about any of it until yesterday, in her backyard, when she let me in for a second. And slammed the door back shut again.

TWENTY-THREE

It's just before dawn. Samson's sitting on the grass next to the garden, watching me replant the green beans by flashlight. I don't know if Sally saw the garden all torn up when she left the house or not. But it's like a wasp flying around inside my head, stinging my eyes, the thought of her seeing it like that. Sally should keep the place, because I know she loves the front porch and the lilacs out back and the washer and dryer right there in the basement. She loves the little bit of a pantry off the kitchen, and the shelves in the living room window for her glass figurines. So she ought to stay. I'm thinking that's what I'll tell her tomorrow (today? what time is it?) when I see her at the funeral. And once I've decided that's what I'm gonna do, the thought of that torn-up garden starts eating at me.

So now I got all the wooden stakes dug in along the rows, and I'm just about done with the beans, digging the roots back into the dirt and wrapping the vines up and around the stakes and the cross-strings. It's like building a fence made of long, skinny green snakes and they're wriggling out of my hand every time I turn to adjust the flashlight. Samson's staying off the dirt, because he's a smart dog and he knows the garden's off limits again, even though we were both sitting smack in it just a while ago.

The outline of trees is starting to cut into the sky, black against purple. I ain't tired anymore. Can't imagine ever being tired again. I got dirt, smooth and slippery like powder, all over my hands, deep in my fingernails and knuckles, making it feel like I got old-man hands. I got a little ache still in my head, but it helps me to concentrate on what I'm doing.

The tomatoes are done. They were the first to go in. Snow peas next, which is why the beans are working so good, because I got practice on them damn peas. There's a couple things I ain't sure what they are, because they're just leafy green stuff, so I try to match up whatever looks alike and hope for the best.

Trees are full shapes now, not just cutouts. The sky is dark rosy pink, yellow gold, still a little purple in places. The yard's smaller now in the dawn. The crickets finally shut the hell up about a half hour before the light started to change. There was exactly nine seconds of total silence, and then the birds started in.

I walk over to get the hose laying against the side of the house, careful not to step on Samson, who's stretched out asleep on the grass. I turn it on soft and soak the garden real good, going one plant at a time. It ain't rained in a hundred years, but it's cool out this morning. Cool and quiet and peaceful, like there's no one else on earth. Harold and the others are gonna be waking up in an hour or so. They all get up early down in Tennessee. I remember that from my visits.

The sun is peeking cool over the treetops to the east. The sky is all milky pink and yellow like roses. Day coming on fast. I turn the water off and coil the hose up neat against the house. Last night seems like a hundred years ago. I look around and everything seems strange because it's so normal and familiar. Samson's still sacked out on the grass.

No reason I can't go in the house and lay down for a couple hours. But I don't move, because I'm not done thinking. There's something whispering in my brain, but it's too soft to hear what it's saying. It's about what I'm gonna do. It's my secret whisper voice that's telling me what I really want, what I really deep down want. But it's too soft to hear because I haven't listened to it in ten years.

"What?" I say into the pink and yellow air. "What?" *Jean, Jean, Jean.*

I think what she's doing right now. It's still early, but I know she's probably up. Setting food out on the back porch for the lousy cat, enjoying the cool when it's too early for the humidity to set in. Pouring a cup of coffee and sitting at that kitchen table where she can look out the screen door, watch the lousy cat eat breakfast. Sitting in the peace and quiet of early morning by herself. She's sitting at the table by herself. Maybe she's eating some cornflakes or toast. She's there right now. Now, while I'm standing here in the yard. I can see her. Hair's mushed straight up on one side where she slept on it. If my arm was long enough, I could reach out and smooth it down. She's all by herself in the quiet of the morning, like she has been all the mornings between the day she moved out of Ma's house and today. Even if there was some guy once in a while sleeping upstairs, she's still at that table in the early morning, alone. I wonder how many times she's sat there, wondering what I was doing right then. Wondering when I was gonna come back. It's dawning on me now, she's been waiting for me to come back to her. All these years, I thought it was over and done. I thought she hated me or, worse, had no more feeling for me than if I was a bug underfoot. And all this time she's been waiting for me to get back to myself, my real self, the one who couldn't be away from her for more than a day. *I thought you was something you ain't.* But I am. I am that something.

Right then. Right then it slams into me like the earth slams into you after you've fallen nine thousand feet. I run to the truck, slide across the seat, and reach for the keys. They aren't there. I got to get to her, and the keys aren't there. I start to panic, because the weight of all the years I wasted are bouldering over me, and every time I try to think straight, I get flattened down like a cartoon character. Got to find the keys. *She's waiting for me.* Keys are in the house. *She's been waiting for ten years.* Just go look in the kitchen. *Jean, wait!* Look on the counter, not there. Look on the table, there they are. *Jean, hold on!*

I need to see her so bad it's like I'm suffocating. Something's taking my breath and squeezing it out of my lungs like two hot sponges. I stop in the middle of the kitchen and breathe through my nose like Randy taught me. Can't pass out. Got to get in the truck and drive. It's only a few minutes' drive to her house, to her kitchen table. But when I breathe through my nose, I get a whiff of myself. When was the last time I had a shower? I look down at the blood all over my clothes. I duck my head and sniff an armpit to see how bad it really is. *Jesus.* I got the keys in my hand now. To hell with it. I run out the door and get in the truck.

Maybe later we'll come back here. Jean can sit at the table and I'll take a shower and change into my good pants and we'll go to the funeral together. Making plans in my head is keeping me calm. I'm pulling out of the driveway and I remember I bought new long-sleeved T-shirts yesterday. Are they laying in the yard with all the other stuff I threw out of the truck last night? I don't need to go busting into her house with blood all over my clothes. A clean shirt wouldn't be hard to manage. I push the pedal down and fly. One hand's on the wheel and one hand's groping around for the plastic T-shirt package. I feel something hot against my ear—it's Samson breathing into my face. He's in the bed of the truck, poking his head in through the back window. Fresh from his snooze. I look in the mirror. I'm gonna have to do something with myself before the funeral. It's today, for Christ's sake. *Jean's waiting.* Samson's grinning and panting, his tongue hanging down out of one side of his mouth. I rub his head hard and laugh.

"You ready, boy?" I yell. "You ready for this?"

Everything's gonna be okay now. Jean's waiting for me and I'm on my way. Now that I'm moving, now that I'm doing something, the boulders ain't running me flat no more. They're rolling right behind and pushing me forward. I hit the pedal harder. The sun's looking me smack in the eye, so I flip the visor down. Feels like it's burning my eyelids off, but it's okay. Everything's okay. I still ain't found those shirts, but I don't remember throwing them out of the truck. I lean way down, feel under the seat. The sun's got me completely blind, so I can't see the road. I sit up and yank the wheel to swerve away from the ditch. I'm going a little faster than I ought to be, and the rear tires start to slide up around the cab, making the truck sidewind like Samson when he walks. I yank the wheel around the other way, steering into the skid and tapping the brakes. It don't take but a couple more swipes across the road and I'm all straightened out. But just when I'm taking my right hand off the wheel, I hear the siren behind me.

I pull over, thinking for a second that he's gonna go around me, but I don't know who I was kidding. I'm starting to think that me and Sheriff Keith are gonna be up each other's ass forever, when I look in the rearview and it's Sue getting out of the car. The one with the nice shoulders, who brought me coffee. She's in full uniform now, short-sleeved shirt and those awful pants that make a person's ass look lumpy.

If I was Billy, I'd be thinking right now how I got nothing to worry about since it's a woman. But I catch my reflection in the mirror, and it ain't looking good. What time is it? Why didn't I grab my watch while I was in the house? Where is it, anyway? My head decides now is a good time to start pounding. I adjust the visor again and wait.

"Good morning, sir," says Sue in her best cop voice.

"Morning," I answer. I wait for her to recognize me, but she acts like she doesn't. I guess they got so many murder suspects running in and out of that station, we must all blur together after a while.

"May I have your driver's license and registration, please?"

What I want to do is slam the door open on her so she doubles over, then coldcock the back of her head. But I know that's no solution, and besides, the door's stuck. So instead I hand her my license which is still in my wallet which is still, thank God, in my pocket. But when I go for the registration, the glove box is empty. Stone empty. I can see the pile of papers and maps and trash lying in the yard near the truck. *Shit.* I think about Jean still sitting there at her kitchen table, and my stomach sprouts wings. It's soaring around in circles inside me. I cross my arms to keep it from zooming around the cab of the truck.

"Registration, sir?" says Robocop.

"I ain't got it," I say, mimicking her flat voice.

"Excuse me?" she says.

"It ain't here."

"Where is it?"

"At home."

"You're supposed to keep the registration in your vehicle at all times, sir," she informs me.

"No shit," I answer. I got no reason for why I say it, except I'm thinking she ought to just shut up and give me the goddamn ticket because I got somewhere I got to be.

"Step out of the vehicle, please." Her voice is hard and cold now.

"Oh, come on. You know who—"

"Step out of the truck."

"The door's stuck. I got to get out the other side."

"That's fine. Just step out and come around the front of the vehicle."

She's giving me a real pain in my ass now, which I may have muttered to Samson on my way across the front seat. He's leaning way out of the truck bed, trying to get a good sniff of old Sue, who's patting his head and waiting for me to get out.

"Follow me, please," she says.

I tell Samson to stay where he is and we walk back to the patrol car. Her ass really is lumpy and awful in those pants, which might account for the crappy attitude. Shoulders are still looking great, though. I got to give her that.

"I'm in a hurry," I tell her.

"You got someplace you got to be?"

"Yeah. A funeral."

"Funeral isn't till one o'clock."

I don't say anything to that, but she looks annoyed now, like I tricked her. So I tell her the truth to soften her up a little.

"I got to get to my sister's house." She's reaching in the patrol car, and stops when she hears this. It's just a little pause, but I see it.

I got to get to my sister's house. I'm breathing through my nose like crazy, not thinking about the time I'm wasting just standing on the side of the road like this. Not thinking about how I could've almost been there by now. Not thinking of breaking Sue's neck just to get away from her.

"You know how fast you were going?" She's pulling out the shit they use to test for drunks. She's gonna put my balls through the wringer, all right.

"Look, I know I was going too fast. I'll take it easy." I hate the sound of my voice almost as much as I hate the sight of her. "This is a family emergency."

She's holding the goddamn mouthpiece at me and telling me to breathe, sir. But I'm in the middle of telling her something, so I push it away from my face. Not really rough, but not really gentle either. She gets on the horn and calls for backup. Then feelings between us get real sore. She tells me I'm under arrest for driving under the influence and I tell her she can go fuck herself because I ain't drunk. That's when she starts telling me my rights and I decide that remaining silent is the way to go. Stupid bitch ain't interested in hearing anything I got to say.

I look at the name by her badge. Platt. I'm about to ask her if she's got a sister named Ella, but I clamp my jaws tight and don't say a word. Must be a family trait, butting into other people's business for a living. I figure out a plan. Once the backup gets here, I'll be as polite and cooperative as I know how to be. That'll make old Sue Platt look like an asshole, which is what she is. So when another patrol car pulls up, I'm just sitting in the back of Sue Platt's car, hands on my knees, looking like an angel. I even give my face a spit wash with the clean part of my shirt.

The other officer is young, blond, pudgy-faced like he still ain't lost his baby fat. They talk awhile outside of earshot. The backup comes and opens my door.

"Your dog bite?" he asks me.

"Only if you make like you're gonna hurt him," I answer in a friendly way.

"Well, we got to get a choke collar and a muzzle on him before we take him into custody."

"He under arrest too?" This gets a little laugh, so I go on. "I promise he ain't drunk."

Pudgy is warming up to me a mile a minute. "It's just that we got to impound both the vehicle and the dog."

"Well, anything I can do to help, just say so." God, I couldn't be more sweet and reasonable. But my brain is spinning in somersaults, thinking how I'm gonna get out of this. If I don't get to Jean in the next fifteen minutes, I'm gonna start screaming like a boiled pig.

"What's his name?" asks Pudgy.

"Samson. You could probably manage the choke collar, but the muzzle's gonna be a problem." I tell him all this like I'm doing my best to help him. But really I'm trying to get him to skip the whole thing for being too much bother.

"Problem, huh?" he says, looking over at my truck where Sue Platt's rubbing Samson under his neck. He's slobbering all over himself, no loyalty at all.

"He's a good dog," I say, "but I tried to get a muzzle on him once and he bloodied me up pretty good."

I know what Pudgy's thinking. I know he wants to drop the whole thing; it's just gonna be a big pain in the ass. And here I am being so friendly and calm. And totally sober too, although I guess they can still smell last night's liquor on me.

"It's regulation, though," he says. "Choke collar and a muzzle."

Pudgy and Sue Platt have another conference out of earshot. They look at Samson, look at me, look at Samson. Time is gushing by and the morning's starting to heat up. Finally Sue comes and leans into the front of the car, grabs the radio. She's calling for a tow truck. *Damn!* Pudgy goes to his squad car and opens the trunk. Sue Platt's blocking half my view, so I have to lean hard to see what he's doing. He's got a rifle in his hand. He's got a goddamn rifle in his hand, and he's walking over to my truck.

"Hey! Hey, wait!" I try to open the car door, but it's locked. Sue Platt won't get out of my way, so I have to lean to see him raise the gun. I holler and bang on the partition between me and the front seat. I'm looking at Samson and screaming now for them to stop it, he'll be a good dog, I promise he'll be good, don't hurt him, when I hear the shot and Samson jumps just a little to the right. He takes two steps sideways, looks around for me, then falls down into the truck bed where I can't see him. I'm screaming and banging my head and my fists into the partition. Sue Platt puts down her radio and pulls out her nightstick.

"You goddamn cunt! You goddamn miserable cunt!" I'm yelling, screaming, hollering my head off. "Stupid bitch, I'll kill you! I'm gonna break your fucking neck!" I know now that I'm not gonna get to Jean. I can feel something awful coming, and I'm not gonna make it to her in time to save her. Everything's over, finished, done. *Samson.*

"Don't you threaten me, buddy," and she hits the metal partition with the stick, just missing my fingers.

"You killed my dog!"

She looks at me like I've lost my mind. "It's a tranquilizer," she says.

I don't hear her, or it doesn't sink in, because I keep telling her again how I'm gonna break her skinny neck and what a stupid goddamn cunt she is. So she yells it at me. "It's a tranquilizer. He's not dead, he's asleep."

This sinks in. This gets in my ear and trots around my brain a few times.

"Oh Jesus," is all I can say, and then relief sucks all the muscle out of me and I lay my head against the window and cry. I don't give a shit who sees me or how much snot rolls down my lip. I cry without the energy to really bawl. Just tears falling out and wandering down my face with no place to go.

Sue Platt walks away from the patrol car, nursing a grudge because I called her some rough names. Through a blur, I see Pudgy carrying a collared, muzzled Samson over to his car. Sue Platt opens the door and they load him into the back seat. He's all limp like water. Then she gets behind the wheel of Pudgy's car, and he walks over toward me. I wipe my face and blow my nose into my shirt. The front door opens and he slides in. I'm never gonna forget, as long as I live, that I near got Samson killed with my big mouth. So I go back to my earlier plan, which is remaining silent.

"I'm sorry about this," says Pudgy. "I know it's a bad day for you and your family." He's surprised at first that I don't answer. But he gets used to the quiet. Samson and Sue Platt stay where they are, waiting for the tow truck to show up. We pull out and drive past them, slow. Watching through the window, it feels like we're going past a car accident. Like it's not real, just a dream. The only thing keeps me sitting quiet and patient all the way into the station is the notion that I get a phone call, and I can call Jean. She'll come and pick me up, post a little bail. We'll get Samson and the truck out of the pound, then go to my house so I can take a shower and change my clothes. And we'll have a talk and we'll get to the funeral on time and everything will be all right. That's my plan at this point, and it seems like it ought to work okay.

Pudgy does the booking. The charges are DUI and resisting arrest. I don't argue, much as I'd like to. Sue Platt comes in a while later and starts writing up a report. She's not talking to me or looking at me or anything. I really caused some hard feelings, and I don't care. I get my phone call, but there's no answer at Jean's house. She doesn't have an answering machine. Nothing but my heart dropping another notch every time it rings. That's when it first occurs to me that maybe I'm wrong. Maybe she ain't been waiting for me all this time. No silence in the world like the dead space between those rings. Maybe I'll find her and she'll tell me to go to hell.

I hang up finally, and now the black panic balloon is blowing up in my chest. Pudgy says I can make another call, but I can't think who to call, who might know where she is. Can't call Billy; he's dead. Can't call Sally; she's gone. Can't call Joe Lee; no telling what he'll do. I think of Randy, but no. Bastard talked to the cops yesterday. Harold. Pudgy gets me another outside line and dials the number for me. More ringing and more stomach sinking. I look up at the station clock. It's nine forty-five already. How the hell did it get so late? Where is everyone? They're all up and over to Ma's house. I don't want to call Ma. I do not want to call Ma.

All through this, I don't see Sheriff Keith anywhere. I want to ask where he is, but I bite my lip and shut up. I'm remaining silent as much as I can. Pudgy dials a third number for me, which is annoying the hell out of Miss Ramrod-up-her-ass. I listen to Ma's phone ringing and ringing, thinking how this is feeling like an episode of *Night Gallery*, when a strange voice answers.

"Ed Lavoe's residence."

Pause.

"Who is this?" I finally ask.

"This is Sherry's sister-in-law," she says.

"Aunt Evelyn?" I squeak. No shit, my voice comes out like a high-pitched fart.

"Ray?"

"Yeah. It's me."

"We were wondering if you were all right," she says.

"I'm fine," I say easily, like this is a casual, friendly call. Sue Platt nicks a glance over at me like she could twist my head till my neck snapped. "I was wondering if Jean was there," I say. Pudgy and Sue Platt exchange a look. It's not my imagination, either. They really do.

"Well, I haven't seen her. Hold on just a minute, okay honey?" I can hear dishes clattering and muffled voices rising and falling through the phone line. Someone's laughter from another room. Just a big, happy family reunion. I can see Ma's kitchen filled with casserole dishes and plastic silverware, people everywhere for her to boss around. I try to make out Jean's voice somewhere in the rumble, but it's useless. My mouth gets dry and I swallow three or four times. I got no idea in the world what I'm gonna say to her. Maybe just tell her to come bail me out and worry about the rest later.

There's a bang in my ear, like someone dropped the phone on the other end. Then Ma's voice saying, "Ray?"

"Hey, Ma. Is Jean there?"

"No, she's not here. Where are you?"

"Harold there?"

"They called a few minutes ago. They're on their way." That means I just missed them. Shit. "Where are you?"

"I'm fine," I say, which is not really an answer. I can't think who else to ask for.

"Where are you, Ray? Are you coming over here or not?"

"Listen, Ma. When Harold gets there, do me a favor, okay?"

"What?"

"Ma?"

"What's the matter? I can hardly hear you." I can tell by her tone that she's not listening to me. She's directing casserole traffic.

"Ma, tell Harold to come to the sheriff's office quick as he gets there."

Ma hollers into the phone, "Sheriff's office? Did they find him? Did they catch the guy?"

What? What the hell? "No, Ma. Hold on a second. They didn't catch the guy." But she's already yelling for Ed. She's completely out of her mind, which is how she gets.

"Ma?"

"I can't hardly hear you, Ray. Hold on." Then her voice is faint as she tells Ed to talk to me. I can feel both Pudgy and Sue Platt trying not to listen.

"Ray?" Ed's voice sounds like it's wearing a little thin.

"Hey, Ed. Do me a favor?" I say.

"What's up?"

"When Harold gets there, send him up to the sheriff's office right away?"

"They catch the guy who did it?"

"I got arrested," I finally say.

There's no answer for a long time. I can hear Ma behind him like a parrot on his shoulder, asking questions.

"Ed?"

"I'll be right there." And he hangs up. That's it. Click, and the casseroles and the family reunion all go dead.

So I'm in the holding cell, which is a first for me. I'm rethinking my plan, figuring what I'm gonna do, what the hell I'm gonna tell Ed. My head hurts, so I lay down for a second. Just to close my eyes. Try counting backward from a hundred to keep my brain empty, occupied. I keep counting, but in my mind I can see Jean. She must have been in the shower when I called. She'll probably wear the cut-off shorts and Detroit Lions T-shirt she wore that summer. Her hair's longer too. There's a ton of people in her house when I get there. I just see the back of her head through the crowd, and she turns and looks smack into my face and smiles. She looks like she might make her way over to me, but then her husband is next to her and she's laughing at something he's saying. Old Whaley is telling me something, and I turn to ask him what time it is. He hands me a shotgun. I know I got to do it quick. I take aim with the gun. I don't remember why I have to do this. I wish I could stop it, but I can't. I pull the trigger. Jean flies up above the crowd and straight at me. Covered in blood from where I shot her in the head, she's flying through the air with her arms out to me, saying my name over and over. I yell for her to leave me alone.

"Mr. Johnson?" I come awake hard, half jumping out of the cot. Pudgy's standing outside the cell. "You okay?"

"Yeah."

"Bad dream?"

"Yeah."

"Yeah." He looks at me all sympathetic, then says, "You want to follow me, please?"

I get up and my shoulder's gone stiff where I skinned the shit out of it. Face is aching too. I'm following Pudgy back out the way we came in, and we pass Sheriff Keith's office. It's got a glass wall separating it from the hallway. He's in there with his back to me, busy hollering at Sue Platt, and I mean hollering hard. This is what I hear before Pudgy hurries me along:

"I'm in Adrian getting the arrest warrant and you're here—" Sheriff Keith.

"He was on his way to her house." Sue Platt.

"—screwing up the entire investigation." Sheriff Keith.

"He was drunk and belligerent." Sue Platt, of course.

"I don't care if he was waggling his dick in your face. You went against—" Sheriff Keith.

That's all I hear, because Pudgy reaches back and takes my elbow, gentle but firm. He looks like he might have been an offensive lineman in high school, so I let him lead me away. But I think I heard enough. Old Sheriff Keith is hatching a surprise for the Johnson family, and Sue jumped the gun. That arrest warrant can't be for me, because I didn't do it. Sue was figuring on holding me here to keep me out of the way until Sheriff Keith had Jean in custody.

I slam the brakes on that line of thinking and follow Pudgy down the hall to the front of the station. Ed's sitting in one of the molded plastic chairs, waiting for me. At first I don't recognize him, because he ain't standing next to Ma. He looks like someone else right now, like someone who has his own grandchildren, his own business, a big circle of friends that I'm never gonna meet. I try to think if Ed was someone who I knew from over to the metalworks, what kind of guy would I think he was? If he wasn't married to Ma, would I like Ed or think he was an asshole? He looks up from the floor and right at me. It's the first time we ever looked at each other. I can tell he's thinking the same thing. *If this wasn't Sherry's kid . . .*

"Hey, Ed."

"Ray. Looks like you're all set," he says, putting a hand on each knee to push himself up out of the chair. Pudgy makes me sign fifty forms. Turns out the charges were dropped. Free to go with no bail, and forms for getting Samson and the truck with no fines.

I tell Pudgy so long, and me and Ed head out into the front lobby, where they got a gum ball machine and posters for the Policemen's Labor Day Pig Roast coming up. I'm counting how many minutes it'll take before me and the truck and Samson all roll into Jean's front yard.

"Say, Ray?" It's Sheriff Keith, catching up with us. Ed's halfway out the front door, so he just keeps right on going after a nod to both of us, a nod that says he'll be waiting in the car. I'm pretty much feeling like the injured party here, and for once it's easy to keep my mouth shut.

"Jeez, I'm sorry about all that," he says. I don't say anything. I'd say that it was all right, but it ain't all right. And it won't be until I'm out of this building and back on the road.

"I know you got a hard day coming up," Sheriff Keith goes on. "I'm sorry about it."

It feels good to be quiet. Not to care what he thinks, not to be afraid. So I figure what the hell, since I really ain't afraid anymore, I say, "Where were you this morning?"

"Had to drive over to Adrian," he shoots back, smooth as butter.

"What'd you go to Adrian for?"

"Police business."

"You went for a warrant," I tell him, not believing my ears.

"I'm sorry about it," he says again.

"Sorry for what?"

"Oh hell," he sighs, like he's giving up. "Folks tell me good morning on the street. Most times, they're thinking about how they're gonna pay the electric bill, or getting that filling fixed that fell out last night while they were eating pork chops. Or maybe they're thinking about a divorce, or they're waiting for a call from the doctor, telling 'em whether it's cancer or not. Can't help but have all these secret things in your head every day, stuff you aren't gonna say out loud, stuff no one's gonna care about but you."

Something's bothering him. I don't take my eyes off his face. He doesn't seem that much older than me, even though he's got a teenage son. I wonder where he's from, how he met his wife, why he ended up here.

"But something like this happens, someone gets killed, and it all breaks free. People are given permission to let it out, tell the truth. Like a hard punch upside the head, and you might as well talk because no one's fooled anymore. I got people telling me who they're seeing on the side, how much they had to borrow for that new SpeedJet, how their daughter's seeing a shrink doctor over to Adrian once a week. Like the whole town's a boil that's burst open."

"Who's the warrant for?" I ask him.

"The reason I'm not telling you," he says, "I want to keep you out of it much as I can."

Right. It's not that he doesn't trust me, it's for my own good.

"I got to go," I tell him. He reaches out his hand and shakes mine like he means it. I do too. I do mean it.

"Sue ain't so bad," he's telling me. "She just got it wrong this time."

TWENTY-FOUR

I head out into the August morning, which is bright like another planet. Ed pulls up with the Buick and I climb in. It smells new inside.

"Where to?" he says. He means where's the truck. I pull a bunch of forms out of my back pocket, look them over, and give him the name of the towing service. I'm dying for a smoke, but I don't want to stink up Ed's new car. I just want to get this over and get away from him. But on the drive over there, Ed surprises the hell out of me. He says, "When you said you got arrested, I thought it was you who killed Billy."

I'm so surprised I don't absorb the words. They bounce off me, off the windshield, the steering wheel, like Ping-Pong balls when they draw the lotto numbers. I don't say a word. We're driving along Sullivan Street, which is the way to the towing yard and also the way out to Jean's. The morning sun is low and putting a hell of a glare across the hood of the car. I want to roll the window down and get a little breeze on my face, but he's got the air conditioner on. The towing yard isn't for another ten blocks or so, but he slows down and pulls into an empty parking lot next to Peterson's Hardware. I figure he's got to pick up something quick for Ma. He parks against the brick side of the building, with the Beech-Nut Chewing Gum ad painted on it fifteen feet high.

Ed turns off the ignition, but he doesn't get out of the car. I wish he'd hurry up, because we're only about three miles from Jean's house and I could practically walk out there from here. But no, he's not moving. I'm gonna have to sit through a lecture. I keep my eyes on the second *e* in Beech-Nut. The sign's been on that wall since I can remember.

I'm waiting to hear all about how I let Ma down and she's gonna need me to be strong and stand by her today and what the hell was I doing driving drunk first thing in the morning and who knows what the hell else he's gonna lay on me. It's too bad, because I was leaning toward liking Ed. He must be needing a lot of nerve bolstering, because he's just sitting there scratching his knee and thinking. It's starting to look like we'll be here all day if someone doesn't say something.

"Look, Ed," I start. But he starts up at the same time and cuts me off.

"You have to figure someone did it, right?" he says. "It sure wasn't an accident." He pauses like he wants an answer. I tell him no, it wasn't an accident. The sun's baking that Beech-Nut sign, beating it into those crumbly bricks.

"I know it's not your way to talk about things," he says. "Your mom and you kids, not a lot gets discussed." I almost give a snort at this one, but I don't.

"So I don't expect you to say anything to me or anyone else." What the hell does that mean? I'm staring straight in front of me, not moving a muscle. I couldn't turn my head and look at him for anything on earth. I can tell by how his voice is hitting off the windshield that he's doing the same thing.

"Your mom's had too much," he goes on. I feel my jaw tighten, so I start counting to ten. Ed's voice rides up and down the numbers in my head. "I don't want to see her hurt any more." *Two, three, four.* "Losing Billy is hard enough on her," he says. "And I'll tell you right now." *Seven, eight.* "She's not going to stand it if someone she loves goes to prison for it."

This ain't what I was expecting. My eyes have dropped down to the *G* in "Gum" on the wall. Someone put a "Keep on Truckin' " sticker smack in the center of it, like Billy used to have on his Harley hat. What the hell is Ed saying? I could hop out of the car now, go get my truck, and to hell with him. But I don't move. Finally he lands hard on what he's been trying to say.

"I have money I keep in the house for emergencies. I brought it with me." He scratches his knee for a few seconds while he's thinking some more. "I want you to hold on to it." I wait, but he doesn't say anything else. More knee scratching.

"I don't need no money," I say.

"If you don't need it, maybe you know better than me if someone does." He keeps going fast so I won't interrupt. "Tell you the truth, I don't care who killed him. But your mom, well . . ." He doesn't finish. "Just hold on to it. If there's no call for it, give it back in a month or so."

I'm staring at the "Keep on Truckin' " guy, at his big nose and long beard and buggy eyes. There's a wasp banging himself against the brick, like those buggy eyes are some kind of flower.

"All right, then," I say after a while. All right, then. He pulls something out of the inside pocket of his windbreaker and hands it to me. It's a white envelope, sealed. For a second it feels like a movie. Or Ginch Littlefield. It doesn't feel real. I tuck it inside the waist of my jeans, under my shirt.

"It's four thousand dollars," he tells me. "Not much, but it's cash."

Jesus, I can't get over old Ed keeping four thousand dollars cash around the house. It occurs to me again how I don't know this guy at all.

"Thanks." There's nothing else I can say. Ed starts up the Buick, and the air-conditioning blows out on my bare arms, giving me the shivers so hard the whole seat shakes.

"You okay?" he wants to know.

"Yeah." But I ain't okay. I feel the envelope against my stomach, and now I'm a fugitive. Now I'm guilty. Now I'm wanted for something and I ain't even sure what it is. We pull away from the Beech-Nut Gum and head out of the parking lot. Neither of us ever said her name, but we both know there's only one kid left after me.

My truck is parked right by the front gate at the towing yard. It seems all right, but there's a look about it, small and foreign, like seeing yourself naked in front of a bunch of strangers. Paul Jorgenson comes out with the keys.

"Hey, Ray," he says. "Norm called, said you were on your way."

Norm? Must be Pudgy. Poor guy, with all his baby fat and a name like Norm. I hand Paul the papers I signed and he holds the keys out with his plastic right hand. Lost the real one in a combine when he was thirteen. He was a year behind Jean in school.

"Ain't none of my business, but I'm sorry," he says.

"What?"

"I'm sorry about your brother," he says again.

"Oh. Yeah. Thanks." Wonder if I'm gonna keep forgetting I have a dead brother for the rest of my life. I walk over to the Buick, and Ed's window fades down.

"I'm all set," I tell him.

"Go get yourself cleaned up," he tells me. "I'll see you in a bit."

"Yeah, I'll see ya." I reach my hand in and set it on his shoulder for a second. "Thanks."

"That's all right," he says. I step away from the car, the window fades back up, and the Buick ghosts out onto Sullivan Street.

I walk once around the truck, checking for I don't know what, but I don't find anything, so I check the driver door. It opens smooth as you please. I don't know how I knew it would, but I knew. Try it a few more times. All fixed. I climb in and measure the distance to Jean's house. I can go pick up Samson after I've talked to her. I start up the truck and ease to the edge of the driveway, about to head out on Sullivan. Then I see the turn of Samson's head when he looked around for me, right before he fell over in the back of the truck. Shit. It'll just take second. And I can call Jean from a pay phone at the pound.

I start up the truck and pull out heading west, with the sun behind me. It's a small miracle, not having the damn glare in my eyes. I'm not feeling too good now. That lump I got in my gut ain't going away, and it's starting to get clammy around my forehead, like the flu. All I need is some sleep. The pound is next door to the sheriff's office, it turns out. Makes sense, putting the dog jail next to the people jail.

I go inside and try to look respectable for the woman behind the counter. Her name badge says "Kathy." She seems awful old to be a Kathy. She's looking me up and down pretty hard behind tinted eyeglasses. Big plastic ones like Elvis wore just before he died. She's got little gold letters glued to the corner of the lenses. K.A.K. Kathy Ann Komenski. Katherine Angela Kirkland. Kathleen Arlene King. At any rate, she's taking in the bloody shirt and the general state of my appearance, and she ain't liking it.

I hand over my forms, fill out some new ones she hands me, and sit down to wait. They got pamphlets about dog adoption and rabies and shit. All of them have a picture of a golden retriever and a kid on the cover. Usually a little boy, sometimes a little girl, but always a golden retriever. There's a dumb dog for you. I close my eyes and lean my head back against the painted cinder-block wall. Think about what I'm gonna say to Jean when I catch up to her. I got no idea what I'm gonna say to her. None.

"Mr. Johnson?"

I open my eyes, and Kathy's glaring at me from behind that wall of tinted plastic glasses. I stand up, walk over to the counter.

"When did he last have his rabies shot?"

"I don't know. Couple years ago."

"Do you have the paperwork on that?"

There are some words that sound bad anytime, and "paperwork" is one of them. But coming out of Kathy's mouth, it's like she said, "Why don't you eat a handful of baby shit."

"No, I don't," I tell her.

"Well, he's supposed to have his vaccination tag," she says, real snotty.

"Yeah, well he don't wear a collar," I tell her. "I got the tag at home." Somewhere.

"I need to see one or the other," she says. "The paperwork or the tag."

"You're not gonna see one or the other, 'cause they ain't here. They're at home."

"I can't release the animal without proof of rabies vaccination. You're gonna have to—"

I tell her he ain't just some animal, his name is Samson. I tell her what's gonna happen to her if I don't see Samson in about one minute. I tell her what Sheriff Keith is gonna do to her, and I tell her what I'm gonna do to her. Her Elvis glasses wobble up and down, she's so surprised. I'm surprised too, but I keep going. I tell her a few more things I'm gonna do to her, and that's when she picks up the phone, punches a button, and asks to speak to Sheriff McCutcheon, please. She don't take her eyes off me and I don't take mine off her. I want to ask if her maiden name's Platt. I hate her. I don't hear what she says into the phone. I don't hear anything except the blood rushing back and forth between my ears. It's got to be getting on to ten-thirty or eleven. I got to find my sister and bury my brother, and she won't hand over a lousy dog.

"Give me my dog," I yell like a two-year-old. I knock over a cardboard heartworm display, and pamphlets fan out across the counter, dribbling golden retrievers onto the floor.

"You settle yourself down, mister," says Kathy, hanging up the phone.

Right about then the door opens and a lady walks in, holding a leash. Kathy and I both go into a deep freeze as the lady comes up to the counter, stepping over the pamphlets.

"I'm here for Hoodoo."

"Terrific," says Kathy, with a smile that makes me want to slap her jaw around behind her head. "Just have a seat."

The lady sits down, with the empty leash on her lap. Kathy hollers down the hall for someone to bring Hoodoo out. Don't know why she's yelling, since half a dozen coworkers are lurking just behind the open door that says "Authorized Personnel Only," listening to me carry on. One of them trots off to get Hoodoo.

"Give me my dog," I tell her, low and mean as a badger.

"Who's your vet?" she says, all professional and smooth now that we have an audience.

"Don Watersmith."

"You wouldn't happen to have his number on you now, would you?" I'm picking up a definite odor all of a sudden. Can't tell if it's her or me, but it's thick.

"No, I wouldn't."

"Well, hold on a minute then."

"You gonna give me my dog?"

"Yes, if you'll shut up."

I'm a little surprised she told me to shut up straight out like that. Surprised enough to stand there quiet while she looks up Dr. Watersmith's number. You'd think they'd have it around somewhere, him being a vet. The smell's getting worse, and I figure it's got to be me. I walk back and forth along the counter, stinking up the place as much as I can.

She's getting the rabies shot confirmed over the phone when a door opens into the waiting room and one of the pound flunkies comes out, holding an animal. He's got it wrapped in a big old towel so he won't have to touch it, on account of that's where the stink's coming from. It ain't me after all. I stop pacing and watch the flunky hand Hoodoo over to the lady. She shakes the towel off and it's the biggest gray squirrel I ever saw in my life. About twenty pounds easy. The lady's making a bunch of baby sounds about Hoodoo this and Hoodoo that and hugging and petting this thing, and it stinks like it ate something dead and now it's farting it out. It meows. It's no squirrel; it's a damn cat. Got one eye missing and a big old clump of matted fur and mud on its back hip. Gray tail like a squirrel's, only twice as wide around. Face all torn up and one leg gone crooked. The lady's making a fuss over him and he's sitting on her lap with his scabby shoulders all hunched and his yellow eye half closed.

I look at him. He looks at me.

"You got to sign this, please." That's Kathy, nice as pie. The lady finishes putting the leash on old Hoodoo, sets him down on the chair next to her, and comes up to the counter.

"That's three times now in five months," says Kathy. "You know we got rules about controlling your pets."

The lady signs a paper. She has perfect fingernails. A professional manicure, it looks like. "He tore the screen out of the window," she says.

"Next time we'll have to fine you."

The lady laughs, a proud parent. "I just can't seem to keep him in the house."

"Try," says Kathy.

I look over at Hoodoo hunched in the chair, going from one jail to another. I look at the lady's arm as she hands the pen back to Chatty Kathy. The wrist and forearm are all torn up with old scars and fresh scratches. Looks real bad next to the blood-red manicure, like she did it to herself.

Kathy must have noticed the same thing, because she chirps, "You ought to have him put to sleep."

"C'mon now." The lady laughs at Kathy. "How would you like it if someone murdered you the next time you acted up—" She breaks off, shoots a look at me, and turns red like a balloon about to pop. "Sorry," she says to me. She goes over and picks up Hoodoo, who stays stiff like he's stuffed with cement. She shoots out the door without another word. I get one last glimpse of Hoodoo, looking back over her shoulder with death in his eyes. That leaves just me and Kathy, who's eyeballing me top to toe, like I have my fly wide open or something. The whole town may know about Billy getting killed, but old Kathy ain't putting two and two together. For some reason, that makes me hate her a little less.

"Give me my goddamn dog, will ya?"

She doesn't even bother to answer, just grabs my forms off the counter and huffs and fluffs back through the Authorized Personnel Only door. I want to run outside and try the pay phone, but I'm afraid of what she'll do to Samson if I'm not there when she brings him out. Cut his throat all over the tile floor maybe. I reach in my back pocket, but Ginch Littlefield ain't there. Can't remember what I did with him. I sit down and lean my head against the cinder-block wall again. Close my eyes and think about the sparkles on Sally's ice cream cone, the bangs hanging in Deena's eyes, the dead and bloated raccoon out on Junction 10 by Billy's house, Whaley's red eyelids sagging and wagging back and forth. About how much I'd like to set Hoodoo on that worthless tiger cat of Jean's. About Bojo, and how Lula chewed the emerald eyes off of him later that summer and Ma and Jean pasted them back on. About how Jean's out to her house right now waiting for me, and I open the back screen door but Billy's already there and he's sitting at the kitchen table and Jean's standing over the sink washing dishes and she won't turn around to look at me even when I say her name over and over, and Billy's holding the glass with the red chickens and laughing and laughing because Jean's dead now too.

I come awake with a jerk, banging my head against the cinder-block. Samson's coming through the door on a leash that the flunky snaps off as soon as they're clear of the door.

"Samson!" I say, like I ain't seen him in months. He walks over to me, sits close to my leg, yawns. Still groggy from the dope. I scratch his good ear, and his tail slaps like a flyswatter on the tile. "Let's go, boy."

And out we go without a look back. If there's any more forms to sign, fuck her.

TWENTY-FIVE

First thing I notice is Jean's truck is not in the driveway, and it's not in the back. I open the driver's door, telling Samson to stay where he is. He climbs through the back window into the truck bed and stretches out on the hot metal, grinning, glad to be a free dog again. Second thing I notice is all her flowers are gone. The place is green and bare, no starbursts of color anywhere. They all been cut right off. Pointy stems stick out of the ground, up the sidewalk and around the porch. No hanging fuchsia, no wild roses climbing up the trellis. It's all been stripped away. I open the screen and knock on the wooden frame of the kitchen door. No answer. I try the knob and it opens with an old-wood groan.

"Jean?" I holler into the house. It has that quiet of an empty house in summer. She's got breakfast dishes drying in the drainer, a checkered dish towel tossed over the edge of the sink.

"Jean?" All the windows are wide open, and there's a good cross-breeze going from the kitchen into the living room. Yellow curtains blow out above the sink, and white ones suck in above the couch, flapping themselves back against the screen like fish tails. I go to the stairs and holler up to the bedroom.

"Jean?" I wait, but there's no sound of her. I take the stairs two at a time, get dizzy so I have to lean against the wall in the upstairs hallway. The bedroom door is open. More breezes blowing more curtains, blue and white this time. The bed's made, with a white bedspread in that nubby pattern like Ma had years ago. I think what it'd feel like to lay myself down on that bed and close my eyes. The breeze in here is cool and cucumbery. It's still and peaceful and I can smell Jean in every room. Whatever's kept me awake the past twenty-four hours is leaking out my ears now, because I just want to lay down and die in this house, in this bedroom, on this white nubby bedspread.

I never been in this bedroom before. The curtains are a bunch of blue windmills and wooden shoes against a white background. Dresser made of bird's-eye maple, with a matching mirror over it. She must have stripped it down and refinished it herself, because it's in too good a shape for as old as it is. Not much on the dresser except a clock radio which I check, alarm set for 6:00 A.M. But the thing that stands out is a photograph of me and her. We're sitting on the back porch of the house on Cutler Road when we were about six and four. I haven't seen that picture since I don't know. And now here it is, old and fuzzy like we're a couple of ghost kids staring back at me. Jean's wearing a yellow dress with tiny white polka dots all over it. She wore that dress every day for near a month that summer. It was just a sleeveless dress with a full skirt down to her scabby knees, but she said nothing bad could happen to her in that dress, it had magic in it. Maybe she was right, because I don't remember anything bad happening that summer. She even wore it to bed. Put on her pj's until Ma tucked her in, then got out of bed and put the dress on over her pj's. When Ma took it away to wash it, Jean screamed like someone was scalding her. Said Ma was trying to kill her.

Now here she is grinning at me out of the picture with that magic yellow dress on, sitting next to the ghost me on the porch. I got one arm around her sunburned shoulder and Ma's trying to get us to look decent. But I'm crossing my eyes and acting up, and Jean's giggling and pulling her bangs straight back off her forehead and sticking her tongue out. Finally Ma snaps the picture right when we run out of goofing around to do, and there we are, smiling and looking straight at the camera. About a half hour after that picture's took, I get stung on the ear by a wasp and holler "Damn" loud enough for Ma to hear me. She takes me in the bathroom and washes my mouth out with Ivory soap. Scrapes it against the back of my teeth so the taste'll hang around for about a week. Jean's waiting for me when I come out of the bathroom, to see how bad it is. It's plenty bad, but I don't let on like it bothers me. Tell her, "Good thing I didn't say fuck." She laughs so hard she pees her pants, yellow dress and all.

I take a look in the spare room. Nothing but chairs with no one sitting in them, a desk where no one's working, and two dressmaker dummies with no dresses on them. I go back to the bedroom and look out at the yard through the blue windmills. Nothing out there but the lousy tiger cat sleeping by the door of the barn, and one crazy bird swooping up and down under the big oak in the center of the yard, yattering at all the other birds.

I head down the stairs and back toward the kitchen. Open the door to the basement, but all that comes up is the cool, inky smell of cement floors and centipedes. Maybe she's over to Ginny Honey's, helping with the kids. The phone is a rotary-dial phone. It feels serious and heavy like this phone will last forever, which is about how long it takes to dial all seven numbers. I got the phone to my ear, looking out the kitchen window. I see that same bird, a robin, going up and down, round and round that big oak like a merry-go-round pony all glassy-eyed, mane flying. Someone picks up after the second ring.

"Hello?" It's Trish. My brain fills up with everything I want to ask her but can't. "Hello?" This one comes out a notch higher, anxious.

"It's Uncle Ray," I tell her.

"I'll get my mom."

"No, that's all right." I stop her. "I was just wondering if Aunt Jean was over there."

A small pause. "Why?" says this little icy voice.

"Because I got to talk to her before the funeral."

"She in trouble or something?"

"Naw. Is she there?"

"No."

"Trish?"

"Huh?" Voice getting smaller by the minute.

"Can I ask you something?" I'm treading real light. The robin outside is still hopping around that tree like crazy.

"I don't know," she says.

"Why'd you say that you done it?" Little-kid silence on the other end. I can almost see her chewing on a strand of hair, eyebrows bunched together. "Ain't nothing your fault," I say.

She gives a huffy sigh like she's all out of patience. "I asked for it. Every night."

"Asked for what?" I'm trying not to rush her, even though I know Ginny Honey's gonna come in and hang up that phone any second.

"In my prayers every night. Asked for him to go away. I made him die."

"It ain't your fault—"

But the phone line goes dead. I hang up and step out the back door. Over at the oak, that robin's chirping and wailing like a crazy thing. She's all fluttery and skittery and chirpy and upset, with her red chest pumping up and down like a torn-out heart.

"Where? Where?" She shakes her whole body all at once, throws her wings out to each side, and flies straight up into the tree. I take a few steps closer so I can see through the leaves to a newly empty nest. She perches on the edge of it and cranes her neck so her beak is high in the air.

"Where are you?" she cries over and over. The wail flies out in all directions like a radio signal. She falls out of the tree headfirst, skimming the ground in a circle and coming to rest in the same patch of grass.

"Where?" she says softly.

She jerks her head in my direction and tilts it sharp to one side. Looks at me out of one pebbly eye, like a pirate. But I ain't what she's looking for. I'm nothing she's ever thought about or ever will. Not me, or Jean, or Billy. She could care less about any of us.

"Where?" she whispers.

She blinks twice and flies back up to the nest, and then the chirping stops. There's no sound except a few of the nearest leaves brushing against one another, whispering comfort. She's deep in her nest, where no one can see her, and she ain't coming out anytime soon.

●

Jean's got a bad reputation around our town. From what I've been able to put together, she goes along just fine for four or five months, then she finds some guy to take home for the night. The selection ain't so great, but she picks from what's around at the moment and takes him home, fucks him, makes him breakfast, and that's the end of it. I heard it first from Al Halsey, the miserable prick that I laid out up to Dewey's last night before Joe Lee put a cap on the party. Said him and a buddy of his were knocking back some beers and shooting the shit up to the Bowl 'n' Bar with her and some other folks one night. This buddy of his is sniffing around Jean's tree, and she up and says, "Okay, then, let's go," and they leave. Plain as that. Al sees this piece of shit a couple weeks later over to the bike shop and he's telling all about how she took him to her house, to the white bedspread, and fucked his brains out. He wakes up in the morning and she's got fried eggs and sausage and toast with blackberry jelly. He's sitting there in her kitchen thinking what's he got himself in for, because he's already got a girlfriend, the rotten shit. And he's worrying how maybe Jean thinks he's gonna be around now. So he finishes eating and he's on his third cup of coffee, trying to think how best to get his coward's ass out of there. And Jean tells him it's time for him to go because she's got stuff to do and for him not to call her. He says maybe in a couple weeks they could get together and she says no, don't call her. But of course he calls, and she doesn't want to talk to him. He tells Al she wasn't sore or mean about it. Like he was asking if she wanted to buy a used rototiller and she was saying, "No, thanks, got no use for it."

That was the first I heard about it. Years go by and I get the same story about half a dozen more times, always secondhand. No one's got the balls to fuck her and tell me about it to my face. Always hear it through some miserable prick like Al Halsey. And it always ends the same, a kind of offhand no thanks to every one of 'em the next day. It's like Billy telling me about his power of rejection theory. We're out in my garage, going over the carburetor on my truck, and he's telling me why he can get any woman he wants.

"Don't never underestimate the power of rejection," he says. "You tell some bitch to stay the hell away from you, she'll be hanging around like a whipped dog till you finally give it to her."

He's right and I know it. I just couldn't get women to come close enough for me to tell 'em to stay the hell away from me. And with Sally, I was too afraid she'd do like I said and that's the last I'd see of her.

"Your problem, Ray," he says while he tightens a nut with an oily socket wrench, "your problem's that you got to get some balls. You ain't never had any balls."

I ask Jean once if all the stories are true, about her and those guys. We're over to Ma and Ed's house, having cake (German chocolate) and ice cream (butter pecan) for one of the kids' birthdays. Ma don't let us skip the birthdays, ever. Cake and ice cream and presents, even if no one's talking to anyone. She's always kept up appearances real good. It's early summer, so we take our plates onto the deck out back, off the kitchen. Sally's inside helping Kyle get his ice cream away from his cake, because they're soaking together and getting him hysterical. Me and Jean are on the deck, watching Ed showing off the flower garden to Billy and Trish. Billy's got his hand on Trish's shoulder, like he's trying to keep her from floating away, like if he lets go she'll take off sideways and upward like the rose petals blowing around at their feet. Trish keeps her head down.

I tell Jean I heard a couple of these stories, ask her if they're true.

"Yeah," she says through the butter pecan in her mouth. "What about it?"

"You fuck these guys and don't care the whole town knows it?"

"You fuck Sally," she says to me. "Don't the whole town know that?"

"That ain't the same thing," I tell her. Ed's kneeling in the dirt, pinching off old blossoms and checking for bugs. Billy says something and Ed looks up at him and laughs, nodding his head. I wonder what Billy said to make Ed laugh like that. Trish's head stays bent.

"Why ain't it the same thing?" she bulldogs me.

"I love Sally, that's why." I hate the words the second they leave my mouth. Jean stops in midchew for half a second, then goes on like nothing happened. But she's looking at me with eyes that are a rough, ripply green like lake water before a tornado.

"Well, that's real nice, Ray," she says.

"You know what I mean," I say.

"No, I don't," she tells me.

Ginny Honey comes to the sliding screen door and hollers out to Billy does he want ice cream with his cake or not. She has to holler twice, because they're out at the far end of the yard and he ain't paying her any mind. Jean's going at her cake with no problem, but mine is sitting on my knee, soaking up melted ice cream faster than Kyle's. My stomach's closed up good and tight. Billy yells yeah to the ice cream.

"How 'bout you, Ed?" shouts Ginny Honey over my head.

"Just cake'd be fine," Ed hollers back at her.

"Come on and get it, then," Ginny Honey bellows, and she returns to the kitchen after a look at me and Jean.

"I don't like it," I tell Jean when Ginny Honey's out of earshot.

"Don't like what?" asks Jean.

"You and them guys," I tell her, keeping my eyes on the three out in the garden.

"No one asked you to like it." She says it like my opinion ain't important enough for her to get mad about. So I try a more direct hit.

"Ginny Honey says half the town calls you a slut." I'm being a shit, but I can't stop. I take a bite of cake. It's sawdust in my mouth. Jean's shielding her eyes with her free hand, looking out toward the garden like I am.

"What does the other half call me?" she says in a smart-ass voice.

"A whore, I guess." But I got a mouth full of sawdust cake, so it comes out like "A whoo-ah, ah gush."

Jean turns her head toward me, surprised.

"A whoo-ah?" she says. Our eyes meet, and we're laughing together, hard enough for me to damn near blow German chocolate frosting out my nose.

"God, Ray, you're such an asshole," she says once she catches a little breath. Ma calls out from the kitchen, wanting to know what's so funny.

"Ray called me a whoo-ah," Jean tells her.

Silence from the kitchen and Ma says, "A what?"

Trish is looking up at us from the end of the yard. Ed's got his nose buried in a white iris. Jean gets up and goes into the kitchen. Pulling back into herself, away from me.

TWENTY-SIX

I light a smoke. Stand there on her flagstone walk and think where she is. What if Sheriff Keith already arrested her when I saw him at the station? What if I been moving further away from her every minute since I left there? What if she doesn't want anything to do with me once I find her? I cross my arms hard and inhale deep on my Salem. Fingers feel for the skin inside the crook of my elbow. Pinch hard and don't let go till the whole arm is tingling like there's ginger ale in my veins. I make sure the kitchen door's closed tight, walk back to the truck. I'm just gonna drive straight over to Ma and Ed's house. No more screwing around.

It won't start. I turn it over three or four more times, not believing it. *What the fuck?* I jump out. Can't think straight. Whistle for Samson, but he's disappeared. The cat's gone too, so there's no mystery there. They could be anywhere by now. Jesus, everything's going all to shit and I gotta get to Ma's house. I run once around the yard, hollering for Samson. Jump in the truck and try her again. Nothing but a thin whine and a battery running low to boot. *Shit!* I get out and slam the door hard enough so it'll never open again.

It's about three miles into town. If no one stops to pick me up, I'll hit Carter's Diner in about an hour. Find someone to give me a lift west a mile or so out to Ma and Ed's. It's got to be getting on toward noon or something close to it. I'm never gonna make it walking. I'm too tired, too hungry, too tired and hungry and confused. I can't remember where I'm supposed to be, and where the hell is Sally anyway? When Sally's around, I don't get confused like this. When Sally's around, I eat and sleep when I'm supposed to.

I walk along the dirt of the driveway, looking down at the steel toes of my boots as they slide in and out of my sight with each step. It's the same powdery, pebbly dirt as the shoulder of North Lake Road. There's even the same leftovers of broken beer bottles, brown bits of glass like drops of dried blood. How long ago was that? Two, three days? Four? Why was I looking for Billy? I been all full of questions for him until he's in front of my face and all I can think to do is tell him to go to hell. When Ginny Honey first said he was dead, I was just surprised. Like you'd be surprised if you're raking leaves and the rake disappears when you're in midswing. Like if you're working on a rose trellis for the side of the porch and the whole thing disappears when you're nailing the third slat to the cross-beam. You're looking down at empty hands and you can't finish what you started and you thought you had all the time in the world. But hell no, you don't.

I thought if I could just have a minute alone with the coffin up to Snell's, then maybe I could talk to him and feel okay about him disappearing in midswing. But it's no use. I'm never gonna be able to finish what I started with him. Tears are prickling behind my eyeballs, and I let 'em come.

Billy was a rotten prick, but that was just Billy. He caught me out back of the garage with a pack of the old man's Salems. Taught me how to inhale. Covered for me when I got sick and threw up two hours later at the dinner table, said there was a bug going around at school. He'd fish the old man's *Playboy*s out of the trash and let me have them when he was done. He taught me to swing a baseball bat like it was one of them spiked balls on the end of a chain like they used with suits of armor. Guaranteed line drives dropping just short of the center fielder. He told me every single detail the first time he fucked a girl. Sandy Ottman, on the floor of her parents' family room, with *Saturday Night Live* blaring to drown them out and her yippy little cockapoo dog sitting two feet away, watching and whining.

He didn't deserve killing. No matter what he done. Then I see Trish's sharp little face. I see her eyes looking back at me, her thinking I was gonna come after her next. That eleven-year-old stony face already knowing she ain't good for nothing else. Did she deserve that?

Jean, what did you do? Because I know now, I've known all along, that it's Jean who killed Billy. How could she, though? Not that she's not strong enough. Me and Billy's the skinny ones. Jean takes after some other part of the family, the part that's got some heft and muscle to them. She could squash skinny old Billy like a worm on the sidewalk, no problem there. But the feel of the rock, the weight of it coming down—I can't imagine it. I hit the end of the driveway and step out onto Sullivan Road.

I look down and see Billy lying half in the ditch, half on the shoulder. He's got blood on the side of his head, dripping down over his eyebrow like a raw egg. He's calling me a bitch and telling me he's gonna kill me. I swing my boot back and send a kick straight into his face. Blood shoots out of his mouth and he rolls down into the ditch. He don't say anything now. I got a rock in my hand and I never felt so happy in my life, so strong. He lifts his head. I raise the rock high above me, drop to my knees, bring it down hard. He grunts and stays down this time.

I'd picked him up at Dewey's, told him Ma was sick. Said I'd drive him to the hospital. He was blind drunk and weak. So I opened his door, shoved him out onto North Lake Road with my truck going 100 mph. Pulled into the woods and set out to find him laying here in the ditch.

And now here we are in the weeds, breathing hard.

"Sorry now?" I ask him.

"Fuck you" comes out all bubbly because of the blood and the spit rolling down his chin.

"Say you're sorry," I tell him, waving the rock near his nose.

"Bitch." He's getting his bearings back, leaning on his elbows toward me. The rock comes down again as his hand clamps onto my leg. It lands solid and makes a sound like if you dropped a clay pot wrapped in a towel, muffled but with no doubt that it's broke. His hand stays clamped above my knee. I pull each of his fingers back until he lets go, and his hand drops into the dirt, raising a little dust cloud. My lungs are swollen up like yellow daises full of happy. My arms tingle light and airy, like tiny ants marching.

"Sorry now?" I whisper, bending low over his ear, close so I smell the blood spreading down along his ear, his jaw, his neck. I can tell he's trying to say something, because bubbles are foaming out of his mouth again. I lean in even closer. "Jean," he says. "Jean?"

"I'm right here," I whisper tender to him.

He whips out quick as a snake and grabs a handful of my hair. Yanks it down so my neck's twisted and I'm looking up at the trees. And behind them, a black sky with gray clouds wisping.

"Kill you." His voice is just a wet hiss next to my head. I still got the rock in my hand. My aim is off because my head's all twisted around, but I bring my arm up sideways and graze the left side of his face. Then my head is free and I sit up, scootching out of reach. I light a cigarette, taking a minute. He's breathing all wet and ploppy, his head swollen and turning different colors.

"Hang in there, Billy," I tell him, biting the Marlboro at the corner of my mouth. "We ain't done."

"Who you talking to?" I look around and there's Whaley's truck inching along next to me on the side of the road. "Ray, you okay?"

I look closer and there's Whaley inside the truck. I turn and look for Billy, but he's not in the ditch and there's no rock in my hand, no blood, nothing. Just me walking down Sullivan Road.

"Where's your truck?" He's raising his voice like I'm deaf. I can tell he's getting a little pissed.

"Back at Jean's," I say. My throat's dry and swollen and I sound like Clint Eastwood in *A Fistful of Dollars*.

"Broke down?" he yells.

"Yeah."

"Git in." Whaley's truck is a brand-new Dodge Ram Charger. It's big. About as big as one of them buses they got for the mentally retarded kids to go to school in. Time I yank that big door open, I'm wondering where I'm gonna get the sprint to climb up into the seat. I lean my head against the hot metal for a second.

"You sick?" says Whaley, not hollering as loud now.

"Yeah."

"Here." Whaley clamps his left hand on the wheel and leans across the seat, with his right hand out to me. I reach up and he grabs my wrist, uses the leverage he's got with his left hand on the wheel, and pulls me into the truck. His grip is like a steel clamp, like he has one of them metal hooks they give Paul Jorgenson when he first lost his arm in the combine, before they give him the fake plastic arm. Like a red-tailed hawk getting a grip on a field mouse. I swoosh up and onto the seat of the truck, half expecting Whaley to start yanking off my skin with his beak. He's looking at me over his drippy red eyelids.

"Thanks," I say, letting my head drop back on the seat. I wait for him to put the truck in gear, but we're just sitting there.

"Who were you talking to?" he says, friendly.

"When?"

"Just now, when I pulled up."

"Oh." I try to think. Who was I talking to just now? I was on the side of the road, doing something. Oh, right. "Billy."

Whaley nods. My stomach's prowling around like a cranky grizzly bear, so I got to look away from the runny eyelids. I don't want to get sick in Whaley's big new truck.

"I'm heading into town," he says.

"Okay."

"Where you going?"

"Ma's."

"You want me to drive you round there?"

"Ah God, Whaley." And I lean so my head's resting on the window, close my eyes.

"Okeydokey," he says, putting the truck in gear. Whaley's got air-conditioning just like Ed, so the window's rolled up tight. I'm shivering with the cold air blowing on me. Whaley tells me to close the vents or turn 'em to blow on him. I look at the dashboard in front of me and it's like the control panel of a little four-seater airplane I went up in one time. I don't even start poking around trying to find air vents.

That money Ed gave me, the criminal money in the white business envelope, the four thousand dollars cash, is in my truck. I stuck it in the glove compartment. Thanks, Ed. Thanks anyway.

"Can you drop me off at Ma's?" I ask Whaley. I can't remember if I told him where we were going.

"Sure," answers Whaley.

There's a smell in the truck, under the metal smell of the air-conditioning. Like dust. Smells like rooms that no one's been in for a while, all dusty and clammy feeling. Smells a little like Elizabeth

Rollins, the dead old lady I saw the other night. She was close to Whaley's age.

"You know anyone named Elizabeth Rollins?" I ask him.

"No." He frowns, thinking about all the people he knows and the ones he don't know. Which gets me to thinking about all the people I don't know. Folks who don't know me or Jean or Billy, and probably wouldn't care much if someone was to tell 'em I was going to Billy's funeral and how he got killed. Just a story from some other part of the country, far as they're concerned. All of a sudden it's my whole life, the beginning and middle and end of my whole life, and they might read about it in the paper over breakfast and then skim on to the day's weather, giving it no thought at all. This line of thinking is making my stomach slide around inside me. Got a life of its own these days.

"Who's that?" Whaley wants to know.

"Who's what?"

"Elizabeth Rollins."

"Some lady up to Snell's, died same day as Billy," I tell him.

"Was she killed?"

"I think it was old age," I say. "She was pretty old."

"How old?"

"Old like you."

"Oh, Elizabeth Sharpely." Whaley nods. "Yeah, I knew her."

We drive along quiet for a while, coming up on town. Whaley turns left and skirts up Left Street, which is really a dirt road you cut into when you don't want to get into the whole business of Main Street, like if you had too much to drink and you'd just as soon skulk home the side way.

"I thought it said her name was Elizabeth Rollins," I finally say.

"She married Carl Rollins summer after my sister married Gil Fletcher," Whaley tells me. "Bettie Sharpely. Good-looking girl. She's passed on now."

I tell him how I sort of stumbled on her the other night.

"Ain't seen Bettie since she . . . since she . . . well, let me think."

I let Whaley think. It's nice that he knew her. I feel better about her being dead. I feel better about the clammy smell of dust in the truck, about the fact that Whaley's gonna die someday pretty soon and the same people I was thinking about a minute ago won't even read about it over breakfast. I feel better because I know Whaley and Bettie Sharpely'll be somewhere shooting the shit, not minding being dead the way Billy minds it.

"She was Catholic," I tell him.

"Oh, well sure." Whaley nods slow, like that's the most obvious thing about her. "Well, yeah. And she went ahead with that divorce, see. That was talked about for a time. Long time, actually."

We're passing the Little Creek Party Store. I was there earlier today. Or yesterday. I was there not long ago, and Randy's brother wasn't working.

"Weren't hardly no divorce back in your 1930s, you know," Whaley's telling me. "Weren't no divorce in our town anyway. And them Catholics, it just don't never happen, 'cause they send you straight to hell."

"Who?" I ask.

"Who?" Whaley asks back.

"Who went to hell?" I ask him.

Whaley thinks for a minute. "No one," he says finally. "But Bettie gets tossed out of the Catholics. Comes to the Lutherans down the street 'cause that's as close as you're gonna get to the nuns and priests now, I guess."

I nod slow, putting the whole story together. They never bury real Catholics up to Snell's. I knew something was wrong with her.

"What was the divorce for?"

"Bettie's?"

"Yeah." I'm so happy now, talking about our friend Bettie.

"Carl Rollins was a mean old shit." That's all Whaley's gonna say about that. So she divorced a mean old shit and they wanted to send her to hell for it.

"Ain't like she killed him," I figure.

"Wouldn't have been no tragedy if she did," Whaley says real loud. He looks disgusted. Old Carl Rollins must've been a world-class mean old shit.

"Mean as Billy?" I ask him.

"What's that?"

"Carl Rollins," I say. "Was he mean as Billy was?"

Whaley squeezes the steering wheel a couple of times in his little talon grip. He's thinking hard now.

"Don't know," he finally tells me. "Couldn't tell you for sure."

I think about how it wouldn't have been no tragedy if Bettie had killed mean old Carl Rollins. On the one hand you got the whole commandment of You Shalt Not Kill. No one deserves killing, especially if it's someone you love. Some folks'd say Jean's got to be punished. On the other hand you got a miserable prick who fucked his own kid and wasn't about to be sorry, let alone change. Which would lead other folks to say he deserved killing and Jean ought to get a reward.

But maybe there's something between the two. Something like it's no tragedy what she did. I chew on that one for a bit.

"We're about there," Whaley says.

"What time is it?" I ask.

Whaley looks at the clock in the dashboard. I hadn't seen it in the middle of all them airplane dials.

"Getting on close to noon," he tells me. We're coming up on Ma and Ed's neighborhood now. It's a sort of a fancied-up subdivision called Forest Glen Estates, and it's considered real swank because all the houses are set back in some trees and they made a little lake in the middle. Just a cheesy pond with a couple of ducks, really. Between the water and the trees, the mosquitoes make the place damn near unlivable. Ed got himself a lot at the end of the development, so his backyard stretches out about a hundred feet. He likes his vegetable garden and his rows of little fuchsia bushes along the back deck, the morning glories creeping up and over the cedar fence on the far side of the driveway. Him and Jean'll get talking about planting perennials and how soon to put the daffodil bulbs down, and you might as well go inside and watch some football for all the conversation you're gonna get. I think about that money Ed gave me. Wonder if it was just on account of Jean's green thumb. Like there's some sort of secret gardeners brotherhood like with the Masons.

Whaley pulls up near the house and there's cars all in the driveway and up and down the street. Nice cars. I don't see Ed's Buick, but there's some Lincoln Town Cars and even a Cadillac. A handful of minivans, a dark-green Land Rover and, parked way down the street, a couple of car lengths away from everyone else, a white Mustang convertible. But no pickup truck.

I tell Whaley thanks a lot for the ride. He tells me he'll see me in about an hour. I slide out of the monster truck and Whaley's peering at me over his red eyelids, wanting to say something.

"What?" I say.

"Our job is just to mourn the dead," he tells me.

"Okay, Whaley."

"That's all. That's all our job is."

"I guess so." Words like "mourn the dead" make me feel like I'm listening to Oral Roberts on the radio. I know Whaley's trying to tell me something, so I smile and nod to show him I appreciate it. Then he smiles real big at me and he's got some teeth left which look pretty strong. "I ain't gonna worry 'bout you, Ray," he says. "You'll do all right."

I take this to heart, I really do. Because I ain't so sure I'm gonna do all right. But it helps to know Whaley's got faith in me. He pulls out and I cut across the front lawn, still looking around in case I missed Jean's truck the first time. Maybe I can get Harold and the minivan to take me—where? Where the hell is she?

I go around through the garage to the kitchen door. Think maybe I'll slide in quiet and find Harold, ask him if he's seen her. I can hear all the voices in the kitchen. There's a stale smell in the garage, like rotten hot dogs. I look for where it's coming from and realize it's me smelling like that. Shit, I can't go in there. But maybe Jean loaned her truck to someone. Maybe she's in that kitchen right now, and one of the voices mixing and buzzing on the other side of that door is hers. I yank on the door handle, take a deep breath, and walk into the kitchen.

Clatter clatter Judy would you grab the napkins please dishcloth flopping on the counter no I want the red one Mommy slices of ham with beans and onions hush up now water running anyone seen Sherry little girl in a checked green dress chewing on a naked paper doll I'm out of town usually four days out of the week Ray your mother's been looking for you.

No Jean in the kitchen move quick for the living room quieter lower voices rustle of paper hand me the home section if you're through oil painting of a bald eagle above the couch it's a three and one pitch to the outside and Maren takes another walk who's driving Aunt Judy she'll need the wheelchair fat guy at one end of the couch looks at me funny Ray where you been?

No Jean in the living room, so I head back into the hallway toward the bathroom just to get a little peace and quiet to clean out my head. But the knob won't turn, so I try again and then the door says, "I'll be done in a minute."

So I wait for the door to be done, standing on one foot and leaning against the wall. There's pictures hanging in the hallway, pink and green and blue hummingbirds in wood frames.

"You done yet?" I ask it. It doesn't bother to answer this time, just opens up. There's a pretty redhead standing there looking at me. But instead of getting the hell out of my way, she grabs my arm, pulls me into the bathroom with her, and locks the door behind us.

"It's Nan," she says.

"Hi," I say back.

"Where'd you guys disappear to last night?" she asks. "I looked for you."

"We went out."

"No shit. Where'd you go?"

"I don't remember."

"You stink." She don't say it mean, though. I do stink.

"I know."

"You need a bath or something."

"You seen Jean anywhere?"

"No."

"She ain't here?"

"Not that I've seen."

I sit down on the side of the bathtub, try to think. There's a knock at the door.

"Just a second," Nan calls to the ceiling.

"I can't think," I tell her.

"Yeah." She's sort of rubbing my shoulder, thinking herself. "Your ma has another bathroom upstairs, doesn't she?"

"I guess so."

"Let's get you upstairs, then. Too many people down here." She's trying to lift me off the edge of the tub. "You drunk?" she asks me.

"Tired," I tell her.

"Okay, let's go. Hold my hand."

"Okay."

Nan opens the door and says something to someone about Harold, and then she leads me down the hallway to the stairs. Up we go, step step step, upsy daisy. There's a bedroom, there's another bedroom, there's a closed door, there's an open door. Big house with lots of rooms. What's Ma and Ed need all these rooms for? There's the bathroom. Whoa, everything's yellow. Nan lowers the toilet lid and tells me to sit down and stay there. Okay.

"I'm coming right back," she tells me.

"Find Harold for me, will ya?"

"Okay," she says. She closes the door and I turn on the shower, start peeling off my work boots, greasy pants, poor old bloody brand-new long-sleeved T-shirt. Once I'm naked I climb very careful into the tub and sit in it, letting the shower pour down on me. Peace. Everything's still yellow, even now that I'm wet and peaceful. The tile, the tub, the walls and curtains and the furry thing covering the toilet seat, even the soap and the soap dish, all different shades of yellow. I'm yellow too. I'm a baby chick, small and yellow and quiet. I sit under the streaming water and rest my head on my knees. Think about Ma. About what she did that night up to Snell's, ruffling my hair and saying how she loved me. I'm a little yellow chick and she's ruffling my chick feathers like when I was a kid. And now Billy's here with me, cupping water in both hands and squirting it out, farting under water so the bubbles come up all around him.

"I'm sorry I told you to go to hell," I tell him.

" 'S okay," he says. "Hey, want to play submarine?"

Nothing's wrong. We're small enough so we both fit in the tub, and we're playing submarine. Me and Billy and Jean are making a train out of the kitchen chairs while Ma's mopping the floor. Ma and Jean are singing to scratchy old Patsy Cline on the phonograph. Ma's packing a brown-bag lunch for all three of us because we're going out to Cabbage Pond for the whole day, just us kids. Gonna teach Jean to catch crawfish. We chase tadpoles all morning and Jean picks buttercups to take back to Ma. When we eat our lunches, there's little faces on our napkins that say "I love you." Ma drew them when we weren't looking.

TWENTY-SEVEN

Harold's here. Harold's handing me a yellow washcloth. I'm still sitting in the tub and water's still pounding down on me.

"Where you been, Ray?"

"Got arrested."

"No shit? Here's the soap."

"It's yellow," I tell him.

"Yeah." He disappears behind the shower curtain. I soap up the washcloth and start in on two or three days' worth of dirt and sweat. Scrub from my broken toes up to my belly button.

"Harold?" No answer. "Nan?" Nothing. I don't hear anything over the shower. So I keep going, still sitting down in the tub, working my way up to my face. Taking it slow and easy around the right shoulder, where bits of gravel are working their way into the skin and I got to pick 'em out. Go extra careful around my face, with the matching cuts over each eye. Ease my way around the three cuts I gave myself yesterday. Jesus, I'm a mess. Rinse the soap off and stand up to look for some shampoo. My hair feels like baling twine.

"Hey, Ray," says Harold on the other side of the curtain.

"Yeah?" I'm squirting myself a handful of Herbal Essence, trying not to get dizzy.

"Take a look at these, will you?" I poke my head around the curtain, and Harold's holding out two shirts. One yellow, one powder blue, both button-downs with short sleeves. He asks me, "Which one you want?"

"They yours?"

"Ed's."

"Blue," I tell him. I'm pretty sick of yellow just now. "Think it'll fit?"

"Yeah. Little big is all."

"Yeah. Okay." I suds up my hair, sitting down again before I fall down. I take a handful of lather and cover my chin with it. Make it all pointy and holler for Harold.

"Hey! Hey, Harold!"

He comes back into the bathroom. "What?"

I stick my head out of the curtain. "Who am I?" I ask him.

"Who are you?"

"Yeah. Who am I?" I waggle my sudsy chin at him for a clue.

"I don't know."

"Abraham Lincoln." I stick my head back under the shower for a final rinse. Grab a yellow towel that Harold hung over the shower curtain and fluff myself all over. I'm awake now. There's brown boxer shorts and black socks sitting folded on the toilet seat, so I put 'em on. I look like the old man.

"Nan picked these out for you." Harold's coming in with a pair of pants. "Ed says they're his smallest, can't fit into 'em no more." They're dark-blue cotton trousers with pleats in the front. Pleats in the front make me look like I got dog teats where my dick ought to be, but okay, okay. Nice of Ed to loan 'em to me. Harold hands me the powder-blue shirt, which is soft like silk. The pants are hanging a little low, so the dog teats are halfway to my knees. Harold hands me a belt and I'm in business. Nan's in the bedroom, hanging clothes back up in the closet. I pull my work boots on and we go in to show her.

"Lots better," she says. "You look just like Ed."

They hustle me downstairs to the kitchen. Harold says he's going to see what happened to Jim. Who's Jim? Nan says she'll give me a lift up to the funeral home and that's settled.

"You seen Jean today?" I ask Aunt Lois, looking at a casserole dish full of rice pudding and thinking how it looks like maggots.

"She's up to the funeral home, setting up the flowers for the service."

"It's not a wedding," says Aunt Weazy, who's carrying two fistfuls of clean silverware.

"She wanted more flowers, just let her be," Aunt Lois tells her.

Up to Snell's. She's up to Snell's right now. I turn around to tell Nan let's go, but she and Aunt Weazy are busy fixing a plate of food for me.

"Let's go," I tell her.

"You have to eat," says Nan.

"We got to go," I answer.

"If you eat," she promises. She's got a knife, fork, napkin, glass of 7UP, and a plate full of food all laid out on the kitchen table. I don't know what happened to the herd of people that was in here when I first came through. They all cleared out except the aunts. They're probably all on their way to Snell's right now.

I put a heaping forkful of something in my mouth. It ain't the rice pudding—thank God for that. I chew and chew and swallow and knock back some 7UP to help keep it down. Like sucking down dirt.

"Hey Nan, let's go," I holler. Aunt Weazy tells me to hush.

"Where's Ma?"

"She left a while ago."

"Where's Ed?"

"He just left with aunt Judy and the wheelchair."

The whole damn world is up to Snell's but me. "Where the hell is Nan?"

"Why don't you eat a little bit more?" Now it's Aunt Evelyn, trying to elbow Aunt Weazy and Aunt Lois out of my face. They're doing it again, flower clustering like they were the other night when I first saw 'em.

"Stop it," I tell them.

"Stop what?" says Aunt Weazy.

"You know what. Stop it." Aunt Evelyn is looking at me funny. She's wearing glasses like awful old Kathy was wearing up at the dog pound. Big plastic frames, tinted lenses, except she doesn't have the gold initials in the corner. There's a coral pin sitting crooked on her dress. Just hanging there on her blue dress, crooked. Big tears pop out in my eyes. I wonder if she was still in love with Uncle Jerry when he died.

"I got to go," I say to the coral pin. All three aunts have shut up now. I look toward the door leading out to the garage, to the street leading toward town. There's a purse and a set of keys on the counter by the door.

"Maybe I'll wait out in the car." I give them a smile so they won't worry about me. "Okay? Tell Nan I'm out waiting in the car."

I get up and head for the door. Turn around to see if they're watching me, but they're back to clearing away the last of the dishes. I push open the door and palm the keys on the way out. Finger through 'em for what looks like the ignition key. They're on a key chain that says "Quality is Job #1," which is Ford. So I start with the gold Taurus at the foot of the driveway. Not locked. Climb into an oven of sweating upholstery and a hot plastic gearshift. Doesn't anybody roll down their windows anymore? Got to leave the door open just to breathe. Key ain't fitting.

Climb out and move on to the Crown Victoria across the street. Can't pull the seat forward because it's all automated with buttons and the buttons don't work until the car's on. Finally scooch my butt up far enough on the edge of the seat, holding on to the wheel, to figure out why the key don't fit.

Work my way over to the white Mustang convertible. Slide in like I own it, turn the ignition, and start her up. I ain't been in a convertible since high school, since Randy's yellow MG. Me and Randy and Jean heading out to the lake that summer, a couple of six-packs in the back seat. Jean tossing her lighter back to me and it flying out the back of the car and Randy pulling over and all three of us tramping up and down Half Moon Road looking for a dark-purple Bic. I don't remember why she was so attached to that stupid lighter. We found it, though.

I pull out and head for town, for Snell's. The wind flying by my head is hot and smells like biscuits and gravy. I got my eyes squinted down and I'm keeping my mouth shut tight so I don't get another bug down the throat. Hair's whipping itself back and forth against my face, dancing, excited to be half dry and flying loose. The powder-blue shirt is beating and flapping against my chest. Mailboxes go by, friendly and full of possibilities. Front porches with Big Wheels and pots of geraniums on 'em. Maple trees with signs nailed to 'em saying "Garage Sale One Mile." Everything friendly and wishing me well.

What I want to do is run into Snell's just long enough to grab Jean, drag her out to the car, and keep on driving. Drive for about two or three weeks and see how far we get. And when we're hungry we can go to a Wendy's drive-through, and we can take turns sleeping and driving.

Just skip the damned funeral and run away. And if she doesn't wanna come with me, I'll tie her up and throw her in the back seat.

I'm in town now, slowing down and driving past women with kids in strollers, girls on bicycles. What time is it? Is it one o'clock yet? I ease into Snell's parking lot, pull up nose-to-nose with a green Vega, and turn off the car. There's two dozen or so Harleys all lined up near the door. They're gonna do the damned Harley chopper escort with the flags and shit right behind the hearse. Billy ain't ridden in about four years, but he still hung out with 'em. I think about the Lincoln Town Cars on their way from Forest Glen Estates. Think of one of them Town Cars bumping a bike, sending the whole row down like metallic dominoes. I look over at the far end of the parking lot and finally see what I been looking for. Jean's truck is parked in the shade at the very back. Jean's truck. Fear gets me in its jaws like a grizzly bear. What if she says no? She can't say no.

I look out over the lake of car hoods, twinkling and shining like water rippling under the sun. The sky's bluer today than it's been in weeks. Humidity down to just about nothing, with dry, crackly heat. All the colors are sharp and clear: the red of the zinnias lining the sidewalk, the snaky blue of the gas tanks on the choppers, the green deep-pile carpet of Snell's grass. Like pictures in an old Sunday school book of a blue-eyed Jesus. Jean used to say the colors were out. Days when there was zero humidity and everything looked like candy, Jean would run outside and holler for me to come on, come on and look, the colors are out. And I'd run outside in the yard and there they'd be, all the colors in the world just beaming as loud as they could. The world was bright and wide awake and we knew it would be a magical day. Because when the colors are out, anything can happen. And the colors are out today.

TWENTY-EIGHT

Inside Snell's, the stillness is closing around me like warm thick water, muffling the sound of someone laughing downstairs. A voice next to me says, "Your ma's looking for you." I nod and walk down the hall. Come up on the room where Billy's laid out. Lots of people sitting around, not looking at that gunmetal coffin. I step into the room, and that's when I see what Jean's been doing all morning. Now I'm laughing. I can even imagine Billy standing next to me and shaking his head, saying, "Crazy bitch," and laughing too.

She brought all her flowers over to Snell's. All the wild climbing roses by her back porch are scattered over the lid of the coffin. Lilies are wove around the steel handles, marigolds lining the base of the coffin pedestal. And she rigged up four columns of gladiolus, look like table legs, all orange pink yellow red. And it's not just the coffin. She's got cattails fanned out in one corner, with purple cactus-looking thistles mixed in. Black-eyed Susans hanging from the windows, mixed with goldenrod. Everywhere I look, the room's sagging with flowers.

And on the seat of every empty chair there's a couple of flowers tied together with a bit of twine. Mums, zinnias, a wild sunflower or two. I look at folks in their seats. Whaley's got a bunch of asters, and there's Randy just picking up a cluster of geraniums. Chairs are filled with little bouquets made of everything from crazy old hawkweed to petunias. This is where she's been all morning.

I take a couple of steps further into the room and there's Jean. She's off to the side, behind the rows of chairs, and she's got Kyle holding two vases up into the air, one in each hand. She has a matching spray of white snapdragons in each vase and she's filling them in with green ferny things. Finally she nods to him to go ahead. He carries 'em across behind the chairs and places each one on either side of the sign-in book. I ain't taken my eyes off her, and she only just now sees me. I must still be laughing, because she gives me a smile like I ain't seen since then. Since she quit being in love with me. Oh God, since I ruined a whole lifetime full of love in one night.

I walk behind the chairs, and in about nine steps I'm next to her. I grab hold of all of her in one motion. She doesn't push me away. She holds on to me tight as she can and puts her head close next to mine. I can feel our breathing together at the same exact pace, just like always.

"Hey, Jean," I say into her hair. "The colors are out."

The answer comes quiet and close to my ear. "Anything can happen," she says.

"Let's go," I tell her, taking her hand.

"Not yet." She keeps hold of my hand, but she ain't budging. "Not till it's over." She's got that set to her jaw, but I give it a try anyway.

"Sheriff's looking for you."

"He ain't gonna show up here," she says, scowling around the eyebrows.

"Soon as it's over, we leave?"

"Yeah," she says. And I kiss her. Smack on the mouth. There in Snell's, surrounded by everyone, I kiss her. And I got my whole self back again. Jean was right, in a way. She thought I was something I wasn't. And I wasn't, so long as I didn't have her. But now, now I got her with me, we'll hash out the rest of it later. We stand close together and watch as people try not to look in our direction. There's the front couple of rows roped off for family. Ginny Honey's already sitting down, with the two girls next to her. I look back at Jean, making sure she's still here next to me. She's wearing a long green cotton dress with no sleeves. She's got shoulders twice as nice as old Sue's. The green of her dress blends into the background of plants and flowers, like her arms are branches and her gold-brown hair is blooming. I look at her eyes, the same snowy green as Billy's, and she's looking at me funny.

"What?" I say.

"Where'd the shirt come from?" she asks.

"Ed."

"Pants too?"

"Yeah."

I take hold of her hand, warm and dry and strong. Ma's voice is out in the hallway. Ed's standing next to Ma, right where he belongs. Now that I'm holding on to Jean, keeping her from floating away from me, I can inspect the rest of the room.

I see the old man at the opposite end, standing in a group of men. He's got a brown suit jacket hanging loose on his shoulders. He's standing right next to Shiner LaVonn, who's in the middle of telling them some story.

"Ar! Ar! Ar!"

I watch him for a while. He ain't saying much. Listening and smiling and nodding, but he's quiet. Standing there with Shiner, he almost looks like a young guy. His eyes slide across to me and Jean, but slide away again.

There's flower shop bouquets mixed in with all of Jean's flowers. Arrangements in baskets, in wreaths, in vases, all with white cards sticking out of 'em. There's a pink glass bowl with hard candy in it: butterscotch and red and white peppermints in cellophane wrappers that people crinkle crinkle crinkle after popping the candy in their mouth. I hear a quiet voice in my ear, "So sorry, Ray."

I look around, but there's no one there. Just a little potted plant whispering on the table next to me, random green spears growing out in all directions. It's got a card stuck in it. "Book Fiends." I lean over and look closer. What it really says is "Joe and Marva at Book Fiends."

I freeze, looking at it. Joe and Marva don't even know Billy. I go in there once or twice a month over to Adrian. They back-ordered three or four of the Ginch Littlefield books so I could read them in order. I look at the green spears, confused at first. They sent that for me. Not for Billy or Ginny Honey or even for Ma. It's for me. I nudge Jean and point to the card.

"Who's that?" she says.

"Friends of mine," I tell her, surprise all over my voice. She looks at me and tugs my hand to say "Follow me." We walk real slow in a circuit around the room, looking at each basket, each wreath. Some of them are pretty, some butt ugly. But they all got cards, and all the cards got people's names on them. A lot I don't recognize, but Jean and me figure who most of them are between the two of us. A small wreath of yellow roses, "Mrs. Wagner's Bible School Class," for Deena; gold and brown asters with a tiny fake-feathered quail in the center, "John and Gilda Keilman" (that's Randy's ma and dad), for me; white carnations wrapped in a blue satin ribbon, "All of us at Kelsey's Lumber," for Jean; a plant with a silver cross in it, "Cindy and Tammy," from the hair salon that cuts Ginny Honey's hair; red mums from Ed's poker club. By the time we're halfway around the room, I realize that most of these flowers ain't for Billy. They're for us, all of us left alive.

I look around at all the people here. I can see Jill Thompson sitting two rows in front of Mrs. Barnes, our old baby-sitter that I thought was dead. Rick, the bartender up to Dewey's, sitting next to Al Halsey. (Who has two black eyes. I must have jammed his nose halfway to his brain last night.) There's the guys from grinding up to O'Donnell's, the ones made me think of the Three Stooges the other night. All three of 'em about as uncomfortable as you can be, but here they are, dahlias on their laps. Like Paul Jorgenson with his plastic arm and Phil Junior, who must've gotten someone to cover his mail route. Even Phil Senior, who owns the barbershop I used to live over, sweating in suspenders over a dark plaid flannel shirt, legs spread in his chair to make room for his belly. He's laughing and nodding and listening to old Whaley, carrying on with a whole world that don't have much to do with Billy being dead. But he's here.

I feel seen. Like there ain't really been a black hole wandering around in my place all these years. There was a person, me, that people saw. And today they see more than just Ray Johnson, you know, the one with that sister. Mrs. Keilman sees the boy who squeezed mashed potatoes through his teeth at the dinner table, and made Randy laugh and spit a mouthful of milk all over the meat loaf. Old Mrs. Barnes sees the kid who holed himself up in a corner with *Green Eggs and Ham* or *Curious George*. Phil Senior sees the guy that ran over his garden hose out back with the mower, nice kid but dumb. These people have seen my whole damned life.

Now the tears leak out, a little river flowing down the side of my nose. I grab some Kleenex off a table and use them to cover my whole face. Jean's squeezing my hand hard as she can, but it's no use. I'm bawling because I can't believe all these people are here, and it ain't for the gossip or the "I told you they was no good" or anything like that. They're here because something bad happened to us, and they're trying to make it better.

And now everyone is taking a seat. The old man sits down behind Ginny Honey, Shiner right next to him. It's dead quiet all of a sudden. Ma and Ed sit in front, with Kyle between them. Jean and I slide in behind, near the old man. I got a bit of boneset in my seat. Jean holds a giant zinnia. I take hold of her hand again and decide not to let go ever. There's a box of Kleenex on one of the chairs between me and the old man. I pull out a couple and hold them out for Jean in case she needs them. She looks at me and rolls her eyes. I hold them clenched in my hand.

A guy in a black suit with a cross around his neck walks up to the podium near the coffin. There's some last-chance coughing and cellophane crinkling going on around the room, and then quiet. The guy at the podium introduces himself as Pastor Hodges. I can tell it's going to be one of those upbeat, happy funeral services, full of God's promise and what a great afterlife we can look forward to when we're all dead like Billy. I wish they'd just tell the truth for once. Stand up and wave their arms around and holler, "Oh my God, this is awful! This hurts! No fair, God! No fair!" But instead we're getting a gullet full of tired old John 14:27, "Let not your heart be troubled." *No fair! No fair!*

It takes about forty seconds for me to get used to his voice enough so it becomes the background noise. An up-and-down rhythm of blah blah blah behind the steady hum of quiet. I concentrate on the tiny lightbulbs burning in the table lamps, the soles of shoes rubbing over the carpet, the heavy curtains. Trying not to think about arrest warrants, just hanging on till we get out of here.

My head's down, hiding my wet face. I got Kleenex in my right hand and Jean's hand in my left. I try turning my head a little, just a little tiny bit, and look around the room to see if Sally's here. I catch a glimpse of her brown hair bent down, like she's staring at something in her lap. Barb's on one side of her, Berry's on the other. Berry's looking sorry as hell, but I'm not sure what for. Who's she feeling sorry for? Sally? Billy?

She sees me and looks right into my eyes. Me. It's me she's feeling sorry for. I turn around and face front again, so as not to bother Sally. I know how far away she is from me now, how much she's let go of me. And that there's no way we're ever gonna be together again, no matter what happens with me and Jean. Sally's gone. I close my eyes and say good-bye to her, good-bye to the hurt I gave her, good-bye to my friend. And I stop crying. That's it. I just stop and let the comfort come in. From Sally, Whaley, everyone in the room. I'm quiet now, quiet and comforted.

I shoot a blurry look over to the old man. His elbow's resting on the arm of the chair and he's got his chin propped up on his clenched hand. It's exactly how he was sitting at Grandpa Eddie's funeral when I was eleven. That's as emotional as the old man gets. He's not looking at Pastor Hodges, he's not looking at Billy's coffin. He's staring at Jean's cattails in the corner like he's waiting for them to explode any second and send cattail fuzz floating over everyone's head.

I look down at Jean's hand, rub my thumb along hers, feel the calluses and the torn cuticles. Little nicks and cuts cover her knuckles from all the tangling with electric sanders and rusted branch trimmers. Innocent scars from working hard, working with her hands. I look at my bare arm next to hers, dotted with white circles and crescents like a bunch of moons coming and going. Some are burns from cigarettes, including the ones Jean gave me years ago, faded now. Some are cuts from jackknives or the metal lids off Campbell soup cans, whatever I could get my hands on at the time. The white moons look sick and shameful next to Jean's strong, honest scars. I try to imagine Jean hurting herself. She'd never do it. Never in a lifetime. She'd pick up a rock first, bring it down with both hands on whatever was bothering her, and smash it all to pieces.

I look up at her face, at the freckles across the bridge of her nose, the line of her jaw, the light-brown springs of hair waving like little flags at her temples. I know this face better than I know anyone's. She turns her head and looks at me.

All the hurt and confusion about Billy being killed is like a big forest fire that's burned through everything in me. Burned clean through all the underbrush of when we were little, all the deadwood memories. Even the big strong trees that I thought would live forever, blocking all the sun. Everything burned bare until there's nothing but a sweep of air coming across the empty space. Jean and me, we're looking at each other now in that empty, burned-out place. And the sweep of air blowing between us, it's carrying nothing but love. Everything else slips away. Ma, the old man, Randy, Sally, even Billy. Everything's okay. We got plenty of room now, just me and Jean, and we're gonna be all right.

Someone's cranking out music on the organ, keeping it soft and slow. ". . . sweet the sound that saved a wretch like me . . ."

Folks are really bawling now, like it's a cue whenever "Amazing Grace" starts. I think about how you could call Billy a wretch, but mostly I'm the one who feels like I been saved. Like some sort of grace found me along with the people bringing sympathy from all over town. Like I got me a second chance.

TWENTY-NINE

The pastor says a few more words. It's over now, and me and Jean can walk out of here in about five minutes. Folks start past the coffin in a slow shuffle. Some stop for a minute in front of it, some just rest their hand against the lid as they go by. A few are crying. Most are looking down at their shoes. They're like soldiers in a parade, marching by the flag. Like the coffin is something holy.

"Miss Johnson?"

Both me and Jean look up at the same exact time, like our heads are attached to the same string. Sheriff Keith is standing over her shoulder. He's asking Jean to come with him please. My hand holds tighter to hers. I look back over my shoulder, and Sue's standing at the room's main door. I check the other exit, the side door. But that's where everyone's going out after a last once-over of the coffin. I guess Pudgy's either covering at the station or standing further down the hall, by the door leading outside. It's a dirty trick, bothering her here. I knew I should've drug her out with me right away.

Jean stands up and follows him past the rows of chairs, mostly empty now. I get up to follow her and see Ma turning around in her seat. I don't stop, just follow Jean up the empty aisle.

"Jean?" Ma's voice is reedy and sharp behind me, a kettle boiling too long. "Jeannie baby?"

It's not until I see the look on Sheriff Keith's face that I figure out what's going on. He's not here to question her. Oh God, he's not here but for one thing.

We're out of the room, out in the empty hallway. Jean doesn't look at all surprised, just disappointed. Ma's still kettle-whistling behind us, with Ed's voice like steam trying to smother the sound. Sheriff Keith's voice is saying the words. Saying the words and making it real.

". . . under arrest . . ."

There's no other sound anywhere. Where is everyone? Where's all those people come to help us? I say no, but nothing comes out. All I hear is Sheriff Keith.

". . . for the killing of . . ."

The freckles are standing out on Jean's face, pale and dusty. I got my arms crossed over my chest, fingers digging hard into the biceps.

". . . anything you say . . ."

This was supposed to be the rest of our lives. This was supposed to be our fresh start, our turn to have what we should've had all along. And someone's taking it away. Someone's taking her away. What the hell did I think was gonna happen? Me and Jean living happy ever after with the worthless tiger cat and the flagstone walkway? The whole town forgetting that Billy was killed, just letting it go since he was a miserable prick anyway? Ma shaking her head at the Memorial Methodist Church and smiling. "Kids. What can you do?" The stupid truth is, I didn't think any further than getting to Jean. Like it would all magically fix itself once she took me back. I got no plan, I got no idea how to help her, how to keep her with me.

Sue reaches in the back of her belt for the handcuffs, leaving a wide hole at her side, wide open and showing me the way out. The plan builds itself in my head in the three seconds it takes for me to reach across the space between me and my old enemy Sue. One hand drives hard into her shoulder, palm open and flat, knocking her back and off balance so the cuffs flip up out of her hand in an arc, two silver fish jumping and looping through the air. My other hand goes straight to the belt at her hip, jerking the gun out and free and now it's in my hand and Sheriff Keith's letting go of Jean and Sue's still off balance falling against the wallpaper, sliding down to the floor.

I flick off the safety while Jean takes a step toward me. I can't read the look on her face. Sheriff Keith reaches for her and I swing the gun up and straight at his face. He stops, and his hands go high and harmless. Jean floats past me down the hall.

"Jeannie? Baby?" Ma reedy, Ma screaming when she gets a look at the gun. Where's Ed? Why doesn't he shut her the hell up? Sheriff Keith's moving his mouth at me, but I hear something else instead. It's the old man coming up the empty aisle.

"What the hell, boy?" He's moving fast at me, so mad. The arm holding the gun swings toward him, stopping him flat just like the sheriff. People are yelling, but I don't see 'em. Are they around the corner? The gun's sweeping back and forth, restless like a lion in one of those nature shows. Pacing, pacing, waiting to bite.

Sheriff Keith motions for Sue to stay down. Pudgy comes up the hall, but Sheriff Keith tells him to stay where he is. Jean's voice is coming from the other end of the hallway.

"C'mon, Ray," she's saying.

I want to run after her, but I got all these people here now, each one staying back just enough, just enough not to get bitten.

"Ray," she says. And I follow her.

. . . *got a gun . . . oh God . . . they're out back . . . hurt anyone . . .* Flutter of voices chasing us down the hall and out the door. We're back at the old service entrance. The delivery truck for Spillman's Florist is parked right by the door. Barely room for both of us to squeeze out. Then we're in the parking lot, where Jean's already halfway to her pickup. Sheriff Keith comes around the front of the building with Pudgy behind him. He's got his gun out and his mouth is round and loud, aimed straight at Jean. She turns to see where I am, still so far from the truck, and Sue coming out the service door behind me.

"Goddamn it, Ray!" She's got the truck door open, and Sheriff Keith lines up the gun straight in her direction. I'm running fast as I can, but I can't get to her. I'm seeing my life ending right here. Here in the parking lot, he's killing her, killing us, our second chance. My hand jerks up and a blast goes off next to my ear. His gun jumps suddenly high into the air and his hand waves, fingers spread like a little kid patting a sand castle. He spins away toward Pudgy and goes down onto the thick green grass. Sue's gun is hot now in my hand. I get to the cab of the truck and throw myself in. Jean's backing out, arm slung across the seat and hair alive and curling wild all over her head. Tires are squealing like in a damned movie and she's bringing it around, shifting gears. I'm firing the gun in the air just to keep everyone ducking for cover so we can get the hell out of there. I look back at the patch of green grass that looks three hundred miles away now. Pudgy's kneeling over someone lying in the grass. He's talking into his walkie-talkie and he's crying. Face is all wet. The face of a kid who's never seen anyone really hurt in his life. And there's Sheriff Keith bleeding on the grass. I picture that kid of his with the champion steer.

"My dad was killed in a shootout at a funeral home."

My stomach closes up and I taste rusty metal in my mouth. Lean out the truck window because I think I'm gonna throw up. I close my eyes and there's the picture still: Pudgy's wet face and Sheriff Keith crumpled up on the grass like a big sleeping Saint Bernard.

Me and Jean aren't saying anything. Like we're wondering if any of it really happened. Jean's steering the truck through the town, a speeding ghost, heading for the back roads that crisscross and snake through the woods north of town. It's quiet and calm like when you wake up from a bad dream and nothing's moving in your bedroom. Soon we're out of town, zigzagging northeast. She's heading toward I-96, a good two hours' drive on the back roads.

"Do you think I killed him?" I finally ask her.

"Who?"

"The sheriff," I say.

"Only if they leave him there to bleed to death."

"Yeah?"

"You got him high up on the shoulder," she said. "I thought that's where you meant to hit him."

We're quiet again for a little while.

"Why'd you lie to me?" I finally say. I'm talking about that morning on my front porch when I looked her in the eye and said, "Did you?" And she looked right back and said no. That's what I'm talking about, and she knows it.

"Why'd you lie?" I say again.

"Because you wanted me to," she says. Just stating a fact, not picking a fight. And I can't say anything, because she's right. I didn't want to know. Being the coward I always been. She's driving steady, not speeding anymore, but sure not slowing down too much for the railroad tracks either. We don't talk about where we're going. Only one place to go, and we both know it. So that's where we're headed.

"You sure he's okay?" I ask her.

"The sheriff?" she asks.

"Yeah."

She nods, brushing back curls that are blowing into her eyes. "He's okay," she says.

"Don't lie," I say. I look hard at her until she looks back.

"Shoulder wound," she says. "That's all."

I think about that while my stomach unclenches and my lungs grow back. I'm breathing through my nose, slow and easy now. I'm breathing. I'm breathing. I'm smiling.

"You picked a hell of a time," she says. "I waited all these goddamn years for you to get your thumb out of your ass, wake up and do something." A little edge of bitterness lines her mouth, gone when she smiles. "But you sure picked your moment."

I don't answer. Lean back and let the sound of her voice fill my head, my kneecaps, my fingernails.

She looks over at me. "You looked like fucking Jesse James with that gun, Ray," she says. Jesse James was her hero when she was a kid.

"Yeah?"

She chuckles a little. "Just like a bank robber, no shit."

I didn't kill Sheriff Keith. Everything's okay, and me and Jean are driving down the road.

"Knocked old Sue flat on her ass," I tell her.

"What a hero," Jean says. And now we're laughing. The colors are flying by, the sun is shining, and we got a full tank of gas.

"Got a long drive ahead of us," I tell her.

"Yup."

"I'm hungry," I say. Ha ha ha.

"Oh Jesus, don't start," she tells me.

"I got to go the bathroom." Ha ha ha.

"When we gonna be there?" she says in a little-kid voice. And we crack up. Kids riding in the back seat to the hunting cabin. Ma and the old man up front, both in a good mood because it's a week vacation. Me and Jean and Billy in the back seat, counting out-of-state license plates, fighting over every square inch of territory on the seat.

"Ma, he's touching me with his foot!"

And it's me and Jean and Billy driving down the road, and the colors are out. We're waving at the trucks so they'll honk their horns. Clicking the metal ashtrays up and down, up and down, until the old man threatens to pull over and whip us. Dodging the ashes that blow back on us from Ma's cigarette. Me and Jean and Billy, on our way to the cabin. We haven't learned to hurt each other yet. Haven't learned to hate. Driving down the road. We got our second chance, and we're taking it.

I'm sitting on the back porch of the hunting cabin, watching the black outline of geese bobbing on the water. Been here since about eight o'clock. We got as far as Manchester, going along the back roads, when Jean pulled into a Foodtown parking lot and we left her truck behind for a shiny green Toyota Cressida with easy wiring. We decided to avoid I-96 and stick to the dirt roads all the way up past McBain. It meant a six-hour drive and getting lost twice, but we made it.

Stopped to use the pay phone at a McDonald's in St. Johns and called Randy. Didn't give myself time to think about whether or not I could trust him. Just picked up the phone and dialed information. Asked him to go over to Jean's and get the money out of my truck before Sheriff Keith impounded it and grab Samson if he could find him. Jean said not to bother with the tiger cat; he was wild to begin with.

Now her voice comes through the kitchen window just a few feet away.

"Come get a load of this thing," she says. "I'm not kidding." She's got a gray spider cornered behind the crusted old Mr. Coffee, trying to get him onto a long wooden spoon so she can carry him outside.

"Bastard's as big as my hand," she's telling me. "I can see his teeth."

"Spiders ain't got teeth," I tell her, watching through the window screen. I didn't know there were spiders that size in Michigan. She doesn't answer, just carries the monster out the back door. Halfway across the porch, he makes a run up the spoon handle at her. Her free hand closes over him, pulls him off the handle, and flips him onto the grass.

"Fucker," she mutters.

"Same to you, lady," I hear him say as he hits the grass running.

"Jean?"

"Mmm?" She's heading back into the house. Stops with one hand on the screen door.

"Why'd you go out to the old man's?" I ask her.

"He tell you that?"

"He lied and said he hadn't seen you." I'm watching the water, afraid she's gonna go back inside without answering. But she closes the door and leans on it, thinks for a minute.

"I don't know why I went out there. Seemed like the only place to go." We're both quiet then, thinking about what she didn't say. *I couldn't come to you.* Then she goes on. "And I wanted him to know it was me, I guess. I was afraid I'd never get a chance to tell him myself, tell him why. You know?" She's nudging my leg with her foot, still leaning on the doorframe. "He sat in that La-Z-Boy for a long time, like he hadn't even heard me. Then he made me wash myself up, gave me some clean clothes, and buried mine out back."

She doesn't say anything more. Neither do I. One thing I know: Sheriff Keith may have nailed her on fingerprints or whatnot, but he got no help from the old man. I turn around and look up at her. Yeah, maybe he helped her. But I can see she's still a long way from forgiving and forgetting everything that came before.

A car pulls into the driveway. It's 11:00 P.M. and we got no lights on (no electricity hooked up), so it looks like no one's here. I take a careful look around the corner of the cabin. There's Samson jumping out the window of a rusted Impala, stopping long enough to pee on the front tire. I come around and step into the headlights where mosquitoes are swarming thick. Samson sees me and starts sidewinding up the sand driveway, growling and snarling with his head low to the ground.

"C'mon, Samson. C'mon, you old asshole dog." His tail's wagging so wide his back legs swing like a hula dancer. Randy climbs out of the Impala and limps up the driveway. He exaggerates the limp so I'll feel like even more of a bastard than I already do.

"Hey, Randy," I say, scratching hard behind Samson's good ear.

"Hey, Ray. Hey, Jean."

She's come off the porch behind me. Randy hands me Ed's envelope.

"Thanks," I tell him.

"No problem," he says. He's looking at me, so I make myself look him in the eye. I make myself do it. He's waiting because he knows I'm gonna say I'm sorry and he's been waiting ten years to hear it.

"I'm sorry," I tell him.

"You sure are," he says. "This was in the truck." He hands me my Ginch Littlefield. I shove it in my back pocket. Says he's got a couple of six-packs in the car. I go get them and join him and Jean out on the back steps. The moon is sending silver shots across the water at us. There's the sound of a motorboat a couple miles away, further up the chain of lakes. I settle on the stairs, a few steps above Jean. She leans back between my legs, elbows resting on my knees like I'm some kind of throne she's sitting on. Samson's stretched out near her feet, cocking his ear at the frogs and the crickets.

"Where you gonna go?" asks Randy.

"Don't know yet," Jean tells him.

"Canada maybe?" he wants to know.

"I don't know," I say. "How's the sheriff?"

"He's okay," Randy says. "Clipped him on the shoulder."

"That's what we figured," I say. Jean's quiet. The heat's broke and there's a breeze coming in off the water. Randy talks, filling in for ten years of quiet. Got a kid by some girl I never met over in Dundee. I'd heard about that from Ma, heard he was a father. He doesn't see the kid much, but he sends money every month. We talk about a few of the guys up to O'Donnell's. Talk about his folks and my folks. We talk some about Billy. And for a little while at least, it feels like when we were kids, eating barbecue and drinking beer, the world far away.

Round about midnight Randy says it's time to go, on account of he's got to be up in the morning and it's a long way back. He leaves the rusted Impala with us, a present from Joe Lee. Gonna drive the hot Cressida as far as Big Rapids and dump it, take the Greyhound back down home.

Once he's gone, me and Jean close up the hunting cabin behind us. We don't know where we're going except in the general direction west. Don't know what kind of life we're gonna make for ourselves. Where we'll live or how we'll work. Police'll be looking for us, but we're both awful good at getting invisible.

We pile into the car, Samson in back and me behind the wheel. Jean is scootched up next to me in front. She's brushing a curl away from her eye and smiling as we back out of the driveway. I don't care who done what or who deserved what or even what's right and what's justice and what's fair. Me and Jean, we're cutting out of the whole deal. We're just going to see what comes. Holding on to each other this time. We're just going.